THE PENTUM MISSION

To Andrew & Margy —
Best of friends — always
   Joe Fontana
   4/18/98

The PENTUM Mission

JOE FONTANA

ORCHISES
WASHINGTON
1998

Copyright © 1998 Joe Fontana

Library of Congress Cataloging-in-Publication Data

Fontana, Joe. 1939-
   The Pentum Mission / Joe Fontana.
      p.   cm.
   ISBN 0-914061-72-0 (alk. paper)
   I. Title.
   PS 3556.049P46   1998
   813'.54dc—21   97-44196
                                                CIP

Manufactured in the United States of America

Orchises Press
P. O. Box 20602
Alexandria
Virginia
22320-1602

G6E4C2A

PREFACE

This novel would not have existed without the help and encouragement of my good friends of many years, Aileen and Bill Murck, both of Washington, D.C., who provided me with a great deal of insight and indispensable assistance in the preparation of the manuscript. They were not reticent in offering their own advice and I must now admit, I bought into all their recommendations, which were solid and meaningful. To them, I shall be grateful for a long time.

Friends of long standing, Judy and Jim Clear; Susan and John Keys, Tibby and David Ford, Washington, D.C.; Julian and Zelda Block, Larchmont, New York; Cecil Lyon, John Beiter, James Gerard, Bob Dobrish, New York City, all of whom took the time to read and reread various portions of the manuscript giving me the benefit of their own experiences and views.

An especial thanks to Victoria Wood, San Francisco, for her support and encouragement and most important, her keen eye regarding the story line; Duane Davidson, a lifelong friend and classmate from Colorado, who was more than generous with his time, and offered many good suggestions; Ed and Irina Hazelwood, Alexandria, Virginia, who provided me with excellent advice regarding their own experiences in the old Soviet Union and the new Russia; Syndicated columnist, Georgi Ann Geyer, Washington, D.C., an author in her own right and student of Soviet and Russian history as a well as a regular commentator on PBS's "This Week in Washington," for her wise counsel and encouragement.

Thanks to Nadine Block, a graduate student at Yale University, who labored over the original manuscript with diligence and great energy. Of course, my unfailing gratitude to Ralph Baxter, a colleague at George Mason University, who took the various drafts of the manuscript and carefully edited them with precision and importantly, patience. His energy and vigilance, kept me going forward. Appreciation to those, both in the public and private sector, who wish to remain anonymous and who contributed mightily their experiences in the new Russia, and who took the time to offer advice on various aspects of the novel.

I owe a great debt of gratitude to Roger Lathbury, President of Orchises Press, the publisher of this novel. For his boundless enthusiasm, encouragement and expertise, I shall be eternally grateful.

Lastly, to my wife Barbara, and our children Greg and Paul, who, for the past few years, when the lights in the house, except for those in the basement computer room, were turned off, would wonder what their husband and father was up to, I owe the greatest thanks. But, at least I was now home, and not traveling to places no one had to go to but me.

Author's Note

This is a work of fiction. Although many of the characters and events portrayed in it are based on real people and real episodes, the story is fictional. For ease of reading, I have used the Russian term *mafiya*, which is the generic translation term used across Russia to denote groups of criminals and/or corrupt officials. At times, the reader will see the term *vor,* which translates into English as "crime lord."

Note further that the Russian language sometimes but not always takes the letter "a" after a woman's last name, but the "a" is absent from a man's. For example, he is Vadim Makorov but she is Svetlana Makorova

The events occur within a twenty-four-hour period. The time variances are due to the different time zones. There is a five-hour difference between Washington and London; a one-hour difference between London and Zurich; a three-hour difference between London and Moscow.

CHAPTER ONE

London
Friday
Local Time: 6:00 p.m.
The Lowndes Hotel, Room 452

Robert Altman, age 25, was happy he was there. The money was good and he had no qualms about what he did for a living. It was necessary, he assured himself, as he did so often during the four years he had sold himself in this manner. He kept his eyes closed, for he really didn't want to see the balding, bobbing head of the old man work his private member to climax. After one hour with the trick, Robert would go home and take his friend of two years to dinner. "Maybe Scott's," he thought. Yes, that's where they would go. The old man would probably give him a tip in addition to the one-hundred-pound note, so there would be plenty of money to spend on the celebration.

    He felt a slight chill from the wind blowing through the door opening onto a small balcony that overlooked the garden court behind the hotel. Although it was a rainy and cool September night, the old man had insisted on keeping the door slightly ajar, "to let in fresh air," he said. The room was dark except for the twilight filtering through the sheer beige curtains, which were drawn tightly over the floor-to-ceiling windows. Robert closed his eyes tightly as his climax was about to be reached, and he began to moan, falling into the joy as his body reacted to the smooth and quick mouth action of the trick. Robert's hands held either side of the man's head, guiding him in the proper movement when it suddenly stopped, and for an instant he felt a warm liquid on his groin. Just as he reopened his eyes, he saw the quick flash of light on steel as the small, slender knife neatly and silently slit Robert's jugular vein.

    The double murder took only 30 seconds.

James Davidson left as he had entered—through the open, glass terrace door. It was still drizzling as he slipped over the balcony rail, and dropped lightly onto the balcony below. He was angry that the blood from the younger man had spurted out and onto his right sleeve. For a moment, his skill had faltered and the neat cut he applied, which would have limited the blood, did not work as planned. Perhaps he was a bit flustered at what he saw in the room. Silently closing in on the old man from behind, he put his hands over the man's eyes and the slit was noiseless and perfect. But as he moved toward the young man, he was struck by the strange beauty of his face. Yes, that was the reason he told himself, a momentary distraction. "It is dangerous to lose focus," he said to himself. "But then, the face had such a disturbing quality about it . . . white and smooth . . . unblemished . . . perfect," he said to himself.

The blood had also splattered onto his latex gloved hands, as well as onto the sleeves of the black jogging suit he was wearing. Those he would discard at a construction site trash container at Hans Crescent, across from Harrod's department store, a short, five-minute walk from the hotel. He had carefully checked the layout of the container and the construction site during his daily jogs each of the four days he'd been in London. Davidson had considered all the arrangements necessary to avoid any record of his presence.

He entered his room—352—identical to the room above where he had just been—and as he hurried into the gray and white tiled bathroom, he glanced at the digital clock on the nightstand, adjacent to the left side of the bed and saw that it was 6:15 p.m. "Good," he thought, reflecting that he had plenty of time to change and go to the theater to accomplish his next task. Without apparent reason, he went to the bathroom sink and began to wash his gloved hands of the blood. After a few seconds as he watched the pink waste water flow down the drain, he reached instinctively for a hand towel, wiping the gloves. "What am I doing?" he wondered as he pulled off the gloves, angrily throwing them with the towel onto the bathroom floor. In another moment, he had his jogging suit off and in the same pile.

As he entered the shower, he turned the water on full force while placing his hands over his face and quietly repeated his confessions of faith and submission to the will of Allah, a God he believed would reward him for taking the lives of the two unbelievers and blasphemous.

Strangely, his thoughts were interrupted by the vision of the pretty, flawless face of the young man whose throat he had just cut. In anger, he began to slap himself hard on both sides of his face as he thought about the young man. Allah would understand this penance for such thoughts. But why would Allah create such beauty? And why not in him?

"I am so holy, my God, so holy, and look at me, my God, look at me!" He looked at himself in the small, handheld mirror he used as he was shaving, angrily flinging the mirror through the partially opened shower curtain down onto the heap of clothes on the floor, where it bounced a few times before coming to rest, unshattered, underneath the sink. As he pushed aside the shower curtain, he grabbed the towel and, in the full-length mirror on the back of the bathroom door, looked at his own body, taut, muscled, and the product of many days of workouts and jogging. He knew he had physical grace and took great pride in his body.

Yet his large and deep brown eyes were not humorous, but sad and somber. His elongated nose, in conjunction with a thin upper and protruding lower lip and broad and high cheekbones, created a combination that made him look gaunt.

As he dried himself, the thoughts of the face made him strangely excited and he began to lose himself in fantasy until the ringing phone broke the momentary pleasure he was beginning to feel. He did not pick up the bathroom wall phone as he was not expecting any call. The only prearranged call had come earlier in the afternoon from his employer in Moscow. Regardless he never answered any unplanned call. After several moments, the ringing stopped.

He dressed swiftly, tense and humiliated that his penis was still rigid as an iron rod, without hope for relief. "Forgive me, God," he kept repeating to himself. "Oh! please forgive me. This terrible need makes me shameful, but I will control this shame, my God, for I am nothing without you." He took one quick look around the room, picked up his passport wallet, opened it to check for his theater tickets and money, smiling at his assignment name: James Davidson—as far from the reality of his true name, Ruslan Ishaev, as possible. And every time he would look at his photo in the blue and gold British passport, he would grin, for at age 28, he certainly lacked the features of an Englishman, as his new name so clearly implied.

No matter. His client had given him the name a month earlier while he was in Moscow to discuss the assignment. It was perfectly acceptable and, in fact, unimportant from his point of view. In any event, he had held many names and he promptly forgot them after each contract. He put on his black raincoat, grabbed his gym bag, where he had placed his jogging suit, shoes, and gloves, closed the door behind him, and hurried down the corridor to the left exit stairs which led four flights down to the back of the hotel. No one would see him. Ruslan Ishaev was now ready to attend to his next and, for this assignment, his last murder. It was 6:45 p.m.

The London dampness made Ruslan raise the collar of his raincoat, and he buttoned the two collar flaps together so his neck was completely covered. There was no need for an umbrella because the rain had stopped and, in any event, he would have had to go through the front hotel reception to get one—an exit he determined to bypass. Besides, he would avoid the hotel checkout because he had prepaid cash for his room. He had incurred no other costs and, in fact, had a credit balance which he knew he would never receive. He didn't care whether he did. The home address in Manchester he had given the hotel clerk when he registered was false.

Ruslan had been in London for three days, and, like all cities, he disdained it. He believed all cities were the same: a jumble of modernity alongside old and worn-out buildings; noise everywhere from the crowds of people, scurrying this way and that, seemingly impatient, to the uproar caused by workers either tearing down a building or constructing a new one—and the traffic, a whirlwind of cars, truck, cabs, all headed somewhere. It was the countryside of his home, more than five thousand kilometers away, outside of another city, Tashkent, Uzbekistan, that he always longed for—days clocked by the planting and harvesting of cotton, the fall of the rain, the vast solitude of the mountains that surrounded the cool quiet of the fields, and his family house, where he had grown up and which he still called home. Cities, he concluded, are places of ruin—"Shitholes," he said to himself.

His stride was quick as he walked the four blocks along Lowndes Street, passing the graceful apartments that flanked the street, to the busy intersection with Knightsbridge Road. He crossed Knightsbridge and turned left along it, joining the late evening throng of shoppers, passing the front of Harrod's department store, turning again at the end of Harrod's, and walking along the back of the store to the construction site, where a small four-story office building was being renovated, directly across from Harrod's delivery entrance. In a few minutes, he was standing at the rear of the refuse container, invisible to anyone on Hans Crescent street. This container had an open top, and Ruslan heaved his bag up and into the container. He knew that, once the construction resumed, the bag would be buried under debris. In any event, if the bag was found, he would be long gone.

Glancing at his watch—it was already 7:00 p.m.—he crossed the street to the taxi stand where a lone cab was parked. As he approached the cab, the driver lowered his window. "Where to, gv'nor?"

Without even looking at the driver, but simply opening the cab door, Ruslan answered, "The Savoy Theatre. I must be there on time, seven thirty. Please hurry."

"I'll do my best, but it's a wet evening, as y'can see; traffic is normally slow, but I'll get y' there with a few minutes to spare. I promise y' that gv'nor, indeed I do," the driver replied.

Rather than answer, Ruslan stared out the window at the few pedestrians walking into a restaurant adjacent to the taxi stand. As the cab picked up speed, Ruslan was confident that his God would continue to be with him. He was proud to be an assassin and to be in the state of grace that he received as a result of the killings he had just accomplished. But there was one killing he could never forget.

It was his first, and at times like this, when he knew he was in a holy state, he would ask Allah's forgiveness for what had happened so many years ago. He still could smell the distant scent of his first and only prostitute, to whom his father had taken him at the age of twelve, and it still made him, even today, nauseated. But each killing brought back those memories he could never erase. He remembered being so frightened . . . over and over again he remembered the prostitute laughing at him as he tried to have an erection. He could bear the laughter . . . he couldn't bear the humiliation, so he picked up a chair aside the bed and hit the woman sharply. Jumping on her before she could recover, he held his hands tightly around her neck until she became lifeless. Then, in a fit of despair, he ejaculated on her bare stomach. He still remembered staring at her body in disbelief, vomiting in the gray ceramic washbowl, on the wood table next to the bed. He had told his father, a Communist Party member, and regional farm collective boss, a lie—that she refused to have sex with him, and that is why he killed her.

His father said nothing to him, and Ruslan believed his father knew he was not telling the truth. Nothing was said. Absolutely nothing came from his father's lips. His father took him back to the house where the prostitutes lived, brushed aside the entreaties of the three other women, and took the body to the mountains where it was dumped amid the underbrush. They both knew that the mountain animals would take care of the dead woman. And the money he had tossed at the women would take care of them. They would be silent and no one would ever know. He never discussed it again, nor did his father ever ask him about having women. He would never be rejected or ridiculed. He was a man, after all, and deserved respect.

"I'm sorry, gv'nor, that we've not been able to move faster," the driver said, again trying to start a conversation with Ruslan. "Traffic is very heavy, I'll get y' there on time. I hear that the play is a very funny one with an American bloke as the star. You should have a good time, I suspect, a bloody good time, gv'nor, yes, a good time."

Ruslan didn't comment. He didn't hear the words, but only the raised voice of the driver, made necessary because the glass partition between the two sections of the cab was only partially open. The voice, deep, yet precise, snapped Ruslan from his intense and almost spiritual reverie. His stomach turned with fierce nausea, and he felt beads of sweat coming down his forehead, his body burning.

"You will not punish me this way, my God. I was too young. You must not do this to me," Ruslan mumbled, as he unbuttoned the collar flaps around his neck and opened his coat as well as his inside jacket. His shirt was damp from the sweat and he was angry that he had let his long past nightmare come to bother him, and in such a manner. But God would not let him forget. Yes, that was his punishment and he must accept that punishment without complaint. He must accept the pain that God brought as a gift. God knew he hated that woman and he was glad she was dead, but God also would never erase the memory of that night. Every time he would kill, he would remember the first time death came at his hands. Memories never die, and he had to accept that.

As rapidly as the burst of uncontrolled sweat had come, it stopped. Ruslan inhaled deeply, the sweet smell of his sweat still clinging to his nostrils. But he felt more comfortable, the wave of nausea having passed. He shifted in his seat and straightened his jacket, rebuttoning it, but leaving his raincoat open. He couldn't understand why he was nervous. After all, to him all assignments were fairly routine. This assignment should be no different, but it had started out strangely. He never expected to have to kill, along with Boarders, another man, and one whose face was having an inordinate fascination for him.

Yet to each client, he knew, assignments were never routine, but just the opposite, and there was always a certain nervousness in clients' voices whenever they phoned him at his home in Tashkent and sought his services. Of course, he knew every request was urgent and it was the same this time when the call came from Moscow and from Boris Shenin, a high officer of Bank Alliance Russia, a bank Ruslan knew to have strong connections with the *mafiya* and especially to the Moscow *vor*. He had done three assignments for the Moscow *vor*, yet he had never met the man titled by his peers as *vor*, the crime lord, for the entire Moscow region. Always his assignments came through underlings and this he knew would be no exception.

After receiving the call, he had left for Moscow, and it was there that the anxiety of Shenin became evident. Ruslan never had any deep understanding of the reasons for any of the assignments nor did he ever ask. Odd, he thought, that the people he dealt with always seemed nervous and frightened. Were they afraid of their own actions, or of his?

As the cab wound its way through the damp London streets toward the Savoy Theatre, around Buckingham Palace, and down the Mall flanking the meticulously groomed St. James Park, Ruslan realized that this assignment—the only one for which the client actually would come to check up on whether he had been successful—couldn't be considered routine. The client's demeanor at their Moscow meeting some two weeks earlier was of fear, abnormal fear.

That late August afternoon meeting at the client's offices on Leningradskiy Prospekt was delayed for thirty minutes because a thunderstorm had brought unusual, heavy rains to Moscow. Ruslan had waited until the rain tapered off before walking the four blocks, past nondescript Communist era office blocks, from the Aerostar Hotel, to the gleaming, marble and glass headquarters of Bank Alliance Russia. He walked into the spectacular, plant-filled, three-story atrium lobby resonating with a black marble interior fountain, water shooting up in a steady, singular stream and falling majestically down into a pool lit by interior white colored lights—all casting a shadowy wave on the adjacent walls. He walked directly to the dark gray, marble top security station where two uniformed guards were viewing the television monitors discreetly hidden under a ledge. Ruslan placed his briefcase on the counter. "I am Ruslan Ishaev to see Boris Shenin."

"Please . . ." one of the guards said as he motioned to Ruslan to open the briefcase, which Ruslan promptly did. Apart from the two pads of lined paper and some black felt pens, the guard found it empty.

"Thank you." During the brief inspection, the other guard had dialed Shenin, saying, "Mr. Shenin, a Ruslan Ishaev is in the reception area. Shall I send him up?" After a moment, the officer, still holding the receiver in his hand, said, "Please go to the twelfth floor. Here is your security card. Return it on your way out." The free standing twenty-five-foot black marble wall behind the security desk had an engraved gold seal with a modernized spread eagle as its symbol. On either side the flags of Russia drooped aimlessly from eighteen-foot brass poles.

At the elevator, Ruslan took off his olive raincoat, folding it inside out and placing it over his left forearm. In a few moments, he was on the twelfth floor. The elevator doors opened onto reception area where a tall, broad-built, elegant man with graying hair was waiting. "Ruslan Ishaev, I am Boris Shenin. Welcome to Bank Alliance Russia."

"Thank you for meeting me," Ruslan responded.

"You had a good flight? The accommodations are to your satisfaction?" Shenin asked.

"Yes. Everything is fine. Thanks for asking," Ruslan said.

After these preliminaries, they walked in silence down a rosewood paneled corridor with scenes of Moscow centered on each panel, illuminated by track lighting.

"Here we are, Ruslan," and Boris Shenin opened the door to his own office reception area. "Please," and Boris motioned Ruslan to continue toward the open door leading directly into Shenin's office.

"Would you like some tea, Ruslan Ishaev?" Boris Shenin asked quietly, as he directed his guest to sit across from him in one of two identical black leather and chrome chairs separated by a black marble coffee table. On the table was the annual report, in English and Russian, of Bank Alliance Russia.

"No, no tea, please. Just mineral water," Ruslan responded gently, sounding almost childlike. With that request, an assistant appeared through the door behind Boris Shenin. Carefully arranged on a tray were a glass, a small crystal bowl of ice, and a bottle of water, unopened, together with an opener. Custom dictated that the bottled water be opened by the guest; one was always uncertain what an opened bottle of water might contain. After placing the tray in front of Ruslan, the assistant left, without saying a word.

"What an unholy man," Ruslan thought to himself. Ruslan glanced at the heels of the table separating him and Shenin. "That is where the microphones are. How stupid. Boris Shenin is not smart. His assistant comes in with a tray without Boris even calling him on the intercom. His lackey must have been listening through the hidden system. How else would he know that I wanted water?" Ruslan stared at Boris as this thought kept going through his mind.

His hands twisted, Boris Shenin gazed with evident interest at the man sitting across from him. He noted that they were the same height, but without any similarity beyond that. Shenin was a White Russian, age sixty, a far cry from the deep olive complexion and obvious youth of his visitor. He knew that this was not the time for lofty conversation, nor did he care to engage in any with this stranger he was about to employ. The man sitting across from him was there for one reason only. The meeting would be simple and direct.

Boris attempted a small smile. "I understand that you have much talent, Ruslan Ishaev, and that you serve your religious brothers well. This a good trait. Loyalty to a brother is the highest honor to which a man can aspire. Admirable, Ruslan Ishaev, admirable!"

Ruslan's response was barely above a whisper and his eyes were stiff and indifferent. "In my homeland, we are all brothers, Boris Shenin. Loyalty, unselfishness . . . I have met with nothing else from my brothers and this gives me the confidence in my life . . . along with my belief in Allah . . . always. Are you, Boris Shenin, unselfish? Loyal? A believer?" Without waiting for the reply, Ruslan continued slowly, "you now have need for me. Correct?"

"Yes, thank you for coming," Boris responded in a business-like fashion. No friendly jesting now, he thought. "We naturally are anxious to have you go to London as soon as possible. The targets, which you will eliminate, have destroyed several of our business arrangements, and have murdered our representatives with impunity. It is essential that they be stopped."

Ruslan reached for the bottle of mineral water and the opener. Slowly twisting the opener in his hand for a few moments, he stared at Shenin and asked, "Would you like some water, Boris Shenin? With ice or no ice?" Deliberately, he opened the bottle and waited for Boris to respond.

"No, thank you, Ruslan Ishaev. I have tea," Boris replied with obvious discomfort, wondering why this man would ask him if he wanted water when he was already drinking tea.

"Yes, of course." Ruslan poured himself some water, but avoided the ice. "Boris Shenin, you must appreciate that timing is critical in these kinds of tasks. I cannot rush, nor can you ask me to perform hastily.

There is the correct time to do the tasks at hand. I know that you realize this. You do, don't you?" Ruslan asked, arching his dark eyebrows in a manner suggesting that it would be inconceivable to him if Shenin thought otherwise.

Without waiting for Shenin to reply, Ruslan continued in a tone that left no doubt that he would decide when the assassinations would take place. "Boris Shenin," Ruslan said, staring directly at him and reaching over to place his left hand on top of Boris' right hand, "this is not stealing other people's money, as you do. What I do requires serious planning so that nothing will go wrong," Ruslan replied.

"Yes, I understand," said Shenin. "But, I have to emphasize that it is our intention to demonstrate by your good work we can reach anyone—anywhere, anytime—who harms our interests."

"Of course," Ruslan responded. "You must appreciate, also, that absolutely nothing can be left to chance. The files you sent me on both men are very sparse. Other than some photos of them and their London office address, which I suspect is now closed, there is nothing, absolutely nothing."

"Yes, that is so. However, we suspect, but cannot prove, they are with the American security services. This is just a suspicion. Both targets will be at the Savoy Theatre in London, the second Friday in September. The older target usually stays at the Lowndes Hotel; the younger one will be at the Carlton Tower," Shenin concluded.

"Good. I shall tell you after the deed is done; I will not tell my plans before. Nothing can be left to chance. If you do not have the information, then you will not make the mistake of telling another. Correct? Nevertheless, I realize that you are anxious for this task to be completed, and, Boris Shenin, it will be completed . . . and to your complete satisfaction."

Shenin looked at this man and, for a moment, admired his confidence—a man who had probably murdered many and probably would kill him, if someone hired him and paid him to do it. Despite all his years as Deputy Minister of Trade in the old USSR, and now as Managing Director of Bank Alliance Russia, he could never understand how someone could be brutal and yet talk of brotherhood. It made no sense.

More critically, he now depended on these dark skins to help keep The Bank Alliance's functioning. They provided the necessary force. He shuddered to imagine that it was probably true that the bank needed them as much as they perhaps needed the bank. He felt very uneasy sitting across from this man who showed no emotion and spoke so softly it was hard to make out what he said.

"Your requirements will be met, Ruslan Ishaev. Two million U.S. dollars have been deposited in the account you designated in Zurich, at the Credit Suisse. Two million U.S. dollars will be deposited upon the successful completion of the tasks. Does that remain suitable?" Shenin asked.

"Yes, Boris Shenin, the funds will be used by those fighting for freedom in my brother countries. And, Boris Shenin, the one hundred thousand dollars for expenses in London. . . ."

Before Ruslan could finish, Boris interjected a quick, "Of course, of course."

With that, the same man who had brought the water came in again and placed a black briefcase on the table in front of Boris. Boris slid it over to Ruslan unopened.

"Please count the amount if you wish," Boris suggested, but knew the offer unnecessary. If, by any chance, the wrong amount was in the case (Boris had counted it himself), not only would the assignment not be carried out, but his life would probably end.

"No need, Boris Shenin. I trust you," Ruslan replied, and Boris, of course, did not believe him. He knew a man like this could trust no one, and he understood why this had to be the case.

"Good, then we are finished, I believe," Boris said in an almost relieved, courteous tone.

"I shall have Georgi escort you to the car and our driver will take you back to the hotel."

"No, that will not be necessary. It is but a short walk back to the hotel," replied Ruslan as he rose from his chair. Boris also stood up and walked him to the door.

Shenin slowly opened it and said, "Your own briefcase, Ruslan.

Don't you wish to take that also?"

"No, I have the correct briefcase," Ruslan said, smiling as he lifted the briefcase filled with the money Shenin had given him.

Shenin bowed slightly to Ruslan, extending his hand to shake, but instead Ruslan leaned over and kissed him on both cheeks, a gesture he accepted without feeling.

"Goodbye, Boris Shenin. And, thank you."

"My regards, Ruslan Ishaev. It was good of you to come. Good luck."

"And, luck to you, Boris Shenin, luck to you," declared Ruslan with a wide smile crossing his face.

The meeting ended like all the others, an exchange of good luck wishes. Not honest wishes. Ruslan could care less for the client, and he never needed the client's good wishes. He was serving the will of God. He was in God's graces.

"Gv'nor, we'll be at the theater in just a few minutes," the driver said, turning his head and talking in a more normal voice, as he reached over to open the dividing glass further.

Again, Ruslan did not acknowledge his words. He had this last assignment to complete, a dinner with Boris Shenin and his lackey, and after that sleep, and he knew he would sleep well tonight. Success brings calmness and a certain serenity. Sleep follows easily. Tomorrow, Saturday, he would be on the 9:00 a.m. Lufthansa flight to Frankfurt and then on to Tashkent to visit his mother and sister. He had the family responsibility, because his father had died when he was twenty-five, and his mother now lived alone with his younger sister, Alia. They depended on him. As much as he wanted to see them, he looked forward to riding through the rugged foothills adjoining his family fields on his horse, an Arabian stallion that he had named "Nevermore." The rides brought him a peace that he had felt nowhere else.

At times, he was ashamed of what he did on his horse. Suddenly, she became a hard, frenzied mountain of flesh, where he rode until his passion was released. He needed a woman, but he was afraid. But sometimes he couldn't breathe because of the need to suppress his sensual nature. After the lonely rides, he would have a view of himself floating in the heavens, promised by Allah, without suffering loneliness, far away from the currents of life, with joy as his only companion. What he did while riding "Nevermore" brought strange thoughts into his head. But God was good to him. He must never doubt that, he told himself repeatedly. God was always his companion and those thoughts will vanish. "God, I am your servant . . . always . . . always."

Ruslan stared out the cab window. He kept dwelling on the assignment in a fashion that was unusual for him: the fearful client, the request for the client to come to London to verify whether he had accomplished his task, the scene of the first murders, the young face, the blood, too much blood . . . too much blood. The general order of all his earlier assignments spanning several years seemed gone. This assignment was on the verge of disorder. Ruslan's mind, normally of euphoric grace, was now uncharacteristically worried and concerned. As the cab made its way along a slow line of cars dropping off passengers at the Savoy Theatre, a fleeting lack of confidence swept over him, and his only thought was that pretty face and how he wished that young man were still alive, and he could not understand why he had that desire. "They were sinners, my God, weren't they?"

"We're here, gv'nor, the Savoy," the driver said as he looked back to see Ruslan, who was vacantly staring straight out his seat window, not moving at all. "Gv'nor . . . gv'nor, we're here. Five pounds twenty, please."

Ruslan reached into his coat pocket and handed the driver a ten-pound note, opening the door and getting out, without acknowledging him. He joined the throng of theater goers and entered the marble and mirrored, art deco foyer, looking at his watch as he descended the stairs to the lower lobby. It was 7:18 p.m.

Moscow
Friday
Local Time: 7:00 p.m. (4:00 p.m., London)
Sheremetyevo Airport
VIP Lounge

Boris Shenin turned and looked intently at his assistant Georgi Ivashkin. Earlier in the afternoon, in a call to Ruslan in London, he had verified that he would be meeting him later in the evening to receive a report from Ruslan. Until he secured that report, he would be uncertain as to any success of this particular contract. There was no other option, his eyes indicated, none whatsoever. The target, David Harrison, had fooled everyone connected with Bank Alliance Russia, and had in fact killed the very people that were being sent to check on the business deal gone sour. Actually, he never expected that from the Americans. They are too moral, Boris thought to himself. Too moral? A fraud. Harrison, like all Americans, was a fraud.

The missile shipment had been stopped when the ship was blown up as it was approaching Benghazi, Libya—right in front of the purchasers. Everyone on board the ship, including the bank's own technicians, had been killed. There were no survivors. Shenin had never understood how they were able to do it. Perhaps an underwater charge placed by divers from a submarine. Perhaps, but he was unsure. Then, on top of this atrocity, the $65 million was never delivered to Bank Alliance Russia from Harrison's company, which was buying the missiles on behalf of the Libyans. This, despite the fact that the payment was by a Letter of Credit from Barclays Bank, London to Bank Alliance Russia. Barclays had said that the account had been closed and the money withdrawn before payment under the Letter of Credit could be made. Payment was to be made upon shipment from the Black Sea, but there was a problem with the documents, according to the bank. Despite the fact that the ship left, the document problem took five days to resolve—the exact number of days to reach Benghazi. The ship disappeared and so did the money. Bank Alliance Russia couldn't afford to lose another transaction such as this. Bank Alliance Russia was a bank, but more important, was an organization of many enterprises in which the *mafiya* had substantial interest.

"Do you think he will succeed, Georgi?" Boris asked almost to reassure himself because he knew what his assistant's answer would be.

Georgi's reply was offhand. "Yes, why not? Isn't he the best? He has always succeeded for us and others. Have you not been told this by others?"

"Yes, yes! I have been told many, many times. The report I have on him is of a man who was a superior member of the Spetsiainkoye Naznacheniya [Special Designation troops]. His marksmanship was sufficient to qualify him for the Olympics, but he was not sent because of his military duties. But this Ruslan is his own man. Beholden to no one. I don't like this at all, Georgi, not at all, but we have no alternative. David Harrison is a chameleon. Harrison is also a killer. I met him twice in discussion about the deal. He appeared so honest and forthright, and his partner, a much older man, very timid."

"They were the consultants to the Libyan government ... also fooled ... in fact they approached us ... they knew about us. The Libyans checked and cleared him. When I sent Aleksandr and Viktor to talk to him after the ship was blown up, they never came back. They had an auto accident coming from Heathrow. In fact, this David Harrison called to ask why they were late. He was lying. He knew they were dead. He killed them or had them killed. The driver of the car was never found and neither were our boys. The car was incinerated. Strange, that the event never made the newspapers. We checked with the dispatcher of the limousine service and they verified the accident."

"I know, Boris Shenin," his assistant reassured him. "This means that the Americans know of our projects, but how, Boris? How? And, do you believe that they now know of the special project with Iran? And does our colleague Peter Bradford have any ideas on how the Americans knew of our earlier Libyan project?"

"That shithead pervert, he doesn't know anything except to skim as much money as he can on these and those other projects he fronts for the *vor*. Why we work with him, I'll never know, Georgi. I'll never know. But, so be it. Our hands are tied. I don't know how the Americans get their information, but I will say this, whatever information they have, they will carry to their graves. Come, Georgi. We have a plane to catch and an evening of celebration in London."

CHAPTER TWO

Washington, D. C.
Friday
Local Time: 2:00 p.m. (7:00 p.m., London)
Department of Justice, Room 6610

Mary Auriello, Deputy Assistant Attorney General for Intelligence Policy, was furious. Her hazel eyes scanned the various intelligence reports on her desk. One was sealed in a special envelope. It lay directly on top of the other reports, filed in order of time developed. The blue folder, with a big red "X" on its cover designating "for the eyes of the recipient only," contained a dozen, two-paragraph reports, which she tossed aside with evident distaste. "Usual shit," she muttered. "Someday, I'm going to tell whoever puts this shit together that I also read *The New York Times*, and I don't want to get supposed intelligence from our agents quoting that newspaper."

The one sheet she fingered contained a cryptic message, centered in bold lettering on a blank page, in a code only she knew: "North east rising sun arriving today." Mary stared at the message for several moments and then threw all the other reports into a basket marked "Destroy." She fed the one message she had just dwelled on into the shredding machine next to her desk; the remaining ones would be burned. In reality, she didn't care, for the other reports were so broadly disseminated throughout the security apparatus of the U.S. government that the contents were too widely known to be useful. Actually, at times, the reports sounded as if they had been lifted from special country reports given to subscribers of *The Economist* magazine.

"And, this headache. I can't get rid of this headache," she muttered to herself. But, she knew what was causing the headaches—too much drinking, drinking alone at her house in Kensington, Maryland, which she had inherited from her parents, both of whom had died within six months of each other, just this year. She had moved into her parents' home to help her father when her mother's health deteriorated and to give him comfort and company. It was only emotion that kept her coming every evening to the home of her birth. She knew that she should go back to her townhouse in Bethesda and put her parents' home on the market, but she couldn't do that. Their only child, she couldn't yet leave the house which had brought so much happiness to her . . . and to them.

Of course, she missed her father, who died in his sleep of a heart attack, but she couldn't forget her mother's suffering, dying of a rare cancer, ocular melanoma. The doctors had removed the tumor behind the eye, but the cancer had gone into the blood stream, and no amount of treatment by specialists could reverse the inevitable. Mary believed that her father died of a broken heart as he watched his wife waste away.

It was first one, then two, then three martinis as she joined her father every evening, taking turns to help her mother. Then he was gone, and she was left alone.

During her mother's illness she couldn't take time off to help, so private nurses took turns, and Mary knew there was no hope at all. In those last few months, her mother insisted that the bedroom be darkened, with just a dim bedside lamp on all the time. When Mary would go in, usually very late at night, having worked until about nine, a drink in her hand, and in the calm of the moment, she could make out in the faint light the wide, king-size bed her father finally died in, the headboard with wave-like scrolls intricately carved by her uncle so many years ago in Ireland and given to her parents as a wedding gift. There she could glimpse her mother, lying in the same bed, unable to see, a devastated body, hooked up to a tube giving minute doses of morphine to kill the pain—and those rosaries—held so tightly in her mother's hands. In order to help her sit up, the nurses propped her up with pillows, combed her sparse white hair, and covered her shoulders with a lace shawl that Mary didn't even know her mother had. She could barely talk and only made sounds. Mary would lean over, kiss her, hold her hands and then she would recite the rosary aloud, her mother moving her lips as best she could, mouthing the prayers.

That last night, Mary stayed until the end. She exploded in sobbing, not only for the memories of her mother, but also for the exhaustion that comes with watching your own die . . . and so slowly, and for the rage that had been gnawing at her for being unable to stop the suffering of her mother. But it was over. Doctor Telnick, a family friend for years, acceded to Mary's request and he was there, along with the two nurses, and Monsignor Hanrahan of their parish church.

There were many things she wished she'd said to her mother, many moments she wanted to share—all gone, dead, and in a bed of pain. She buried her head in her mother's withered hand, and the rage did not stop. The rage she knew so well rose to her head, exploding everything, injecting her eyes with fury and her lips with curses—"How could you, God. How could you do this to this woman? You allowed a saint to suffer. How could you . . . how could you . . ." and she fell on her knees, not embarrassed that she had an audience while she continued to curse the only person who could have saved her mother.

Two days later, Mary buried her mother. Then came the drink. It was all she had for solace, and her work, which was prodigious, became all-consuming. So now this headache . . . always a headache and always beginning in the morning and increasing in intensity by early afternoon.

"Here, Mary, two aspirin and some Evian water. Take it. Mary, shouldn't you see a doctor? . . ."

"No, I shouldn't and I won't. Don't mother me, Beverly. I know what I am doing."

"Well, I just think that maybe you . . ."

"Please, Beverly, don't lecture me. I have enough on my mind. This shit that comes across my desk? Can't you sort it out? Do I have to read all of it?"

"Mary, it is sorted. By the way, Jim Foster's also waiting to see you. He wants just a few minutes of your time. What do you want to do?" Beverly asked.

"I don't need Jim to come and ask how I am. Tell him I'm fine . . . okay. Tell him I'm fine."

"Mary, he wants to see you . . . I don't understand, Mary, I don't understand what you're doing to yourself," her secretary of many years, Beverly Peterson, replied, and then left the office, after placing the aspirin and the small bottle of water on Mary's desk.

Mary buried her hands in her face, fighting back tears, muttering, "Shit, God, I can take anything, but why did you do this to my mother?" Her words became slurred.

"Mary, hey, Mary."

"Who let you in?"

"For openers, I did. Besides, I had a meeting in the building, so I thought I'd just by. You do remember that you and I are supposed to be together? Mary, it's been three months since your mother passed away. Look at me Mary. I know it must be hard, but you have to forget—"

"Don't tell me what to do. Don't you ever tell me what to do. Do you understand? Now get out of here," she shouted at the only man that had been consistently in love with her for these past three years.

Jim Foster, age 45, divorced father of twin daughters, a senior partner of the law firm, Watson & Stewart, took Mary's tirade in stride. He knew it was momentary, and it was, and his love for her too great. He admired her, but loved her more.

"No, no, I don't mean that, Jim. I'm sorry we haven't seen much of each other. But I need a little space right now. You know how much I care for you, Jim. I'll see you for lunch. Pick me up in about an hour. Okay?" she smiled as she walked over and hugged him, holding him a few moments.

"I know how you miss your mother and father, but you have to let go at some time, Mary. You can't dwell on this forever."

"I know, Jim. I know what I have to do," she said as she raised her eyes to see his, knowing by his look that he was genuine in his feelings for her. She kissed him lightly, took him by the arm, and accompanied him through her secretary's office to the hall door. "Thanks, Jim. I'm sorry I've been such a shrew. I'll make it up to you soon. I will. Lunch at three. I promise I'll be there—at 701—I promise."

But Mary's calmness didn't last.

Returning to her desk, she took the pencil that was stuck in her shining chestnut hair, pulled into an untidy bun, and flung it across the room, hitting a picture of the new attorney general. "Stupid shit," she mumbled. At five-feet, four-inches tall, forty years of age, and 110 pounds, with immaculate skin and high cheek bones, and until recently a daily aerobic participant at the department gym, Mary looked years younger than her age, and she knew it. More critically, she was the Justice Department's senior official regarding intelligence policy, as well as in charge of the most sensitive mission the United States was undertaking, code name: Pentum.

Pentum was a special unit set up in early 1992 to prevent the sale of contraband armaments, missile technology and nuclear weaponry by countries of the former Soviet Union, by targeting and eliminating those key leaders of the Russian *mafiya* who were trying to sell to countries on the United States' embargo list. The president's National Security Council Finding 92-3 avoided the words "target and eliminate." These were Mary's interpretations of the words the president used which were "prevent and contain." This special unit's identity was limited to the president, the director of Central Intelligence, the attorney general and the director of the FBI. But even in that limited group, Mary said little, and all her reports to the president and the others were only oral briefings. Nothing was ever reduced to writing—at least by her. What the president told others, if at all, was his business. In fact, Mary's view of intelligence information sharing could be summed up in two words: "No sharing." She trusted no one.

"My God, I've got to get rid of this headache." She gulped down the aspirin. "I can't go on this way . . . I just can't. Beverly's right—I have to see a doctor, but I hate them too. Shit, this is just shit."

It was now after 2:00 p.m. Washington time, 7:00 p.m. in London, and she hadn't received the transcript from the wiretaps placed on the phones of Bank Alliance Russia's Washington representative, a Mr. Valery Kalischenko, a one-time agent of the KGB in the Washington Embassy of the former USSR, who held a mid-level job at the embassy. After the collapse of the USSR, he had offered his services to the FBI and the CIA, for a sum of course, to detail certain historic secrets of the spy system which the KGB controlled from the embassy. The FBI wanted to pay but the CIA balked, so the deal was off. In any event,

Bank Alliance Russia was suspected of being a front for the Moscow *vor,* and Mary asked that Kalischenko's phone be tapped and his mail intercepted.

Mary's unit at Justice drafted the request for clandestine, electronic surveillance, and then, as required by federal law and Justice Department procedure, had the surveillance request approved by a federal judge. Naturally, she was responsible for the final request that went on to the judge. She also answered any of the court's questions regarding the request. Still these requests were carefully controlled because several of her colleagues kept bringing Mary's attention to the constitutional limitations against such searches. Mary had no patience with these people, who, she believed, in their own narrow view, abused the freedoms they espoused to protect. Sometimes she fished for the justification, but who said fishing was bad? You might catch something and, if you didn't like what you caught, you could always throw it back, couldn't you?

When she believed the surveillance to be critical, as it was in this case, the approval went through regardless of those who thought otherwise. If she had the time, and felt inclined, she would remind the questioners that such surveillance had produced major intelligence successes. Usually, she ignored the questioners . . . but she also remembered who they were. She never feared being held accountable and never fled her responsibilities. Despite her disagreements with the attorney general, her requests for electronic surveillance were always approved by him, and never turned down by the special federal judge overseeing the request.

Single, brilliant, and totally dedicated to Boarders and Harrison, who were the other members of the Pentum triumvirate, and fearful of no one in the political or bureaucratic field, Mary thought herself a genuine patriot. Others thought her acerbic, with an exaggerated sense of hatred when she felt betrayed, and a streak of apocalyptic vengeance that frightened many in the FBI and the CIA. The new administration thought her insufficiently loyal to its wishes. Did she care about the new administration's feelings or thoughts? No, she did not.

Those transcripts were due early in the morning, at seven, she reminded herself. She needed time to digest them, and, if relevant, send a summary to London, where Boarders and Harrison were staying. Her rage was also directed at the new attorney general, who in his zeal for budget reductions, had cut the number of Russian translators employed by the Department of Justice. Since the breakup of the USSR, he didn't believe that the United States needed all this spying stuff. Stupid. What did this idiot think? The Russian bad boys were going away? Do American bad boys go away? The attorney general was a political hack and joke, but he also was the president's former law partner, which, in Mary's eyes, made him even more dangerous. He had the ear of the president, who rarely had an original thought but then the president knew how to move people with his oratory: that was how he had been elected.

"Beverly, get me Howard," she shouted to her secretary.

As she waited for the call, she glanced out the window and saw that the weather was getting worse. A rainstorm was coming and that meant traffic gridlock in this city where no one knew how to drive in inclement weather. As Mary's anger grew, the phone buzzed and a soft voice said, "Mr. Breedon on the line."

"Howard, what are you doing? I needed the transcripts by this morning. This morning is not two p.m.," Mary shouted over the phone.

"Come on Mary, you know how short handed we are. The number of taps requiring Russian language translation has grown to thirty plus, and you're the one who authorized them. And we have only three translators. And, you won't let me get other translators from the other intelligence agencies in the U.S. government to help translate these taps. Give me a break, Mary.

"Go to your fax machine—the encryption is on its way now. Sorry, my good friend, we're up shit creek if we don't get more help. This is madness . . . madness . . . I'm repeating myself, so you understand . . . madness. Does anyone in main Justice realize that nothing, repeat, nothing, has changed in that place they now call Russia? Hey, Mary, how about a drink after work?" he laughed, knowing what her answer would be.

"No," she said as she curtly hung up.

Simultaneously, she heard the ping of the fax machine coming on, and the pages began to come through at the rate of one every six seconds, all gibberish which she promptly took to her encryption machine, and out came language she could understand—English. She scanned the ten pages and then carefully read each page, zeroing in on the message on page eight: "I believe that everything will be taken care of at 7:30 p.m., Friday. It will be a wonderful performance, I am sure."

"What the hell does this mean?" she pondered. She grabbed David's schedule in London and immediately noted his 7:30 p.m. theater date. "Christ," she said to herself, "Bob Boarders and David will be together. No way," she said to herself, "the *vor* hit man can't possibly think of taking them out at a theater. But then, why not? Remember Lincoln? The most unlikely place is the most likely place to assassinate," she reminded herself.

Her wrath was now directed at the new attorney general. "I'm going to let him have it at the next staff meeting. This new administration and its cost-cutting bullshit. What simple-mindedness." The last attorney general who understood gathering intelligence was Bobby Kennedy. "And he was a Democrat," she said to herself. "The present incumbent was out to lunch—way out. Besides, she couldn't trust him with anything. He had a penchant for leaking things to the press. He loved the press and he loved seeing his face and name in the news. He thought that by cozying up to the press he'd be immune from criticism for some of his nuttier policies," she pondered, as she toyed with the telephone line. "Something doesn't fit, though . . . something just doesn't fit," she kept repeating to herself.

"Mary," her secretary buzzed, "a courier from the NSA is here. You have to sign for something. You coming out or do I send him in?

"I'll come out, and, Beverly, thanks for the aspirin. Call Jim and tell him I'll be there for lunch. I told him I was going to, but call to confirm it. I've been a bitch, haven't I?"

"You really want to know?" her secretary inquired.

"No." Mary laughed.

"I didn't think so," her secretary responded, joining in the mirthful moment.

Mary went into her secretary's office where the courier had his two-key lock satchel with him. Mary took out her key and placed it in the lock, turning it one way. He put his own key in and turned the lock in the opposite direction. He lifted the cover, exposing a large manila envelope bordered in blue with the familiar red "X" and Mary's name on the front. She took out the envelope. "Thanks. Hope you're not stuck in traffic back to Ft. Meade. Looks like rain."

"Hope not, ma'am, hope not . . . Oh, Ms. Auriello, you have to sign here," he said, and she turned the envelope over to see a receipt, the back of which adhered to the envelope. She signed and he tore the top off, leaving her copy still affixed to the back of the envelope.

Mary went back to her desk and opened what she knew to be real time electronic surveillance:

> Key Coded
> NSC/cycle 155-890-cycle begins
> Caller Moscow 1500 GMT
> Recipient London 1200 GMT
> Moscow No. 235-4700
> London No. 212-4000/352
> Voices/English
> First Pickup
> "Lowndes Hotel, Good Evening."
> "Room 352"
> "Thank you. One Moment, Please."
> Voices/Russian/TransEngl
> Second Pickup
> "Yes"
> "Good evening, this is Richard. Will you be able to join us this evening?"
> "Yes, with pleasure. I look forward to seeing you after all is accomplished.
> "Wonderful, we will see you later. Good bye."
> End, no voice
> Voice data base unknown London/voice data base known Moscow
> voice data base entry Moscow retrieval prohibited
> Pentum restrictions in place
> Retina scan access only
> NSC/cycle 155-890-cycle ends at 155-900
> Key Coded

Mary knew Moscow voice data bank meant Bank Alliance Russia people, whom NSC had begun monitoring before the Libyan missile deal. She didn't care who they were. "Data base unknown London" meant that the voice that responded with one word "Yes" was not identifiable in the massive computer voice storage of the National Security Agency—the eavesdropping unit of the United States. But, Mary didn't have to know the name identity. She knew whoever he was, it was the man sent by the *mafiya* to hit Boarders and Harrison.

"And that is . . . Oh! My God . . . isn't Boarders? . . ." Before she could finish the sentence, she shouted, "Beverly, get Boarders at the Lowndes and if he's not there, call Harrison. Hurry, Beverly."

Her mind was racing. She . . . she had earlier this morning talked to Harrison as well as to Boarders.

"Hurry, Beverly, please hurry. . . ." Mary looked at her office clock, noting it was 2:20 p.m. Washington time, 7:20 p.m. London.

**London
Friday
Local Time: 7:00 p.m.
The Carlton Tower Hotel, The Landsdown Suite**

David Harrison was very worried and he didn't like to worry. He liked being in control and now he felt otherwise. It was 7:00 p.m. and Bob's absence bothered him. Bob Boarders was his business partner of the past five years and before that, way before, his instructor at a special U.S. Army military intelligence program, Ft. Riley, Kansas. He had called Bob's room at the Lowndes Hotel and left messages, but there was no return call. This was a special occasion that he and his wife Betty were to attend, and they expected that Bob would be there. Bob had said that he would be there. And David trusted him. He always did.

The open window of his suite let in a slight breeze and he looked out from the tenth floor at the misty evening, enjoying for a moment the quietness of the view below and the orderly landscaping of Cadogan Square in front of the hotel. He had been to London many times, but this time was different and special. He thought of the unreality of it all—he was going to a command performance at the Savoy Theatre where his only child, Timothy, was the star of a hit comedy.

Just earlier that day, he and Bob had finished the final details on a mission that was about to be concluded. And yet, in a few minutes, he and Betty would be meeting the Queen of England. And no one, even Betty, his wife of almost 30 years, knew what he really did on behalf of the United States. To all he was an international businessman, with business in Europe and Russia. And it was that person that would be in attendance tonight. That was fantasy. The reality was far different. He looked around at the flower-filled suite and momentarily wondered what it would be like to just lead a normal life as a father and husband. He would never know.

He walked over to the mirror and finished fixing his bow tie, completing his costume for the evening and staring for a moment at his slim, six-feet, two-inch frame. At age 52, he was still in reasonably good shape. He knew that age was creeping up and that the agility of his early years wasn't there anymore. This would be his last mission, he silently told himself. He looked through the open bedroom door and saw Betty putting on her make-up and gazed longingly at her. He wondered whether she would still be beside him, if she knew the truth. There were so few people like him. Maybe it would be better if his kind didn't exist on either side of the equation. But that was an illusory thought, and he knew it as such.

"The only time Bob is late is for a social function. Thank God, that's the only time," Harrison grumbled to himself. Although the years had passed, as had the many missions, he could still recall the day and time he first met Colonel Boarders. It was 1965, at Ft. Riley, Kansas, after he had graduated from Notre Dame with a degree in engineering and a commission as a Second Lieutenant in the U.S. Army from the university's ROTC program. Vietnam was the war that everyone wanted to win during that year and he accepted his military service willingly and with eagerness. He had decided to go into Military Intelligence after his Army testing, and counseling had indicated that would be the best area for him. Besides he knew Russian and Arabic—one he had learned at the university and the other while growing up in Saudi Arabia, where his father was an engineer for ARAMCO, the Arabian American Oil Company. Even his academic counselor thought Harrison unique because engineering students rarely took Russian, but David enjoyed the class and the language. David never knew his mother because she died when he was only three. He father had never remarried and had died five years earlier. Except for his wife and son, David had no relatives.

David's first impression of Colonel Robert Boarders was of a man eager for a fight: someone in relentless warfare, with imposition of his will paramount. Boarders was short, with thinning hair, even then, and huge arms which he kept close to his body, as if he were always preparing to fend off an attack at any moment. He didn't look kind-hearted.

The special training cycle that Bob directed at Ft. Riley was the most strenuous. His motto—"Be not afraid" sounded like a biblical statement from on high, and the manner in which Boarders said it every morning at five convinced the trainees that he was God making the statement. And of course, to them he was God. He would start every day with the same question: "Of what should I be afraid?" The answer always to be given was "Be not afraid." The fact was that Harrison and all his fellow trainees were afraid, of Boarders in particular and of the training tests in general.

Yet Boarders knew all to be humans, not robots, and he knew all of them, including himself, to have imperfections, but he never let on about this soft side of himself. Regardless, he never wanted his recruits to be like shifting sands, unsure, unstable, uncertain. "Be not afraid," yet they always were, and Boarders knew it. Whatever fear remained after the training would be controlled, constrained or, if need be, suppressed.

As part of the program, the trainees parachuted at dusk to an isolated section of the Arizona desert. Left there with nothing but a supply of water and a radio, they had seven days to accomplish the goal of getting out alive and well. David succeeded, along with three others from the class of ten, in trekking across miles of grueling Arizona desert in the middle of summer. Harrison had no trouble in the desert. His father had taught him to make the desert his friend. His love of the solitude and his own stoic approach to life made the journey a happy time for him. If he had told anyone, they would have thought him strange, but he liked the peace and serenity of the desert at night. The anger of the desert came during the day when the brutal sun demonstrated that it was king. Night was tranquil and radiant. It was the queen.

The last phase of the program was a sample mission overseas to Amman, Jordan. Only David completed it. During the training, David had almost killed the target, a paid informant of the Central Intelligence Agency who had volunteered for the test. David captured the target and had so intimidated him that he spewed out everything, including the fact that he was a paid informant of the United States. David felt that if he could get that information from him, his loyalty was limited, so there was no reason to keep him alive. Colonel Boarders intervened just in time. As part of the test, David had to check in with the colonel by pressing a prearranged signal on his radio, so Boarders knew his location at all times, as he had intended. When Boarders arrived at the site, he saw that David had tied up the target in a grotesque manner, so any move the man made would inflict more pain, and, after a while, death. While others had shied away from the prospects of taking a life, David hadn't.

When Colonel Boarders called David at the National War College, where he had been teaching for five years, having given up active intelligence duties, he responded without question. Their mutual friend of long standing, Mary Auriello, would be in charge of the special mission.   The special unit set up the Pentum Trade and Investment Company, London, to handle the mission's assignments. David knew why he was selected by Boarders. They had been together on some of the most successful overseas assignments ever for the United States. Few people knew of those assignments, and all records had been destroyed. Cover records had been inserted in their place. Nothing that Bob or David did was legal and, in fact, their activities were specifically prohibited by law. Colonel Boarders never understood, nor did any psychological profile of David ever explain the calmness in David's killing. David demonstrated no feeling in any testing—paper testing or event testing. It was as if he were two men. Sometimes, even Boarders, who was no stranger to stealth killings, was taken by the coolness with which David would carry out an assignment.

Survival was their key, and both were capable of as much violence as those they challenged. But David seemed to be inherently fond of all games of hazard. That is why he was successful. He was an assassin, an American assassin.

Harrison walked back into the parlor of the suite, heading toward the phone, which was ringing repeatedly. "Honey, are you getting the phone?" his wife Betty shouted from the bedroom.

"Yes, I hope it's Bob. Probably in Singapore when he should be here."

"Bob," David shouted, "Where the hell are you?"

"No, Mr. Harrison, this is the concierge. Your car is ready."

"Yes, thank you. We'll be right down."

"Where the hell's Bob?" he wondered. "Where the hell is he?" He was aware that, for months, Bob had been working with a woman in the Moscow *mafiya*. She had provided sufficiently good information allowing them to terminate the missile shipment off the coast of Libya. Bob was the only one to have met her and he described her quite well, but David had no picture of her. He was to meet her tonight at the theater with Bob.

"Christ," he said, and headed toward the closet to get coats for himself and his wife. "Honey, let's get out of here. We don't want to be late. To hell with Bob. If he doesn't think enough of us to come, to hell with him." Yet, even as he said this, he reached for the phone and dialed Boarders' hotel one more time. Again, the hotel operator put him through to the room, where he heard only a recording to leave a message, which he did. "Bob, you SOB, where are you? Remember, the Savoy Theatre? My son has a command performance and you'd better be there," he said as he hung up in exasperation.

He looked at the flower-filled suite, reflecting on the divergence which always appeared in his life whenever his family was involved. He could never relax and enjoy both his wife and son. Something always encroached—but he could never say that he was surprised by the intrusion. He thought that just maybe, only just one time—but that thought he knew to be naive.

His son knew that his mother loved flowers, so he had many sent, with several notes thanking them both for supporting him in his quest to be an actor. Harrison was against, Betty for. But both knew Tim's drive would get him to the top—which is what had happened.

"Well, how do I look?" Betty asked, laughing, as she walked gracefully from the bedroom. "Am I young enough to be the star's mother?"

"You'll always be young for me," he said, reaching to hug her and cup her breasts as she recoiled.

"Oh, not so fast, my young man. Later."

"Coat, honey?" And with that he helped her into her tailored, long, black velvet coat. She did look stunning wearing a simple black dress and the diamond and emerald necklace he'd bought her—"Man, I'm so proud tonight," he told himself. She held onto his arm as they walked down the corridor, stopping in front of the elevator bank, where he pressed the down button. "My, we look like an elegant couple, don't we?" he said as he held Betty close to him, looking at the glass covered elevator door. Betty leaned over and gave him a quiet kiss.

It didn't seem that long ago, really, he told himself, that he had met her. Like few memorable events in life, he remembered every detail of that first evening. She was at a Saturday Christmas party that he and his roommates had impulsively decided to attend even though they had senior exams the next week. The party was at a dorm house on the campus of St. Mary's—adjacent to the main Notre Dame campus. She was the first girl he saw as he walked in. She was wearing a short, navy blue skirt and matching sweater which showed off her form well. The blue eyes, big and so innocent, told him it was going to be a challenge getting her into his bed. And it was. He couldn't let her out of his sight that evening, even though he tried to a few times. He wanted her badly ... not like the others who provided a physical outlet for him, for which he had a typical Catholic guilt feeling. "No, this one is different," he thought. When he introduced himself, he reached out his hand and touched Betty's, holding hers for several moments. In a moment of bravado, he pulled her gently toward him.

But she clearly resisted, by dropping her hand immediately and placing it on his chest, firmly saying, "Wait a minute, David." She kept her hand in that position for no more than a few seconds, but to David, it seemed forever. He wanted her so badly, but it was hopeless, and his buddies teased him about the fact that he went home without her.

The next day, she relented and had coffee with him. They were inseparable from that point on. He had never thought of love until he met Betty. They married after graduation. She received her degree in history, and he in engineering. She stayed with her parents in Arvada, Colorado, the beautiful, sprawling suburb of Denver, while he undertook his military training. Thereafter, she went with him to his first posting in Washington, D.C. where he was assigned to the Central Intelligence Agency for special training. He finished first in his class of twelve. No one had ever achieved a perfect score in the year-long training cycle. David was the only one. But the training took him away from his wife. He could see her only six times during the year-long period.

Rather than complaining, Betty busied herself with history courses at George Washington University. Her parents visited her frequently, as did several of her college classmates. She wrote David every other day and mailed the letters to a special PO box he'd given her. He received her letters in bundles, and brought them home with him every time. He never discarded one of them.

It was five years into their marriage, and after several miscarriages, that Timothy was conceived—on July 4. He remembered that day because it was the first day of a two-week holiday that he could spend with Betty before he left for further training in Morocco, in preparation for a mission. Betty stayed behind in Washington; and although he visited her twice in a six-month period, he was gone when Timothy was born. Betty never said a word about that. Her mother and father were with her and David was thankful for that.

She'd been through so much with him—and had always been gentle, kind, and understanding. Betty was tender when they made love and he would clasp her in his arms, never wanting to leave her. There were times when his joy was supreme, his happiness so deep, that tears would come to his eyes. He'd be embarrassed and start to apologize. Betty would keep kissing him and holding him even more tightly. Their love making was like a new invention, as if they were discovering each other for the first time. Their intimacy was deep and total. Whenever he was away from her, he realized that life would be unbearable without her. Yet he continued and she never asked him to do otherwise.

The concierge was waiting for them as they stepped off the elevator. "Good evening, Mr. and Mrs. Harrison. This way, please," he continued as he led them through the lobby and to the front entrance where the driver was holding the rear door open to a Bentley limousine.

"My, my, David, haven't we arrived? Or should I say, hasn't our son arrived?"

"Our son, honey. This is our son."

"Have a good evening, sir," and with that the concierge saluted them, and returned inside.

As the car sped off, the phone at the concierge station rang. "Howard, this is Allison at reception. Have the Harrisons left? There's an urgent call for them from Washington."

"I'm afraid they just left for the theatre, Allison."

"The party is waiting on the line wanting to know if there's a number at the theatre for patrons. Do you know, Howard? The party seems anxious."

"I'm sure there is. Let me look it up. Give me a moment." He flipped through his directory of theatre numbers but could find only the general theatre number. "Have them try 71-836-8117. That's the general number. Perhaps they'll be able to do something."

Betty sat close to David. "This is just beautiful, David. Never in my dreams would I have thought we'd be seeing our son on the stage and the queen present. We should be so proud." She leaned over and kissed David, whose mind wanted to join her in this happy frame.

But he blurted out, "I'd be happier if I knew where Bob was. He should be there."

"He will be, David. You know he's never let you down. He'll be there."

Washington
Friday
Local Time: 2:20 p.m. (7:20 p.m., London)
Department of Justice, Room 6610

"Mary, there's no answer in Colonel Boarders' room. None. And there's no answer at Mr. Harrison's room either."

"I am on hold with Harrison's hotel, asking for a number at the theater where we can reach him. See if the limo has a cell phone in it," Mary replied. Her heart sinking fast, she stared vacantly at her office TV which was always on to CNN, but without sound. "If you can't get through, call Commander Robinson at the Yard. You have his special number at the palace." She looked at the clock; the curtain at the theater would rise in ten minutes . . . in ten minutes. And she could reach no one . . . no one.

London
Local Time: 7:00 p.m.
Heathrow Airport, Terminal Four

The British Air flight from Moscow, scheduled to arrive at 7:00 p.m., was to be one hour late, which worried Stephen Thomas, a chauffeur employed by Mayfair Car Hire. He was at the VIP lounge to meet a party of two from Moscow, from the Bank Alliance Russia. Stephen would hold up a small slate right outside the Customs Hall with that name chalked in large letters. He was to take them to the Dorchester Hotel. He looked at the television monitor and saw it change again; the British Air flight would be an hour-and-a-half late.

In accord with company procedure, Stephen called his dispatcher on his cellular phone to notify him of the delay. The dispatcher told him to stay and carry out the pickup as planned. He went back to the parked car and moved it to the other side of the roadway. The lane he had been in was in was thirty-minute pickup only.

He followed these instructions, taking another look at the inside of the immaculately clean, black Mercedes, placing a *Times* newspaper, neatly folded and ready to read. The rain was still falling and he instinctively pulled his blue cap down as he strode back into the terminal. He headed for the small coffee bar adjacent to the Customs Hall for a coffee and some relaxation before his clients arrived. He had all the time in the world, he mused to himself, but his clients' time, unfortunately, was limited.

London
Local time: 8:00 p.m.
British Air Flight 911 from Moscow
On approach to Heathrow Airport, London

"BA Flight 911, this is Heathrow Air Traffic Control. You're to hold pattern until further notice. We have had to close a runway temporarily; a plane skidded off on landing. We should have the matter under control in thirty minutes."

Captain Richards responded methodically and quietly, "Copy. BA Flight 911 is to hold pattern until further notice."

"Correct. Hold pattern. Please."

Captain Richards turned to his first officer, Tom Miller, who had heard the same instructions and looked amused. They had plenty of fuel for alternate airports, including Manchester. "Better tell Meredith that we're about to make this announcement," Captain Richards told his first officer, referring to the chief cabin supervisor. He then buzzed Meredith, asking her to come forward.

"I guess we shouldn't worry," Meredith said. "We're already one hour behind schedule. The baggage situation at Sheremetyevo Moscow airport hasn't improved at all. It takes security forever to screen the baggage and that's always a delay. The Russians are really ill equipped for capitalism. We'll have some very frustrated passengers."

"You're right. But there's little anybody can do. They just don't have their act together yet. And, I guess we don't either," Captain

Richards said quietly. "We'll wait. Okay. Tom, give the announcement."

"Ladies and gentlemen, this is First Officer Miller. We've been advised by Heathrow Air Control to hold our altitude under further notice. The airport is congested but this should last no more than thirty minutes. I'll keep you advised. We should be on the ground shortly."

In First Class seats 2A and 2B, Boris Shenin turned to Georgi Ivashkin. "We shall be late for our appointment, won't we? But he'll wait for us." Without expecting a response, he returned to reading his magazine.

**London
Local Time: 7:00 p.m.
The Lowndes Hotel
Room 352**

Sarah Williams had twenty rooms to serve before she could go home. She had the rooms and suites on the first through the fourth floors.

"Night service," she said as she knocked on the door. Hearing no answer, Sarah used the master card (the doors were all electronically coded for entrance with a wallet-size card that looked like a credit card) and turned on the lights by pressing the master switch as she entered the room. She noticed that the balcony window door was open slightly and the wind was blowing briskly. She closed the door. She went to the bed and pulled the coverlet down, folded it into a perfect square, and placed it in the chest at the foot of the bed. Expertly, Sarah turned the sheets down, fluffed the pillows and placed the breakfast menu on the pillow with a small chocolate.

Next, Sarah went into the bathroom, slightly annoyed that all of the towels, including the face towels, had been thrown on the floor, on top of the bathmat. She couldn't understand why guests never put the soiled towels into the hamper, next to the bathroom basin. As she gathered them in her arms to take them out, a handtowel fell and she noticed how red it was. It couldn't have been a shaving accident—no, there was too much blood. "God, what is this?" she wondered. Suddenly, she became frightened and tossed the towels into the bag attached to her night cart and hurriedly brought in clean towels, straightened a few chairs, and left quickly.

CHAPTER THREE

Moscow
Friday
Local Time: 4:00 p.m. (1:00 p.m., London)
10 Tverskaya, Suite 1400

Peter Bradford, like the few other American expatriates who were allowed into the old Soviet Union in 1978, was careful. In rare moments, he would also admit he was very lucky. He had a quiet, almost liquid way of speaking that betrayed little or no emotion, and at times, little energy. He wouldn't make mistakes because of hasty action, never fidgeted nervously, always remained suspended in some kind of strange calm. Bradford was a fanatic about disorder.

The desk where he sat was devoid of any papers—all having been filed appropriately and out of sight. Not one book in his two matching bookcases on the left wall in his modest office was askew; all were arranged according to height. The two guest chairs that faced his desk were positioned 32 inches apart—always. Whenever a visitor would leave, pushing the chair back, as soon as appropriate Bradford would rearrange the chairs to spots he had carefully outlined on the dark gray office carpet with small bits of colored tape. At times, he would check the measurements on either side of a large painting of the Kremlin, which hung behind his desk, to make sure that it was equidistant between the walls. He believed that whenever he closed the door to his office, or to the adjacent conference room, the painting would be off center. The only way to prove to himself that it was centered was to measure. Only then did he relax. Unless the meeting was confidential, he kept the doors to the office or to the conference room open.

He actually enjoyed anonymity. That is probably the reason he lasted in this city of many faces . . . and for so long.

He had heard from Boris Shenin that Shenin and his aide Ivashkin were on their way to London to verify the success of the assassin they had hired. To continue with the Moscow *vor*, Bradford had to demonstrate that he had eliminated those responsible for the failed Libyan missile delivery. To do otherwise would have been stupid and, if anything, Bradford wasn't stupid. He also wasn't a wave maker, and he never wished to offend the Moscow *vor*, whom he had known since the days of Brezhnev, nor did he want to make any more errors.

Bradford was proud he had been accepted by the *mafiya*, but it had come at a price ... the killing of a fellow American. That killing brought him the respect of the *mafiya*, and he carried that badge of approval with great honor. If the killing was brutal and memorable and if it had saved him, it had also destroyed the myth that he was a loyal U.S. citizen.

When an officer from the Inspector General's office of the Department of State was getting too close to the truth regarding the payment of certain in-country invoices, which were inflated in price, and in many cases, payments for nonexistent services and goods, he invited him over for dinner and killed him with a poison provided by the Moscow KGB. Without flinching, he and two members of the KGB then cut up the body and took it to one of Moscow's city dumps about thirty kilometers north of the city. The official investigation concerning the disappearance of the State Department officer Thomas Sewell depended heavily on Bradford's testimony, who said he dropped him off in front of his hotel and that was the last he saw of the young man.

When the murder occurred, Bradford was one of three project managers for the construction of the new U.S. Embassy in Moscow. He still found it hard to believe how he got the position. It was 1978 when he answered an advertisement in *The Washington Post* for a "construction supervisor" and supplied his background to a post office box. Shortly thereafter, he was called for an interview by the American company that had won the contract to construct the embassy. It was clear that the contractor was interested in nothing other than how cheaply he could hire Bradford. Bradford did have experience, having been with a large home construction company in the Washington area. But he had never been outside the United States. He was divorced and hadn't remarried, and his only child, a daughter, lived with her mother. By choice, he rarely saw her. She reminded him too much of his former wife, whom he despised.

He seized happily the opportunity to leave the United States. Seldom had he felt such eagerness. Soon after his arrival in Moscow he took what he considered a good opportunity to enhance his income by selling what he knew to the KGB. He felt distinguished—that he, a lowly construction supervisor, without even a high school education, would be sought after by the Soviet spy agency. And the KGB cultivated him, by providing him money and also girls—young girls to whom he had a compulsive attraction.

He was proud of his height—about six-feet, three-inches tall. At age sixty, he was beginning to fulfill the genetic promise that he would be a bald man, and he was self-conscious about his thinning hair. And totally out of the character of calmness and disinterest he always wished to project, he was addicted to chewing on pencils—a habit he had acquired when giving up cigarettes years earlier. He placed the damaged pencils in his top desk drawer, lining them in accord with their length.

Today, however, nothing he did could forestall a wave of anxiety that was slowly taking hold.

The sale of battlefield surface-to-air missiles, stolen from the Soviet inventory as its troops were leaving what was then East Germany, was his idea. Those missiles were at the bottom of the Mediterranean Sea, thanks to the operations of the two men now being hunted in London by the hit man Shenin had hired on Bradford's behalf.

His second idea, the sale of an off-inventoried one kiloton Russian nuclear weapon to Iran, and for a price he had negotiated—some $350 million in American money—must, under any circumstances, succeed. He was apprehensive because the *vor* neither forgave nor forgot a blunder—and he had blundered badly on the Libyan missile sale and that blunder had seriously damaged his credibility—a credibility he had built over the years. But Bradford believed he could make up for that miscalculation by having his new deal bring into the *mafiya's* coffers much more money than was lost on the Libyan debacle.

He sat in his office suite alone, waiting for the arrival of the Moscow *vor*. The double doors to the conference room were open and the eight chairs stood around a simple, highly polished mahogany table. There was no other furniture in that room. The only door to the conference room was through his office. The only door into the suite was from the reception area and he could see the reception room from his desk through the one-way glass he had installed in the door. He was afraid. Too many people had disappeared after mistakes occurred.

As night was falling slowly, thickly, he was relieved to be delivered from the day. He liked the night. Darkness was a kinder element for him. His fair complexion made it necessary for him to stay away from the sun because of the cancers that developed on his face. Careful examination showed small scars remaining from multiple operations to remove cancerous lesions from his forehead and nose. He contemplated plastic surgery, but never thought seriously of changing his appearance—which gave him the air of a street fighter. This he didn't mind—but again it was a fantasy in which only he believed.

He didn't ask his secretary of these last five years, Svetlana Makorova, to come to this meeting. Although he spoke passable Russian, many times he had her act as his translator and note taker. But there wouldn't be a need for her at this meeting. She was on a well-earned vacation in Cyprus, where the sun was shining, according to her morning call to him. He knew he loved this young woman, but he also knew that she had suitor who was a young member of the Moscow *vor's* team, as well as a favorite of the man coming to see him.

Besides he had been living with a woman since he arrived in Moscow. She had been his Russian language tutor and, unlike his former wife in the United States, she treated him with respect and honor. Although he had no children with this woman, by a former marriage she had two sons, both of whom were now married.

Svetlana, his secretary, was something special that he could never have . . . and he made up for this by paying her well. He shouldn't have thanked himself, because the *mafiya* expected this practice from one of their own. People who worked under the auspices of the Moscow *vor* presumed generosity from its members.

The air was still as he looked out his window—no wind and only a light rain falling on this late Friday afternoon. The dim face of the clock on his office wall told him that it was 4:00 p.m.—1:00 p.m. in London. Earlier in the day, he had received a call from Boris Shenin that everything was on course. In a few hours, Boris would board his plane for London, so it would be much later before he would get a report from Boris about what happened in London. Bradford's hands were trembling, for a moment; he was uncertain, fearful, as he reached into his desk drawer and made sure that his 45-caliber Colt pistol lay in place and fully loaded—not that he would ever have a chance to survive if he tried to take on those who were coming to see him. Perhaps, he thought, he could get one, perhaps even two, but they would finish him off, regardless. He closed his eyes for a moment while he silently slid the desk drawer back into place.

As he stood up, he muttered to himself, "It wasn't my fault that the deal on the missiles went down. Why is it my fault? Why?" Before he could answer himself, he looked down at the street and saw two black Mercedes draw up. As the doors to the cars opened almost simultaneously, Dimitri Gravev, the crime lord of Moscow, the Moscow *vor,* was the first to step out. He stood on the sidewalk, looking more solemn than ever. In the shifting light of the street lamp and rain, he glanced at the building and, followed by his four bodyguards and two aides, entered the building—a shapeless one built during the early 1960s. The two guards at the entrance merely nodded when the group came in. There was no need to ask for identification. The visitors were well known.

Hearing the door knob turn, Peter immediately rose from his desk and headed toward the door. Dimitri opened it fully, blinked and tossed his head slightly, reaching to hug Peter and kissing him on both cheeks. Peter didn't restrain himself and he hugged back. Perhaps even a handsome figure, almost as tall as Peter, Dimitri stood erect. His face, broad with high cheek bones, was complemented by a generous mouth and deep brown eyes. His hair was black with slight traces of gray. The Italian designer suit was perfectly fitted to him and his tie was a subdued red against a flawless white shirt. Dimitri had one small wedding band on his left hand and no other jewelry—not even a watch. The eyes looked at Peter steadily without any expression whatsoever. Gravev controlled the merchandise that had gone down off Benghazi, Libya, and he was here for a report on what was being done to correct the situation. A larger and more important shipment was being prepared to be sent, and he needed confirmation that the problem had been solved.

The four body guards stayed in the reception room. Dimitri and his two aides came into Bradford's office and then moved through to the conference room. There was no conversation until all were seated. Unless asked to by Dimitri, the aides would not enter into the conversation. Protocol dictated that Peter sit in the first chair on Dimitri's left. Unopened bottles of mineral water, Pepsi and glasses rested at each spot.

"So, my good friend, Peter, what news do you have from the city? Is our man in place?" Gravev asked in a quiet tone.

"Yes, he is in place," Bradford answered. "The matter will be concluded in a few hours."

"Good. I am pleased. Now, my friend, on the other project—the special sale to our friends to the south. Are you confident that the sale will go through . . . unhindered? We certainly do not wish to get into the same situation as before, do we, Peter?"

"Of course not, Dimitri, and we won't. I am confident of that," Bradford said, looking directly at Dimitri. For several moments, there was silence except for the humming of the ventilation system.

"Good, Peter. Good. I always admire a confident person. Your confidence makes me all the more certain that you will succeed this time . . . unlike the last. Peter, my friend, my good friend of all these years, we can't keep losing our sales and our money. Now can we? You do understand, don't you?" Dimitri spoke suspiciously, his eyes continuing to look directly at Bradford.

"Yes, I do understand. Everything is in place. We shall be successful. I assure you of that, Dimitri. I assure you," Bradford replied.

"Good. Everything is in place. All we have to do is to wait. Correct?" Dimitri inquired earnestly.

"Correct. All we have to do is wait. I shall call you directly once I get a report from London, which shall be in several hours. May I call you at home quite late this evening?" Peter asked in a solicitous tone.

"Of course, Peter. Call anytime, please. I want to know. By the way,

Peter, it will not be necessary for you to attend this evening's meeting at my dacha. There is no need. Besides, Peter, I want you to get some sleep. You have very dark circles under your eyes. I am worried about you, Peter. Yes, you should get a good night's sleep, a gentle sleep, Peter, a gentle, good night's sleep," Gravev said as he rose from his seat.

"Yes, I shall try, and thank you for being so concerned, Dimitri," Bradford said as he also stood up, not understanding Dimitri's use of the words "gentle sleep."

Normally, Bradford would have been asked to accompany Dimitri and his group to the bank of elevators, but not this time. Peter gritted his teeth and he had a terrible sense of desolation. He closed the door behind him, returning to his desk where he sat still for several minutes. "Gravev may be more ruthless, but I am smarter," he said aloud. "Yes, what I have planned is much smarter," he murmured, clenching his hands together, "and Gravev will soon find that out. He was nothing until he came to me. I made him what he is today, that fuckin' SOB."

Peter then rose and looked down from his fourth-floor window to see the two Mercedes leaving the curb, speeding away down Tverskaya.

London
Friday
Local Time: 7:20 p.m.
The Savoy Theatre

The Royal Security Service section of Scotland Yard had placed metal detectors at the three main entrances to the theatre. Ruslan Ishaev had, as everyone else, to show his ticket first and then go through the detector. This was done very smoothly because security was well aware of the on-time arrival of Queen Elizabeth and her entourage.

The crowd mingled in anticipation of an elegant evening, and many were unaware that they had to be seated before the queen would arrive with her party, which included the star's parents. The excitement was evident even to Ruslan. The main entrance to the theatre, adjacent to the Savoy Hotel, was directly off the Strand through three sets of stainless steel double doors. When the theatre was full, as it was for this command performance, movement was restricted. At the urging of the ushers, the crowd was slowly funneling into the proper channel for the stalls and the balcony. Everyone knew that they would be able to see the queen's party, because the seats in the Savoy were so placed that the royal box was easily viewed.

Ruslan lingered by the entrance to the stalls, thinking what better way to murder the American than in this theatre. It would demonstrate that the *vor* could reach anywhere. Although he could have attempted the assassination at the hotel where Harrison was staying, he selected this manner for maximum publicity . . . but he knew it entailed maximum risk as well as maximum surprise. He had been to the theatre three evenings in a row, plotting his deed. Getting to Harrison's box seats would be simple. He only hoped that the client had given him the right information. The silencer insured that his specially designed pistol made virtually no noise. In tests he himself conducted while in Moscow, the sound of the speeding bullet would be no louder than a short cough, hitting the target with a muffled thud. Ruslan would be gone before the target would slump over dead. "No," he said to himself, "killing Harrison would not be difficult."

He glanced at the clock above the Circle bar, and then disappeared into the men's room, a few steps down the corridor from the bar. When he went into the men's room, he was surprised to see a security officer there.

Ruslan look bewildered for a moment, as the officer spoke calmly. "Sir, this room will be closed for several minutes until the performance begins," the officer politely told Ruslan. Ruslan said it would only take a minute, as he had to go into the loo.

The officer thought nothing of it at all and smiled with a jog of his head to indicate okay, saying, "I understand."

"Another lapse," Ruslan thought. First, the momentary hesitation at the hotel when he looked at the face of the young prostitute, and now this. The ticket provided him by the client gave him no indication of this special occasion. The client didn't tell him, or didn't know. If he had known that the queen would be in attendance for the performance, he would have realized that security would be tight, as it was wherever the queen went. Once he had gone through the metal detectors as he entered the theatre, he knew that the evening would be different, and all his carefully made plans would be jeopardized. Now, he would have to improvise what needed to be done. Regardless, he would go through with the assignment because he had never abandoned one before.

His earlier visits to the theatre didn't include this kind of security, so he was surprised when he arrived this evening. Regardless, he had to put the gun together. The parts were in the bottoms of his shoes and time was moving rapidly. His shoes were carefully constructed in Moscow by his client and it was relatively simple to put the weapon and silencer in place, but he needed at least two minutes. He had practiced the procedure many times. It was almost 7:25 p.m. and the officer would be hovering over him until he left. And, more importantly, if the officer looked at the bottom of the loo, he could see Ruslan's feet, because the door was a partial one. Silently, he leaned over and slipped off his size-twelve right shoe and unsnapped the entire bottom with a quick turn and pulled out the specially built pistol, placing it in his jacket pocket. He repeated the operation on the left shoe after replacing his right shoe. He withdrew his silencer and placed it in his other coat pocket. Quickly, he flushed the toilet and opened the door to see the officer staring at him.

"Something wrong with your feet, sir?" the officer inquired calmly.

"They are a bit tight because they are new . . . you know how these dress shoes are . . . very tight to look good, I guess," Ruslan replied as he walked to the sink to wash his hands.

"Yes, I'm happy I'm not wearing them myself," the officer said.

Ruslan went over to the washstand next to the outside wall, leaving his jacket open and loose. As he reached for the paper towels to wipe his hands, the bulge in his right pocket, which were not there before, now became evident to the security officer who had been watching him closely. He started to walk toward Ruslan asking "Sir, would you mind coming with me to go through the detector again? Just a formality."

"Of course, of course. I've gone through it once tonight. No matter again," he said smiling.

But as the officer turned slightly to open the door, Ruslan grabbed his neck, and in a moment had broken it. He held the man without looking at him and slowly took him into the loo, placing him on the very seat he had occupied just a short while earlier. His pulse racing, he felt a painful sensation of doubt about the mission surface in his mind. "God must not abandon me. God would not abandon me," he kept repeating to himself.

He didn't know that when the security officer asked him to go with him to the metal detector checkpoint, he had pressed a button on his pager, alerting the station that he had a potential problem.

Ruslan looked at his watch and saw that it was almost 7:30 p.m. He had to get to his seat. No one would be allowed to enter the auditorium until after the royal party was seated. He left the men's restroom quickly and reached the stalls, where the usher asked him to hurry. As he sat down in Seat H-2 in the brightly lit gold and red auditorium, "God Save the Queen" began to play over the sound system.

He had no fear of what lay ahead. He knew this would be a different mission. He just had to wait; be very efficient as he approached Harrison during the fifteen-minute intermission, getting close enough to fire his weapon but from a sufficiently far enough distance allowing for an unobtrusive escape. He was always successful, so why not now? The job would take no more than a few seconds by his steady hand, carefully aiming an ultra silenced weapon. He was trained for this business, and his anxiety passed out of his mind. On this occasion, however, the unexpected presence of the queen inflicted maximum danger in carrying out the assignment. Why should that matter? He deliberately made the decision to continue, realizing that, for him, a skilled and precise killer, it was not a hopeless situation. Ruslan continued, thus, to make adjustments to his earlier, carefully organized and rehearsed plan, and he began to feel satisfaction that he could carry out the assignment. He was a superb assassin, wasn't he? He had just murdered three people, silently and quickly.

No longer feeling uncomfortable with the changing circumstances, the auditorium lights now dimming, Ruslan shifted in his seat slightly, a smirk crossing his hard face, his eyes now fixed on the gold trimmed red velvet curtain as it parted for the first act of the American hit comedy, "Breakfast with Olivia."

Now self-assured, Ruslan would do the only thing possible for him: kill Harrison. He was too near to his mark and he was confident he would not fail. Nothing would now make him uneasy, and he was ashamed that he had a fleeting, frightening thought that maybe he would have to sacrifice himself in the attempt on Harrison. This hesitation, this brief period of fear momentarily angered him, for such a sacrifice would bring him his supreme Paradise. Shouldn't he welcome such a death? *In the name of God the Almighty, I am nothing but your servant ..."*

London
Local Time: 7:30 p.m.
Buckingham Palace
The Royal Security Command Center

Commander Michael Robinson, assigned by Scotland Yard to head the Royal Security Service, couldn't believe what he was hearing over the phone. One of his men had been murdered in the men's bathroom at the Savoy and the queen had arrived and was in the theatre. He pressed the preset button on his phone for the Royal Limousine.

"Stewart here."

"Have the queen and her party entered the theatre?" Commander Robinson asked quietly.

"Yes, they've just gone in," came the reply.

"Thanks, Stewart. I'll be right over."

"Is there a problem, sir?" Stewart asked.

"No, just a precaution," he said looking at his watch. It was 7:30 p.m.

THE PENTUM MISSION

London
Local Time: 7:30 p.m.
The Lowndes Hotel
Room 452

Sarah Williams was still worried about the blood on the hand towel that she had taken from room 352 directly underneath. Well, no matter, she would report it on the laundry turn-street. She had placed the cloth in a separate plastic bag and had tagged it accordingly so the laundry personnel would know how to treat it. Anyway, she was near the end of her shift and room 452 would be one of the last. She looked forward to going to her sister Amanda's house in Inslington and playing bridge with her bridge club and having a little sherry—yes, she smiled to herself—even workers like herself had sherry.

Her sister was a widow who had been married to a civil servant in the British Foreign Office. Sherry had been his favorite drink. Although she recognized that her sister had married well, Sarah had never married, and was happy being a maid. She thought back to her sister's marriage, and how happy it had been. But the marriage failed. Later, her husband had gone off with a younger woman from the office. Sarah couldn't say she was unsettled when she heard that he had died in an auto accident in Kenya. She and her sister were good friends and that was all that counted, she supposed.

She rang the buzzer, said her usual "Night Service," and waited for a response. No one answered, so she let herself in by pushing the master electronic card key that she carried on a long brass chain attached to her belt. The room was dark, so she instinctively reached to the left of the door and the second switch which would turn on all the lights in the room simultaneously. She felt the breeze from the open balcony door—"Why," she thought, "would people keep their balcony doors open in this rainy weather?" It took her five seconds to walk through the short foyer into the room, and then she stepped onto the oriental carpet, which she instantly noticed was wet.

She looked down to her feet, realizing she was standing in blood. She then looked at the bed and saw two naked bodies in a grotesque manner—one's bloodied head on the left thigh of the other. "Good God," she uttered quietly. She pressed the emergency button on her pager and ran out into the hall, collapsing on the floor. "Oh good God, oh my good God, this cannot be, this cannot be," she cried. Overwhelmed by nausea and utter fright, her body shook uncontrollably.

London
Local Time: 7:45 p.m.
London Metropolitan Police Station
Sloan Street, Belgravia

Dean Goodwin was small. When he slid down in his chair as he did when he was tired, he appeared even smaller. And tonight he was tired from boredom. He had been at the station since nine and had expected to go home at the normal hour of three, but his captain had asked him to take another shift, because the on-duty officer had called in sick, and it was a very slow day, with the night predicted to be no busier. So why not stay at least until eleven, his commander had asked him, with a slight smile. No matter; he could catch up on some files and report writing. Besides, it would mean double pay, and his wife was pregnant with their second child, so he could use the extra money.

Being the duty officer at the station had its ups and downs. As a detective, he knew that his hours were never his own. Yet, here at the Belgravia station, the services of the detectives were in little demand, because the crimes mostly involved stolen vehicles, break-ins, and assaults. Nothing serious, he mused. Unlike other parts of London. He thought that everyone that lived in Belgravia was civilized or at least appeared to be. The common police room—where all the officers had desks—was quiet. He and Dudley Arrison were the only ones in a room that during the day bustled with as many as ten detectives and scores of other officers.

The station was an old 1920s' style, four-story building on Sloan Street. The only modern equipment, in an otherwise nondescript building, consisted of the telephones and the computers hooked up to the central police system and, of course, to Scotland Yard Center. The desks were old, but the station had an aura of warmth and comfort and chaos at times.

Goodwin loved being a police officer—it was his whole life and he had been in the police force since leaving the Royal Navy some fifteen years earlier.

"Dudley, if you're going out, get me a roast beef and no mayonnaise," Goodwin said. "I want some chips . . . and one of those diet sodas. You know, the ones with zero calories," he added, as he tapped his middle that was getting too soft and too round. He would have to start working out at the police gym to get his weight down before his annual physical, due in about ten weeks. And he didn't want his name on the fat list posted in every station—the new rules of the new police commander—who of course was as trim as he could be at fifty-five. "Why," he thought, "is everything that's so tasty so bad for you?" Imagine Pilsner ale not good for a man. "Silly, these new health fads," he thought. His wife was a vegetarian, and that was a source of conflict, although not serious, in their marriage. After all, she would tell him, he could have his meat at lunch, and she was right.

Dudley looked up from his file and held out the palm of his hand for money. Before Goodwin could respond, the intercom rang. It was the station's receptionist, who said that the night manager from the Lowndes Hotel was on the line reporting that there were two bodies in his hotel.

"Come on, Graham, some kind of joke? How long have you been on duty?"

"No, sir, here he is," and he clicked off without responding to Goodwin's comment.

"Detective Goodwin. Can I help you?"

"Yes," a nervous and unsure voice, speaking rapidly, came over the phone "Ernest Stirling here, the evening manager at the Lowndes. Can you come over right away? We have had a terrible tragedy in the hotel. Please, though, use the back service entrance in the alley off Lowndes Street. Don't want to disturb the other guests."

"I understand," Goodwin replied, with some distaste. "But what happened?"

"Two men are dead; one is a guest of the hotel. The other I don't know. It is a gruesome sight. Please come over right away. This is just horrible. I don't know what to do. . . ." His voice trailed off.

"Be there in five minutes," Goodwin said and hung up. No, he said to himself, not in Belgravia. He would have to call Scotland Yard for help . . . but not right now, and only after he knew exactly what was going on.

"Dudley, don't go anywhere. We're going to the Lowndes. Some interesting work ahead, I think."

"No food then. And what is the interesting work—a Rolls double parked?" Dudley joked.

"How about two bodies?" Goodwin replied in a surprised tone.

Dudley stared at him and caught the keys to the car as they were tossed to him. "Two bodies . . . at the Lowndes?"

"Yes, Dudley, two bodies at the Lowndes," he replied as he shook his head incredulously.

Washington, D.C.
Friday
Local Time: 3:00 p.m. (8:00 p.m., London)
Department of Justice: Room 6610

"Patching you through to Commander Robinson. Please hold on," the Scotland Yard dispatcher said quietly. As the various computer generated tones sounded over the phone, Mary knew that all the precautions that had been taken had collapsed. Somehow, someway, the Moscow *vor* knew of the location and schedule of Boarders and Harrison. Her thoughts as to how that could have possibly happened were interrupted by a deep, baritone voice.

"Commander Robinson here. Mary—good to hear from you. How can I help?"

"Commander, you know of course that our David Harrison and a Colonel Boarders will be in attendance tonight as guests of the queen.

THE PENTUM MISSION

We've just received information that they both may be the targets of an assassination attempt. It's my strong suggestion that you get them out of the theatre as quickly as possible. Is that do-able?"

"Yes, Mary, it is. Earlier this evening, one of our security officers was murdered in a men's room in the theatre: neck broken neatly by someone who knew what he was doing. Now what you're telling me confirms my worse fears. It was that incident that caused me to ask that the queen leave. Harrison and his wife are here, but I don't believe that Colonel Boarders is here.

"The queen and her party will leave at intermission. I'll notify Harrison as well. They are well-guarded and I am speaking to you on a cell phone just a short distance away from their boxes. No one, I repeat, no one will be allowed to leave the theatre until the queen and her party and the Harrisons leave. I assure you that he'll be safe," Robinson said.

"You must have Harrison call me directly. Advise him I'm leaving for London within a few hours. I'll notify him of my ETA in my call to him."

"I assure you they'll be fine. We'll post guards at their hotel."

"Thanks, Commander. I owe you one. Are you coming to D.C. soon? And aren't we on the same program this December at the Interpol meeting in Bern?"

"Yes, Mary. We're supposed to discuss terrorism and modern government leader security. Know anything about it?"

"No." She hung up.

"Sweetness in one breath; anger in the next," Robinson told himself.

**London
Local Time: 8:45 p.m.
The Savoy Theatre**

The peal of laughter from the audience as the curtain closed on the first act made the Harrisons smile even more as they saw the memorable performance their son had given. But this moment of happiness was tempered by the fact that David's closest friend, Bob, wasn't there. The old colonel wouldn't do this. "He always notifies me about where he's going to be, just as I notify him. Something's wrong," he thought. Could it be that he picked someone up? Is the old man taking too many chances now? He's probably stuck with some . . . and he let his mind close on that thought. He turned to his wife and both rose from their seats to join the queen for intermission.

"Honey, what do I say to the queen?" he asked as he took Betty's arm. But as he looked over to the queen's box, he noticed that her party had already left.

"You thank her for coming to our son's performance," Betty said and leaned over and gave David a small kiss on his left cheek." This is one of the happiest days of my life."

Distracted by the emptiness of the Royal Box, David did not acknowledge his wife's comments, but asked,"Did you notice the queen and her party leaving?"

"No, I don't think so. But, of course, I was looking at our son on the stage . . . where your eyes should have been as well," Betty replied, firmly tugging on his arm.

"Mr. Harrison," he heard someone say to his left. He turned to see an usher next to him. The usher handed him a note which he read quickly. He looked up and asked when it was received.

"Just a few moments ago," the usher said. "A gentleman is waiting outside for you."

"Honey, we have to go now," Harrison said as he looked at his wife who stood listening to the conversation with obvious interest.

"What's wrong, David? What's wrong?" she asked.

"I don't know. I just don't know. Maybe it has to do with Bob," he said as he took her arm and led her from the box.

The usher parted the velvet drapes to the box and standing outside was Commander Michael Robinson with two security officers that David recognized as those watching the royal box and his own box.

"Mr. Harrison, we earlier notified the queen that she must depart because of a security concern in the theatre. She's on her way to her car and we ask that you come with us as well. One of my men has been found murdered in the first-floor men's room. We don't know whether the killer is still in the theater or whether this is an isolated incident. But we must ask that you, your wife, and your son leave now. We know your situation, sir." He left the comment hanging. "Two of my men are already on their way together with the manager of the theater to get your son. He should be in your car when you and Mrs. Harrison arrive. The remainder of the performance will be canceled. The manager will make the announcement after we have left and the intermission is over. We must move now, Mr. Harrison. Please. Further, Mary Auriello asks that you call her on an urgent basis. You have a car phone?"

David, holding firmly to Betty's left hand, said to Robinson, "Of course . . . yes, I'll call her directly," and followed him toward the exit stairs. He realized that the matter that Mary Auriello spoke about had gone sour in some fashion. David began to think the unthinkable about Bob. He must be in serious trouble. Something wrong had occurred, very wrong. And what about Bob's contact? Where was she?

Ruslan Ishaev thought the play was pointless. Laughing about the breakdown of a marriage and having an affair with another woman. "Sick," he thought. He knew he didn't understand the dialog. But then, he was educated in a country where the premium was on family and the sanctity of mothers. Slowly, he looked at the royal box and the Harrisons' box. "It will not be difficult," he thought, "not at all." The area to the royal box and the adjacent boxes were closed to all the public until after the performance. So he could go up the stairs, but not much further beyond the corridor leading to the boxes. But he also noticed, as he left the area for the foyer, that the security was much more intense and that the men's room, where he had been earlier, displayed a sign saying it was closed. In fact, security officers stood at the landings on the stairs as he looked up. He wouldn't be able to get through, that way.

Ruslan went to the Circle bar and asked for a bottle of mineral water, paid for it and turned before he could get his change from the ten-pound note. The waiter called after him with the change of some seven pounds but he waved the waiter away, saying it was a good tip for good service. Ruslan mingled with the crowd and marveled at how the English lived, all orderly and mannerly and enjoying a play he believed to be immoral. As he wandered over to examine the theatre announcements hanging on the wall adjacent to the ticket booths, he noticed that many in the crowd were looking toward the entrance. Ruslan began to make his way in that direction where he overheard several comments that the queen had already left. "Does this mean," he thought, "that the Harrisons will also be leaving?"

Rather than go back to his seat, he hurried toward the front entrance doors facing Savoy Court, only to be stopped by a security officer who asked him to stay inside. Through the glass doors, Ruslan saw the queen's limousine and security cars leave slowly, followed by the Harrisons' limousine. As calmly as he could, he headed toward the fire exit adjacent to the entrance to the stalls, slowly pushed open the door and found himself in Caring Lane, a small alley behind the theatre.

"They will not get away," he said to himself.

Feverishly running down the alley to the Strand, he saw the queen's fleet of four cars slowly make its way to the intersection of the Strand and Trafalgar Square. The Harrison car was behind the last security car.

At the intersection, Ruslan stood for a moment in the crowd, which was being held back by a patrolman so that the queen's entourage could pass. Ruslan waited, and then bolted toward the Harrisons' car just before it reached the intersection, flinging himself in front and rolling forward to allow the car to stop without running over him. He guessed right. The car came to an abrupt halt a foot or so from Ruslan. Harrison rushed out from the car, followed by his son and the driver. When Harrison reached Ruslan, rather than immediately turning him over, he waited for a few seconds, holding back his son who kept shouting, "Dad, see if he's okay."

Without replying, he quickly looked at the man and thought it odd that he was wearing a tuxedo. In the quivery instant it took to realize that the situation was wrong and this wasn't an injured man, he fell on Ruslan and tried to keep him down. But it didn't work.

Ruslan pushed him off, firing one shot into the air, rolled over, and, as he got up, fired the next one, hitting the driver; the third slammed into Timothy's right shoulder. At this point, Betty leaped out of the car and ran toward Timothy. David grabbed Ruslan's arm, twisting it so that the remaining three shots scattered, one hitting a rushing police officer. Ruslan kicked David in the right leg, making David lose balance and fall backward toward Betty. In one moment of fury, Ruslan brought his gun down full force on David's forehead, causing blood to gush. Betty, reaching over to David, felt a blow on her right chin, falling on the pavement, unconsciousness.

Within ten seconds, Ruslan had injured six people. But he knew that police would soon be there and that he had to get away. As several people from the crosswalk ran towards him, he waved the gun and rushed headlong down the ramp before the Charing Cross Hotel, turning left into a door marked "Heaven."

Inside, a short, rotund lady was vacuuming the front foyer.

She yelled at him. "Stop! Stop! The club is closed."

He pushed her aside so that she fell against the wall, her cleaning hose slipping from her hand, the noise reverberating in the quiet lobby. Ruslan rushed up the stairs, where he saw a restroom. He ran in and collapsed. He knew he had little time left, but he needed just a few minutes to rest, just a few minutes. "My God. Please, my God. Don't leave me. Please."

No one came up the stairs after him, but he knew they would soon. Ruslan splashed water on his face, and discarded the gun in the bathroom trash bin, useless now that the specially-made bullets had been used and he had no more. Ruslan then brushed his hair with his hands and slowly walked out. As he went down the corridor following the exit sign, he noticed the many large pictures of naked men and he began to run. "My God, what are you doing to me? Why are you bringing me this madness? I am carrying out your will. Why are you doing this to me?"

He ran down one flight, throwing open the exit door, which faced an alley leading to the Charing Cross Hotel delivery entrance. He walked in. Only a delivery clerk was present. The clerk waved him on, thinking him to be a bartender. He wandered into the lobby and sat down. He needed to sit. Soon he would leave. But he would just sit . . . and pray. The noise of the ambulances and police vehicles wouldn't bother him. His prayers would eliminate all noise. His sins were pardonable by God.

Nothing he did was dark, greedy, or fearful. What he did was beautiful, graceful, holy. Tomorrow the world would be good to him again. Allah would command such. God would never abandon him. Tonight would be glorious. God would send him dreams of a radiant, golden morning. There would be nothing menacing in the morning . . . only joy. Pure joy. As these thoughts raced through his head, he closed his eyes and placed his hands over them, cutting out all the violence he had just created.

At Trafalgar Square, the driver and Timothy lay unconscious. Betty was stirring and awakening, crying. She tried to reach Timothy, but her strength failed.

David, conscious but bleeding, crawled over to her.

"Honey, I love you so much, so very much," he said. He cradled her in his arms, collapsing on her.

London
Friday
Local Time: 9:00 p.m.
Heathrow Airport, Terminal Four

British Air flight 911 arrived exactly one-and-a-half-hours late, at 8:30 p.m. Boris Shenin and Georgi Ivashkin as they walked the long, brightly lit terminal corridors, finally reaching Passport Control. Nevertheless, because the lines of arriving passengers were so long, it was already 9:00 p.m. when they exited directly into the Arrivals Hall, which at that hour, was also crowded. Boris was the first to see Stephen Thomas holding the "Bank Alliance Russia" chalkboard. In a dark blue uniform, with the crest of Mayfair Car Hire on his left jacket pocket, his blue cap smartly positioned on his head, Thomas was standing formally behind a maroon-colored rope with other chauffeurs, all holding similar boards with various identities of passengers.

"Good evening. I am Boris Shenin of Bank Alliance Russia."

"Welcome to London, Mr. Shenin. I am Stephen Thomas of Mayfair

Car Hire, your driver while you are in London. Please, may I take your bag?" Thomas said, as he reached over to get the one small overnight suitcase Shenin was carrying.

"Thank you very much. This is my associate, Georgi Ivashkin."

"Mr. Ivashkin, welcome also. Your bag, please, sir."

"Yes, thank you," Georgi said, as he handed his case over to Thomas.

"Did you have a nice flight?" Thomas asked.

"Yes, but we were delayed because of the air traffic here at Heathrow. Other than that it was uneventful," Shenin replied, slightly annoyed at being asked, not because the question was untoward, but because he could never get used to the intrusive nature of the service personnel in the West. In Moscow, his chauffeur remained silent, unless Shenin asked him a direct question. But here in the West, Shenin thought, "everyone talks as if they have known you forever." He missed the old Communist days when position meant something serious and the perquisites of office brought the respect lacking in the freedoms of modern Russia. Shenin hated the familiarity with subordinates and he even kept his distance from Ivashkin, his aide of several years.

"Air traffic is always delayed whenever we have rain, which, by the way, we have had all day. But I shall soon have you at the Dorchester. Traffic should be light at this hour, so I'll have you there in about 30 minutes. Usually it takes about 45 minutes to an hour during rush hour. But you came in after rush hour, so we'll speed along."

Shenin didn't reply, but in Russian he said to Ivashkin, "He talks too much. This driver talks way too much. But enough; we shall make our appointment with your friend Ruslan in due course."

The Mercedes had been altered so that the back seats, although fully padded and leather covered, lacked any frame except for the rim. The back of the seats was six-inches thick—so that specially tipped 9mm bullets from a Smith & Wesson Model 39 pistol with silencer would penetrate with ease directly into the back seats. The pistol Thomas would use was called "Hush Puppy" because of its extreme silence and its use in clandestine missions of killing humans and guard dogs.

It was still misty with a slight drizzle as Stephen Thomas led Shenin and Ivashkin out the electronic doors from the Arrivals Hall and to the crosswalk that would take them to the driveway where the limousine was parked. Within a few minutes, they had reached the car. "Here we are, gentlemen." Thomas put down Shenin's case while he opened the rear door wide to allow Shenin and Ivashkin to easily enter. "Please, gentlemen, the latest *Times* is for your reading pleasure. Directly in front and in the middle is a small compartment with some cold Cokes and Perrier water, if you wish. Please make yourselves comfortable." Shenin and Ivashkin didn't reply as Thomas closed the door. Each picked up the neatly folded *Times* prior to sitting down.

Thomas walked to the back of the car, opened the trunk, placing first one case and then the other gently down. He reached into a small canvas bag and pulled out the pistol, quickly removed the safety feature, and fired, in quick succession, four shots following a faint line that had been drawn across the back of the car seats. The only sound was equivalent to dropping suitcases into the trunk. He placed the gun back into the bag and closed the trunk door. The entire operation took one minute. As he walked past the right side of the limousine, he noticed that his passengers' heads were down. There was no movement. The bullets had penetrated the bodies neatly and, rather than exiting, had expanded on impact, causing massive internal bleeding. Thomas settled himself into the driver's seat, starting the car, and driving slowly toward the exit, passing the security control booth where he would turn in his parking permit for the evening.

"Looks like your passengers are exhausted," the guard commented.

"Yeah, they really need their sleep. Thanks. See you again," Thomas replied.

Thomas sped along the exit motor way from the terminal complex and onto a feeder road taking him to a roundabout which led to the main motor way to London. He went, however, around the roundabout and onto an ancillary road where he then drove to a turnoff about a mile from the roundabout and about one-half mile from a small commercial strip where his rental car was parked near a pub called "The King's Rest."

He stopped the car by the side of the road, locked all the doors, and then began to walk toward the pub. About twenty-five feet from the limousine he turned, faced it, and pressed a button on a small radio receiver he had taken from his coat pocket. Within two seconds, the signal activated the detonator, located directly underneath the small compartment where the cold drinks were located. The one-pound plastic explosive blew off the top of the car. Flames reached the full fuel tank, causing a massive explosion and forcing Thomas to fall to the ground. Nothing would be left of the bodies in the limousine and very little of the limousine itself. But he had to hurry. He knew the explosion would soon attract the police.

It would take Thomas fewer than ten minutes to walk to his car parked by "The King's Rest" pub, where he would pick up his cellular phone and call a special number, leaving the message, "The rain has stopped." Then he would drive back to Heathrow, board a plane for Paris, and then on to Montreal. He would return to London again only when called by Colonel Boarders.

Thomas's real name was Pierre DeLattre. He was an expert in using explosives for sabotage and a veteran of several missions with Colonel Boarders and David Harrison.

As he drove away back to the airport, he smiled as he thought of the code name Boarders had given him: "Valuable."

CHAPTER FOUR

Cyprus
Friday
Local Time: 10:00 a. m. (8:00 a.m., London)
Larnaca International Airport

Svetlana Makorova was fleeing, but not in the hysteria that an escape can take, unplanned and unsettling. And she wasn't depressed. Far from it. In her heart fluttered a sense of elation—of freedom—a feeling that she had never had before.

Seated next to her mother, Galena Makorova, Svetlana was distracted from her thoughts by the woman sitting to her left in the airport lounge, cradling a baby. The boy was crying loudly, despite the efforts of his mother to quiet him. She momentarily glanced at Svetlana, with an evident air of disillusion and frustration. The infant quickly smiled at Svetlana's quiet, receptive gaze and reached out to touch her, which with his short arms and small hands, he couldn't do.

Svetlana's mother, her hands tightly held together in her lap, normally would have engaged in conversation, but she remained silent. A woman of splendid build, she always looked polished; her black silky hair, with strands of white throughout, gave her an almost regal appearance. Still, the emptiness of her life, since the death of her husband some ten years earlier, made her look older then her fifty-seven years. The long periods of solitude and unhappiness had taken their toll.

The expression in Svetlana's light blue eyes, as she looked at the baby, was of somebody who knew what lay ahead, without illusions of hiding the truth. Svetlana knew she had to get through this day, and many more to come. At twenty-seven, her life was being altered beyond anything she ever imagined. Regardless, anxiety couldn't overtake her. She realized the importance of that fact. Svetlana must move calmly and in accordance with the plan outlined by Colonel Boarders.

Her lover, Moussa Berdayev, was to have joined her in Cyprus for the weekend, because he believed that her mother was returning to Moscow on the evening flight. But, when Moussa would arrive at the Cyprus Sheraton Resort Hotel, where she and her mother had registered, neither would be there, and the search for them would be on. She knew that he would go into a frenzy. He would be aggressive and persistent in his hunt. Immediately, he would call Dimitri Gravev, the Moscow *vor,* who would have some of his aides go to the apartment on Pirogoveskaya, which she shared with her mother. This, of course, would be a futile gesture. He knew they wouldn't be there.

Colonel Boarders had instructed Svetlana to leave everything in the apartment, taking only some clothes needed for the holiday in Cyprus. Nothing in the apartment would be removed; even the framed photographs of her father, placed on the piano that her mother enjoyed playing, were left behind.

There were no relatives or friends to question, or to be harassed by Dimitri's men. Her only girl friend, Marina Vladimirova, had left for Israel some six months earlier, her own mother and father having died in a fiery auto accident on the Boulevard Ring Road in Moscow. The driver of the other car, an official of the Federal Security Service (the new name for the old KGB), was drunk. Although injured severely, he recovered and was never arrested. When Marina tried to bring charges against the man, the Moscow City prosecutor took her statement, and nothing was done. So much, Svetlana thought, for the new "freedom."

No one could be hurt by Dimitri's men, because there was no one left. Her own mother had secluded herself since her husband's death. Svetlana's cherished Aunt, Yelena Fyodora, her mother's only and older sister, had died a year earlier. The sad fact was that they would never return to Russia, with all its memories, however sad or tender. She couldn't say she really cared otherwise. Svetlana's life had, for the past several years, been a lie. Living a lie is as fatal as an incurable disease. The cost of such a life had become unsustainable, because of her belief that what was being planned by her employer, Peter Bradford, was too horrific and abhorrent to be left unchecked.

Svetlana was born in the afternoon at three, on the anniversary of

Lenin's birth—April 22, 1969, at the Moscow Central Clinic. The clinic was reserved for senior Communist Party members and their families—her father, Dr. Vadim Makorov, and her mother were both members. Dr. Makorov, a nuclear physicist, had just been elected to the Academy of Sciences; her mother was a landscape artist of some note. She was their only child, and born when her father was forty, her mother ten years younger.

Yelena Fyodora, Svetlana's aunt, an eccentric but well-known spiritualist and hypnotist, claimed that being born on such an important date would make Svetlana's life "shine bright as a golden star." Svetlana's father dismissed Yelena's supposed gift of prophecy when she said this, but his dismissal wasn't serious, because he was happy with the prediction. Besides, Yelena was a leading member of a small but growing parapsychology group that the Communist Party let flourish, in large part, because several prominent party officials sought her guidance. She was always present, it seemed to Svetlana, and always brought gifts. What intrigued Svetlana were the various shades of lavender that her aunt always wore, as if from an apparition. Hanging from her neck were several strands of multi-colored crystal beads and red stars. "The red stars are to make our Communist comrades comfortable," she would tell Svetlana with a wink and a smile, indicating that she cared little about they thought. What was important was what she told them from her readings of astrological charts and what came from her obvious clairvoyant talent. It was said that even Brezhnev had called on her at her studio. But Svetlana never knew whether that was true.

Svetlana would look at her aunt's extraordinary alabaster face, framed by a mound of brilliant red hair, and believe that her aunt was from another world. On Svetlana's tenth birthday, Yelena gave her a plain gold bracelet, from which hung a small heart with the inscription, "Svetlana, bright as a golden star. 4.v.79." Thereafter, Svetlana placed it on her right wrist every day, regardless of what other jewelry she was wearing. Svetlana loved her mother, but adored her aunt.

Svetlana's mother's health had been precarious since her husband's death. She had serious bouts of nausea and dizziness, refusing to go to any doctor, despite Svetlana's entreaties. This time, in Cyprus, however, the medical problem was fictitious. Svetlana made certain that the concierge at the Sheraton knew that they were going to Larnaca Hospital, where her mother would see a doctor to check on a supposed early morning episode of dizziness. The concierge wished them well, as he escorted them to the lobby entrance doors where the doorman had a taxi waiting. During the silent ride, her mother held Svetlana's right hand tightly while keeping her own eyes closed.

Once at the hospital, they sat in the reception room for a few minutes, pretending to wait for a relative or friend. After a few minutes, Svetlana and her mother left in another taxi for the airport. As they did in Moscow, they left everything in their hotel suite untouched. Nothing was taken—no clothes, jewelry, cosmetics, nothing. They brought only their handbags that they normally would take if they were going out shopping.

Colonel Boarders had instructed Svetlana and her mother to walk to the departure lounge at the Larnaca International Airport, buy the day's edition of the *Herald Tribune,* and sit in the third row of seats, on the aisle, facing the Swissair counter, with her mother seated next to her, pretending to doze. A middle-aged man and woman would find them; both would have small red crosses in their lapels. The man would be wearing a dark blue suit and white turtleneck shirt; the woman would be wearing a white suit. A blue bag would be hanging from the woman's shoulder. The woman, who would be able to identify them, would be carrying a copy of *Der Spiegel* magazine. She would approach them, with the man standing at the entrance to the row of seats where Svetlana and her mother were seated. They were not to rise from their seats to meet the woman. They were to remain seated.

The woman would come over and, in German, ask if she could borrow the paper. Without replying, Svetlana and her mother would get up and follow her to where the man would be waiting. The woman would speak, again in German, "It is good to see you. We have such a lovely day as the wind is coming from the north east." Svetlana would reply in German, "Yes, the day is warm as we had a rising sun." The man would then come over and take her mother by the arm. Svetlana would hand the *Herald Tribune* over to the woman, and the woman in return would give her the magazine *Der Spiegel*. No other words would be spoken.

Svetlana turned her gaze from the baby boy that had finally fallen asleep toward the couple approaching their row of seats. She gently touched her mother, who looked at her and followed Svetlana's eyes to the couple now a few feet from where they were seated. The meeting was over in less than a minute. She saw her mother walk with the couple toward the very entrance through which they had entered earlier. She hoped that she would see her mother again, but then she wasn't sure. Colonel Boarders had organized a special charter flight bound for Frankfurt where her mother would then be put on a special US government flight for the United States . . . and a new life and home. Svetlana was to join her on Monday, but first she had her own assignment to accomplish. As her mother exited the airport and disappeared into the crowd, Svetlana thought of that first encounter with Colonel Boarders, and how unusual the meeting was some six months earlier.

At the time, she and her lover, Moussa Berdayev, were on a trip to Zurich. In his usual expansive manner, Moussa, who knew nothing about opera, decided to take her to see *La Boheme* at the Zurich Opera House. She had seen the opera once in Moscow when the Metropolitan Opera from the United States performed. Peter Bradford had obtained tickets for her as a birthday gift and she had taken her mother and her aunt. She recalled that the ending was unhappy because the heroine died, leaving her lover distraught.

For the occasion, as he had often done before, Moussa flamboyantly bought her jewelry from one of the shops on the Bahnstrasse, the main shopping street in Zurich. This time, the purchase was a five-caret blue topaz pendant in an oval setting surrounded by diamonds. "To match the color of your eyes, my Svetlana," Moussa said. She feigned surprise and happiness. Svetlana was not in love with Moussa. He treated her with respect; perhaps that is all that she could expect of a relationship that was never completely fulfilling.

Sightly older than Svetlana, Moussa had a handsome, good natured face, strong and sinewy, and dark in complexion. He had unusual strength for a man of his small stature—he was a few inches taller than Svetlana, about five-feet, seven-inches tall. He appeared always conscious that he was not taller and, to compensate, wore shoes with a higher sole. His eyes were striking in their darkness, deeply set under thick and overhanging eyebrows. There always seemed to be an unnatural luster in his eyes and Svetlana saw them lose that luster only after they made love. He seemed like a child when his deep passion had been spent. Not the intense passion which is necessary to experience genuine love, without remorse. But she could never tell him that. He was good to her . . . and to her mother.

She had also seen his wilder, violent temper directed at others, but never at her. Moussa was never cruel to her, and he always seemed determined to please her, never to upset her. Moussa would always bring a gift, no matter how small, when he picked her up in Moscow. He appreciated her elegance and was never indifferent to her clothes, always complimenting her on her choice of colors and styles. Moussa adored her beauty, and was intrigued by her long, light brown, almost blond hair. As she lay her head across his broad chest after they made love, he would spend moments caressing her slender, pale body, and stroking strands of her hair, extolling how silky it was. Sometimes, though, she felt as if she were a mere trophy . . . something Moussa paraded before his friends in the *mafiya,* and at the parties she went to with him when businessmen from Europe or the United States were present.

She knew that at some point she would have to break off with him. Moussa would always say to her, "I'll never let you go, my Svetlana . . . never." And, she knew that he meant it. When she would think of her situation, she would enter one of her long periods of silence. She was a prisoner in a system that she was just beginning to understand and determined to leave.

She first met Moussa when he came with Dimitri Gravev to visit her new employer, Peter Bradford. Svetlana had graduated with honors from Moscow State University and excelled in languages. She could speak four languages in addition to Russian: English, German, French and Arabic. The KGB was in the process of recruiting her, when the 1991 coup brought down the old USSR and the Yeltsin reform government was installed. Like many Russians, she found the coup changed her life forever. She was looking for a job, and one of her friends informed her that a position as a translator was available at a new American company. Svetlana was excited and told her mother about the opportunity. "An American company, mama. Maybe I will go to America!" Svetlana expected so much when she went for the interview, which was perfunctory. Peter Bradford hired her immediately.

Russia was in the midst of a violent quarrel with itself that year. Svetlana and her mother were worried about their own survival. For several months after the coup, her mother's pension stopped coming. Then, when it came, it was less than the full amount. The new Yeltsin government kept promising that the full amount for all pensioners would eventually be delivered, but his words, however much he meant them to be true, were never carried out. Prices skyrocketed and Svetlana's mother was becoming increasingly anxious. That became the overriding concern of Svetlana and her mother . . . a concern that they had never had before. Russia was convulsing toward changes that neither understood, but felt. With her mother's approval, Svetlana eagerly seized this opportunity to work for an American company. And the salary of $200 a week, in U.S. dollars, not Russian rubles, Svetlana received in absolute wonderment.

On the second day of her employment, Moussa came in. She felt very uncomfortable as he stared at her. When she brought the tea into the conference room, where Peter, Dimitri, and Moussa were meeting, he stood up and helped her with the tray. Both Peter and Dimitri smiled, as they observed what he did. Later that day, Moussa came by and brought her a small bouquet of pink roses. That is when she noticed his wedding band. For days she would not respond to him, even though he would come to the office on any pretext. Peter Bradford would say nothing and appeared not to encourage her one way or another. But Moussa was persistent. When he would come in, he would smile that broad, sincere smile of an adolescent seeing his first love. His warmth was so genuine that Svetlana became eager to see him, although she wouldn't demonstrate that eagerness to him.

Finally, she had dinner with him at the Metropol Hotel, and to her surprise, she enjoyed the evening, especially his laughter and his kindness toward her. Two weeks later, he asked her to go to St. Petersburg with him. She refused, but she knew that at some time in the future she would say yes. She never understood her own feelings at that time, knowing that he had a wife and one child, a six-year-old boy, living on the outskirts of Moscow. Those feelings would be known later, and they would be different from the kind that she had wished.

When Svetlana's mother met him, he was respectful and conversed with her for some time over the dinner that Svetlana and her mother had prepared. He even asked Mrs. Makorova if she would sell him one of her paintings. "No, I cannot do such a thing, Moussa. These five paintings are all that I have left. I no longer paint since my Vadim died some years ago. I hope you understand." After she said that, he leaned over and kissed her hand, obviously sorry that he had asked. Whenever he came to the apartment for Svetlana, he would bring gifts of food—usually fruit—for her mother. Svetlana's mother resigned herself to a fact that she could not alter and never questioned Svetlana on the relationship—which, in her heart, she knew would end someday.

Moussa had even purchased a small two-bedroom dacha about thirty kilometers southwest of Moscow, so that Svetlana and her mother could visit a place away from Moscow. But, as she found out what he did for Dimitri (Moussa's bank position was illusory), she knew that there would never be a time when she could truly have a deep affection for Moussa—a killer, an extortionist, a bully, and sycophantic follower of Dimitri Gravev, the Moscow *vor* leader. Moussa always seemed despairing when he came back from a meeting with Dimitri, but the smile would be broad when he saw her. She recognized that, for a while at least, she needed him . . . until the fateful meeting at the Zurich Opera House.

Moussa was enjoying the evening at the opera. He seemed more ebullient than usual. Maybe, she thought, it was the excitement of going where he had never been. She didn't really know. He asked her many questions about the opera and Svetlana tried as well as she could to tell him about the theme which was love and death. "Ah," he said, "what is one without the other?"

Svetlana smiled and said, "One is better than the other."

Moussa squeezed her hand gently and asked, "Which one?"

She smiled and they walked up the marble staircase leading from the opera foyer to the box that he had bought for the evening. He had purchased all six seats in the box in order to be alone with her. They were seated for only a short time, when a short, balding man, dressed in a black evening suit, parted the curtains and asked if this was Box N; he quickly corrected himself, as he noticed the small brass plaque identifying it as Box M.

"Excuse me, I am so sorry. These old eyes are having their usual trouble." He spoke in German, which Moussa didn't understand. Moussa's only languages were Russian, and some English. Moussa looked at him, somewhat irritated at the interruption, but said nothing. Svetlana saw the stranger sit in the adjacent Box N with a group of men and women who greeted him warmly. As one woman rose to kiss him, Svetlana overheard her say, "Colonel, good you are here." "A military man," thought Svetlana. "No, impossible, he doesn't appear to have the bearing of such a man. No, impossible."

"You are interested in the short, old man, my Svetlana?" inquired Moussa.

"Oh, no, how silly of you, Moussa," she said as she placed her hand on his right thigh. "I hope you like the opera, Moussa," and she reached over to give him a small kiss on the cheek as the lights dimmed for the opening scene.

At intermission, Svetlana and Moussa went out into the burgundy-carpeted foyer fronting the entrances to the box area and adjoining the corridor where the crowd was making its way down the winding stairs to the champagne bars in the brilliantly lit, massive, marble-lined lobby one floor below.

"You like the opera, Moussa?" she inquired softly as she took his arm.

"I can understand only a little. Why do they sing in another language?"

"Italian is the language of opera and the author is also Italian. Of course, they could have done the opera in German, but then perhaps it wouldn't be the same." She knew he was having difficulty with the opera, but he wouldn't admit it.

"Svetlana, my Svetlana, I want to have a winding staircase, just like this, in our new home. I shall build you a new home . . . soon, my Svetlana . . . and you will live with me and have my children," he said, as he took her arm. She frowned, looked at him quizzically, for a moment before speaking.

"But, Moussa, my mother and I have a very nice apartment. And, you have provided us a dacha outside Moscow. Moussa, I can't live with you, and I can't have your children."

He didn't respond, and she saw that he was hurt.

"You must understand, Moussa. You must understand why I can't do what you wish. You are married and have a child."

"I do what I want, my Svetlana; I do what I want," he said, as he held her arm tightly. For the first time, she was frightened in his presence. She pushed away from him and walked slightly ahead.

He reached for her, and said softly, "Svetlana, please, I am sorry . . . I am sorry I said that."

Svetlana didn't reply. He tried to hold her hand, but she refused. As they reached the end of the stairway, she said, "Moussa, I must go to the washroom. I will see you later."

"I will be waiting for you," he said, leaning over to kiss her.

She turned her face away and left without looking at him. As she turned from the foyer into the corridor leading to the washrooms, she noticed the man that had earlier come to her box in error. He was walking toward her from the washroom area. Only when they both were in the middle of the corridor, and out of sight of the foyer bars, did he approach her saying, in German, "Excuse me, Svetlana Makorova, I hope your mother is fine. Tell her that her cousin sends greetings."

Startled, she tried to reply, but no words came out. Colonel Boarders stared at her intently for a few moments before he continued in the softest of voices.

"I have but a moment, Svetlana. Please call me at this number. You'll hear a recording telling you that tickets to the Bolshoi Ballet are available for a given date in Moscow. I'll be seated next to you when you arrive at the theater. I hope to see you and your mother then. There will be nothing else on the recording. Once you've called, you won't be able to call again because the line will be out of service. Memorize the date. I'll assume that you'll be there. Tickets will be sent to your mother's apartment by messenger, one day before the performance. We need your help, Svetlana. You're our only hope in preventing the *vor* from carrying through a tragic and unforgivable project."

She looked at him, and could see in his eyes the sad worry that comes with heavy responsibility. Yet his voice was so even, so hushed. His face was agreeable and bright, with pointed eyebrows and high forehead. He was small, but big boned. As he extended his hand to say good bye, she shook it, feeling the roughness of the palm, a roughness that comes only from hard, manual labor, she thought to herself.

Svetlana looked at the card and realized that the city code was for Zurich.

"It's good to have seen you. Isn't this performance beautiful? I hope that you're enjoying yourself," he said, bowing slightly. "Oh, by the way," he turned, edging even more closely to her, and whispered, "we should keep this meeting to ourselves. Moussa Berdayev wouldn't understand," he said, bowing his head again as he hurried toward the bar area.

Surprised and confused, she lingered for several moments, staring vacantly at the large posters of operas that had played in years past. She was frightened, but strangely calm. Her mother had no cousin anywhere. Her aunt never married, nor did her father have any siblings. And, how did the old man . . . colonel, as she remembered him being called by the lady in the adjoining box . . . how did he know Moussa's name? She remembered her father using the expression, "visiting my cousin," which always puzzled her, because she knew of no cousins. It appeared to be a joke between her parents, she thought. Yet, Svetlana also remembered that when her father said that to her mother, she looked worried. She never smiled. But that was long ago, Svetlana thought, so very long ago.

She glanced down the corridor toward the washroom and noticed the sign for telephones. She hurriedly went down the hall where the phones were positioned directly opposite the ladies' washroom. Svetlana fumbled for some Swiss coins, praying that she had enough. She found only one Swiss franc coin and quickly deposited it, knowing that it was more than enough. The ring seemed eternal, and then, her hand shaking while holding the receiver, she heard a woman's voice come over the line, speaking in German. "Welcome to the ticket data bank. Bolshoi Ballet tickets, Moscow, are available for the evening of April 22 at 7:30 p.m. Thank you."

The phone line went dead. She pressed the new call button on the phone, picked up the receiver and dialed the same number again. In German, a voice came indicating that the line was no longer in service. "He was telling me the truth. My God, what's going on? What is going on?"

She couldn't call her mother from Zurich. Moussa left her virtually no free time, and he would hover over her if she did make the call. Even now, she knew, he would be waiting for her. With him, she never had a moment alone.

Regardless, she was fearful about the phone in her mother's apartment. She had been fearful of her calls being monitored for some time. It would have been easy for the *vor* to get into the apartment and place a device on the phone. She didn't think that was the case, because she had tested the phone by making certain statements. If he knew about the statements, her employer, Peter Bradford, never acted as if he overheard the statements . . . which were critical of him. Svetlana knew that Bradford, however, had a penchant for recording every conversation. His conference room and his own office, even his car—all contained recording devices. He was paranoid, Svetlana thought, and the more she pondered his behavior, the more she wanted to get away. She always wondered if Dimitri knew. "He must," she assured herself. "It would be dangerous for Peter, if he didn't. But maybe Dimitri didn't realize that even his discussions with Peter were recorded."

Svetlana would have to wait until she returned to Moscow the next afternoon. Her mother would know what this was all about.

Hearing the tone indicating that the performance would begin in a few minutes, she glanced at her reflection in the glass enclosed opera poster. She aimlessly toyed for a moment with the gold bracelet that her aunt had given her. "Bright as a golden star," she said to herself, "bright as a golden star."

She knew Moussa was waiting for her. The blur of the crowd was protective as she hurried from the corridor directly to the main lobby. Svetlana quickly spotted Moussa looking out the lobby windows, holding two glasses of champagne. She came behind him and said, "Moussa, we must go back to our seats."

"I missed you, my Svetlana," he said in a soft, appealing tone, as he placed the glasses of champagne on the bar ledge. "I think you are angry at what I said to you. I am sorry, my Svetlana . . . very sorry. I have something for you. I wrote this myself," he murmured as he haltingly handed her a piece of paper he had torn from the leather covered note pad he always carried.

"Moussa, what is this, now?" she asked as she took the piece of paper and noted that he had written a poem. He had never done anything like this before for her. He had written the poem in Russian:

> *To Svetlana, my love*
>
> How soon we fly on
> To what is ours
> And stars bid us welcome
> To the life of love
> How soon the steps are then lighter
> I am like a rock, lonely, scattered, joyless, hard, unknown
> Amid your beauty which makes my light
> With you, I cry in love
> Without you, I am alone and life is not again.

"Moussa, my dear Moussa, come here," she said as she took his hand and kissed him on his right cheek, not caring about the crowd. "I shall keep this forever. This is the best gift you have ever given me."

"You like it, then?" he asked in his childlike manner. "You really like it? I have many poems I've about you, but have been afraid to give them to you. You think it not manly to write poems of love, Svetlana?"

"Of course not. You are kind to me and I'll never forget what you have done for me."

He held her hand tightly and smiled broadly, as they walked in silence up the winding marble staircase. She marveled at the beautiful tear-drop crystal chandeliers and the magnificence of the patrons. How contradictory her life was. This poem was the most generous present he had ever given her because he had done it on his own . . . but she also knew that she couldn't stay with him much longer.

When they were seated, she looked over at the adjacent box. There was an empty sixth seat. The colonel was gone.

On her return to Moscow the next afternoon, she told her mother the story of the strange meeting at the Zurich Opera House. Her mother didn't reply at once but busied herself with rearranging some books in the bookcase adjacent to the window, without any apparent reason. "You must tell me, mother, who this man is. Who is your cousin?"

Svetlana's mother looked forlorn and she continued to take books from the case, dust them, and replace them. "Your father read all of these. Svetlana. Did you know that? He enjoyed collecting and reading books on subjects I could never comprehend. He was a gallant man, Svetlana . . . a brave man . . . I miss him so much." She began to cry softly. She took her hand and wiped the tears from her cheek and reached for Svetlana. "Too many tears, too many tears, my dear daughter. Tears never cover the true sadness of your mother. Those were stormy years while you were a child . . . very stormy years . . . come let us sit together on the couch," she said as she took Svetlana's hand. "You will see Colonel Boarders, and you will help him, Svetlana. He knew your father . . . it goes back so many years ago. Do you remember that bitterly cold night in January, 1984. . . .

"I had invited several of your school friends, as well as our neighbors, Yuri and Elena Vadykin to join us. You remember the evening. It was to celebrate your receipt of the Komsomol award for the best presentation of an essay you had written about my art and the landscapes it depicted.

"You had given an address at the school on the day when the children had spoken about their parents' work. My art was chosen because you said you did not understand your father's work. Your father and I were so proud of your speech; I actually had gone to school to listen to you as had other parents to listen to their children. When they announced you as the winner, you ran off the stage to where I was seated. You were so excited.

"Just as you and I were placing the cakes and sweet cookies on the table, Yelena Fyodora knocked loudly at the door, shouting, 'Galena Makorova, my sister, open the door. My sister, open the door. Please hurry, please hurry!'

"'Yes, yes, I'm coming,' I called, as I rushed to the door, trying to open the two latches, failing in my nervousness on the first try. 'Yelena, I'm here. Do not worry. I'm here,' I shouted through the door as I finally freed one, then the second latch, opening the door to see Yelena covered with snow and crying in such grief.

"You ran from the kitchen where you were gathering dishes for me. 'Mama, mama, what is wrong? Why is Aunt Yelena shouting?' My Svetlana, you were so frightened at seeing Yelena in such a state. And so was I.

"I was not successful in calming Yelena. She continued to cry, throwing her arms around you and me and muttering, 'He is dead! Galena, he is dead!'

"'What do you mean, my sister? Who are you talking about? Speak to me, Yelena. . . . Don't frighten me like this. Why are you doing this?'

"It was then that Yelena told me that your father had died on that very day.

"My Svetlana, you remember what Yelena told us. She was conducting one of her spiritualist sessions with the wife of Admiral Pyotr Portugalov, when she terminated the session to come to our apartment. Yelena said that she saw a vision of a massive flame engulfing Vadim. 'You must believe me, my sister, you must believe me! The image is too strong . . . too strong. Oh, Galena, I wish, I wish it were not true, but it is, my sister. It is!'

"She was correct of course. But, I knew from the beginning that your father would never come back. This a burden that I have carried for so very long and I now share with you. Days earlier when Vadim left for the East to conduct tests for the institute, I knew that we would never see him again. You remember that evening a few days earlier, when he spent so much time with you, asking you many questions about your school and speaking to you in French. You had just started that course and stayed after school to take the special class. He was very proud of you, my Svetlana, very proud.

"But I should start further back. I ask you to understand. Times were very different then. I can close my eyes and remember the exact moment your father came home, distracted and distraught . . . characteristics unlike him.

"It was January 14, 1984, exactly one week before the evening of your celebration. He was in attendance at a meeting called by General Secretary Andropov to discuss the Afghanistan conflict. . . ."

Interlude

On January 14, 1984, Dr. Vadim Makorov, the USSR's most prominent nuclear physicist, member of the Academy of Sciences, author of numerous scientific articles, representative of the Soviet Union to the International Atomic Energy Agency, General Director of the Kurchatov Institute of Atomic Energy, and Senior Member of the State Atomic Energy Inspectorate, was in attendance at a meeting in the Kremlin called by General Secretary Andropov to discuss the Afghanistan conflict. The war had been going on since 1979—some five years, with no end in sight.

At that meeting, the general secretary announced that he had decided to employ a tactical nuclear weapon in Afghanistan. "You, my generals, have told me that the only way to end this war is for an infusion of many more divisions, together with a large occupation force after we are victorious. With these suggestions I cannot agree. We must demonstrate that we mean business. Comrades, no one should doubt the force of this nation. The Soviet Union is not a joke." The last few words were stated by the general secretary slowly and with determination. He looked around the room filled with his most senior military advisors; he knew that none would disagree with him, the former head of the KGB. He knew they were all cowards . . . and he knew all their secrets of life as well . . . except for one, Dr. Makorov.

"Dr. Makorov," he continued, "you are our expert in the field of nuclear weapons. I must have your assurance that no harm will come to our troops, nor to the neighboring countries of Iran and Pakistan, although, at times, I believe they should also be taught a lesson. In addition, our comrades in our surrounding brother republics of Turkmenistan, Uzbekistan, and Tajikistan must not be injured in any fashion. Can you assure me of this? What, Dr, Makorova is your answer to my question? Please respond," and he stared directly at Dr. Makorov as if to warn him not to disagree with his earlier announcement.

"Comrade General Secretary, I cannot agree with you more that this war should be concluded. But, of course, I can offer no advice on military matters because you have experts around this table who are more knowledgeable than I. However, as Comrade General Secretary knows from reports on the test of our own nuclear weapons, we can predict with only modest certainty the extent of the blast, the damage, and the fallout. Weather conditions at the site of the detonation will determine the extent of all of those aspects of the blast. In this instance, we would program the weapon for ground blast. This would produce the worst blast damage at close range and the worst fallout because the earth and surface debris would be dragged up and vaporized within the fireball. But this would be containable in the area, no more than ten kilometers around the blast site. By contrast, an air burst would spread its heat flash and therefore its burn effect, and secondary fires would extend over a much larger area than a ground blast. And a higher altitude blast would spread the effect over even a much wider area.

"As the General Secretary is aware, when the Americans air-dropped nuclear weapons on Japan, in August 1945, they used 2 four-kiloton weapons, each bomb equivalent to 20,000 tons of TNT. The injured and death toll from the bomb dropped on Hiroshima was approximately 150,000 people; the one dropped on Nagasaki injured or killed some 75,000 people. In both cases, firestorms lasted some six hours, destroying everything within an area of ten and a half square kilometers," he responded gently in a steady monotone. Dr. Makorov reached over for his tea and sipped it slowly. Looking around, he noticed the stunned faces of everyone, but the general secretary, who showed no emotion, was lightly tapping his finger on the table, indicating that he wanted to end the meeting.

"Yes, Comrade General Secretary, there should be no problem in using such a weapon," Dr. Makorov continued. "Of course, I would recommend that we test the weapon first, just to be certain of its effect. This test would not delay the intended date of its use in Afghanistan. I would recommend that the test be conducted one week from today at our test facility in Dushanbe, Tajikistan. As the General Secretary knows, it has topography similar to Afghanistan and the facility is equipped for such a test. We shall use a ground burst, a one-kiloton weapon, mounted on our intermediate-range missile, the SS-20, which has a sufficient range to reach targets in Afghanistan. This test would give us up-to-date precise data. Having these data will eliminate any worry about any harm coming to our brave comrades."

The general secretary knew that Dr. Makorov was stalling; yet he wanted his approval, even though he needed no one's approval for this action. He waited for a few minutes, absorbing the silence of the room with satisfaction. He knew no one would speak at this time, unless he spoke first. "They are all sheep," he thought, "frightened sheep."

"Dr. Makorov, my dear Vadim Makorov, you know, especially you, who convinced me to announce, some few years ago, an agreement with the United States on a moratorium on nuclear testing, that we cannot conduct a test. Of course, the use of nuclear weapons to defend vital interests is not covered by this agreement. Is that not correct, Dr. Makorov? The Americans know this. No test, Dr. Makorov. I gave my word and I will keep my word. Unless there are military reasons against launching on January 21, I will set that day as the time to send our greetings to the criminals in that bastard country. Any further comments?"

Rather than wait for a response, because he knew there would be none, he turned to Dr. Makorov and said, "Please, Dr. Makorov, attend to any details as to the use of the weapon with Col. Gen. Maximov Sheluko. . . . Good, this meeting is adjourned." As the assembled ten military and defense ministry officials rose from their seats, Andropov asked, almost in passing, "Dr. Makorov, please stay for a moment."

After everyone had filed out, Andropov motioned to Dr. Makorov to come and sit directly next to him. "My comrade, Dr. Makorov, why did you recommend a test? Are the results from prior testing incorrect?"

"Yes, Comrade General Secretary, the test data we have are generally accurate, but we have not conducted tests, as you correctly stated, for two years. Without a test, we cannot verify the accuracy of the weapon and its circle of damage. Thus, the use of the weapon may result in less damage or perhaps more. We are unsure, for reasons I explained earlier."

"I intend to end the war before I die. Do you understand?" Andropov raised his voice for emphasis, as he again started to tap his fingers on the table.

"Yes, of course. But, your health is fine, Comrade General Secretary," Makorov replied courteously.

"Don't patronize me, Dr. Makorov. I know that you, as well as many in this room, realize that I am very sick and some wish me dead now. No matter. I will die, I assure you, but before I do, the weapon will be used, and you will be at the site to supervise its launch. Yes, you will have your up-to-date test results. You can send a team to Afghanistan to count the bodies." A thin smile broke across his pallid, pasty face. "Well, it is time for us to part, dear Dr. Makorov. Do you have any questions?"

"None," Makorov replied.

"Thank you for coming, Dr. Makorov. By the way, do you know that in my apartment we have one of your wife's paintings—the one we have is of Gorki Park in the winter—just admirable, just admirable . . . the painting is so realistic you can almost touch the snow on the trees. I have a deep admiration for her work. My regards to her and to your daughter. I understand that your daughter has just received a gold medal from the Komsomol for her outstanding school work. She has perfect grades in all her class work as well as in attendance. You are to be congratulated. Again, my best wishes. I hope that I have not kept you too late. I know that you will want to go and enjoy your family," he said, again with that feeble smile that so disturbed Dr. Makorov.

Dr. Makorov always marveled at the personal information Andropov had ready. He always seemed to place personal notes in any conversation as if to warn the listener that families would be harmed if they disagreed with him or his policies. He may have believed that he knew everything, but Dr. Makorov knew that this time he did not.

"Yes, we are very proud of her. Very proud. Thank you, Comrade General Secretary. I shall tell my daughter of your good wishes. You are most kind to remember . . . most considerate." Dr. Makorov could barely conceal what he was truly feeling for a man who was ordering the slaughter of countless human beings.

"Do you have a driver, Dr. Makorov?"

"Yes, thank you."

"Good, we are finished." He rose, pressed a button nearest to the phone at the head of the conference desk, and an aide immediately appeared, holding the door open for the general secretary to come through. Andropov, however, motioned for Dr. Makorov to go first. He shook his hand and again said, "Good bye. I look forward to positive realistic test results," again smiling in a fashion that parted his thin lips in an offensive fashion.

"If there is evil on this planet," Dr. Makorov thought, "I am looking at it in the person of this insane man." He also realized how apparent it was that Andropov would not live much longer. Although his voice was strong and his confidence supreme, the mechanical and slow manner in which he walked and the ghastly pallor of his face and his darkened eyes made it clear that Andropov's time was limited.

As he hurried down the long Kremlin corridor, led by two security officers, he tried to forget what he had just heard. The few minutes it took him to get the elevator, which would take him to the garage where his driver was waiting, seemed an eternity. He knew he would never come back here, and this senseless order from an aged and ill general secretary would never be carried out. There would never be a launch of nuclear weapons against Afghanistan.

Coded Message Strike
January 21, 1984. Time: 5:45 A.M.
To: Deputy Minister of Defense, Aleksandr Likhachev
From: Col. Nikolai Nozyrev, Strategic Army Rocket Forces, Far

East
Site: Dushanbe Rocket Launch, Facility No. 2A

At 5 A. M. today, an SS-20 carrying a one-kiloton nuclear device exploded in place, destroying the mobile launcher and surrounding buildings, including a temporary blockhouse set up to monitor launch. Nuclear warhead was inert because it was preprogrammed to arm ten seconds from impact at designated target. Area of devastation, nevertheless, is two and one-half kilometers around the accident site. Facility 2A obliterated. Known dead from temporary block house:

> Dr. Vadim Makorov
> Defense Minister Leonid Zonov
> Col. Gen. Maximov Sheluko, Chief of Staff, Army Group, Afghanistan
> Lt. Col. Boris Sergeyev
> Yuri Zinoviev
> Seven Technicians, Strategic Rocket Forces
> Five officers, Strategic Rocket Forces
> Col. Gen. Oleg Manolev, Commanding Officer, Dushanbe

Investigation is underway to determine cause of misfiring. Our condolences to Comrade General Secretary on the loss of Comrade Zinoviev, Comrade General Secretary's personal assistant, and Comrade Lt. Col. Boris Sergeyev, Comrade General Secretary's military aide. Nothing of these brave comrades remains. Please advise, Comrade General Secretary.

Signed: Nikolai Nozyrev, Col. Deputy Commander, Dushanbe

National Security Agency's Satellite Control Facility
Ft. Belvoir, Virginia
January 21, 1984, 8:45 p.m.

Colonel Boarders turned to David, quietly saying, "He did what he said he would. Dr. Makorov is a man of incredible daring." They both looked up at the three large screens showing identical pictures of the explosion at Dushanbe.

"How did he do it?" David asked.

"We'll never know," Colonel Boarders responded. "But he did, and he took with him some high powered people. Old Andropov will do nothing now . . . at least not before he dies." Colonel Boarders' face became sad. His eyes closed for a moment.

Then he turned away from the bank of monitor screens, walked up the short steps to the exit doors, turned and called, "Come on, David. Let's have a drink." As they exited into the dimly lit corridor, Boarders, his voice breaking with emotion, asked, "David, have you ever read *Profiles in Courage?* Kennedy, in speaking of courage, said each man must look into his own soul. Makorov showed us what courage is all about. He followed his conscience and gave the ultimate. We should never forget him, David, never. One of the great heroes of this ugly war. A hero among heroes, David." For the first time, David saw tears come to Colonel Boarders' eyes.

Coded Message Strike
January 22, 1984. Time: 10:00 a.m.
Dushanbe Rocket Launch Headquarters
To: General Secretary Yuri Andropov
From: Likhachev, Deputy Minister of Defense

Comrade General Secretary:
Attempting to determine reason for misfiring of missile on January 21. Entire area incinerated. Fire from missile ignited launch and nonlaunch fuel lines leading to area near block house, completely destroying block house and surrounding buildings in an instantaneous explosion, incinerating everyone in the area. Possible fuel leak as cause still being investigated. Final report within five days.
Signed: Likhachev

Coded Message Strike
January 23, 1984.
Time: 7:30 a.m. Moscow
To: Deputy Minister of Defense Aleksandr Likhachev
From: Andropov

Oral report to me only. No written report needed. Compile none.
Signed: Andropov

The Kremlin
January 23, 1984
8:00 a.m.

"Maya, my dear, please bring in the transcript of my meeting of January 14 with the General Staff and Dr. Makorov, together with the tape. I want to compare your excellent notes. As usual, Maya, you have kept no copies?" Andropov pushed the listen button on the intercom.

"Yes, Comrade General Secretary. I shall bring them to you right away." In a few moments, Yuri Andropov's secretary of many years, dating back to his days as head of KGB, came with her notebooks, the transcription of her notes, and the accompanying tape recording. She knew, from experience, she would never see them again. "Tea, Comrade General Secretary?" she asked.

"Yes, a fresh cup. Thank you, Maya. Thank you very much." Andropov continued, "And, Maya, please place a call to Mrs. Makorova. I wish to ask her permission to come to see her and pay my respects. I shall go only with my military aides and the usual security. Dr. Makorov is a hero . . . yes, a hero of the Soviet Union. Please remind me to sign the appropriate award papers in due course," he commented as he turned to the transcripts, placing them in his brief case, along with the tape recording. They would be burned in the fireplace at his apartment.

Andropov never signed the award papers. He died on February 9, 1984. No records of a nuclear launch order were found and those in attendance felt it wise to avoid discussing that fateful meeting. There were reports, however, both in the Soviet press and in the Western media, that an inspection team to Dushanbe Rocket Launch Facility was accidentally killed when a new rocket engine misfired.

When Andropov visited Mrs. Makorova, he stayed only ten minutes, telling her that her pension would be substantial and that she could stay in her apartment, which was reserved for the "high scientific community, of which your husband was such a senior member." Svetlana was away from home, in school. At the time, her mother had mentioned the meeting to her, but the sadness over the death of her father overcame any memory of this event.

In London, a visitor entering the chapel of the Tyburn Convent, Hyde Park Place, a short distance from Hyde Park, Victoria's Gate, and adjacent to Bayswater Road, would find a brass plaque above the stand that holds holy water. On entering the church, the visitor would bless himself with this water, in accordance with Catholic tradition. Just as the visitor would cross himself, his eyes would fall on the following:

> *Chapel Donated In Memory of VM*
> *God Be with you my friend, always.*
> *Anonymous. 1984*

Prayers are said twenty-four hours a day, every day, by groups of four nuns of the Benedictine Order of the Adorers of the Sacred Heart. The nuns pray at each side of the altar and in the form of a cross.

"You have the full story, now my daughter. Perhaps I should have told you earlier. But little did I realize at the time that you would meet Colonel Boarders, or that he would need your help. I honestly believed that I would go from this earth, never having to tell you the truth about your father's sacrifice. Now, I have done so, Svetlana, I am too weary ... too sad and weary." Svetlana's mother rose from the couch, holding Svetlana's hand. "I will rest now, Svetlana. You must accept what he wishes you to do absolutely and without a trace of reservation, and with profound conviction. He would not be asking you for your help if he did not believe it necessary. When he saw me before you left for Zurich, I told him that I had no doubt that you would assist. It is I who gave him your itinerary, Svetlana. He found you as he wished. Remember what I have said: behave bravely as your father would have and I now know you will do."

"This is very confusing, Mother, very confusing. I must think what has happened and what you have said. But, tell me how Colonel Boarders and father met. Please, I must know everything. I must!" Svetlana said, in an anxious voice.

"I cannot, my daughter. Not now. There is no need. Please, we shall talk later. I must rest, but you will do as Colonel Boarders asked. You must promise me this. Do you?"

"Yes, I promise." With that, Svetlana's mother let her hand drop from her daughter's and walked to her bedroom, closing the door behind her. Svetlana stared for a moment at the closed door, turned and went to the bookshelves her mother was earlier cleaning. She took the discarded dust cloth which lay on the window ledge and proceeded to take each book and dust it, just as her mother had done earlier. And the tears flowed more than ever.

CHAPTER FIVE

Friday
Washington, D.C.
Local Time: 4:00 p.m. (9:00 p.m. London)
Department of Justice, Room 6610

The dark blue coffee mug, with the bold logo WETA of the local Washington public television station, sat directly in front of her, its decaffeinated coffee untouched and cold. She fingered the handle, caressing it, picking the mug up and slowly shaking it gently as if to stir the black liquid inside. Under a six-inch paperweight bronze figure of the Sphinx, purchased in Cairo several years ago, rested a pile of phone messages written carefully on small oblong light gray paper by her secretary Beverly, all organized by time received, and all needing to be returned.

A sculptured silver antique framed picture of Mary with her mother and father at her parents' 40th wedding anniversary sat next to her in-box, with files neatly stacked, a few loose papers on top. Opposite this, next to her out-box, was a similarly framed picture of her with Jim Foster at one of the overlooks in the Skyline Drive, some 100 kilometers from Washington, D.C., taken the first year they'd met. He held his arm around her while behind them glowed the spectacular color of fall foliage. She was smiling a warm, genuine smile. She was happy . . . it showed. She looked at neither photo, but kept moving the mug in a circular fashion, aimlessly, not yet placing it down.

It had come at last—the day Mary never wanted to rise to see, never to be a part of. That black lit darkness that comes to everyone, sometimes expected and sometimes not, but it comes—and it had come for Boarders. He also had no asylum from death. None. For her, she knew nothing would ever be the same again. Mary didn't shudder; she didn't have to imagine what the consequences would be of his death. She knew them.

No one had to tell her that Boarders was dead. He had failed to respond to messages at the Lowndes Hotel where he was registered, and he wasn't with the Harrisons. She retraced as best she could Boarders' whereabouts during the past twenty-four hours, ending with his coded call to her this Friday morning, 6:00 a.m. Washington time, 11:00 a.m. London.

Between that hour and now, his program was unknown—even to Harrison. But Boarders had never, in the years she had worked with him, missed an appointment without offering an explanation. If Boarders was anything, he was deliberate. He planned everything, and yet he rarely told anyone, including Mary, his complete schedule. "I'll call you" was his comment. And, of course, he always did. But, not now.

She brought the mug to her lips, looked at its contents for several seconds, then placed it, again untouched, on a coffee-stained small white napkin near her phone. Her silence continued as she gripped the front of her desk with both hands as if to steady her gaze—a gaze directed at nothing in particular—certainly not the wall directly ahead on which hung her myriad diplomas and awards, nor the wall along the right side of her office displaying several pictures of her with various governmental officials, and one large one with the President. No, it was a gaze trying to ignore an inner demon that was showing itself in a persistent and disturbing way. She needed a drink badly, but that indulgence she knew would become pampered self-absorption, and she couldn't afford that luxury at this moment. Slowly, though, Mary reached into the bottom left drawer and took out an amber colored plastic tumbler, together with a partially filled quart bottle of Bombay Gin, from behind some files. For several moments she stared at both, then twisted the cap off the bottle, and began to pour the clear liquid into her plastic glass. She recapped the bottle and placed it directly in front of her. Suddenly, and without warning, she stopped all movement, her fury sending a wave of blood immediately rushing to her brain. "Fuck. Fuck everyone . . ." she cried. She picked up the glass, hurling it across her desk, into the air, spilling the contents across the desk and onto the two guest chairs in front of the desk and the blue-gray office carpet. It fell abruptly, bouncing in several places, finally resting on the floor next to the mahogany glass front bookcase holding Mary's briefing books. A second later, Mary hurled the bottle in the same direction. It struck a framed Admission Certificate to the U.S. Supreme Court, smashing the glass frame. The impact shattered the bottle.

Hearing the turmoil, Beverly, rushed in, stared at Mary, and was paralyzed with disbelief. "Mary . . . Mary . . . what in God's name is happening? Mary, Mary . . . ."

"Fuck everyone! Everyone!" Mary shouted. Then, Mary slowly raised her hands to her face, and pushed herself away from her desk. Lowering her voice to a soft murmur, she hesitated. "I'll clean up the mess, Beverly. I'll clean it up . . . don't worry. I'm fine . . . I'll be okay. It's over . . . I'll be fine, Beverly. I'll be fine . . . just fine . . ." she said as she reached for tissues and began wiping the gin off her desk and the files.

Mary had been out of Georgetown University Law School for seven years and was Special Counsel at the CIA, when she first met Colonel Boarders in early 1987. After law school, at which she finished first in her class in June, 1979, and despite the entreaties of her law dean, and the wishes of her family to clerk for a Supreme Court justice or to work at a prestigious law firm, she decided to serve as a counsel to the United States Senate Select Committee on Intelligence, primarily because it was there that a fellow student, John Reilly, with whom she was in love, had obtained a job. Both were law clerks, doing research and the other menial bidding for Committee senior counsels as well as for the Senators on the committee.

Reilly, a strong, sinewy, gregarious man with a great deal of energy, but not particularly handsome, soon left the Committee. After six months, he became bored with the tedium of research and, unknown to Mary at the time, applied for and received a job offer from a law firm in Chicago, his home town. When he told her he was leaving and wanted her to follow, she was angry that he had carried on a job search without telling her. And, in her mind, to add insult, Reilly told her late one Saturday morning while they were in bed together and after they had

had sex. Feeling used, hurt, angry at the deception, she slapped him across the face, said nothing, and left. Despite his calls, letters, deliveries of flowers, and the intercession of their mutual friends, she never spoke to him again. The breakup was all the more painful because she loved him, believed in him, cared for him, trusted him. It was a long time before she forgot John Reilly, and only she knew of the pain of that separation.

After she left Reilly, Mary threw herself into her work even more prodigiously. Her photographic memory, her command of the law, and her obvious fascination with foreign intelligence collection brought her to the attention of the Director of the FBI, who asked her, in 1983, to come to the Bureau as Special Counsel for intelligence matters—the youngest and only woman to have held the position. Mary was 27 at the time of the appointment. Four years later, she was sent to the Central Intelligence Agency, also as Special Counsel. Her portfolio was vague and her appointment closely held information. It was in that capacity, on June 5, 1987, she met Colonel Boarders.

Mary had flown to Paris for a special meeting regarding the targeting of certain leaders in the Middle East. It was the agency's secret of secrets, a project so important and vital that it had to be carried out—regardless of domestic law to the contrary. It was true that the hostages in Lebanon had been released, but the President, whose anger at this sorry chapter never abated, turned the other way when briefed, changed the subject, and winked at Mary as he did so. The CIA never forgave itself for not rescuing its premier Middle East agent who was tortured and killed by Middle East reactionaries. To punish those who had done this, a series of assassinations would be carried out . . . regardless of whether those assassinated actually pulled the cord that strangled the CIA operative or mistreated the hostages. Early messages had been misunderstood. The message sent by this assignment would not be.

The meeting, held over dinner at the Hotel Plaza Athenee, in the small Relais grill adjacent to the main dining room, was long. Her memory of the first meeting with Boarders was vivid because he said so little. It was at this meeting that she also met Harrison, who reviewed the plans both had devised. After the waiter set the coffee on the table,

Boarders leaned over and softly said, "Mary . . . once we start . . . there is no turning back. There is no retreat. Understood?" There was no inflection in his voice, just a calm, straightforward comment. "We can stop the beginnings, Mary; but once the beginnings start, we don't stop."

"No stopping" was her only comment. From that moment, it was clear that the three were comfortable with one another. The closeness grew and the results of this collaboration, even to this day, were shrouded in deepest secrecy. The partnership had begun, and the results of the efforts had been significant.

"You did call Jim and tell him about . . . lunch?" Mary asked, remembering that she had promised that she would meet him at three and it was now after four.

"Of course, Mary, when I saw you were going to be late, I called him. He understood, and asked that you call him when you have a moment," Beverly replied, as she picked up the broken pieces of glass, placing them in the waste basket she was carrying.

"I'll do that, Beverly, please." Mary began to pick up the remaining slivers, carefully placing them in her left hand, then discarding them in the waste basket her secretary still carried. Neither looked at the TV—the sound had been turned off—and both ignored the CNN special report logo coming across the screen.

The ringing phone broke the awkward silence that had descended as both continued to collect the remaining glass pieces. Mary didn't stop her movements. Beverly put the waste basket down, walked over to Mary's desk, and said, "This is Mary Auriello's office." After a few seconds, she turned to Mary, saying, "Mary, it's Commander Michael Robinson . . . London."

Mary put the remaining bits of shattered glass into the waste basket, brushed her hands over it, and then took the phone Beverly was holding for her. "Good evening, Commander Robinson. Have you taken care of everything?" Mary asked quietly.

"We tried, Mary. We tried."

"What do you mean? 'You tried'?" she demanded, her voice rising.

"An attempt was made on Harrison's life as his car left the theatre.

A man jumped in front of the car. Harrison and his son rushed out to see if he was hurt. It was then that the man took out a gun and shot at David and his son. His son was hit in the arm. Harrison was struck with the pistol across his head. So was his wife. She had also left the car. I'm sorry, Mary. I understand that a special report has gone out over CNN. Did you hear it? And Colonel Boarders, Mary, was found murdered at his hotel in bed, with a male prostitute. We don't yet know the motive for that murder, but suspect it may have been committed by the same man who attempted to take out Harrison. I'm sorry, Mary. I really am. I know—"

There was a long silence. When Mary finally did speak, the ferocity of her response surprised even Beverly, who continued to search for any remaining shattered glass and to wipe the spilled gin from the carpet and the wall where it had splattered, using two small hand towels from Mary's private bathroom.

Mary's voice rose with anger and frustration. "You're sorry, Commander? You're sorry ? What the fuck were you doing? You gave me your assurances that the Harrisons would be protected. Didn't I call you? Didn't I call you and warn you? What planet are you on? Where was Harrison's car? Commander, did the Harrisons have a security escort? Did they, Commander?"

"Yes, but—well—. Not really for them—the security cars—one was in front of the Queen's limousine and one behind . . . and after that came the Harrisons' car," Robinson tried to reply.

"What are you telling me? That the Harrisons had no security? You have to be joking. Why do you think I called you? Because I had nothing better to do? Didn't you tell me that you would make sure nothing would happen to them? Didn't you tell me that? Why should I have trusted your word? After all, my Commander of the New Scotland Yard," Mary's voice dripped with sarcasm, "you were the one on duty when some kook scaled the fence around Buckingham and found his way into the Queen's bedroom. Whom did you blame then? Oh, I remember. When I saw you after that incident, you said, and correct me if quote you wrongly, 'These things happen.' Things don't happen and things don't sort themselves out. People make things happen and people sort things out."

"Mary . . . Mary . . . calm down . . . please try. Everything is under control . . . please," Robinson pleaded with her.

Mary broke off his solicitation, continuing, "Don't 'Mary' me, Commander. I told you of Harrison's work for the United States. Why on earth wouldn't you have a security car assigned to Harrison? Is that too much to ask? Aren't we supposed to be on the same side? Or do I have that incorrect? I should blame myself for believing, perhaps just this once, something right would happen when I asked counterparts in England to help me. But was I wrong? Isn't that the case? Isn't that the case?"

Ignoring her temperamental outburst, which he had never experienced, Robinson replied remorsefully, "Mary, I'm sorry you feel that way." He had made a mistake. An ice age would descend on their relationship. She had that ability . . . and would use it. "Mary, about Colonel Boarders—"

Mary didn't reply. Her body shaking with fury and scorn for a man she considered irresponsible and embarrassing. And to think, also against her better judgment, she gave information about Harrison and Boarders to Robinson, who had insisted on disclosure because Harrison would be a guest of the Queen. Certainly, she didn't tell him the entire story, only that "Harrison was on a special assignment for the United States and would be accompanied by a retired U.S. Army Colonel." Now she knew it was imperative to protect both their identities and Colonel Boarders' reputation.

She waved Beverly to leave.

"Commander Robinson, about Colonel Boarders. I will say this only once. Please follow these instructions. I must ask that you follow them without deviation. In other words . . . don't screw up this time." Her mind churned with worry that Robinson would do just that, but she needed him, for a while at least. It was necessary to control what was spinning out of control.

To that end, she lowered her voice and spoke as if addressing a group of children. She chose every word carefully, calling Robinson by his first name. "Michael, it's vital that you remove Colonel Boarders' body from the hotel as quickly as possible. An unmarked ambulance must be used. Use your most trusted drivers for this. You are not to confirm to any press that an American officer was murdered at the hotel. In fact, he was not even there. The hotel records must be expunged and substitute names must be inserted. Try a different spelling for Boarders . . . try Borders. This clerical error can easily be explained. Find another body to put into that room. I don't care where you get it from . . . but find one. No publicity under any circumstances must attend to this murder. And there can be no tie to the Harrison hit. Do you understand? If you feel that you can't do this, then tell me right now, Commander, right now. This isn't a game. I will leave in a few hours and should be in the London area around five or six tomorrow, Saturday morning. Michael, you mustn't fail me this time. You mustn't," she spoke quietly.

"If you have any problem, call Inspector Charles Franklin if you have any qualms about doing what I have just asked. He knows me well," she concluded, her voice taking on an unnaturally calm and soft manner.

"Mary, I'm sorry. I truly am. I'm responsible, but I really don't know why there was a security lapse regarding the Harrisons. I take responsibility. Yes, I certainly shall do what you ask me to do."

Robinson really had great admiration for Mary. She was well known by police and security departments around the world. She had given lectures at the Interpol Academy. Her knowledge of police history, technology, and security issues was legendary. Her friendships spanned the globe, and yet he knew her to be secretive and protective. She never let slip what she didn't want the listener to hear. A consummate agent, but he could never prove that. It she were an agent, her public persona made everyone think otherwise. Robinson knew that he had been caught short, and that she would never let him forget it.

"In this business, Michael," Mary continued softly, and in a manner devoid of the faintest trace of sympathy for Robinson, "as I'm sure you're aware, there can be no room for mistakes. It will take all of our skill to control and solve the matter at hand. People like Harrison and Boarders depend on you and me. I know that you're as determined as I am, Michael, to prevent this from escalating into something devastating for everyone. Please have Colonel Boarders' body at Alconbury when

I arrive. I need you as well as the police officials investigating these cases at the airport.

"In the meantime, find the assassin who killed Boarders and attempted to kill Harrison. He must still be in London. I assume you have a description. If you have to go public, I urge discretion and no mention of Boarders. Harrison, I'm sure you understand, is an innocent American businessman, who happened to be caught in an untoward attempt on your monarch's life by a deranged man. If you find the assassin, kill him. I don't want him alive, and you'd better not want him alive either. We don't need him. I know who directed this hit, Michael, and there are ways of reaching that individual as well. Do I have your understanding, Michael, on how to proceed?'

"Okay, Mary, okay. I understand . . . fully—I understand fully."

"Fine." More in sorrow than anger Mary said, "Michael, we both have much to do. But you have to understand how one would get moderately upset at this kind of lapse in judgment. There can't be another failure . . . there can't be, Michael. I'll see you tomorrow. I'll call from the plane."

"I'll wait," Robinson said, but the phone line had already gone dead. Mary had hung up on him.

She had one more call to make, and she couldn't make it in her office.

She rose from her oversized, government issue, brown leather desk chair, grabbing the page where she had written a message, reached for her purse from the lower right hand drawer, and took it, placing the note in the purse's open back pocket. Walking quickly, she grabbed her black raincoat hanging on the rack by the door and walked over to her assistant's desk, adjacent to her office. "Beverly. Did I shout too much? Or was it normal, medium normal, high normal?" she smiled as she reached into the candy jar on Beverly's desk, helping herself to some M & Ms.

"Well," Beverly said, "and before I answer that, the AG has been on the phone and wants to see you. Something about a CNN special report describing a supposed attempt on the Queen."

"Hmm . . . Later. I'll see him later . . . about a half hour. Okay. Now,"

Mary said, smiling, "I want you to be truthful. Did I shout too much?"

"Are you sure you want to know?" Beverly asked.

"Of course, Beverly, always. How bad was it?"

"High normal."

"Good, I just wanted to be sure," Mary broke out into a big smile and shrugged her shoulders. "I must be getting meek."

They both laughed.

"My, my. Well this proves I'm becoming a more pleasant person. Anyway, I'm going to walk over to the Old Post Office Building for quick bite, and to get some air. I'll be right back—maybe fifteen minutes. I'll need a plane to get me to London. Make sure I still have a toothbrush in my permanently packed suitcase. Yes, before you ask, I'll see the AG before I leave."

Mary now knew she didn't have enough time. The call from Commander Robinson didn't bring her comfort. The mission had gone awry—a first for her, Boarders, and Harrison.

"I've already ordered the plane. The CIA is providing a contract carrier for you. Because the Director had to approve of the special flight, he asked if you would be so kind as to brief him before you take off," Beverly said with a wide smile, anticipating what Mary was going to say.

"My God. William Miller wants to be briefed? He's joking, isn't he? Well, we'll have to do it when I return."

"He's on your side, Mary," Beverly said quietly.

"Then he'll have to wait. I have more important things to do right now. By the way, Beverly, thanks for helping me clean up the mess. I suppose what I did is one way of clearing up a problem. Maybe even the more effective way. Who knows? Thanks," and with that she grabbed Beverly's umbrella propped aside the office door and left.

Mary's office was at the end of a long corridor where portraits of all the attorneys general hung. As she often did, on her way to the bank of elevators midway down the corridor, and for reasons she herself only vaguely understood, she paused in front of former Attorney General Robert Kennedy's portrait, wondering why the artist captured him in such a melancholy manner. "He was so good . . . and he suffered so much . . . his brother killed . . . . so much pain in his face . . . so much pain," she pondered, and then picked up the pace, heading toward the elevator.

It was a short two-block walk from Main Justice to the Old Post Office, also on Pennsylvania Avenue. The carefully restored, late-nineteenth-century stone edifice housed offices as well as a food court and specialty shops. Mary, however, used the Eleventh-street entrance across from the IRS building in order to be near the phone booths. Several people were milling around the booths, but she spotted a free one and closed the door behind her, picked up the receiver, dropped a quarter in the slot, and dialed a number.

"Systems Cab Company, may I help you?" came a male voice over the phone.

"Yes, I'll need a cab to meet me at the Pennsylvania Avenue entrance to the Old Post Office Building in a few minutes. Can this be done?" Mary asked.

"I'll be there, at the Pennsylvania Avenue entrance," the voice repeated her statement.

"Thank you," she said and rung off. Mary didn't have to identify herself and she used this phone number only to a special operative she employed occasionally. At one time, the operative, Beke Santos, a tall, heavily built Jamaican American, was part of a Boarders/Harrison overseas team. But he had been injured while on a mission in Algeria, and, as with all their mission members, Boarders and Harrison had made sure he was taken care of. As the helicopter extracted Beke from the desert, a shot hit his left ankle. Despite emergency medical treatment on the helicopter, it was a few hours before the plane landed on a French navy support ship in the Mediterranean. The surgeon on board did the best she could, but the wound was too deep, so Beke could walk, but his limp was noticeable. It didn't affect his sight and he was an expert marksman and demolition man. Mary would use his services tonight.

She quickly left the phone booth and walked briskly to the side entrance, past the stream of people flowing in and out of the food court, going down the six steps, pushing open the heavy windowed oak framed door, and strode to the front of the building where a dark blue BMW was parked. Its plates were District of Columbia, lettered only SCB. She saw that Beke was the driver and immediately got in.

"Good day, Beke. How are you, your family?"

"Fine, Mary. Are you okay?" he asked as he started to slowly pull the car away from the curb. "Yes, I am fine, but I need your help, Beke. Here. . . ."

Mary opened her purse and drew out a note which read

> Kalischenko
> 12445 M. Street, N.W., Suite 1000. Parking Space No. 35
> First level.
> Gray Mercedes. Plates: Md.13346-111
> Phone:202-304-7892
> 12390 Cedar Court
> Potomac, Maryland
> Phone: 301-897-6432

She placed the note in the slot adjacent to her seat and said nothing.

As the car arrived at the Justice building, Mary said, "Take me another block; I want to walk and get some air."

"Sure, Mary. It's a good day to go for a short walk. But it's damp out there."

As he stopped the car in front of the Federal Trade Commission building, Mary opened the door, and said, "David's been hurt; so has his family. Boarders is dead."

"I'll take care of everything, Mary. Too bad about Boarders. He was a king, the best of kings, Mary, the best. Take care, Mary. Take good care."

She smiled at him and whispered, "Thanks, Beke. Here's the key. It's all in the box at Union Station. Throw away the key when you have taken all that's in the box."

Mary knew she would be late for the attorney general's meeting. She had only a few blocks to walk, and she walked slowly, with a short stride and little energy. "Too much for me . . . too much for me . . .," and tears came to her eyes. The distant thunder from a shrouded sky broke through her silent thoughts with the forecast of an approaching thunderstorm. Mary hoped that it wouldn't delay her departure for

London.

She was worried that the information concerning Boarders' death would wipe away years of great service for the country. She would protect his reputation. The sale of the nuclear device to Iran would be stopped, but without him it would be more difficult. She was absolutely confident of the project, yet her confidence was shaken when she heard about Boarders. He was irreplaceable, and she could never work with anyone other than Harrison and Boarders.

All the years of covert activity, of fighting off threats, imagined and real, and of setting thresholds of success greater than the mission before, with two men unique in the field, led her to know she couldn't continue without the three of them being together. They truly believed that, among the civilized, human life is set at risk only to serve freedom. Too often there were other agendas for intelligence agents, but for Mary, Harrison, and Colonel Boarders, it was a singular goal. They believed in what they were doing. It was more than patriotic. It was their faith.

She reached the Justice Department's Tenth-street entrance, paused for a moment, and looked at her watch. It was 4:45 p.m. She kept walking, crossing Constitution Avenue. She sat on a park bench a short distance from the National Museum of American History. "Bob, oh, Bob, why in the hell did you leave us? You deserved honor, dignity, no, not this way, Bob. You have gone too soon . . . too soon," Mary murmured softly to herself, weeping helplessly.

"Hey! Ms. Auriello. How're ya' doin'? You ok?"

Mary looked up to see Dennis Knapp, a lawyer in her office. She couldn't let anyone see her in this state, and yet her heart was so heavy. There was so much to do, and Mary knew she had to keep her agony and grief to herself.

"Actually, yes, Dennis," she recovered quickly, and her official persona came through like a theater star on cue. "My contacts . . . these new lenses . . . I must have something other than them in my eyes. The wind blew some dust or something more serious. But I'm fine now," she said as she opened her purse and took out some tissue, dabbing her eyes. "Awful thing, vanity. I mean, isn't that why we wear these things right on the cornea. Really! Wearing glasses, as you do, is much more practical. You're to be commended."

Without waiting for Dennis to reply, she quickly rose from the bench and continued, "I'm happy you came by, Dennis." She smiled. "Now, tell me about the research. Has the Russian government published a new Criminal Code yet? Or are they still using the old one from the Soviet days?"

"You can guess, Ms. Auriello. The old one. Which, of course, is discouraging. Do you think they'll ever change it?"

"Of course, Dennis, they will. The reason is simple: the quest for freedom is an age-old quest. It hasn't changed since the dawn of man. But let's go, Dennis. I have a meeting with the AG, and you know he doesn't like to be kept waiting. By the way, I want to see you and the other interns for lunch on Monday, next. Make sure that Beverly knows, or I'll forget," she laughed.

As they reached the Constitution Avenue entrance to their building, he opened the door for her. "You're always optimistic, Ms. Auriello, always upbeat. I don't know how you do it. I get down when I lose a squash game. Would you believe it?"

"Yes, I would. You're a man!"

"By the way, the scuttlebutt has it that the AG is after you; at least that's what we hear. I guess you know about that rumor also."

"You shouldn't be listening to rumor. I believe in being optimistic. I hope you do too, and that you never give up in the face of any disappointment. Now, as for the AG, really, now why would anyone spread that rumor? I think he's a very nice man," she said as she winked. When they both reached the elevator, Dennis pushed six on the control panel, smiling at Mary's comments without responding.

As they reached the sixth floor, Mary asked, "Dennis, would you take my rain coat and Beverly's umbrella to my office? Ordinarily, I wouldn't ask, but I want the AG to think that I've been working in my office rather than worrying about my contacts in the park." Dennis took them quickly, and with a wave and "Thanks" she strode toward the attorney general's office, straightening her rose colored suit.

She never carried papers to briefings. Whatever information she imparted was in her head. And she allowed no notes.

Washington, D.C.
Friday
Local Time: 11:00 p.m. (4:00 a.m., Saturday, London)
Apt. 2100, 4501 Connecticut Ave., N.W.

Beke Santos had settled into his evening routine of reading *Newsweek* and watching the late evening news. "Paula," he called to his wife of thirty years, "bring some of that chocolate cake you made today. No coffee though. Some milk."

Paula Santos, a modest size woman with carefully coiffured gray hair came in and stared at her husband, seated comfortably in a maroon leather wing chair she had bought him years earlier, when he retired from the Marines. "Beke, is there some reason you can't get the cake yourself? Are you an invalid? That limp doesn't prevent you from walking," she said, but with a smile.

"Okay, I'll get up to do it. But, you know I like to watch the news. It's the only enjoyment I get these days."

"What? I'll never sleep with you again!" She laughed as she left the living room and headed toward the kitchen.

Without responding, Beke pressed his TV remote button to Channel Nine. Coming across the screen was the logo for the Eleven O'clock Headline News.

"Good Evening. I'm Maxine Lowe. Topping the news this evening is a report of an explosion in the garage at an office building at 24th and M Street, North West. Destroyed in the garage were several cars on level one. The police report that the blast occurred between eight and nine this evening, when most of the building personnel had already left.

The dead have been identified as a Mr. Valery Kalischenko, Washington representative of Bank Alliance Russia, a major Russian bank closely allied with the present Russian government, and a bank many Western banks do business with. Mr. Kalischenko's two assistants, Ygor Rodinov and Nicolai Verneko, who were in the car with him, also died. The police are unaware of any other deaths, but the cars on either side of Kalischenko's were destroyed and the ceiling of the garage above the cars was heavily damaged.

Police are speculating that the car bomb was placed to cause maximum damage to the Kalischenko vehicle. The police state that the killer must have known Kalischenko's exact schedule in order to carry out the attack.

Earlier this evening, in a bizarre twist, Kalischenko's home in Potomac was also the scene of a fire which destroyed the home and adjacent garage. It's been reported that Kalischenko's wife and child were away at the time, in Moscow.

Still needing his snack for the evening, Beke got up and headed toward the kitchen. Mary would be pleased.

CHAPTER SIX

**Cyprus, Lanarca International Airport
Local Time: 10:30 a.m. (8:30 a.m., London)
Aboard Swissair Flight 900 Bound for Zurich from Cyprus**

Svetlana Makorova felt alone because she was alone. Although she oftentimes preferred solitude, this wasn't one of those times. She avoided looking at her seat mate, but rather kept staring out the airliner window. Perhaps she was looking for that miracle of equilibrium and serenity—a sense of peace—which comes only with real happiness. But that would have to wait. It would be deception, she told herself, to ignore the constant agitation that reigned in her life these past five years, loving a man she didn't love, and working for a man she despised. Through her own volition, she had decided to turn on these two: Moussa Berdayev, her lover, and Peter Bradford, her employer. This, she told herself, wasn't the time to be romantic or sentimental. Besides her mother, she knew she had the loyalty of Colonel Boarders, that silent man, whom she would be seeing today in London.

"Beautiful day, isn't it?" the middle-age male passenger, seated next to her, asked.

Svetlana looked at the stout man, her blue eyes smiling, "Yes, it is. It would be a nice day to be on the beach, I suppose."

"Your destination Zurich, or are you going on?"

For what seemed like an infinite time, Svetlana didn't reply. She was unsure how to respond and was saved by the flight attendant reminding her to "Fasten your belt, please." Svetlana turned again toward the window.

She was oblivious to the noise from the Swissair Airbus 320's twin jet engines as they revved up for takeoff. Svetlana continued to stare out of the right side of the aircraft, seeing an Aeroflot Ilyushin passenger jet taxiing to its gate. That flight would be the early one from Moscow. So many times she had come with Moussa on that very flight. The first time, perhaps even the second and third times, were exciting for Svetlana because they were her first trips outside Russia. Moussa's bank—Bank Alliance Russia—had an office on Cyprus, and Moussa would visit the office and, as often as he could, would take Svetlana with him.

Cyprus became, after 1991, the destination of choice for hundreds of Russian businesses. The new Russian government had signed a favorable tax treaty with Cyprus which made doing business from Cyprus virtually tax free. The Moscow *mafiya* followed to make sure that the commitments the businessmen made in Moscow were not forgotten in Cyprus.

She tried not to think of those early times. "Today was different," she mused. She had ended the fighting with herself six months earlier when she decided to help Colonel Boarders. Her freedom had begun then. Questioning and doubts about that decision vanished for she knew that something large, something capable, something perhaps even noble, rose up within her, a liberating spirit that she had never experienced before. Freedom is a splendid comrade and would now be hers.

Over the past six months, she had given Colonel Boarders a great deal of information on the workings of the Moscow *mafiya*. At their last furtive meeting just a week earlier, at the Moscow Arbat-Smolenskaya subway station, that massive station below the crowded market stalls and pedestrian mall, Colonel Boarders told her that it was time to leave Moscow. "I'm afraid, Svetlana, that Bradford will be able to trace the information flow to you . . . and probably soon. We mustn't take untoward chances," he told her quietly, as he stood next to her on the platform as if waiting for an oncoming train. "You must depart Moscow, and you must take your mother with you. Your employers won't spare her if she is left behind and you leave. You'll fly from Cyprus next Thursday, a week from today. Here are your instructions. Memorize them. Then destroy them."

Just as Colonel Boarders was reaching into his pocket, he noticed a man and woman running down the escalator, hurrying toward the platform. "Svetlana, I must go now. You may have some company soon."

Turning away, he bent over as if to pick up piece of paper. "I believe you dropped this," he whispered to her as he handed her a small blue envelope, just as the train slid to a stop. Colonel Boarders joined the crowd entering the car directly in front of her.

She turned to head toward the exit onto the Arbat when a voice cried out, "Svetlana! It was one of Dimitri Gravev's drivers with a friend.

"Vladimir! Do you have a car?" Svetlana said without answering his question. "I must get back to the office."

"Yes, it is outside, parked in front," he said with a broad smile as a driver for the Moscow *vor,* having no fear the traffic police would ticket his car, which was illegally stationed. "And, Svetlana, meet my girl. Katkya Lesnikova, this is Svetlana Makorova. She is in charge of the whole operation in Moscow!" he said with a booming laugh.

"Katkya, if you are Vladimir's friend, you are mine," Svetlana said as she extended her hand to Katkya, and she leaned over to kiss her on both cheeks. "You must come by the office and we shall have a long visit. Do not trust this Vladimir. He says one thing and does another," Svetlana laughed loudly.

"Vladimir, I missed my train. It is leaving. You must stay with me until I get on. You promised," Katkya looked sheepishly at Svetlana.

"I won't tell a soul, Vladimir. I shall take a taxi back. Actually, I may walk. I don't know. You have a good time and don't worry. I have not seen you and you have not seen me. Good luck, Vladimir . . . Katkya. Katkya, you must come and have tea with me. You must," Svetlana walked toward the escalator, taking it directly to the crowded street above.

"Amazing," she said to herself, "Colonel Boarders had seen one of Dimitri's drivers and had recognized him. Amazing, the colonel had memorized all the photos she had given him of the Moscow *mafiya.*"

The day following that secret meeting with Boarders, her heart beating fast, she asked Peter Bradford for time off to go to Cyprus for a seven-day stay. "Peter, my mother has not felt well, and I think, as does the doctor, that the sun will do her good. As usual, I will call you every morning."

"Fine, Svetlana. I mean to take a few days off myself after this special sale goes through. You do know that next Thursday morning, however, I have a meeting on that subject. I suggest that you take the later plane to Cyprus on that day—actually it is one of the few Boeings that Aeroflot recently leased—so it should be a much better flight. I envy you. I would like to leave this rainy weather myself."

The day of the special meeting a week later was dreary. Clouds hung low over Moscow, the inevitable rain falling steadily. In attendance were Dimitri Gravev, the Moscow *vor* leader; Moussa Berdayev, Svetlana's lover; Peter Bradford, her employer; Prakash Farnak, an Iranian businessman in Moscow; Frederik von Hauser, a Swiss banker; Jomhori Shenasi, the Iranian ambassador to Russia; and Major General Yuri Nikolayev. The only one to linger for a few moments at her desk was Moussa. The remaining men greeted her with a smile or nod and moved directly into the conference room.

"Are you ready for the sun, Svetlana?" said Moussa, leaning over to kiss her.

"Not here, Moussa. You have a meeting to go to; you should be in the conference room."

"Ah! my Svetlana . . . always a worrier, but I will follow your advice and go. I will see you tomorrow anyway, in Cyprus."

"Yes, Moussa, you will . . . and hurry down. Don't call me and tell me you are going to be late like you did the last time. You must promise me that you will not be late."

"I promise," Moussa said quietly, as he entered the conference room, closing the door behind him.

Quickly she went to Bradford's office and entered a small closet to the left of the large painting of the Kremlin directly behind his desk. Behind a false panel at the bottom of the right closet wall sat the concealed equipment which recorded all conversations in Bradford's personal office and conference room. The only rooms without the system were the reception area, where Svetlana had her office, and the kitchen and the bathroom. She hastily checked to see if the tapes were running properly, and hurried back to her own desk, where she had several stacks of paper to file while the meeting was going on.

Every evening, she checked the tapes and placed in Bradford brief case the tapes that had been used. She doubted Bradford listened to them. He liked them "just in case," he said when he was showing her the taping system—a full year after she was employed. He swore her to secrecy. And in fact, she told no one, including Moussa. For a while she believed Bradford when he told her the tapes were necessary "for legal reasons, because he did not keep notes." He seldom had her keep notes unless he specifically requested. But it was these tapes that Colonel Boarders always wanted and of which, when she could, she gave him copies, passing them at their meetings at the Bolshoi.

There was not a sound from the conference room—none of the usual shouting or loud voices. No sound at all. After an hour and half, Bradford came out. "Svetlana, can you get us some fresh tea? We should be finished in about another hour. What time is your plane?"

"It leaves at 5:30 p.m., but I can stay until about two or so. Will that be sufficient?"

"Yes, we'll be through long before."

She noticed that Bradford had an uncharacteristic frown on his brow; he looked frightened she thought as she went into the small kitchen, taking a bottle of water from the refrigerator and filling the tea kettle already on the electric hot plate. It took but a few minutes to boil, and then Svetlana poured the hot water through a tea strainer directly into a large tea pot. The pot, purchased by Bradford in Germany, had scenes of Berlin, but Svetlana found the color interesting—a brilliant rose with each scene bordered in gold. Different for an office setting, she thought. Initially Bradford said he had bought the set for his wife, but he never took it home. One day, he asked Svetlana to unpack the remaining cups and use them as the office china, which she did.

She knocked on the door and turned the handle. But as Bradford saw her, he surged from his chair and took the pot from her, the fear and worry still etched on his scarred face. "Thank you, Svetlana."

"Do you need clean cups, Peter?" she asked.

"No, Svetlana. No."

No one looked up from the single sheet of paper that each seemed to be reading—except Moussa who smiled at her. "We should be finished in about a half hour, maximum," Bradford said to her.

"I shall wait, Peter. I shall be here."

Svetlana was filing papers at the bank of four-drawer gray file cabinets along the left wall of her office when she heard the conference door open. Again, everyone silently filed out, but this time, because they had to pass through her office to exit to the hall, one by one they said good bye. Only Dimitri Gravev, followed by Moussa, acknowledged her with a "Thank you for the tea." Bradford still had the look of fear on his face. Saying nothing, he went into his office, sitting for several minutes alone at his desk while Svetlana continued her filing. She knew that she had to get him out of his office in order to get the tapes of the meeting.

"Peter, did you want to have lunch with Mr. Todd Winston? He called as you were finishing your meeting and asked that you join him at the Metropol. Should I call him back?" Svetlana asked as she went back to her desk to get the last pile of folders to file.

"I guess I should. He has some deal he wants me to look at. And, I'd best get my mind off what is bothering me. Yes, call him. Tell him I'll be there in 30 minutes."

Svetlana quickly placed her remaining pile of files back on her desk and called Winston, confirming the lunch. She knew she would have time to obtain the tapes and substitute blank ones in the machine, as well as in Bradford's briefcase. He would not know whether they had been used.

"Peter, are you okay? Is it too stuffy in the conference room? I called the building manager and he sent up an engineer who said the ventilation is fine, but, I think it's too stuffy, don't you?"

Bradford didn't respond, but stared at the one piece of paper he had taken from the conference room and held in his hands. Slowly he folded it, and put it in his jacket inside pocket.

"Peter, don't you want me to file that?"

"No, I'll take it with me. It's nothing really . . . nothing . . . just nothing. I'll come back later to get my brief case, but only for a few minutes. Have a good trip with your mother and Moussa. Now, call me, Svetlana. I may have to cut short your vacation if I need you here."

"Of course, Peter. I understand," Svetlana replied.

Peter opened the closet that Svetlana had just been to, took out his dark brown raincoat, wandered over to the window, murmuring something indecipherable, and walked to the exit door. "Svetlana, good bye. Don't forget to take care of my brief case."

She looked up from her file cabinet. "Peter, yes, of course. Thanks for giving me the time off. I'll call you every day."

Svetlana finished the filing, checked Bradford's desk, and circled the conference room, tearing off a page from each pad so that a fresh page would be evident for the next meeting. She looked in vain for any indication of notes on the sheets she tore off. She checked the waste basket but it was empty too. Rushing back to the closet, she took out the used tapes from the tape machine, replaced them with fresh tape, and placed fresh tape in Bradford's briefcase, after she had written the day on the tape. The used tapes she placed in her purse. Whatever was discussed at the special meeting would all be on the tape. She hastened over to Bradford's computer, turned it on, slipping in a disk to copy what he had been working on since the last time she had made a copy for Colonel Boarders. The tape recordings and the computer disk she would bring with her to Cyprus and on to Zurich. The one thing she was not bringing was the single sheet of paper that Bradford so carefully folded and took with him, as did all the others.

The Swissair flight's lifting from the runway momentarily broke Svetlana's thoughts of that last day in the office and she started to flip through *Der Spiegel* smiling, realizing that right in the middle of the magazine was where her new German passport and Swissair ticket, had been placed by the strange woman she had just left.

Svetlana's name now was Helga Dietrich. Her own Russian passport had been given to the woman by Svetlana in the folded *Herald Tribune*. So any record of Svetlana Makorova was gone. Even if Moussa were to trace her to the airport, he wouldn't find out she left. She knew that Moussa would try to bribe the passport control officers for information. But again, nothing could be passed on, because she no longer existed. Cyprus passport control had no security cameras taking pictures of departing passengers.

It would take about three hours and forty-five minutes to arrive in Zurich. She wouldn't have to pretend to doze. Tension brought exhaustion and sleep.

"Menu card," the flight attendant said as she handed Svetlana a small printed card.

"No, no thank you. I will not be eating. I will just rest for a while. Thank you, though. I think I will try to get some sleep."

"You're lucky," the man next to her said, "I can never sleep on planes, trains, or whatever. I need a bed." He laughed loudly.

"Yes, of course," Svetlana answered, as she turned her head, adjusted her dark glasses, and placed the pillow she had found on her seat when she boarded behind her head, continuing to look out the window. There was always some exhilaration and liberation that came from flying, and she usually liked it but not today. She thought only of what she had to do when she was in Zurich. The sky was a beautiful blue and the beaches were visible as the plane proceeded in a left turn over the airport, climbing steadily over the water and heading in a westerly direction toward Zurich.

For a moment, Svetlana toyed with the gold bracelet that her Aunt Yelena had given her years ago. "Shine bright as a golden star," her Aunt Yelena had said to her. Svetlana thought of her aunt and wished she were sitting next to her. Fortified by some vodka, her aunt would let the stories flow from her about this apparition and that prediction, and Svetlana would be enthralled, wanting her aunt to continue indefinitely. Joyous times are rarely recreated, she thought. Her aunt hid reality behind a mask of mystery. But she made Svetlana cheerful. And Svetlana thought about how much she needed her aunt now. She finally closed her eyes and in a few moments was sound asleep.

London
Friday
Local Time: 8:00 p. m.
The Lowndes Hotel, Room 452

Looking weary from a double-shift day, Detective Dean Goodwin mused in an expressionless tone, "Well, well, well, Dudley, what do we have here?" His gray eyes surveyed the scene from the small foyer leading to the bedroom. He slowly entered the room and placed himself so that he was just about two feet from the right side of the bed. "Mind the carpet, Dudley. . . . Mr. Sterling, has anyone been in the room since you called me?" Goodwin inquired of the hotel night manager, who had followed him into the room.

"No, no one has been in this room since I called you. After the maid, Sarah Williams, discovered the bodies, she fled. Thank God she hit the the panic button on her pager, alerting the hotel security. Greenville, the night security officer, and I came up immediately, attended to Sarah, looked into the room briefly, and again locked the door. No one's been here since I called you, about fifteen minutes ago." Sterling's voice quavered as he stared at the bodies and the blood. There was so much blood that he was filled with fear as well as with anger that this had happened in his hotel, just as he had been appointed night manager.

"Fine, very good. The killer obviously interrupted an entertaining afternoon, it appears," Goodwin suggested casually.

Blood had poured from the bodies into the sheeted mattress and flowed onto the floor, seeping into the dark green, oriental carpet. The head of the younger man was turned sideways, facing the open windowed door leading to the balcony. The killer seemed to have taken the young man's head and turned it slightly to the right as he cut the jugular vein. That would account for the virtual river of blood on the side of the mattress facing the balcony door, with the other side fairly unstained. The older man's head was lying on the right thigh of the young man. His neck appeared, from where Goodwin was standing, to have been cut in the same location. Both were naked. The younger man's thin, but well-defined body was hairless except for his brownish-blond pubic hair, a portion matted with the blood from the old man's slit neck. The older man's body was small but trim, his arms unusually large and muscular, as were his thighs. There appeared to be no other marks on either body.

"Swift, but not brutal. Most likely by a professional. But why?"

Goodwin thought to himself. The room was not touched, except for the multi-colored grey and green bedspread, green blankets and a loose sheet, all heaped in a mound at the foot of the bed. The antique mahogany, Victorian-styled bed was not particularly large, and it was centered as it backed to the wall, to lie parallel to the windowed balcony. Centered above the bed hung two large prints of the Portobello Road Antique Fair as depicted in 1890. A floor-to-ceiling, matching mahogany armoire was unopened. Nothing was written on the note pads placed haphazardly on the one-drawer mahogany tables on either side of the bed. The small coffee table and two grey-green damask covered matching chairs appeared not to have been moved. Scattered on the grey damask covered couch were three magazines, *Time Out, London; Newsweek;* and.*Tattler* The *Financial Times* was folded neatly on the coffee table directly in front of the couch. It appeared to have been untouched.

Standing aside Goodwin, Dudley Arrison, his assistant, said nothing. He began to inhale with some difficulty. "God, what is this? I feel sick sir . . . very sick, sir," he said covering his mouth, as if to gag.

"What is this, Dudley? Never seen blokes in this kind of position before? Men do screw other men. It is a bit strange though. But then, it does happen," Goodwin sighed. "When were you promoted to Assistant Detective?"

Dudley, sensing that he'd better get his emotions under control, ignored the question and, turning to Ernest Stirling, who was standing slightly in back of him, said, "I'd better go down and interview the maid, the security officer, the reception clerk and the concierge." He spoke in a businesslike fashion as he flipped through his note book, hoping that Goodwin would forgive his earlier lack of emotional control. "Mr. Stirling, can you have them in your office, so I may talk to them? I'll call them one at a time. We'll start with the maid. Okay, Dean?"

Turning to his assistant, Goodwin responded quietly, "Fine, Dudley. Also, talk to the bellman on duty. I believe he was in the baggage room . . . you remember we passed him when we came through the back entrance, at the request of Mr. Stirling." Goodwin spoke as he looked askance at Stirling, suggesting that London metropolitan police detectives should have come in the front door, not otherwise. "I want to look around a bit, then I'll be right down. Before you go, though, call on your cell phone and ask district headquarters to send a crime scene team. We need to have them examine this place, get pictures, prints; you know the drill. Try not to get what's her name's team—you know that frizzed hair, red-lacquered nails, tall. . . ."

"Regina Hilson?" Dudley interrupted.

"Yeah, she's the one. She's a good bit mad, isn't she?"

"I believe she thinks the same of you, sir. I'll do what I can, but the duty posting for our station has her listed as on for tonight," Dudley took the cell phone from his pocket, pressing the code for district headquarters, following Stirling out.

Goodwin turned, "Oh, Mr. Stirling, please give Dudley the records of the rooms adjacent to this one as well as the rooms directly above and below . . . and the plan of each floor. I'll need the video tapes from your security cameras for this week. The one over the front entrance, as well as one that directly views the reception desk."

"Yes, of course, you can have the videos, but we have cameras only on the reception desk. They also pick up the entrance, but from a distance. The entrance directly faces the reception area. Our security consultant said we needed only one set of cameras. The records and videos will be ready when you come to join your assistant in my office."

"I'll be down shortly."

The room was cool, the benefit of the misty September night. Breezes blew the curtains, the balcony lights forming a halo around them from the rain that was still gently falling. Goodwin had handled two dozen murders since becoming a detective eight years earlier. He knew instinctively that this was not a routine murder, if any murder is routine, the kind that occurred several hundred times a year in London. Murders of spouses and friends, robbery murders, drug murders were routine. "Contract murders are rare in London, and this is beginning to look like a contract murder," he said to himself as he stared at the bodies.

While undergoing training as a detective, he heard his chief superintendent tell him that "Solving a murder is like taking a strange, unfamiliar, unpleasant journey with the expectation that the destination will be reached sooner, rather than later. The longer it takes to reach the destination, the greater the chance that it will never be reached and the journey will continue to be strange, unfamiliar and unpleasant." From experience, Goodwin knew this to be true. The quicker he solved the mystery, the more likely the perpetrator would be caught. He was saddened by what he saw.

Goodwin stood by the two bodies, pondering what would bring these two disparate people together. "I guess it could have been any of the young male hustlers who cater to the wealthy and lonely. Obviously, the young man catered to the wealthy . . . and he would be discreet," he remarked to himself. He would have Dudley look at recent prostitution arrests to see if anyone knew the young man. Getting information on him would be easy, for other male hustlers were not discrete and would talk . . . if, for no other reason, so that the police would be more lenient to them.

But the older man—presumably in his early sixties, or maybe even older—had lines on his face brought on by extensive exposure to the sun, and his body had the appearance of someone who had worked hard, probably at a job requiring great physical labor . . . but that can't be, Goodwin thought. "What did he really do?" Goodwin stared at the old man's serene face and absentmindedly asked aloud, "What did you do that prompted someone to have you killed?"

Goodwin calculated that the killer had come in from behind, quickly killing the old man first, and then the younger one. There was no struggle; the murders could have taken only a minute or less. Slowly walking around the bed and the pool of blood that had created a large, erratic blot on the carpet, Goodwin reached the open balcony window door, touching nothing. He stood peering though the billowing curtains, and he could easily see how the killer came into the room, "through the balcony, but from where?" Turning away, he walked again to the bed, stared at the bodies, and noticed for the first time that the old man's right hand bore a watch with four small internal dials depicting various time zones. Goodwin bent down to look at the watch and verified that the time it indicated corresponded to the time on his own. "Regina will find out when and where he bought the watch. It's a very expensive one, and they probably don't make many of them," he said to himself.

Nothing escaped her . . . and for that he was thankful.

Goodwin had learned by experience that it is best to spend time observing a crime scene, touch nothing, but think and observe; place yourself in the position of the killer: try to determine the motivation for the killing; spend time thinking . . . thinking . . . and more thinking. He had to make some order out of this bloody scene. For about five minutes, he stared at the bodies, trying to imagine the stealth of the killer, the manner in which the assassin came from behind, how he quickly took the head, slit the throats . . . so quickly . . . there was no time for the victims to scream. No fuss . . . nothing.

His training and seasoning convinced Goodwin he could rely on his own skills and instincts to draw conclusions. He took out his pad and scribbled, "Too neat / professional / old man target / young man / paid / check old man/businessman/probably in money/business deals gone sour/maybe something more/call Yard." He closed his notepad and slipped it into his left side jacket pocket, placing his pen in the same place.

As he looked into the bathroom, he noticed the towels piled right next to the bathtub. Apparently, from the looks of the shower curtain, someone had strongly grasped the curtain, causing tears at the top and in three places where the metal rings held the curtain in place. Most likely both had taken a shower, playing with one another. That could account for the tear at the top of the curtain. There were no clean towels. On the counter over the bathroom sink, in an orderly fashion, were the toiletries of the older man. The only thing out of place was the soap. It was thrown into the sink, which made little sense. The soap in the sink soapdish was untouched and still wrapped. Goodwin looked down at the waste basket and saw tissue, a disposable razor, and the wrapping from the shower soap, as well as a used condom. "They should all have fingerprints on them, but none will be the killer's." Black, very brief underpants—most likely the young man's—and standard white boxer shorts—most likely the older man's—lay on the floor.

Goodwin walked over to the unopened armoire. He guessed that it contained the clothes of the old man and perhaps the younger man's clothes. "How neat these two were. They hung their clothes prior to jumping in bed." His concentration was distracted by a buzz on his pager. He looked at the number. It was the Belgravia station. "What now?" he thought. He reached into his pocket and extracted his cellular phone, pressing the preset number for the station.

"Belgravia Station, Graham, here," came the voice over the phone.

"Goodwin here. You paged me?"

"We just received a flash from headquarters. A car in the queen's motorcade was set upon by an unknown assailant. Luckily, it was the last car. The queen was not injured, probably didn't even hear the shooting. An American businessman, his wife and son were injured in the shootout near Trafalgar. They were guests of the queen at a command performance where their son was the lead performer. The extent of their injuries is unknown. A member of the security officers of the queen's detail was found murdered in one of the Savoy Theatre's men's rooms. It all happened about half an hour ago, 8:30 p.m., maybe later. A city-wide lookout bulletin put out by headquarters describes a young man, age 25 to 30, dark skinned, over six-feet. He fled the scene, and witnesses say that it was this man that attacked the American and his family. I thought you'd like to know."

"Yeah . . . Of course, Graham. Thank you. Is Hilson on her way?"

"Oh, yes, and she said for you to stay out of her way," he replied with a laugh.

"Okay." Goodwin intended to say something further, but decided it unfit for the ears of the junior receptionist to hear from a senior detective.

Again, he turned to look at the two bodies. "Yeah," he said aloud, without apparent reason, perhaps just to reassure himself, "the young man was in it for the money; the old man for the fun; the killer was after the old man, not after the young one. Now find the killer . . . but first, find out about the victims."

"Enjoying the view?" a sharp, deep, voice from behind called.

"My friend and great crime solver, the Lady Regina Hilson," he answered, smiling broadly.

Followed by two aides, both carrying large square black cases, Regina stared for a moment at the bodies. "A little day's sex caught short. What's

THE PENTUM MISSION   125

your first impression, Dean?" she asked in a mockingly solicitous manner. They also enjoyed the repartee that comes from being friends who could joke while talking candidly.

"A professional job. I don't think you'll find anything missing. The young man was probably at the right place at the wrong time. Ditto for the old man. It appears to me that the hit man was after the older man. Probably some sort of businessman into a deal that went the wrong way, or money laundering, or both. I'm guessing. But I don't think the young man was involved at all in the old guy's business. I'll need segmented photos of every part of the body. Well, you know the exercise."

"Indeed I do. Just looking at the bodies, I'd agree with you: no bruises; no conflict of any sort; just neat slices in the neck. Too smooth for other than a professional. Probably wore gloves, so no prints of the killer, but we'll check everything. Are you getting the videos? Any interviews?" Hilson inquired.

"Dudley is downstairs right now doing both. I'm going to join him after I leave you. I'll call the chief inspector but I suspect that he is busy with the trouble at Trafalgar Square."

"Yes, I heard on the radio coming over here. What a strange evening, Dean. Well, I've work to do. Off with you now. See you later," Hilson said with a short wave of her right hand.

With that he took one last look at the scene, trying to fix in his mind how these two strangers had died together. Goodwin then moved into the corridor, instinctively noticing the exit stairs at each end of the corridor. Two patrolmen were coming down the hall from the elevator area, and he waited by the room for them. They would help Regina secure the room and stand guard while she and her experts did all the required investigative work.

"Good evening," he said to both.

"Good evening, Sir. We're here for Ms. Hilson," the taller of the two patrolmen responded.

"Room 452."

Without looking back, he headed toward the far left corridor exit and took the stairs to the first floor. When he reached, he noticed that a left turn from the exit door led into the lobby, and a right turn to an exit door out to the alley through which he and Dudley had earlier entered the hotel. The alley ran from Lowndes Street, along the side of the hotel restaurant and came to a dead end, after passing the delivery entrance and baggage room of the hotel.

The only exit was to Lowndes Street, and someone who used it would have had to pass not only the baggage room, which the bellman attended, but also the hotel restaurant whose windows face the alley, Goodwin thought.

By contrast, all corridors from the right side of the hotel led to the first floor and then into the lobby. There was no outside exit from that side of the building. But on the first floor on the left side, a reception area directly faced the front doors to the hotel. "The assassin used the balcony for entrance into the room. There were no signs that the door to room 452, where the murders occurred, was forced. If it were, it would have made some noise, because even with the proper electrical coded card, the click would have alerted the two lovers in bed. No, it had to be the balcony, which means the person had to be agile, strong, and probably registered in the hotel." Goodwin pondered these thoughts for several moments, before turning down the corridor and into the to the lobby.

It was time to sit in on the interviews Dudley was conducting. This is different, he thought, quite different.

Zurich-Kloten Airport
Friday
Local Time: 1:45 p.m. (12:45 p.m., London)

The Swissair flight from Cyprus landed promptly at 1:45 p.m., taxiing to gate 38—the gate farthest from Passport Control. Svetlana felt as if she needed a hot bath—for some reason she felt untidy, even though her dark green slacks and matching jacket were unwrinkled.

As she stepped from the cabin door, she nodded to the flight attendant, who said good bye in German. She glanced at the free standing, dark gray marble wall bordering one side of the exit passageway and depicting various mountain peaks, over which water silently glided down and then recycled to the top in a continuous circle. It was a peaceful welcome, and perhaps that was what the Swiss wanted the arriving passenger to believe about their country.

She slowed her pace and stepped to the side, allowing the other passengers to go by quickly. Svetlana thought of her mother, who in several hours would arrive in the United States—alone. This separation from her mother was her sole regret.

She stopped at the first kiosk to view the array of chocolates next to the magazine display. In earlier days, when she traveled with Moussa, he would stop here and buy her the biggest box in the case. "Svetlana, for you. You should eat more. You are so thin," he would laugh as he gave her the box. She knew that he was in Cyprus now, turning the island upside down, looking for her. His rage would have no end.

Instinctively, Svetlana picked up her pace, as if she wanted to escape her own thoughts of Moussa. In a few seconds, she saw the passport control and the lines behind each of the four booths. She picked the shortest one. Regardless, they all appeared to move quickly. She recalled that the Swiss never seemed to be too concerned with this element of control.

Just as she was number five in line, a voice from her left called out in Russian, "Svetlana... Svetlana, how are you?"

She didn't turn. She wouldn't turn to see who it was, although she recognized the voice. This time, she felt protected by the dark glasses she still wore.

Within seconds, the man stood next to her. "Svetlana, it's me, Jess Stevens... don't you remember? I was in Peter Bradford's office just last week," he raised his voice as he reached and stood by her in line.

Svetlana turned, and replied in German, "I don't know you. Really, you must be thinking of someone else."

"Are you sure you're not joking with me? It's me... don't you remember?" he pleaded.

Finally, Svetlana reached the head of the line. A young man behind Svetlana turned to Stevens and said coldly in English, "She doesn't know you. Now leave her alone or I'll call the airport police."

"Okay, I'm sorry. . . ." His voice trailed off and he backed away from her. Svetlana reached the passport control booth, showed her passport, and was quickly waved through.

Jess Stevens saw her disappear down the escalator behind passport control to the baggage hall. "Christ, that's Svetlana. I'd know her anywhere. Besides, she had that gold heart charm she always wears. That's Svetlana. I wonder what she's doing here. Bringing some cash for Peter Bradford? Or, maybe Peter doesn't even know she's here. Could that be? No, that doesn't make any sense. I'll call him when I arrive later this evening. Yes, I'll call him. Maybe I'll score some points . . ." He rushed to his own gate for the Swissair flight to Moscow.

Svetlana didn't look back. Because she had no luggage, she went directly to the customs channel with the large green and white sign indicating "Nothing to Declare," and headed to the taxi stand. She immediately got into a taxi and asked to be taken to the Zurich Art Museum. She couldn't believe what had just happened. She knew that Stevens would call Moscow, if not immediately, soon. But she didn't care. In a few hours, she would be leaving Zurich.

CHAPTER SEVEN

Moscow
Friday
Local Time: 6:00 p.m. (3:00 p.m.,London)
Kropotkinskaya, 22, Apt. 70

Peter Bradford's central apartment was large for Moscow, it was the former apartment of a general of the Soviet Air Force. He didn't always live in such luxury. When first in Moscow, Bradford stayed in a dormitory-style old hotel with other Americans working on the U.S. Embassy complex. Once, however, he became embraced by the *mafiya* and the Embassy contract ended, he moved into this apartment. To this day, he didn't know who owned it. He paid no rent. He surmised that it was a perk for being part of the *mafiya*.

A heavy structure with rough surfaced brickwork and bizarre, indecipherable stone gargoyles, the building was constructed, probably in the early 1930s, in a square. It sat on a corner, making it more imposing. A gravel driveway led off the street to a small parking lot behind. Although there were twenty apartments in the building, no more than five cars could fit into the space. On one side were two large areas for refuse, with a decrepit stone barrier fencing off oversized refuse containers, all without tops. The back entrance to the building from the parking lot led through a metal sheeted door. An elevator was a short distance down the corridor. Bradford rarely used this entrance. He preferred the guarded entrance in front.

The front of the building was little better. The small patch of ground directly facing the entrance to the building was barren. The walkway from the sidewalk abutting the street had been recently repaired, and the massive, double, three-inch oak door at the lobby entrance was also new. Although the lobby wasn't particularly attractive, it was clean.

Two olive skinned, mustached, overweight security officers sat behind a faux gray marble counter, staring intently at the four video monitors, one scanning each side of the building. The outstanding feature of every apartment was a set of steel plates on the entrance door. Robberies had reached epidemic proportions in Moscow, and the steel doors helped prevent break-ins. But because the apartment was in a zone controlled by the *mafiya* for whom Peter worked and Bradford was a tenant, the apartment had been spared such problems.

The interior of Bradford's two-bedroom apartment was a mix of contemporary furniture. Under twelve-feet high ceilings, the furniture reflected his own penchant for simplicity and order. He abhorred clutter, so there were virtually no knick-knacks on any table. The bookcases were filled with Russian history written in Russian, neatly arranged by height. The bareness gave the apartment a clinical, antiseptic appearance, several ferns softening an otherwise severe setting. Everything rested in its proper place. The kitchen appeared untouched, plates neatly placed in open cabinets.

Bradford stayed here only some of the time. He had another, even larger apartment where his wife lived, about an hour's drive from Moscow. But this one was for Peter's own use. His wife had never seen it; in fact she didn't even know about it. Whenever she called the office, which was rare, she was routinely told he was at a meeting. He never answered her phone calls. He called her when he was ready to speak to her, rather than the other way around.

It was an unpleasant meeting that Peter Bradford had earlier had with Dimitri Gravev at Peter's office. He told Dimitri that he had heard nothing from Boris Shenin, who had left for London, but that Shenin should be calling him momentarily. In any event, Bradford confirmed that Ruslan Ishaev was in place to carry out his assignment.

Dimitri again expressed concern that there be no mistakes as had earlier occurred with the Libyan matter: "Then, my friend, there is no further purpose for this meeting. I was expecting some good news from you, that our problems had been solved. We must now wait. You can call me when you have news."

With that Dimitri left; the good byes were stilted at best. Peter knew he was in trouble. He also knew that Dimitri would sacrifice him to the necessity of succeeding, and if Peter failed, Dimitri would replace him. It was that simple.

Dimitri had been furious that the $65 million due from the abortive Libyan missile deal had never surfaced . . . and, although he resisted stating his conclusion, he blamed Peter. Gravev never wanted events to go awry. But, at the time, Dimitri had a more important meeting to go to. Peter was upset to be left out, despite the fact that he knew where the meeting was to take place and had been expected to attend. To show his displeasure at the lack of progress, Gravev disinvited Peter by not asking him to come along. It would have been imprudent for him to remind Dimitri, so Peter was left to seek out the pleasures he'd been thinking about all day.

Bradford's thoughts were distracted by the sound of the phone ringing. He hesitated for a moment, almost in a fear that he couldn't understand. Slowly he picked up the receiver, and in doing so, activated the taping system he'd installed in his apartment.

"Bradford," he answered curtly.

"Peter, this is Jess. You remember me, Jess Stevens? You'll never know who I saw in Zurich yesterday. It was your assistant, Svetlana."

After a moment of silence when he was unsure whether this was another one of Stevens' tricks to get him to listen, Bradford responded slowly, "Well, that is interesting. You're sure you weren't drunk? Svetlana called me just this morning from Cyprus where she's on vacation. Did you speak to her?" he replied in a skeptical tone.

"Yeah. I went up to her. The woman denied that she was Svetlana. But it had to be her. She had on that bracelet that she always wears— you know . . . the one with the heart."

"Well, it could have been anyone. The bracelet isn't unique. I've seen several similar in Moscow. Well, no matter, I'll call Cyprus and we'll find out. I'm sure she's there. Thanks for calling, though."

He hung up, without waiting for a reply.

Stevens is a fool, he thought to himself. "He's trying to ingratiate himself. I'll call Svetlana tomorrow, but now I'm going to relax. I don't want this to be as joyless an evening as the day."

He went over to the bar and reached for the decanter of scotch, filling three small gold hued glasses almost to the rim. He placed them on a matching end table and sat on a dark blue, canvas covered couch and waited. "Are you ready, girls?" he raised his voice slightly.

"Almost," came the reply from the adjoining bedroom whose door was slightly ajar.

"Hurry. I'm getting lonely."

Within a minute, two small young women, dressed in black sheer robes and holding hands, came out, slowly walking the few meters to the couch. Both were oriental looking, and had long black hair and childlike faces. Bradford got up, taking his glass of scotch, and moved over to the chair facing the couch, saying, "Girls, okay, let's see what you can do." He raised his glass as each of the girls took one and swallowed the contents in a few seconds.

As the girls undressed, he did likewise. Totally naked, he sat in the chair, fondling his penis as he watched the two girls giggling, still holding hands, He liked them young, very young. These girls, for whom he was paying five hundred dollars, were just fourteen years old, and from Thailand. How they got to Moscow, he never knew, but they were part of the *mafiya* operation, run by Dimitri's cousin, and he felt no misgivings about using them.

For some reason, it took him longer to get an erection, and he began to sweat as he jerked faster on his penis. One of the girls looked at him and smiled, raising her hand, inviting him to join them. Finally, as he began to reach his climax, he got up and went over to the couch, putting one knee between one girl's legs and the other knee between the other's. As the girls' tongues came out, and their own crotches begin to undulate against his knees, he masturbated freely while the girls tried to catch his ejaculate; most of it went on their breasts. But it was a weak spray and he was frustrated.

"Fuck, what's wrong here? What's wrong?" He went back to the couch and sat toying with his flaccid penis, knowing that it wouldn't become rigid for some time. But he would watch the two girls play with one another until their climaxes, and that would give him additional pleasure. He would see a doctor soon, perhaps in Germany. Maybe something was wrong with him . . . it couldn't be the cancer on his face. His doctor in Moscow had said that all was under control. It had to be stress. As he stared at the girls who were both achieving climax and making sounds of pleasure as they each furiously fingered their clitorises, he sank deeper into his chair, looking down at his limp penis, becoming dizzy, without understanding what was happening to him. The dizziness persisted, and he fainted, sliding down from his chair to the floor, his right hand still holding his slack penis.

Both girls looked frightened. They left Bradford on the floor, and dressed hurriedly. They had already collected their money before going into the bedroom to change. Their driver was downstairs waiting because the payment was for only one hour's work. As they fled the apartment, they looked down without a worry about whether he was alive or dead. They didn't care.

Peter woke up about a half hour later. "Christ, what's wrong with me?" he said to himself as he gradually lifted himself from the floor, holding on to the chair. The dizziness had gone, but his stomach felt sour. "Maybe it's something I ate." He knew that he wouldn't go to see a doctor. He disliked doctors ever since the cancerous lesions on his face had formed; he was frightened that he had terminal cancer and didn't want to know about it. He was worried the girls would tell Dimitri's cousin he had fainted. Dimitri's cousin in turn would rush that information to Dimitri. He hoped Dimitri would take it as a joke that Peter couldn't handle the two young ladies. Peter prayed that would be the case.

He was already over two hours late to get to his wife's apartment, about an hour's drive from the city apartment. He quickly went over to the tape recorder and listened to his phone messages. Panicking, Bradford ran to the bathroom, opened the medicine chest and took out a bottle of aspirin. His hands were shaking so severely that he had difficulty opening the bottle cap. Pouring two tablets into the palm of his left hand, he washed them down with a mouthful of water from an opened bottle on the shelf above the bathroom sink. Looking into the mirror over the sink, he noticed that he was sweating.

"Shit, what's going on?" He stepped into the shower, turned the water on full force, and felt the warm, strong flow come over him. Just as the water was beginning to make him more relaxed and he believed he was gaining control, his body started to shake. Bradford grabbed the handle to the shower soapdish and exploded into uncontrolled sobbing.

"I'm dying, I'm dying. Oh, my God, I'm dying." Just as quickly as the terror had struck him, it ended. Vacantly staring at the shower temperature dial, he let the water run over him, unable to move for fear the terror would strike again. Finally, he turned the water off, reached for a towel, and slowly left the stall.

He looked into the mirror again, hanging on to the edges of the sink, fearing that the trembling and shaking would return. Slowly, he felt the anxiety leave and a sense of normalcy return. He would call his wife and tell her he was on his way. He only hoped that he could arrive home before the terror would strike him again.

Moscow
Friday
Local Time: 6:00 p.m. (3:00 p.m., London)
On the Ring Road to Gravev's dacha
Thirty kilometers southeast of Moscow
Near the village of Barvikha

Dimitri Gravev left Peter Bradford's office disconcerted. He was beginning to lose confidence in Bradford. He was unsure about Bradford's stability and had a feeling that things were not turning out the way Bradford had planned. The situation was slipping away, Dimitri believed, but he kept the doubts to himself. He realized, from experience, it was best to remain patient . . . but alert to the fact that matters might deviate from a predetermined path.

Dimitri was also fatigued. He slept only fitfully for the past several days. He was concerned that the Libyan missile project had ended in such a disaster. Dimitri abhorred failure. In addition, he was worried that the shipment to Iran of the one-kiloton nuclear weapon, no longer on the inventory of Russian weapons, would not be accomplished as planned. Besides, he despised innovation, and these two Bradford deals—the dead missile matter and now the nuclear sale—were new business areas for him. He had never dealt in arms before. Predictability was his comfort index. And he couldn't get Bradford to predict this next venture would be any more successful than the last.

Since the August 1991 coup, and the accession to power by Boris Yeltsin, business had been brisk. Dimitri realized he could never have formed a bank under the Communist government, let alone a private business. He knew from his present success that Marxism had been a colossal failure. He would remind his wife, "We are doing very well, Olga, very well. The only benefit we had under Communism, for our children, was a small three-room apartment, then only because I was a bodyguard to the party chairman. Look what we have now, my Olga."

Yet his wife always appeared unhappy. "It was simpler for us, Dimitri. Now things are so complicated. We have more, but things are more complicated with you and all your businesses. I don't understand sometimes what is happening."

Life was much simpler under the Communists yet more fearful. But he supposed some people, maybe even his wife, would surrender their present freedom for the certainty that Communism provided. He understood the view but thought it romantic and unrealistic. Being a bodyguard for senior officials, though, had made him eligible for the apartment, and for that he had been grateful. But he had known the system was corrupt and bound for failure. . . . He realized he was one of the luckier ones that gained from Communism; most had not. As a bodyguard to elite Communist Party leaders, he had felt obligated to join the party, but he had never been active in it and had paid his dues and attended the mandatory political meetings, engaging in nothing beyond that.

Seated in the back of his speeding black Mercedes armored sedan, with his own bodyguard and driver in the front, followed by another car with two aides and two other bodyguards, he wondered aloud why he traveled in such a manner. "All this protection I have against what? From whom?" Not from the government; many of the police leadership were on his payroll, and they would avoid bothering him unless he was stupid enough to get into politics—which meant killing or maiming a politician. Some of the scum contract killers could be hired to carry out this kind of bloodshed, but he knew, in the long run, it was better to buy the politician than to kill him.

When he found out that a *mafiya* underling had taken it on himself to have a member of the Duma murdered because the member had failed to give a political patronage job to his relative, Dimitri had the man who had ordered the killing of the parliamentarian executed right in front of the apartment house where he lived, so that everyone understood that such activity was permitted only with the permission of Dimitri.

The *mafiya* had a fundamental unwritten rule, which Dimitri had originated and had the responsibility to enforce: you had to be disciplined, to stay with your own designated business and avoid touching others'. Turf wars were unacceptable behavior in his view, and he cracked down with a vengeance when the invisible fences between the members of the *mafiya* were ignored. Intrusion into other territories for whatever reason had to be discussed and there had to be reasons for the change, reasons that had to please everyone and advance the monetary take of everyone.

In one such case, when Gravev's view was ignored, he had the errant and disloyal business man slain in the man's own office at noon, so that the death would receive maximum exposure in the press and on television. When this display was insufficient, he eliminated a prominent television personality who was attempting to change the rules of kickbacks on advertising revenues. After these two events, order was restored and a calm returned to the Moscow scene . . . except for the hoodlums, "scum," he called them, who stole cars and broke into apartments. Dimitri left those to the police; they always blamed the *mafiya* for these petty crimes, which would generate less money in a month than Dimitri's businesses made in a minute. Of course the police avoided mounting a serious investigative campaign to find the perpetrators of the slaying of the two *mafiya* traitors. Beyond a note of information in the public record, the matter went no further. The police knew that the *mafiya* took care of its own house.

Dimitri's personal principle was that to abdicate in the face of challenge was an act of a coward. He wasn't a coward. He despised flattery and feigned generosity, and he didn't admire timid loyalty. Loyalty to him had to be total, not out of fear, but out of belief in him. He never wanted bad news disguised or good news exaggerated. That was his concern about Peter Bradford. Peter's news was never delivered with clarity. He seemed to always be hiding something, and only after Dimitri asked questions would he explain the full event.

Dimitri bypassed politics, other than to make financial contributions when requested by representatives of the Yeltsin government. He had to do this. The government's role frankly encouraged his kind of business, and he was loyal to that kind of encouragement. A government needed to maintain order. Otherwise the business which was creating so much wealth for him would be jeopardized. Dimitri disliked political confusion and disorder. He knew of no businessman who felt otherwise. The new political system allowed for the expression of free will. People had the right to live calmly and hopefully. Everything he was doing depended on these freedoms—freedom to buy the cigarettes, the liquor, the electronics, the foodstuffs, the cars—and all of the monopolies he controlled existed only because the market had finally matured for customers to have money to buy the products. He set the established prices that assured him a substantial profit.

In his view, economic instability brought about by chaos was worse than sabotage. Although he kept a substantial portion of his funds overseas, he was a Russian. He loved his country. It was this country that allowed him to prosper, and he was going to let nothing or no one destroy what he had so painstakingly built.

He avoided political rallies of any sort, and would rarely see a politician. He was a businessman, and for him that was sufficient. He had good contacts with the Yeltsin government, although he rarely used them, and in fact had met the president several times, most recently at a reunion of former Kremlin bodyguards. Most, like him, were much older men, and all had businesses which, in many cases, were affiliated with his. Yeltsin knew him by name and reputation, and had invited him to several dinners with visiting foreign businessmen, but Dimitri had always declined. He rarely socialized outside his family. He enjoyed the quiet time at home, and attended only a few official bank functions.

The Bradford deal had an obvious political feature, the sale of a nuclear weapon to a country without it and a few years away from developing one on its own. The nuclear device was diverted from the inventory during the chaos attendant to the breakup of the USSR. Maj. Gen. Yuri Nikolayev, a retired KGB general and close friend of Bradford and the owner of the weapon, had moved and secreted the weapon at a cotton warehouse owned by one of Dimitri's companies. The warehouse was located a few kilometers south of Ashgabat, Turkmenistan, close to the border of Iran.

Dimitri acceded to this request by Bradford, even though the business arrangements remained incomplete. This made him uneasy. He felt that he was now crossing the internal line that he set for himself in business. But the amount of money Peter had negotiated was too large to ignore—$350 million U.S. from Iran for the delivery of the nuclear weapon which the Iranians were going to detonate somewhere in their desert. He supposed this was to frighten the world, especially the U.S. and its close friend, Israel, by insisting that the behavior of those countries toward the Arab world change.

He questioned whether it was a productive idea. "Would the U.S. really be fearful? The Israelis? Probably not," he said to himself, as he looked out at the moonless night. But how to be sure that the weapon would be detonated only in the desert? Dimitri was aware that Iran had the capability of sending missiles to Israel.

"What's to prevent them from putting this weapon on one of their rockets?" he asked himself. "One weapon would not be enough. The Israelis would retaliate with more. No, the Iranians wouldn't use the weapon in that manner," he assured himself, reaching to open a small compartment directly in front of him for a bottle of mineral water. Removing the plastic cap in one twist, he took several swallows before replacing the cap and placing the bottle on the seat next to him.

Peter Bradford had been very useful to him during the Communist days. He had provided the official conduit for a great deal of KGB special money being sent outside the country, money that would move outside the embassy accounts to individuals the KGB wished to pay directly without anyone in the foreign office knowing. Communist intrigue extended deep, and Bradford was an unwitting accomplice to their internal political games. In addition, he brought many special goods in and distributed them from a closed KGB apartment where he stored the goods. He couldn't live there because he had to be with the other workers at the U.S. Embassy site.

Dimitri had met Peter during his days as a Kremlin bodyguard and knew then that Peter wasn't a loyal U.S. citizen but on the payroll of the KGB, providing them with useless information. But more importantly, Bradford was a reliable messenger. The KGB paid him small change, Dimitri thought, but for Bradford, it was more than the U.S. contractor for whom he worked was paying. At times, Dimitri would hand-carry the satchels of money to Bradford's U.S. embassy construction office, and from that start, they developed a business relationship. Bradford actually helped Dimitri start the myriad off-shore companies that were part of Bank Alliance Russia.

Bradford was the one in charge of the more seamy side of Dimitri's business, including the liaison with Dimitri's cousin, Leonid Karanikov, who handled the importation of drugs into Moscow and St. Petersburg, as well as the prostitution rings in both cities. Dimitri's cousin was also the intermediary between Dimitri's *mafiya* and foreign groups that tried to come to Russia to do business. Although Dimitri's cousin needed their cooperation for the drug and prostitution trade, they were unwelcome to enter other businesses where Dimitri had an interest.

Dimitri said to his cousin, "I don't go to Italy; they don't come here. Understood?"

During one instance when Dimitri's cousin appeared ambivalent about a request from an Italian *mafiya* leader to set up an arrangement allowing the Italian to received a greater percentage of the drug profits, Dimitri appeared at the meeting to explain his reasoning.

"I am not in business in Italy. I don't expect you to do business here. Do you have any questions?" To make sure his Italian compatriots understood, he had the Italian delegation detained at the airport for 24 hours and interrogated by his men, dressed as customs agents, with the cooperation of the true agents. Their money was confiscated, along with their suitcases, as evidence. The *mafiya* agents found cocaine in the Italians' personal luggage—a violation of Russian criminal law punishable by ten years in prison. Through Dimitri's intercession, they were released and never came back. But Dimitri also realized that both his cousin and, more likely, Bradford did keep up a relationship with the foreign groups. As long as it didn't cross the line that he had drawn, Dimitri didn't care if they made money on their own.

Dimitri monopolized the importation of cigarettes into Russia, Ukraine, Belarus, and the far east republics of Uzbekistan, Kazakhstan, Turkmenistan, Tajikistan, and Kyrgyzstan. He had majority control in all Western factories set up by his Western joint-venture partners to manufacture local cigarettes. In addition he held the monopoly on certain construction materials in Moscow and St. Petersburg, and took percentages on all hotel and office building construction. Subsidiaries of the companies also had the monopoly on the importation of certain Western foodstuffs and electronics. He had invested in several cotton production facilities in Uzbekistan and Turkmenistan. In Russia, he had branched out, at the advice of his sons, to invest in newspapers and magazines published in Moscow and St. Petersburg. Through a multitude of offshore companies, he was immune to much of the taxation levied by the Russian government.

Dimitri remained aloof, in major part, from the day-to-day operations of the businesses which he had turned over to his two sons, Nikolai and Gregor. His third, and youngest son, Igor, had skirted the footsteps of his brothers, becoming a teacher of history at a small high school in Moscow. And, unlike his brothers, he never asked Dimitri for financial support. Dimitri loved them all, but worried about the professor, as he called his third son. All were married. Dimitri had five grandchildren. When his youngest son's wife had given birth to a twin set of boys and failed to name either one after him, or any family member, Dimitri was furious and threatened not to speak to his son . . . a threat he soon forgot when he saw the two babies. Besides, his third son had a stubborn streak, similar to his own wife's, He didn't try hard to change the decision.

All of his children had gone to college, something that he hadn't done. He was most proud of his daughter, Dr. Marya Gravev, a heart surgeon of some renown, presently visiting at the Columbia Medical Center in New York City. She had received her medical degree in Moscow, but then went to England and studied at the London University College Hospital. Her earlier marriage had ended in.divorce, and as she had no children, she immersed herself in her work. He would visit her on his next trip to the United States, scheduled to take place in two weeks. He was bothered when she told him she had decided to stay in the United States and hoped to practice in New York City. He thought she should return to Moscow. But she always told him that there was nothing for her there except unpleasant memories from a failed marriage. In a way, he agreed with her, but he did miss seeing his only daughter more frequently.

The one business that he took personal control of was Bank Alliance Russia's principal subsidiary, BAR Security International. The subsidiary had over 5,000 employees, principally in Moscow and St. Petersburg, but also in other Russian cities. It was loosely affiliated with a major German manufacturer of security equipment, Breitermann, GmbH, Frankfurt, a privately held German company. Hans Breitermann had met Dimitri in Moscow, when, through mutual friends, Breitermann came to see Dimitri in 1988, and told him of his plans to open a representative office in Moscow in order to sell security equipment. Dimitri became interested and visited Breitermann's tidy, neat factory outside Frankfurt.

After some discussion, Breitermann and Dimitri formed a new company where they both were equal partners . . . Gravev brought to the alliance multiple contracts which Gravev received to upgrade the Kremlin security system and other government installations; he then subcontracted to the German company the supply of security cameras and other specialized equipment. This turned out to be a lucrative arrangement for both. Soon, BAR Security received contracts for major new office buildings in Moscow, the contracts providing for the equipment as well as the manpower. With this infrastructure and, more importantly, access to the computer security codes Dimitri's power was invincible.

So this new arms business of Peter Bradford, a portion of which had gone sour, made him uncomfortable. It had not always been that way, or that worrisome, and at 67, he wanted a more consistent and quiet life.

Gravev had, at one time, been the principal bodyguard for Brezhnev and had traveled with the Communist leader on all of his foreign trips, including those to the United States. His father was a coal miner, working in a mine near the city of Shakhtinsk, in what became the Republic of Kazakhstan.

The family of five lived meagerly in one large room; at one end was a kitchen and next to that a small bathroom with a tub. But they considered themselves lucky to have received this residence. It was one of his father's awards from work. His father managed to build, from scrap wood he foraged, walls separating the kitchen and bathroom from the main living area. At the other end of the large room, he had put up wooden curtain rods from which hung colorful, flowered fabric, dividing the area into two bedrooms of equal size: one for him and his wife, the other for his three sons. It was crowded, yet what else was there to do?

There was never money, though, to buy all the food that was needed, and the coat he wore in the wintertime was a tattered and patched one passed to him from his older brother. The winters were severe and the heat minimum, but the family survived. Dimitri remembered his childhood as one of love from his parents, but also one of privations, discomfort, and hardness. He would always remember how little the family had by way of material comfort.

Along with his two brothers he was expected to work in the coal mines as well. When he was conscripted into the Soviet Army at the end of World War II, he eagerly accepted the conscription and was sent to East Germany as part of the Soviet occupation force. He knew he would never return home. His father and mother were proud of him and the military medals he accumulated. He learned German while in Germany. Classes were optional, but, unlike many other enlisted men, he opted to take the courses, and he did well.

After his tour, he signed on for an additional four years, when he took special training in security. The training, given by a special unit of the KGB, was intensive and emphasized that he would have to surrender his life in order to save the person he was protecting. Initially, he was assigned as a bodyguard for Communist Party politburo members who visited Germany, and received commendations from many. Attentive, unobtrusive, and thorough, Dimitri had the valuable characteristics of a bodyguard. He never had to use his special training to save anyone, and in time he became the head of the Kremlin's bodyguard unit that protected the Communist Party general secretary. Although assigned to the KGB, he stayed in the military, and he reached the rank of major in the Soviet army.

At age 25, he married Olga Limonova, a girl he had known in school. It took him time to fall in love with her, but he did. She was quiet, resourceful, and beautiful. Only when she gave birth to their first son did he realize that an early romance with a East German girl was a youthful infatuation. Now that Olga had given birth to their first child, he would be forever faithful. And he was. Despite the many opportunities given him, he never once succumbed. He felt that giving in to one's physical needs would be destructive in the end, especially if he had a loyal wife at home. He could never look at his wife and be ashamed. And shame to him meant being disloyal to the woman who bore his children.

Dimitri remained part of the Kremlin's bodyguard contingent until Gorbachev took power in 1985. At that time, at age 53, he opted to leave after thirty-five years of service with the Soviet military. With the permission of the Moscow Communist Party, and under the new laws that Gorbachev's regime passed that year, he started a private firm to provide drivers and security for the Western companies coming to Moscow in search of business deals. Of course, the new company had the complete backing of the KGB, but, of importance, Dimitri was allowed to keep fifty percent of all earnings, and he gave the other fifty percent to the Moscow Communist Party.

Soon, however, he was able to keep more and more, as he began to realize that the whole political situation was rapidly being altered. With perestroika and glasnost, people's attitudes were changing, and he knew that to be the case as more and more Western businessmen came. When Gorbachev ended the Party's dominance in 1989, Gravev stopped sending money to the Communist Central Committee in Moscow, although shrewdly he kept sending a small percentage to the head of the committee; in this manner he silenced the one person who would have complained.

This business led to others and, when in 1991 the new government headed by Boris Yeltsin allowed for the formation of privately held banks, Dimitri immediately formed his own, pressuring many of the privatized businesses for which he was providing security to deposit funds in his wholly owned bank, Bank Alliance Russia. Soon, the bank began to buy into new enterprises, and, of course, made loans at prohibitive interest rates. If a company didn't pay back on time, the bank then became the owner of the company, although Dimitri continued with the same management unless the managers proved incompetent or disloyal.

His control tightened. Since 1985, he had amassed a considerable fortune, and although shy and avoiding publicity, he made charity contributions in Moscow and St. Petersburg that brought him some public esteem. He rarely spoke at times when he contributed money, and charities to children's hospitals and children's sports were his priority—as well as the Russian Orthodox Church—primarily to please his wife who, after the new government allowed freedom of religion, began to go to church regularly. Dimitri was a nonbeliever, but he went with his wife as often as he could. She expected her husband to accompany her, and he would go for that reason only.

He was immensely proud of the house he was now approaching. Off the paved road, the gravel driveway to the main entrance was flanked by a perfectly lined row of white birch trees. The exterior of the mansion was dark, almost mulberry in color, built with small bricks, and topped by a roof of many irregular planes and gables and a cluster of chimneys indicating numerous fireplaces. He had seen a picture of this English Tudor mansion in a magazine and showed it to his wife, who also liked the style—unlike anything they had ever seen before, and far removed from native architecture. The entrance way was flood-lit to reveal a facade balanced by an equal number of windows on either side of a hand-carved front door of oak, studded with iron and set back under a small overhanging roof. On either side of the slate walkway leading to the entrance sat two bronze lions.

During construction, Dimitri had observed every detail of the seven-bedroom, ten-bath, meticulously decorated home. He wanted an overall appearance of order, peace, and beauty. Fidelity to precision was what he desired. Many of the furnishings were purchased from London antique dealers. All the appliances for the restaurant-size kitchen came from Germany.

The mansion had three floors with a majestic staircase that made a half turn in itself and wound up to the second-floor hall, on the left side of which were three equal size bedrooms, one larger guest bedroom, and on the right a master bedroom suite occupying about three quarters of the other side of the mansion. Two bedrooms and one bath completed the third floor and were used by the housekeepers. There was also a sitting room for them and a small kitchen for their use. A small office, library, and storage area made up the remainder of the third floor. Dimitri would often go to the top floor to place his calls, read, and meet, from time to time, with certain members of the *mafiya*. He used the first-floor library for more formal meetings, such as would be taking place tonight.

There were two elevators in the house: one adjacent to the kitchen on the first floor, and a private one that led from the master bedroom directly to a small room off the four-car garage. So, Dimitri could leave the house directly if he chose. He never used this elevator, but it was there. Above the garage were two bedrooms and two baths for the security officers who accompanied Dimitri wherever he went.

The basement of the mansion was divided into the laundry room, utility room, wine room, and a large drygoods room, where everything from canned food to cereals was stored by the housekeepers preparing the meals. Two large freezers as well were located in the store room. A portable generator could provide electricity, if the power from the local village was interrupted.

The architect followed the picture as closely as he could, guessing, however, what the interior would be like. Dimitri became exhilarated when he came here. This house became, for him, the image of success; other trappings didn't interest him but this one, this prize, in his mind, made him aware of the dimension of his success. The house was a reflection of himself.

As the car slowly came to a stop directly before the front entrance, Dimitri's thoughts were broken by the ringing of his cellular phone. The number was known by only a few people. Even Bradford didn't know the number. His sons, daughter, wife, and several members of the *mafiya* were the only ones who had access to it.

"Yes," he replied.

"Dimitri. Moussa in Cyprus. I'm worried. Svetlana and her mother aren't here. I checked their room, their clothes are there, but they're not. Nothing has been touched," Moussa remarked anxiously.

"Have you checked with the concierge? Did she leave any messages for you?"

"Yes. The concierge said that she took her mother to the hospital. I went there—neither the mother nor Svetlana registered for treatment."

"Well, they decided to go on a tour or do some shopping. Be patient, Moussa. I will call Bradford and find out if he knows anything. I have your number. I'll call you back directly. Okay?"

"I'm worried. Something has happened to her. I worry about her all the time. You don't think somebody has done something to her, do you, Dimitri?" he asked.

"No, I don't. Svetlana is a wise woman. She will be okay. Moussa, I must go now, I have an important meeting to attend. But I will call you back. Stay by your phone."

As he pressed the end button on his cellular phone, Dimitri thought that Moussa was behaving too excitedly. It was early evening in Cyprus, so perhaps Svetlana and her mother were enjoying shopping. "Moussa is too emotional. I will have to talk to him at some point."

Before going into the house, he dialed Bradford's in-town apartment. He knew that Bradford would be finishing up with the baby girls. Dimitri was disgusted with Bradford's sexual peccadilloes, but there was nothing he could do. The man was sixty and perhaps very sick. Dimitri had seen Peter become less and less engaged, and more and more distant. The phone rang for a long time before Bradford picked up, and he sounded terrified.

"Yes . . . who is this? Yes . . . ."

"Peter, my friend, this is Dimitri. You sound very unsure. Is there anything wrong, my friend. Did you not have a good time with your girls?"

There was a long silent pause.

"Peter, are you still on the line? Peter . . . ?"

"Yes, I'm here. Do you want me to come to the meeting tonight?" Bradford asked, hoping the answer would be yes.

"No. No. That will not be necessary. Why I am calling is to inquire whether you have heard from Svetlana. Moussa just called me and said that neither she nor her mother are at the hotel in Cyprus. Would you know where she is? Has she moved to another hotel?"

"No, I don't believe so. I heard from her this morning. And, she said she was having a very good time. The sun was out, and she planned to go to the beach with her mother. But, if I hear from her, I'll call you directly."

"Thank you, Peter. I know that you will. I will check with you later. Will you be at home? Or at your apartment?"

"I'll be at home."

"Take care of yourself, Peter. Perhaps you are having too many girls. You should learn to relax, and you should, perhaps, get some exercise. Next time I go swimming and to the banya, I will call you. You must come with me. Swimming and the steam cleanse the system. Peter, please call Moussa in Cyprus and tell him what you just told me. I told him I was going to call him back after I spoke to you, but I have to attend to the meeting here. Tell him that I told you to call him. Thank you, Peter, and good bye. My regards to your wife." With that, Dimitri placed the cell phone in the holder directly in front of him.

The rear car door was opened by the bodyguard who had accompanied Dimitri in his own car. "Thank you, Yakov. Thank you very much." he nodded to his personal bodyguard and assistant of many years. The two aides and two other bodyguards left their own car and followed Dimitri into the house. Once inside, the guards went ahead to a small room adjacent to the library where Dimitri would hold his meeting with the Iranian ambassador and others. His two aides, Sergei Mironov, a young lawyer and son of one of Dimitri's closest friends who had his own security business in Tel Aviv, and Andrei Leskov, the financial executive for Bank Alliance Russia, would accompany him to the meeting. Andrei had at one time been a senior executive of Rosvnestorg, the state bank of USSR, and Dimitri felt comfortable with his knowledge. He began working with Dimitri in 1991 when Bank Alliance Russia was formed. Since then, he had been at Dimitri's side at every major business negotiation.

"Sergei . . . Andrei . . . go into the library and please tell them I shall be there directly. Please review any papers that they have brought with them, and take care of the preliminaries." Without a nod, they headed toward the library door.

As usual, whenever Dimitri came home, he would spend several minutes with his wife to hear the latest on the family and whatever other news she would bring him. He headed toward the kitchen where she would be waiting with some hot tea for him. He would enjoy this short respite and think of nothing else for a few minutes.

London
Friday
Local Time: 9:00 p.m. (4:00 p.m., Washington, D.C.)
St. Thomas Hospital Emergency Room
Lambeth Palace Road

Emergency Room Nurse Marjorie Evans had a choice of available options, but as usual, her decisions were practical ones, appropriate to what she faced. When she heard over the loudspeaker that five ambulances were coming, she was grateful that, this evening, the emergency room was fully staffed, and she began to direct it in a loud, commanding voice. There was never time to chat; the staff had to act quickly.

She steered the most seriously injured from gun-shot wounds, the chauffeur, directly into surgery; the young man, Timothy Harrison, whose shoulder was badly injured, she also directed into surgery. The policeman that had been hit immediately below the heart was dead on arrival. Nothing could be done for him, and she had him placed in the holding room until the police medical examiner arrived.

David Harrison and his wife both looked dreadful, but in reality, the wounds produced more blood than anything else. Nurse Evans placed each in adjoining treatment rooms where the one doctor on duty would treat Mrs. Harrison, and the intern would attend to Mr. Harrison—who was awake when he arrived but speaking incoherently, usual for that kind of head injury. He would need a CAT scan just to be sure, although from her experience, she believed that he was fine. In fact, she had a feeling that he would be troublesome, and her feeling was correct, as he tried to get up from the treatment table to see his wife, at the same time asking for his son. The intern tending to him, a medical student from South Africa, Dr. Mgana Itani, was unable to control him, as he got up from the bed, still bleeding, and trying to get to his wife.

Nurse Evans had seen this kind of foolish courage before and belted out, "Get back on the table, Mr. Harrison. You are not in charge here. I am. Understand? Your wife is fine and your son is being operated on to remove that bullet someone put into his shoulder. You have all had a busy night. Now, please, lie back and let Dr. Itani treat you. He's an excellent intern. Your face needs attention and all the blood has to be cleaned. He'll give you an antibiotic. Unless you cooperate, we'll be here all evening, and I get off at midnight. I don't like to leave my replacement any trouble. Understand?"

"Is my wife okay? my son?" David asked as he tried again to get off the stretcher. Again, he was held back by Nurse Evans and Dr. Itani.

"I must ask that you cooperate, Mr. Harrison. You must let Dr. Itani attend to you. As soon as he has finished, we'll let you visit your wife and your son. You must understand that we have to get on with taking care of your injuries." Meanwhile Dr. Itani was cleaning the blood off Harrison's face with antiseptic gauze. The soothing aroma and coolness of the gauze brought an unusual calm to him, and he lay still for several moments while Dr. Itani continued his work. The attending nurses had taken off his jacket and tie. The top of his shirt was soaked in blood, and the orderly had propped him up while another orderly took off his shoes, shirt, T-shirt, pants and underwear, covering him with a large sheet, as Dr. Itani continued his work. He felt very sleepy, very sleepy; the valium Dr. Itani had given him was taking effect and he would soon be asleep.

As Nurse Evans turned to check Mrs. Harrison, she heard her code for an emergency phone call. "What now?" she asked herself. She reached for the nearest wall phone, and pressed the operator button. "Who wants me now?" she asked, irritated.

"A call from Washington, D.C. to inquire about Mr. Harrison," the operator replied. "Shall I put her through?"

"Washington? Now what? Yes, put whoever it is through," Nurse Evans said in an exasperated tone.

"Yes, this is Nurse Evans, Emergency Room, St. Thomas Hospital. May I help you?"

"Very good of you to come to the phone, Nurse Evans, as I know you are very, very busy. This is Mary Auriello, a personal friend of Mr. Harrison. Would you be so kind to tell him that I'm on my way to London to see him. It's urgent that he gets the message. I'm sure you'll do that. You're most kind," Mary said in the sweetest tone.

"Of course. He'll be sleeping, I should think for about an hour or so. He's fine. The blow to his head was superficial. He knew how to avoid what could have been a fatal injury. He's very lucky, I'd say. . . . Yes, I shall tell him. When are you expected?"

"That is good news that he will recover quickly. I should arrive sometime in the early morning. I'll call him in an hour or so. You say he'll be awake then?" Mary inquired.

"Yes, I would expect him to be awake, and bothersome. He's difficult to keep down, literally," Nurse Evans said in a voice that Mary understood to be annoyed at her call and query.

"Of course. Thank you, and good bye," Mary replied.

"Good bye."

"Now who put this bloody call through?" Nurse Evans said to no one in particular as she hurried back to the room housing Harrison and his wife.

CHAPTER EIGHT

**London
Friday
Local Time: 9:30 p.m. (4:30 p.m., Washington, D.C.)
No. 164, Cadogan Place**

Ruslan Ishaev mounted the seven brick front steps quickly and nervously placed the key into the windowless six-paneled solid oak front door. The late-nineteenth-century four-story town house, on one of London's most fashionable streets, had been converted into corporate apartments. The door led to a small, softly lit, dark wood paneled hall, which would take him directly to the elevator. He could have taken the brown carpeted stairs, directly left of the elevator bank, but he was exhausted and dazed from the tension of his flight and the hurried thirty-minute taxi ride from Charing Cross Hotel to this house, where the building directory listed BAR Ltd. on the fourth floor.

As he left the elevator, he turned right and walked down the corridor to its end at Apt. 4A, placed the key in the double lock, and opened the door. It took several seconds before he could see in the darkness, and he felt on the left wall for the switch, which he turned on to reveal a small foyer with a large seascape on the wall. Threads of light leaked into the living room directly ahead. He waited to turn on any of the lamps, for he wanted to savor the darkness and the silence of the room. He sat on the dark brown fabric covered empire-style couch, where he took off his specially made shoes, and laid down on the couch. "My God, my God. I have done your will," he exclaimed loudly in the empty room.

The apartment was solemn, with heavy, rococo style, dark walnut furniture, the walls covered mostly by a series of nondescript landscapes—all in heavy gilded frames with miniature brass lights over each. The floor was carpeted wall to wall with a heavy, dark brown wool carpet. The lamps on several of the tables randomly placed throughout were hammered iron with simple beige lamp shades. The living room ended in a moderate-size dining area, with a large pedestal table, around which stood eight cushioned ornate chairs similar to the furniture in the living room. The small crystal chandelier was dark, but the glow of light from the foyer cast a soft shadow off the chandelier against the far wall, revealing a large painting depicting a mountain. The place almost seemed like a private museum rather than an apartment. But Ruslan didn't bother to look at the art. His mind churning, his temples pulsing, and his hands still trembling, he rolled off the couch and assumed the prayer position with which he felt so comfortable.

He would communicate with his God. A forgiving God, a merciful God. A protective God. The mercy of Allah is infinite. His God provides the equilibrium of life and his sacrifices in the name of God would be recorded in heaven. After his prayers, Ruslan knew that he would be transformed into an enchanted man and that God would inspire him to greater deeds. His prayers would not be useless.

Praise to Allah, the Almighty
You are the shining light of my life
You are the great vision in my eyes
You are the hand that guides me
You are the air that I breathe
You are the water that surrounds me
You are the land that feeds me
You are the body that I have
You bring joy and happiness

To me who will always do your will
Praise to Allah, the Almighty.

Forgive me for my impertinence
Forgive me for my vanity
Forgive me for my lack of true faith
Forgive me for my sins of my mind
Forgive me for my hand that did not finish your deed today
Forgive and keep me in the state of grace, always

Praise to Allah, the Almighty.

Over and over again, he implored God not to forsake him. As he got up, he walked to the bedroom, which had an oversized bed with a massive headboard crowned by a series of interlocking triangles carved across the top. Above the bed hung what appeared to be a companion piece, similar to the one in the dining room. The bed cover was gold brocade, and matching pillows rested at the head of the bed. Two similarly colored side chairs flanked a desk, on which lay a holder for a pen, paper and envelopes. The open drapes, which also had a golden hue, revealed panels of sheer, stark white curtains. Ruslan walked over to the curtains and with his right hand parted the panels, looking across the street to a similar apartment building. His eyes looked down, and he could see no pedestrians on the wet street.

Moving over to the closet, he opened it to reveal a number of suits, shoes, slacks and shirts. As he glanced at the clothing, he surmised that all were his size. The client accomplished at least one thing right, he thought to himself as he picked out a pair of black slacks, a grey shirt, a dark gray jacket and black loafers. On the lone shelf in the neatly arranged closet was a small, plain gray box, with BAR logo on its front. He took it down and placed it unopened on the bed.

He went to the bathroom and stared at the shower, as if in fear to enter, remembering the shower he had earlier at the Lowndes. For a moment, he thought of the young man he killed. Shaking his head, he began to recite his prayers again and again, as he undressed, removed his wig of shaggy black hair to reveal a close cropped crew cut, and ran the shower. He was in the shower less than five minutes, enough time to shave off the bushy mustache. He stepped out and dried hurriedly, avoiding looking at himself in the mirror, staring rather at the floor.

Ruslan wondered whether he should leave the apartment because he hadn't heard from the Bank Alliance Russia's representatives. He picked up the phone and dialed the British Airways phone number. After a long wait, he heard a clerk come on the line. "British Air, may I help you?" the agent asked with a cheerful voice.

"Yes, please. The seven p.m. flight from Moscow. Did it arrive on time in London?"

"One moment please. Let me see . . . yes, it arrived, but it was one-hour-and-a-half late. It landed at 8:30 p.m. Is there anything else?" she asked.

"No, no. Thank you for your help." Ruslan hung up the phone, exhilarated that he didn't have to meet the bank's representatives yet.

Metropolitan Police
New Scotland Yard
Broadway
London
Local Time: 9:45 p.m. (4:45 p.m., Washington, D.C.)
Surveillance Team B—Security Intercept Station
Room SB-100

The automatic recording system intercepting the ten units Agent Mason was monitoring flashed a brilliant green warning light, and a short, high pitched *beep-beep-beep* broke the silence of the room. Interception unit no. 8 began recording, startling Mason because this had been a dead intercept for many weeks. He switched instantly to audio, and quickly put on his earphones, pressing the open switch on his console which allowed him to verify the clarity of the brief conversation less than twenty seconds.

At his computer keyboard, he typed in his access code for entrance into the main Yard computer which was programmed to automatically send the recording, in digitized format, on to a designated recipient, in this case, by secure satellite link, the National Security Agency at Ft. Meade, Maryland.

Mason's identity established, the intercept data were fed immediately and reached the NSA computer in seconds. Mason watched his screen for confirmation, which came almost instantaneously. "Intercept SY234-GMT-21:45 accepted. Automatic deletion occurring at initiating intercept station commencing now . . . SY234 deleted." Mason's screen went black.

Mason watched as the tape machine automatically rewound to its start position. No record of this intercept would exist at the Yard. It would be as if the intercept had never happened, the conversation never took place. He had heard the conversation, but he had no idea what it meant. And it was over as quickly as it had started. He leaned back on his chair, put his feet on the console table, and returned to reading *The Evening Sun.*

At the National Security Agency at Ft. Meade, Maryland, the intercept was being computer analyzed for voice recognition. It wold take several minutes for the computer program to identify the voice and retrieve an existing match—which it found. Ruslan's voice was matched to the intercepted call from Moscow he had received earlier in the day at the Lowndes Hotel. A special printout would be sent automatically to an analyst on duty who would listen to the new intercept. The match would be made, but the identity of the person speaking still remained unknown. Until a name corresponded with the voice, the information was incomplete. The transcript and match information, however, would be sent to Mary Auriello's office. It wouldn't arrive until six p.m.

**London
Local Time: 10:00 p.m. (5:00 p.m., Washington, D.C.)
164 Cadogan Place**

Ruslan looked at his watch. It was 10:00 p.m. Boris Shenin and Georgi Ivashkin, his employers, whom he had met in Moscow just a few weeks ago, should have arrived at the apartment.

"Perhaps they decided not to come, and for that I thank Allah," Ruslan mused, because he thought both were indecent and unholy people. He needed some fresh air and some food. Putting on the clothes he had selected out, he stood before the foyer mirror for a moment to marvel at how different he looked. He then reached over and opened the box he had earlier laid on the bed, took out round, silver, wire rim glasses, and a British passport with his new name—Evan Holder. No one would recognize him. Of that he was absolutely sure.

He had accomplished only part of the mission. The elimination of Harrison, whom he believed was injured seriously, would have to wait for another time. Ruslan realized that many had seen him and the police would probably be looking for him, but his looks had changed and he was confident that his plans to leave London tomorrow morning for Frankfurt and on to Tashkent would not change. Yet he couldn't explain his need at this point to avoid fleeing, to have a respite. Normalcy in the midst of danger had been ingrained in him from his days of training with Russian special forces. He was never to act anxious, unsure, unsteady. "Control, Ruslan, control, always," his instructor would remind him. If Shenin did come, he would immediately know that Ruslan had been there and would return. Shenin could wait for him; not the other way around, He smiled at these thoughts.

Ruslan had become an expert in assassinations. He was acquainted with all the methods and means for accomplishing his tasks. Even at his home town near Tashkent, Uzbekistan, people grew afraid of him. Some knew what he did as a profession, understanding that his profession brought the large amounts of money that came to him from sources other than his family's cotton farms.

His friends were his mother and sister. The only diversions in his life were his assignments, his horseback riding, and his religion. He had long ago resigned himself to the fact that his reward would come in heaven rather than on earth. There were certain things that he discussed in private with his mother, but she would remind him that God understood and would show him the way. Outside his family, he rarely spoke to women and reacted timidly whenever one spoke to him. He distrusted women, so his enforced celibacy became delusional—alone on his bed, unable to concentrate, because of the erotic urges floating through his mind, he imagined what it would be like to love a woman—the perfume of paradise, he believed—paradise brought to him only after this life.

As he placed his hands in his pocket, he realized that he had left his wallet with his credit cards and money in the tuxedo jacket. Going back to the bedroom to retrieve them, he instinctively opened his wallet and flipped through the money section, folded it quickly and placed it in his breast pocket, turning off the lights to the bedroom as he left.

He had kept about 1,000 pounds and on his way to London had placed the remaining amount from the $100,000 which he had been given for his London expenses in his account in Geneva. However, in Tashkent he had left his mother and sister $10,000. They could use what they needed and save the rest. Both were frugal, so, although Ruslan modernized their home and bought them other amenities, they would keep the money hidden in the house, along with other money he had given them during the last few years.

But most of his money was in Switzerland, where he hoped one day to live. He loved the mountains and streams, but more importantly, he admired the order and calmness of the people. Yet he realized it would be a long time before he could ever fulfill his dream of living there. With that thought in his mind, he opened the door, switching off the lights as he left.

He walked down the stairs, this time slowly, but with a slight bounce to his steps. Ruslan was pleased that his heart had become pure through his prayers, his thoughts were good, and he had eliminated those who disregarded the will of God.

As he walked down silent Cadogan Place and onto Sloan Street, he breathed deeply, enjoying the night. The walk to Sloan Square was invigorating and cleansing. He avoided looking at any of the windows of the various fashionable shops along Sloan Street; he felt safe, almost happy in the enjoyment of his state of grace and liberty. One block from the Square, he saw a small bistro on a side street. He had eaten only a light lunch earlier in the day, and he was hungry. "Lavandou" said the small painted sign swaying in the light breeze. Ruslan peered into the window and saw a small bar and several tables, which, even at the late hour, were filled. He took the one empty seat at the bar after he walked in, content with the moment. The aroma of the restaurant was pleasing, and he could smell fresh bread being baked—or was that just an image of his mother's kitchen?

The seat he chose had a short cane back on a black frame, and he decided to take his jacket off and place it on the back. He noticed that several others at the small bar had done likewise. An older man, dressed in a white shirt and black bow tie, somewhat dandified, and wearing a black apron with the lettering "Lavandou" on the pocket of the apron, approached him with a carafe of water. He began to pour some into Ruslan's glass, when Ruslan interrupted him.

"No, please. I would prefer bottled mineral water."

"But, of course. Would you like Evian, Perrier, *ou* Hilsons, the English kind?" the waiter asked, mixing some French with his English.

"Perrier will be fine. And, no ice, please," Ruslan said quietly.

"Of course." The waiter left for the end of the bar where a small refrigerator sat underneath the black and white tile counter top, and he opened the stainless steel door, taking out a bottle of Perrier, at the same time reaching for a glass on the counter. He placed both on a small tray, with a slice of lemon on a small plate, and brought them to Ruslan, who was intently staring at the menu.

"*Monsieur*, what would you like? We have a *specialité de la maison*, dover sole with herbs, *ou si vous preferez, petites* lamb chops *avec une sauce de vin rouge. Aussi, les autres specialités* on the menu. Questions?" the waiter asked, still mixing French and English.

Overhearing all of this was a young man next to Ruslan, who looked over and said, "I would take the dover sole, if I were you. It's the best in London, actually. I know because I work as an office clerk at the *Observer*, and that's what our food critic says . . . you should try it."

Ruslan turned and looked into the dark blue, innocent eyes of a very young man, perhaps twenty or twenty-one, about the same height as he, dressed in dark, form fitting blue jeans, black turtle-neck, and navy blue jacket, with an square-jawed, intelligent looking creamy white face, somewhat disproportionate to his body. He was slim but well formed; his light brown hair showed streaks of blond. His eyes sparkled and his voice was exuberant. Ruslan gazed at the young man for so long that the young man, chagrined, blurted aloud, "Is something wrong? Mister, is something wrong?"

"No, nothing is wrong . . . I am sorry . . . I just must be too tired," Ruslan said, beads of perspiration appearing on his forehead. "Allah! Why do you do this to me? This man has the face of the one I just killed in your name. Why do you do this to me? I am so holy. I am your servant!" he silently repeated to himself.

The coincidence with the young man that he had murdered at the Lowndes was too much, too vivid. He closed his eyes and began breathing with difficulty, forcing himself to contain feelings for the young man next to him that he couldn't understand. Again the face, the beautiful, perfect face. He had that image which wouldn't go away and here next to him the image again surfaced. He sensed the scent of the man next to him, subtle, beautiful, his hair, his eyes, the strong jaw. For a moment, Ruslan imagined he had his hands on the young man's face, moving it closer to his own, maybe alone together in an unknown intimacy, trembling with desire and surprise.

Sweat now pouring down his face, he took the napkin, patted his face lightly, saying softly, "I have to leave now. I did not realize how quickly the time has gone. I have to get to the airport. Sorry to have bothered you," he said, as he placed a five-pound note on the counter.

"No bother," the waiter replied, "*mais non*, no *problème, pas de problèmes, merci, et bonne nuit. Merci.*"

As Ruslan slipped off his chair, reaching for his jacket hanging on the chair's back, the young man intently asked, "Are you feeling okay?"

"Yes, I am," Ruslan said. "I must go now. Good bye."

The young man again asked, "Are you sure you're okay? The waiter will call a cab for you if you wish."

"No . . . no thank you. I am fine. Good bye," Ruslan replied, and strode quickly out. He had to escape. This agony had to end. He had to recover from the shock of seeing the likeness of the young male prostitute he had slaughtered a few hours earlier at the Lowndes. He needed to calm down. His mind was too confused, too jumbled, too frightened. Outside, he kept mumbling, "I am a man, Allah! a man! Do you understand? Do not do this to me. I cannot take this feeling any longer. I just can't. You must save me. Don't abandon me!"

Ruslan returned quickly, peering intently at his feet as he strode the several blocks back to the safe house. He needed rest, sleep. Tomorrow he would leave . . . no, perhaps tonight. "Control, Ruslan. Always control." He couldn't complete this mission. It had been wrong from the start. Until then, he had never murdered a bystander; he had killed only the victim selected by his client. But then he had killed both. It was wrong. God would punish him. God was punishing him. He had to leave this city... yes, he would leave right away. He couldn't finish; the money would be returned. He would never leave his home in Tashkent again.

Ruslan was lost in his own fear... fear of succumbing to a temptation he didn't understand and didn't want to understand. The temptation was like a pestilence descending on him, a slow silent killer that he knew would be impossible to shake. He would fear death less than the humiliation of this constant temptation, this unfamiliar desire, this supposed exclusion from life's innermost secrets—desires of men—for men.

He ascended the four flights of steps to the apartment. His hands were quivering as he fumbled with the key, inserting it incorrectly several times before opening the door. For a moment, he was still, feeling even more lonely, the door open, the darkness creating a desperation he had never felt before, in fact he liked darkness, but here, the only light came through the open living room drapes that let in the faint light from the street below. Just as he reached for the foyer light switches, turning them all on... could it be? He thought he saw the young man he had just earlier been sitting next to in the restaurant lounging in the room.

Blinking his eyes furiously, he took his glasses off flinging them toward the image, blurting out, "You... you... how did you get here? How did you get into this apartment?"

"I walked. I wanted to be sure that you were okay. I wanted to be with you. Here, come sit by me. You need to rest. Please sit by me," the young man said as he began to unbutton his shirt. "I'd like to stay here for a while."

He didn't approach. His hands still trembling, sweating with fear, Ruslan shouted, "Stop. You must leave right now. I cannot have you stay. Stop tormenting me. Stop! Stop! Get out!"

"Why don't you want me to stay? I saw how you looked at me. You want me, don't you? Come here, please come here," the image said, a bare chested figure in front of the bank of living room windows, a white figure against the darkened panes of glass. "Don't you want to touch me?" the image asked, smiling flirtatiously, slowly fading. Then the image was gone.

"My God, what is happening to me? You must not do this to me," Ruslan screamed, his body shaking, unable to move.

"Why don't you want me to stay? I saw how you looked at me. You want me, don't you? Come here," the image said, beginning to move toward Ruslan.

In utter panic, Ruslan exploded, "Get out, get out! Here, you want money? Here, yes, you came for money. Here it is—." And Ruslan, reaching into his pocket, drew out his wallet, throwing it into the air toward the image that again disappeared.

There was silence. No one picked up the wallet which had come to rest at the base of the windows. Was anyone there?

"Oh! my God, you cannot do this to me . . . you cannot to one of your faithful—" Ruslan stood still unable to walk.

Then the image began again, softly whispering, "No, I am going to stay. I know you want me," and started to move wistfully from in front of the windows, arms outstretched as if to receive Ruslan in an embrace.

"Pick up the money . . . leave me. Oh, let me alone let me alone. Stop. I must stop you, I must. My God, you believe I have sinned. You have now surrounded me with this fire."

Ruslan's mouth quivered. His hands shook; the uncontrollable dread began to take hold.

"I must kill you . . . like the other . . . like the other. Yes, I will kill you." In a final descent into mania, Ruslan hurled himself toward the image in one frightful leap, flaying away at the air, hitting the table lamp next to the couch, stumbling over the coffee table, plummeting headlong into space. "You shall die!" Ruslan screamed again and again, as he hit the windows with the full force of his body in a rendering crash, trying to push the image into the window, smashing the lower half of the window into pieces, his neck bluntly hitting the wrought iron frame separating the upper and lower panes.

The rush brought him back to reality, but it was far too late. The crash of his muscular body into the window had severely lacerated his face from which blood flowed freely. His head had turned grotesquely sideways from the brute force with which he hit the iron window frame, blood running down onto the rest of his upper body and onto the floor. In a moment of anguish, he tried to lift himself from the floor where he had fallen, straining to crawl over to the couch, blood following his slow movements. In supreme misery, a prisoner in the anteroom of hell, his vision of paradise was gone.

It was 11:30 p.m.

CHAPTER NINE

Washington, D.C.
Friday
Local Time: 5:00 p.m. (10:00 p.m., London)
Department of Justice, Attorney General's Office Room 6111

Mary Auriello had served under several attorneys general, and the present one, Bernard Vennix, was the worst, at least in so far as intelligence and security matters were concerned. He talked too much—to the press, to others in the department, to anyone—in order to prove his importance. He was dangerous, because he failed to understand or to comprehend the necessity of secrecy in intelligence operations. The cold war was over, and he felt that was sufficient reason to forget about intelligence gathering and certainly to spend no money on such an activity. He was stupid, Mary believed, and he knew she thought that of him.

Vennix's strength, probably his only one, was that he was the former law partner of the President of the United States. Although Vennix had a checkered law career (he had his license suspended for one year for destroying documents in a securities fraud case, which he denied, claiming he was framed for political reasons), he had managed to latch on to the president when the president was a young associate in the firm that Vennix had founded in Charlotte, North Carolina. Mary never liked to be with him, whatever the purpose of the meeting. Perhaps it was because she was privy to information about Vennix that colored her perception of him and led her to regard him as unfit for his job.

When she found that the reason for Vennix's first divorce was his abusive behavior toward his wife, whom he had married upon graduation from the University of North Carolina, Mary disliked him even more.

His second wife, and the mother of his three children, stayed with him, although during the presidential campaign it was rumored that he struck her. Always the loyal woman, she appeared at all functions with him, and he managed to avoid being asked an embarrassing question by the media he carefully cultivated.

Mary had no quarrel with his conviction that he was there only to protect the political interests of the president. What appalled her was how he accomplished this task. Beneath his official courtesy, and behind his obsequious speech, Mary detected insolence and obstinacy. Age sixty-five, of ordinary build, he kept his white hair perfectly coiffured, giving him a childish look in contrast to the harshness of his expression and the insincerity of his grey eyes. Without morals, he was conspiratorial by nature. Yet he had accomplished the impossible. He was able to get the president elected when the polls showed him 30 points behind the incumbent. He did it through a mixture of guile, lies, promises, media manipulation, and his ability to use campaign funds in ways he knew to be illegal but easily concealed.

She realized that there would be no euphoria for a long time. Her hazel eyes again teared as she thought of how Boarders was slaughtered. She didn't want to believe what she had heard from Commander Robinson. Deep agony comes when truth is disclosed about someone you love. All she could do was to maintain a certain distance. She needed to get this briefing out of the way and rush on to London.

Although Mary's soul had hardened from years of intelligence operations, a part of her was increasingly vulnerable. Her parents were gone; now Boarders was too. "I'm no good at these things, God. No good," she said to herself as she strode into the attorney general's suite of offices.

The double doors leading to the attorney general's suite were open, revealing a reception area decorated in United States government issue blue leather furniture. A worn-looking couch stood against the left wall on which hung large portraits of the president and vice president. In no apparent order in front of a coffee table sat three matching leather chairs facing the couch. Several nondescript small green plants in wicker baskets clustered on one corner of the table, a stack of magazines at the other end. The center was occupied by a large cut glass bowl filled with potpourri, giving the reception area an unusual, pungent sweet smell. Bright, gold panel drapes framed the large bank of windows overlooking Pennsylvania Avenue.

In the reception area were two large, matching walnut reception desks, only one of which was occupied. Computer terminals perched on both desks, and files—blue, green, manila—were piled on both. Along the right wall, the Great Seal of the Department of Justice hung centered between two American flags. One side of the reception room led to a large conference room, the other to the attorney general's personal secretary, and beyond to his personal office. Mary expected the meeting to take place in his personal office so she was surprised that when she arrived, the receptionist, a pencil thin woman of indecipherable age hiding behind oversized glasses, told her to go directly into the conference room. Mary was not up to meetings, let alone this one, but she needed to brief Vennix before she departed.

"Good afternoon, Bernie," Mary said as she moved into the conference room, taking a seat directly next and to the right of Vennix, who sat at the head of the large, rectangular, mahogany conference table, writing furiously on a pad.

"Come in, Mary. Coffee's in the regular spot. It's regular, not decaf. Regular, O.K.?"

Mary winced because he always asked her the same question, and she always gave the same answer, "No, Bernie. Decaf is what I drink, but I really don't want anything now. What are you scribbling so diligently?"

"I'm writing notes so I don't forget. Age deprives us of the ability to recall. I find I'm writing myself more notes than before. By the way, you know how I'm now outwitting my insomnia?"

"No, Bernie, I didn't know you had insomnia," Mary said, skeptically and with some annoyance, saying to herself, "Who the fuck cares?" Addressing Vennix she continued. "When did your problem with sleep start?"

"Oh—a few months ago. I don't know why. Maybe it's the heat of the upcoming second-term campaign. I just don't know. I haven't had it before. Anyway, I play chess games on my computer for a couple of hours, and then, when my eyes start to droop, I head for bed. It's worked every time. You should try it."

"Well, I will, if I ever get insomnia, but I sleep like a baby, Bernie. By the way, I hope you're not writing things you want to tell me. I don't like notes on anything you and I discuss, Bernie. You know my feeling about that."

Looking askance, his eyes shifting from his notes to Mary, Vennix responded, "These are just notes, notes for the press. I'll see them directly after this. You know I'll discuss some campaign issues and so forth. No, certainly, nothing that concerns you."

Then, rising, he casually walked over and closed the conference room door. "Mary, did you see the CNN report?" he asked, lowering his voice. "The shooting incident, in London—the report even mentioned Harrison's name. Apparently, his car was part of the queen's motorcade and yet the assassin let her pass, zeroing in on Harrison. Do you have anything on this? Anything at all? I have to see the president later, and he may bring it up."

"I didn't see the CNN report, Bernie," Mary responded in a voice even and quiet. "I'll ring the president before I leave for London to give him a 'heads-up.' So you really don't have to concern yourself on that score. I don't like the president getting information about Pentum second-hand. You do understand why, don't you?" Mary said, her gaze fixed on Vennix's eyes.

"Well yes, of course. We should keep the channels straight, shouldn't we? Only you can brief the others in the loop. I was just trying to be helpful. I suppose there are things you tell him that you don't even advise me or your friend Miller at the CIA."

Mary didn't respond to his comment. He knew perfectly well what the Pentum briefing protocol was. Unless the information came directly from her, the information wasn't to be believed. This carefully controlled information flow, in Mary's view, was responsible for the wall that prevented anything from becoming public, but, she knew that Vennix had a few favorite media friends and he loved to give them scintillating tidbits about covert operations just to demonstrate that he knew—and he trusted that they would never report on those operations.

"The Brits knew that Harrison would be there, and they also knew, through our intercept surveillance, that he and Boarders were potential targets of the Moscow *mafiya*," Mary responded. "Somehow the Moscow hoods figured out they were responsible for the abortive Libyan missile deal and targeted both. The intercept from NSA came in just an hour ago confirming the two of them as targets, and I called Robinson of the Royal Security. There were perhaps thirty to forty-five minutes to try to arrange proper security for both—enough in my judgment to put them into place. But it didn't happen.

"Bernie, you should also know that Boarders is dead, probably at the hands of the same assassin. He was found in his hotel room a few hours before the strike against Harrison."

Vennix's face flushed at the news of Boarders' death. Jumping from his seat, he headed toward the window where he peered out, spouting, "Shit! He's the one who carries the ball in these, isn't he? Harrison's injured, Boarders is dead, that leaves just . . . you," Vennix said, turning around and staring at Mary.

"You have a problem with that, Bernie?" Mary asked, still staring at him. "While you're conjuring your response, let me say that, at this moment, we know that our contact, who had provided us the information about the Moscow *mafiya*, has safely left Moscow, and is on her way to Zurich via Cyprus. But at this moment we don't know where she is. What's vital, however, is that we also don't know where the renegade nuke is. We know who controls it, and I know how to control him. So, please, Bernie, don't get excited and don't get confused. Everything's under control. There's been no deterioration. And don't panic. No one knows of Boarders' death except you, me and Robinson in London. Not even Harrison."

"But, that leaves just you—you—," Vennix repeated aimlessly.

"You think I'm not qualified?"

"Of course, not. It's just that his death changes the equation, doesn't it?"

"His death does nothing to this mission, Bernie. I don't want you thinking differently," Mary's voice was quiet.

"Of course. Now, what about the nuke? If it's delivered, the crazies will use it, won't they? And we'll be in a real mess . . . just before the start of the election campaign . . . I can't let that happen . . . nothing can interfere with the campaign, Mary . . . nothing," Vennix said, his voice becoming agitated as he returned and slumped into his chair.

"One could say that you do panic, Bernie. Look at you. Just look at you," said Mary, no longer quiet, her voice cracking with derision. "The Pentum isn't for sissies, Bernie. It was started by this president to do what we have successfully done—prevent crazies from getting Soviet nukes and missiles. Yes, Boarders' death and Harrison's injury leave just me and, Bernie, I don't intend to have this mission go south," Mary continued, her eyes blazing with fury. "The operation will continue and continue successfully. It will be concluded, as planned, by Saturday evening."

"Mary, I think it would be wise to reconsider. Perhaps we should pull out now," Vennix lowered his voice to a whisper. What if some newsperson finds out about Harrison and his connection with the United States? Mary, a campaign's about to begin. All we need; something like this to hit the fan. . . ."

"There isn't any connection. Your thinking that there is is the problem, Bernie," Mary interrupted Vennix's comments. "Some day you're going to slip when you talk to all your press friends, and you'll create the impression that there's a connection, because you think in the wrong direction, Bernie. Repeat . . . there's no connection. There never has been. You do understand that, don't you? There is no connection between the Pentum missions and the United States. Bernie, do you understand that? Cleanse your mind of that thought right now," Mary replied, exasperated with Vennix's insecurity.

"If anyone does ask you to comment on the attempt on Harrison's life, I suggest you say, that, 'We are appalled whenever Americans become targets. We're awaiting further information.' That should take care of that. You must say nothing else. No one will know of Boarders' death; there's no reason to know. His death won't be reported, Bernie. I assure you of that. The only person who now knows and who could possibly talk is you, Bernie."

"What do you mean? Are you accusing me of something, Mary? Leaking information to the press?" Vennix rose from his chair and headed toward the small buffet table behind Mary where he poured himself some coffee.

Her patience ending, her voice rising, Mary replied, "Yes, I am. Listen to me, Bernie. Listen to me: this mission is at the most dangerous and delicate stage. There can be no thought whatsoever of giving in now. We have an obligation—do you understand that word?—an obligation to rescue the contact and to stop that bomb from being delivered."

"Oh, get off that moral shit, Mary. Contacts—even the use of that name is silly—they're turncoats. Who gives a shit whether the contact comes out alive? Come on, even you'll admit that the crazies will get the bomb one way or the other."

"What? Whose side are you on?" Mary rose from her chair and began to walk away. "The contact will be saved, Bernie, and the nuke won't be delivered. If you or anyone here screws it up by talking, or does anything . . . anything to foul up the conclusion of this mission, I'll see that you, and whomever you recruit, will regret that misstep the rest of your life. I mean that.

"And the stupidity of your concern about Pentum's impact on a political campaign. Why on earth would you want anyone to know anyhow? Pentum is a closed circle, and when the mission is over, it'll vanish as quickly as it came to life. But, I'll say this only once, Bernie. If I find out you've jeopardized this mission by even talking about it, I'll see that the world will view some photos of your beaten wife, now in the sealed file of your first divorce, Bernie. You talk, Bernie, and I'll see that one photo is published in your favorite newspaper, *The Washington Post.*

"I'm leaving in less than an hour. I want to hear nothing from you, and I want you to say nothing to anyone. One loose lip, and if this mission goes down, I'll sink you faster than a rock in water. You know I mean it. And, for God's sake, don't you talk to the president about this. The two of you discussing this without me makes me puke. Forget it, Bernie. This mission will be complete and successful."

"What photo?" Vennix shouted back.

Without responding to his question, Mary said, "I repeat, don't discuss this with anyone ... and don't worry about the completion of the mission. I have to go now. I'll call you and the President late tomorrow evening, Saturday, at the White House. I understand you'll be at the dinner the President is giving for the Governors. You'll be happy with the news, I assure you."

"Mary, you're blackmailing me." Vennix shouted as if he wanted others outside the room to hear his words. "You're blackmailing me," he repeated.

"For God's sake, no, Bernie. I'm not the only one who knows about your past. That isn't what concerns me. I want you to understand, Bernie, that I'll let nothing stand in the way of the mission's success—nothing."

For minutes, Vennix just glared at Mary. She stood and looked at him. "Bernie, I have to go. I'm leaving for London."

"The money, Mary. What did you do with the money from the Libyan deal—the payment sent by the Libyans for the purchase? Where is it?" Vennix asked as he got up and walked toward Mary, who was waiting by the conference room exit.

"What did you ask?" Mary demanded. "What *did* you ask?"

"The money?" Vennix repeated.

"There is no money, Bernie. Now, tell me, Mr. Attorney General, do you believe that silence, cooperation and success in intelligence operations are cost free?" Someday, I'll sit down and diagram what happened to the money, but not now. That money, of course, was not U.S. government-appropriated—just so you know that we're not spending those funds impermissibly, not that it would matter for you. We could take lessons from you on that score. Good bye, Bernie. You'll hear from me."

Mary opened the door and left without looking at the receptionist who was talking furtively to the attorney general's secretary. As Mary passed them, she turned and said, "Get back to work. If I find you eavesdropping again, I'll have you both fired." She had no authority to say that. But, then, she said it with a smile.

Mary had bluffed. There was no photo, and even if there was, she didn't have it. It was a guess, and she guessed correctly. "The fucker wanted money. Asshole."

Vennix buried his face in his hands, remembering those photos, that horrible nightmare so many years ago and so hidden, that even in his Senate confirmation hearings, nothing was mentioned. Absolutely nothing. How did she get it, the bitch? He buzzed his secretary, asking her to get his press secretary to tell the waiting press he would be a few minutes late. He leaned over and placed his head on the table, trying to stifle the pain that he had caused himself and his first wife so long ago. And Mary knew. She always knew, that's why she had no respect for him, or trust. What if she told others? His career would be damaged, wouldn't it? He had to deny Mary the opportunity to humiliate him. He would stop her. He couldn't bear life with this hanging over his head, too much was at stake. After all, he was the Attorney General of the United States. Right, *the Attorney General.* He had power. Didn't he? Who is Mary but a bitch that could be replaced. Yeah. *Who the fuck is Mary. Only a bitch.*

Vennix wouldn't hesitate in what he had to do. Saving himself took precedence over the success of the Pentum mission. So what if a bomb drops? Who gives a shit? They could all kill themselves in that fucking desert for all he cared. Yeah! Kill themselves. If the crazies didn't get the bomb now, they'd get it later. No, he had to protect himself.

He would ruin Mary, maybe something more. Self-preservation brings out hidden wishes—and desires and, in the unraveling of such a drama, often brings destruction. Vennix picked up the receiver of his private phone and slowly punched in a number. His unspoken desire would now become a reality.

Zurich
Friday
Local Time: 3:00 p.m. (2:00 p.m., London)

The ride from the Zurich-Kloten airport to central Zurich isn't a pleasant trip on any occasion. Although softened by a center strip where, at regular intervals, multicolored and varied flowers grow, the four-lane concrete highway passes by nondescript office towers and apartment buildings. It is only when the taxi leaves the tunnel carved through the hardened, mountainous debris left by an ice age glacier that the true nature of Zurich emerges, as the old, architecturally diverse, magical center city comes into view. At different times and perhaps in different moods, Svetlana had seen the same scene many times before, but to her it was always magical.

The streets of Zurich have a peculiar appearance, many narrow ones winding through the old city section, flanked by elegant, patrician residences, built, in some instances, two- to three-hundred years earlier. The Swiss are proud of this city, impressive in reputation as a financial center, adorned with a multitude of church towers, spires, antique guild houses with meticulously crafted facades, alongside modern banks, office buildings and expensive shops. Majestic yet compact, because the surrounding mountains restrict growth, Zurich always entranced Svetlana with its brightness and beauty, as it had many Russians who made it a business and holiday destination after the end of Communism.

No matter how sublime the spectacle of Zurich—a city in almost ideal balance—Svetlana knew that she was there at the sufferance of Moussa and for no other reason. Moussa's constant companionship made true enjoyment in the city impossible. This, however, was different. She was alone in the city for the very first time, but her time would be limited.

She kept her hands tightened on the straps of her black leather purse, which contained the computer disk from Peter Bradford's office computer, the two audio tapes of the meeting in his office discussing the Iranian purchase of a nuclear device, and the three signatory cards detailing account information regarding the *vor* bank accounts. Colonel Boarders had asked her to place these in the safety deposit box at Banque Unger & Hausemann. Copies of the tapes, the disk, and signature cards were also with her mother on their way to Washington. Colonel Boarders never told her why he also wanted them in a safety deposit box in Zurich, at a bank she had never visited. Colonel Boarders' strategies had been flawless, so she had no reason to question this part of her assignment.

The taxi sped along the road bordering the Limmath River, an expanse of water that cuts the city into two, as it leaves Lake Zurich, whose own terminus lies at the beginning of the old city. Svetlana, seeing the glittering splashes of the sun off the river, thought of the times that Moussa and she had walked along the path, saying little to each other, but taking in the beauty and calmness that only a river can bring. But even those walks with him she took without feeling. During those walks, she tried to concentrate on the swans floating across the river current, all the while holding Moussa's hand and listening to what few words he said to her.

When Svetlana reflected on the singular airport coincidence of Jess Stevens, she was distressed at such bad luck. Her clairvoyant and mystic Aunt Yelana Fyodorova would always tell her, "if the spirits summon the beginnings to be good, then the spirts will foretell the ending to be equally as good. This is not my fantasy, Svetlana. It is the truth!" Of course, the beginning had been good. She and her mother had left Moscow, and then Cyprus, without problems. Her mother was now on her way to the United States, and Svetlana would soon be on her way to London to join Colonel Boarders and his partner, a man she knew only as David Harrison. Regardless, the airport incident would not alter her remaining plan, so carefully laid out by the colonel. "But," she thought for an instant, "perhaps Zurich is the beginning?" Quickly she brushed aside this idea, by silently telling herself, "It can't be; it won't be." She refused to become anxious over an occurrence that no one could foresee. Although weary, she wouldn't become obsessed with fear.

"Twenty francs, please," the driver announced. For a moment Svetlana kept staring out the window, looking at the large blue and white banner announcing a retrospective exhibition of Picasso. The driver, getting no response, turned around and repeated, "Twenty francs, please; twenty francs is the fare."

"Yes, of course. I was just reading the banner. I believe I will enjoy the show," she said as she reached into her purse and pulled out a twenty-franc note, handing it to the driver. "Thank you very much, and good day," she said. The driver nodded and waited for Svetlana to close the passenger door. She looked at the banner, flapping in the slight breeze, and wanted so much to go into the museum, realizing that the few times she visited this place with Moussa it was a hurried tour. He never had the patience to read the small descriptions of the exhibits. After another glance at the banner, she turned and walked across the street to the taxi stand, entering the first cab and asking the driver to take her immediately to the DHL office. It was but a ten-minute ride by cab. She glanced at her watch. It was 2:30 p.m. in London. She had plenty of time.

The taxi quickly left the stand, following a street which led to the Bahnhofstrasse, the main shopping street of Zurich. Svetlana looked out the cab window, her eyes scanning the many pedestrians, and shops and the sidewalk cafes that border this wide four-lane street down whose middle ran electric cable cars. As the cab turned left onto Schutsenstrasse, she glanced at the meter, opened her purse, and took out a five-franc note which she gave to the driver as she alighted from the cab and walked into the DHL office.

Several people were milling around the counter designated overhead "Pick-up." She waited while the clerk took care of the customers before her, and she reached the counter, giving her name and showing her passport. Apart from mutual "Good afternoons" in German, nothing further was said, and Svetlana received a large DHL envelope which she took with her to the counter closest to the front entrance. There she opened the cover envelope and took out a small, brown, plain envelope which she placed in her purse, unopened. She discarded the DHL cover in the trash container beneath the counter and left.

It was a short ten-minute walk up the Bahnhofstrasse, and then a left turn onto St. Peterstrasse, where Banque Unger & Hausemann was located. The walk cleared her mind of any latent depression. The cool, crisp, sunny afternoon made her regain her good sense and control her nerves. "Just a few more hours," she thought, "just a few more hours." She could stand the rising tension and proceed to the bank, calmly, and with determination. "No longer will I have to lead a life of make believe. No longer will I tremble at the thought of making love to Moussa. No longer will I have to live a lie," she repeated to herself several times as she walked down the street, avoiding a glance at the display cases, keeping her head down, her eyes fixed on the sidewalk.

Quickening her pace, she came to the intersection of Bahnhofstrasse and St. Peterstrasse. From the corner, she could see the bank building just a few paces from the intersection where she now stood. The five-story bank building's facade of stone and brick gave it a silver gray but not monumental appearance. On the right side of a highly polished oak door she read a brass plaque that stated "Banque Unger & Hausemann, banque privé." In Zurich for the *vor*, Svetlana had visited another private bank, Banque Braun & Cie, and knew these private banks catered to an elite group.

She entered the marble-lined entrance hall, which led to an oversized reception area, the end dominated by a massive Louis XIV table with gold trim around the rim of a solid black top supported by four ornately designed legs in black, also with gold trim. An oversized woman sat reading what appeared to Svetlana a computerized sheet of numbers. There were no other materials on her desk. At a right angle to the desk stood a more modern black table for the computer, printer and telephone receiver. On either side of the receptionist's desk, placed about twenty meters from each end, were large, dark green ceramic jars, from which grew magnificent tall palms, framing the desk, as if painting a scene. Svetlana marveled the Swiss admiration of perfection and clarity. She reflected that the reception area where she was standing, carried those themes without question.

As Svetlana stood before the receptionist, the woman, short, cherubic, and dressed in a severe black dress that hugged her stout form, continued to examine the sheet of numbers, diligently checking off each number as she compared what appeared to be an identical list of numbers on her computer screen. Behind her rose a set of twelve-foot-high floor-to-ceiling glass panels. To the right of the panels, and directly adjacent to the wall, was a glass doorway. Looking through the glass door, Svetlana could see that the passage led to a large corridor, unfurnished but carpeted with several medium-size, oriental carpets, and lined with two large wall tapestries depicting the old city of Zurich. At the end, a spiral staircase seemed to descend from the first floor to the floor below. It was there, Svetlana surmised, she would find the vault.

Svetlana waited silently until the receptionist, who seemed rooted to her chair, raised her head. Svetlana then said, "Good afternoon. I am Helga Dietrich and I would like to have access to my deposit box."

"Good afternoon, Ms. Dietrich. Yes, of course. Helga Dietrich," she repeated as she turned to the computer screen and pressed several keys, bringing up a list of names; she pressed another key to highlight Svetlana's pseudonym.

Svetlana could see the screen because she had silently stepped to the left of the desk from the center where she had been standing.

"Yes, you have access. May I see your passport, please?"

Svetlana handed over her German passport. The receptionist took it and, without remarking, handed the passport back.

"You're so lucky! You can go anywhere in Europe! No more passport control in the European Union. Switzerland, as you know, did not join the Union, so here our little country still issues its own red and white passports and we still have the passport control. How ancient. But I suppose the politicians have a reason. I don't understand it, and I voted to participate in the union. Politicians, a strange lot," she said with an air of resignation. "Please go on in. The door is directly to the right."

With that Svetlana approached the door and heard a buzzer indicating that she could enter.

"Good," she said to herself. She looked at her watch, seeing it was three p.m. in London. Her flight, if all went well, would leave for London in about two hours.

She reached the winding staircase and slowly descended, noticing that at the very end was another desk, similar to the one on the upper level, but this one was attended by two security officers and a receptionist as well. The security officers sat at a black marble top table, where three television monitor screens glowed. The table itself was about eight feet behind the receptionist, and directly in front of the security officers' table stood a row of black planters with large ferns. The area was carpeted a soft green.

The receptionist, a young girl with light blond hair tied in a bun, from which hung a long, white scarf with blue trim, spoke first, "Good afternoon, Ms. Dietrich. Welcome. May I see your passport, please?"

Svetlana marveled that the receptionist greeted her by name.

"Yes, of course."

"Just a formality. I have never had someone who was admitted upstairs appear downstairs here with a different passport. Our computers talk to one another," she said with high pitched laughter. "But, please sign here. We'll have to compare your signature on file."

"Of course." Svetlana wondered how they had her signature on file. She signed the form placed before her. The receptionist fed the form into a small box next to her computer and a ping sounded on the computer. Svetlana's name was approved for entry.

"Aren't these new computers wonderful? In the old days, we had to go through card files; now, we just press a button. Let us see, your deposit vault is 2851. Please come with me."

Svetlana followed her. They both walked into the vault where the receptionist turned left to a row of boxes labeled "Aisle A. Boxes 2800-2900."

"Here we are." The receptionist stood directly in front of the box. "Do you have your key?"

"Yes."

"We shall open the front door first with your key and mine. Then, I shall leave you to open the tray in the box. As you know, you have the only key to that." This exercise was accomplished smoothly and the receptionist left, saying, "See you soon. Remember, we close at 5:30."

"Yes, of course. I shall not be very long."

Svetlana took the box to one of the small cubicles lining the vault along the front and sides; the boxes were housed in free-standing aisles in the center of the vault.

She wasn't nervous, but anxious to open the tray, place her own items in, and read the instructions Colonel Boarders had said would be there.

The cubicle was painted light gray. It contained a small birchwood table, and a gray, fabric-covered chair. Directly in front of Svetlana was a small crystal tray containing several precisely sharpened pencils. Adjacent to this tray was another, larger one containing note paper, with the words "Banque Unger & Hausemann" engraved in gold lettering. On the right side of the desk was a phone to call the receptionist. A German sign said that no outside calls could be made from the phone.

Svetlana placed the twenty-inch long, six-inch wide, six-inch tall deposit box on the desk, directly on the soft piece of black felt for this purpose. She reached into her purse for the second key and placed it in the lock. After one quick turn, the top popped slightly, and Svetlana opened the top to its full position, revealing two blue envelopes of equal length. She took both out and recognized that one envelope was thicker than the other. She opened the thin one first. Inside was a folded, light blue piece of paper, with the following typewritten words:

```
    Take the second envelope with you. It contains your
airplane tickets to London, funds for the trip, and a new
passport with your name. Place the passport you are
presently using in this box. This envelope also contains
a smaller envelope if you have to follow the instructions
in the second paragraph. Do not open this smaller envelope
until you have called the number below.
    It is doubtful that anyone will recognize you, but
if you have been recognized, please call the following
Zurich number for instructions: 410-9890.
    Do not take this message with you, but place it back
in the deposit box together with the material that you
have. Memorize the phone number.
                                     My thanks, B.
```

Svetlana read the note several times. "He was here," she thought to herself. "He will not let me down." She wouldn't use the phone in the bank. It would be too dangerous, she thought. She would go to a public phone booth and call the special number. What would these instructions be? She looked at her watch, finding it was close to 3:30. She could still make the 4:30 flight to London, and if she missed that, there were other flights.

Hurriedly, she placed the disk, tapes and signature cards in the box, took it over to the panel containing the open slot, and slid the box in, closing the front door and placing her key in, ready to lock it. She then remembered that she would not have to call the receptionist to come in because, once she had placed the box in the slot and closed the door, it would automatically lock.

She walked back to the alcove she had been using and picked up the phone which automatically dialed the receptionist.

"Yes, are you ready?" came the voice at the other end.

"Yes, I am ready to leave now," answered Svetlana.

In a few moments, the receptionist came in, smiling at Svetlana, "Well, did you find everything to your satisfaction?" she asked.

"Yes, of course," Svetlana replied, "everything is efficient, and for that I am pleased."

"Good. I have been at the bank for over three years, and no one has ever been displeased. Isn't that wonderful!" the receptionist smiled as she escorted Svetlana to the door leading to the stairs which would take Svetlana to the upper level. "Thank you for coming, and have a pleasant day," the receptionist said.

"Yes, I will, and thank you again." Svetlana climbed the stairs to the exit.

The upstairs receptionist had risen from her seat and was holding the door open for Svetlana when she arrived at the upper level. "Well, I do hope you found everything satisfactory," she said.

"Quite satisfactory, thank you very much." The receptionist again motioned her to go forward, opening the exit door for Svetlana as well. As Svetlana stepped outside, she looked for a phone booth.

Svetlana headed directly to the Hotel Schweitzerhof, a few blocks off the Bahnhofstrasse, a hotel whose coffee bar she had visited many times. She knew it would have a public phone.

Her name had become Helene LeFevre, and she was a French citizen. Svetlana felt somehow relieved; she had delivered the material successfully. She had no reason to be concerned, would make her one phone call, and would be on her way. This time, she did scan the shop windows as she joined the throng of pedestrians on Zurich's most famous street. As Svetlana crossed the Bahnhofstrasse to the opposite side, a street car was approaching down the center lane, so she hurried out of its path and just reached the opposite side. She entered the hotel, passed the reception desk and wandered in the direction of the coffee shop, indicated by a small sign to the left of the desk. She noticed a row of three phone booths directly across from the entrance to the shop.

Svetlana placed the one-franc coin in the slot and heard the dial tone ring the number. She was not really concerned and believed this call to be just a precaution. After seven rings, a recording came on:

"Welcome to the Pentum Trade and Investment Travel Office. Your travel plans have been changed. Reservations for you have been made at 64, Steinwiesstrasse. Your apartment is number 10. Please go there promptly. Thank you for using Pentum Trade and Investment Travel Office Services."

Her head dropped as she heard the instructions. She wouldn't be leaving Zurich for London. She marveled at how Boarders had thought of everything. Because Jess Stevens saw her here, Boarders would want her to stay until further notice. She assumed there would be instructions at the apartment he had waiting for her. He didn't want to take the chance that someone would follow her to London. Her trip was ending in Zurich. "Aunt Yelana was correct. If the beginnings are not good, the endings will be the same. Zurich is my beginning and ending," she said to herself, as she lowered her head against the phone box, uncertain what to do. "Colonel Boarders will not let me down. He has this all planned. I will go to the new place, rest, and wait," Svetlana quietly said to herself. Reality was clear for her. Composing herself, she opened the booth door, looked for an instant down to her purse to make sure it was closed, and strode out.

As she left the booth, her dark glasses still covering her eyes, a voice shouted . . . another voice from the past . . . from Moscow . . . my God . . . Oh! my God. She stopped walking and stood still. There was nothing else to do. She stood still and waited as the voice came closer. Too many coincidences . . . God . . . too, too many.

"Svetlana, Svetlana, it is me, Sasha Rodinov, Svetlana . . ." Sasha said as he walked directly toward Svetlana who stood absolutely still. Looking ahead, she felt her heart sink. First Stevens saw her and now Sasha Rodinov. "Svetlana, Anatoli and I are here in Zurich. We did not know you and Moussa were also. That crazy man. He should have told us." Sasha reached over to kiss Svetlana.

Sasha Rodinov, about the same age as Moussa, was a man with unlimited money he earned as an enforcer in Peter Bradford's Moscow drug trade. Thin, with stiff black hair, sad, large, black eyes, and a perpetually hoarse voice, he would always pretend to be ignorant of matters, and, because of his own drug habit, seemed to live in another dimension. She thought him a deformed human being with an exorbitant appetite for drugs and sex. He was vulgar, and she knew that his true vocation was giving himself pleasure every time he beat people senseless if they failed to pay their drug debts to Bradford.

Anatoli Shapov was no better in her eyes. Slightly older than Sasha, shorter, but much larger in girth, with a harsh voice and a dark brown beard, he added gambling to an appetite for drugs and sex. In Moscow, he drove the largest Mercedes fitted with leopard skin upholstery and gold trim, something worthy of an Arabian prince. Anatoli's coarse humor and his general ignorance and inhospitable manner made him someone she tried to avoid. He was no more discrete in his personal habits than Sasha, and he reeked of cologne.

Apart from their claim to have served with Moussa in the Soviet Army, she never understood the close relationship between Moussa and these two. To her Moussa was refined, gentle and courteous. Sasha and Anatoli were just the opposite. She saw them only when they came to Bradford's office. Even Dimitri Gravev was never present, but Moussa was always there whenever they met with Bradford. Moussa told Svetlana, "I like to go to the banya with them—nothing more, Svetlana." She didn't believe Moussa, yet really didn't care after a while. She convinced Moussa to exclude them from any occasion when she was to be present. They were crude and deadly. No one argued with them or answered them back. To Svetlana their manners were those of cannibals.

Svetlana, her mind numb with fear, didn't respond. "It's me, Svetlana—Sasha," he said as he reached over to kiss her, first on one cheek and then on the other. She stood fixed. "Svetlana, are you okay?" he asked as he stepped back.

"Oh! Sasha—I am so sorry. I have had this terrible headache since yesterday! Would you believe it! I am so sorry," and Svetlana leaned over and hugged Sasha. She would lie to Sasha but couldn't hide. Yet she would also get to the new address. She had to.

"Sasha, Sasha, what are you doing in Zurich? Where are all your girls? Oh! Where is my mind? Headaches do terrible things to you, don't they, my Sasha? Don't they?" Svetlana, now composed, said with a wide smile.

"And Anatoli, where is Anatoli?" Svetlana asked with wonderment and amazement in her voice, as she walked with him, continuing to hug him and speaking at the same time. "It is so good to see you," she said, as she took his arm, and slowly walked toward the entrance.

"Anatoli is in the car; the girls are sleeping off sex, drugs and vodka, and we were just driving around after making a delivery," he smiled as he looked at her. "Now, what has Moussa done to you to cause this headache! He has been unkind to you. I will kill him, if he is not kind to you! I swear on my mother, I will kill him!"

"Is Moussa with me? No, I am with Gravev!" she said, her face taking on an expression of delight. "Yes, I have left my handsome Moussa. You are right! Moussa is not nice to me, so I am with Dimitri, my Dimitri," and they both laughed. "Dimitri Gravev—our boss!"

"My Sasha—I am just kidding! You must know that. Now, I tell you a secret. You must promise me, you must promise me," Svetlana whispered, as she leaned over and kissed him on his right cheek. "You must promise me. Moussa and I are on a secret holiday; no one is to know! And, now you find us! What to do! Oh! Sasha, what are we to do?"

"Svetlana, don't worry. Anatoli and I will tell no one. A secret trip! We are here, Svetlana. Can't we get together just once before you leave? We must see Moussa our partner. What do you say?" Sasha responded.

"Oh! Sasha," Svetlana, taking off her glasses, tears beginning to well in her eyes. "Sasha, we must have some time alone. This is our fifth anniversary. Would you believe it has been that long? I want to buy him a beautiful gift. What should I do? Now you and Anatoli are here. I will have no time with him. Sasha, you must promise me; please do not bother us. I must go. Promise me, Sasha. I love you. You are so good to me! Do not bother us though. It is our anniversary!" she said as she walked away, heading toward the cab directly in front of the hotel, blowing a kiss to him as she closed the door to the taxi.

She slumped into the seat, exhausted. "Take me to 64, Steinwiesstrasse. Quickly, please."

Sasha blew Svetlana a kiss as the taxi left the curb and headed up the street.

"Shit, Moussa is so fucking lucky. She is as pure as the first snow. I'd like to be in her. God, I would like to be in her all the way, every way," he laughed at his own words, knowing such a dream would never become a reality.

Sasha looked across the street and saw that Anatoli had parked the car on the opposite side at the intersection. Sasha walked over, and, as he opened the door, said, "Anatoli, it was Svetlana, and she said that this is her fifth anniversary with Moussa. He is here and wants to be alone with just her. And she took a cab and off she went."

"I know. I saw you and her. Why would she take a cab? The hotel they stay at is the Baur au Lac, just seven blocks from here."

"Maybe she does not like to walk seven blocks, Anatoli. She is a princess, you know that!" Sasha responded, again laughing at his own statement.

"No, let's see where she goes. Do you remember what direction?"

"Yes, toward the lake," replied Sasha.

"The only problem, Sasha, my friend," responded Anatoli, "is that I just spoke to Moussa's office in Moscow to tell him we will be coming back to Moscow tomorrow. My friend, he is not in Moscow. He is in Cyprus. She is not here with him. She is with someone else. We must find her, Sasha. We must, and then we will tell Moussa in Cyprus. I have his phone number there. And I wrote down the license plate number of the cab, so we shall have some information. I wasn't a KGB agent for nothing, right?" And they both laughed, knowing that they had something that would endear them to Moussa, who generally thought them to be fools, but enjoyed good times with them, and only that.

CHAPTER TEN

London
Friday
Local Time: 11:00 p.m. (6:00 p.m., Washington, D. C.)
St. Thomas Hospital, Lambeth Palace Road
Room 220 West

"*David . . . David, take that ugly look off your face. I'm not one of your targets. I really am sorry that I missed Tim's performance. You know how much I admire your family, but, now . . . I have so little time to talk to you. You see this bright light behind me? . . . It's brighter than the brightest sun you and I have ever seen. It never gets dark here; there are no midnight stars ever, just the coolness of this light. I like the way it feels, David. Don't gloom over me, and above all don't get angry at what I've done; I've done what I've done.*"

"Bob, cut the fuckin' crap. What the fuck did you teach me and the select few? Your three fucking pillars of life? I mean, come on now, I must have been fuckin' stupid; you were our God . . . our fuckin' God. Pillars. Remember: Discipline, Focus, Determination. Fuck you, man. You screwed me over. My whole family got hit because you were screwing someone you shouldn't have been with. What the fuck do you think? I should be happy? I don't give a shit about that light. Bob, what's wrong with you? Where the fuck is your head?

"*I'm not the hero you always wanted me to be. I am only me, David. The feeling of this . . . emptiness was too much . . . too much. . . . I know that I won't ever be alone again . . . this bright light is a friend forever—*"

"Emptiness? Fuck you . . . try selfishness. Hey! that's a good word, you fucker. Memorize it . . . you were fuckin' selfish. You taught us one *thing and practiced another. Why Bob? I don't want to think that all these years you were false in your teaching those fucking pillars of life. Whose life? Ours or yours? Or maybe no one's? Bob, maybe it's all a myth. Maybe you taught a myth? Maybe you've always been a myth."*

"*Get off the self-centered pity, David. What I taught you is no myth. It's reality in our business. You know as well as I. I should have never come back. I was too old, David, and yes, too weak, after Susan died. Too . . . too weak. You know I love you and Mary. That's all you need to know. I'm having trouble seeing you. Can you see me, David?"*

"*Barely, Bob. Oh, shit! Self-centered pity? What the fuck did you just say? You're the one who's self-centered and wallowing in pity. Fuck you, Bob . . . oh! shit! I'm having . . . hey, Bob. Where the hell are you going now? Bob, you know I don't want you to go now. Bob, don't go now. I just shot my mouth off. I know you've had a rough time. I didn't mean anything I said. I love you too, Bob. You made my life what it is; you've been part of it; you're the reason I'm where I am. Don't go, Bob. Please don't. We can have great times again . . . hey, my big buddy. . . . Don't go, Bob. It's okay. Stay with us, Bob. Oh, God! Stay with us . . . stay with us . . . don't ever go, Bob, don't ever leave us . . . don't . . . don't. . . ."*

The groans and sobs reached the corridor and prompted Nurse Evans to rush into the recovery room, concerned that something had gone wrong. She saw David Harrison sitting upright in bed, tears coming to his eyes. Ignoring him for a moment, she walked over to Mrs. Harrison to see if everything was in order with her. Quickly realizing that Mrs. Harrison was sleeping soundly and comfortably, she turned to Mr. Harrison, who had his head in his hands, his cries muffled, still calling out, "Bob . . . you can't leave . . . you can't."

"Mr. Harrison, Mr. Harrison, what's wrong? You were shouting for someone named Bob not to leave. You've had a nasty blow, and they can cause very bad nightmares, and the medication doesn't help much, I have to admit," Nurse Evans said. "Who's Bob? Whoever he is, you and he had a running conversation for a short while. Now, you must rest. You're a very lucky man, Mr. Harrison. The blows to your head were simple breaks of the outer skin on your forehead. You must have turned your head at just the right moment. I ask you, please lie back now and try to get some rest."

"Nurse," David said, without responding to her query about Bob, "how're my wife and son?"

"They're fine. Your wife is here in the same room with you. I don't think you woke her up with your loud cries, though. If you wish, I'll pull the curtain between the beds and you can see for yourself," Nurse Evans replied. Harrison nodded assent. She raised her right hand, slowly pulling the light blue curtain along the track in the ceiling that divided the room into two.

"Your son is fine as well, and he's also very lucky. The bullet grazed his shoulder, and the wound was less severe than anyone thought when he came in. Actually, the bullet must have gone elsewhere because it wasn't in his shoulder, nor anywhere else in his body. The police have posted guards outside this room, as well as outside your son's room—which is next door, 222," Nurse Evans said. "I have some good news for you too; you should be discharged as soon as Dr. Itani makes his final examination. He'll be here shortly," she said with a broad smile.

David didn't respond. He looked over to his right and saw Betty sleeping, the lower part of her face in bandages, but to David, her face was still flawless. He murmured to himself as he slowly got up, "I'm so sorry . . . I'm so very sorry."

"Easy, Mr. Harrison. We've given you some pain medication. Do you want more?"

"No, I don't want any medication at all," he said, realizing that any further medication would make him even less alert and able to do what he knew now he had to, and quickly. "I do want to know if anyone has called here." Nurse Evans continued to busy herself by arranging the water pitcher and glasses on his bedside table.

"Yes, a Mary Auriello called earlier from Washington. I took the call, and she said that she'd call around eleven or so, London time, which is about now." She looked at her wrist watch. "She wanted you to know that she's on her way to London and will arrive sometime early this morning. She seems very concerned about you. "

Without responding, David slowly rose from bed, put on the slippers that were on the foot mat, and shuffled over to his wife. Nurse Evans stood beside him, realizing there was little further she could do or say. He stood looking at Betty for several moments before he leaned over and kissed her forehead, then her cheeks, and finally her lips, saying gently, over and over again, "Honey . . . oh . . . no . . . not you . . . no, no. . . ."

"Mr. Harrison, you must get back to your own bed, otherwise you'll never get over the headache that is pounding away," Nurse Evans reached for his right arm. As he turned toward her, she saw in his face a look of anger.

"I'd like to see my son," Harrison softly said, as he started to drift to the door.

"Wait a minute, Mr. Harrison. Here, let me help you put this on first," Nurse Evans said as she reached for a navy blue bathrobe hanging on the open clothes rack. She held it as he placed one arm in a sleeve and then the other, with some apparent difficulty. "Mr. Harrison, you really should be back in bed. . . ."

Without responding, Harrison moved out the door and into the hall. She followed, but didn't attempt to stop him. Instinctively, he grabbed the rail on the side of the corridor to guide himself.

"Sir, can I help you?" asked one of two police officers near Harrison's room. Nurse Evans raised her hand, signaling them to leave Harrison alone.

He pushed open the door to his son's room, which was slightly ajar, and stood there trying to adjust his eyes to the semi-darkened room. His son, his only son, Timothy Harrison lay still, an intravenous drip making its way slowly into a needle taped to the back of his right hand. His left shoulder was hidden by a large surgical dressing. He was asleep. Harrison went over, and bent down, kissing him on his right cheek, keeping his lips to his son's face for several moments as if listening for a heart beat, feeling the warmth of his face, making sure that he was alive. "Oh! God, how I love you, Tim. I'm sorry, Tim, I'm sorry." Harrison murmured as he lifted his lips from his son's clear face.

Striving to hold back tears, Nurse Evans stood in the doorway, silent. As he approached her, she put out her hand to take his arm. This time, he let her do so.

"How long will my son be here?" he asked, his voice so soft as to be almost a whisper.

"Not, long, Mr. Harrison, perhaps three or four days. He'll be fine. In fact, he should be awake in a few hours," Evans replied as she walked him back to his room.

"Thank you for helping me, Nurse Evans," he said as he let his arm drop from her hand. He looked at his wife and stopped at her bed gazing at her, mouthing again, "I'm sorry, honey, sorry."

As he straightened himself, and headed toward his bed, he said to Evans, "I need to be alone for a moment, Nurse Evans. Thanks for helping me and my family." But as he said these kind words, the expression on his face didn't change, and his voice was emotionless; his pale blue eyes, which held tears when she went over to tend to him as he was dreaming, were no longer soft. The temples were taut, his lips barely moved when he spoke, and the voice was so quiet, so terrifyingly soft, that she could barely hear. But his anger was unmistakable, although for the moment, controlled. "Nurse Evans, if Ms. Auriello calls, you're to interrupt me for her call. Okay?"

"Certainly, I'll inform the operator and the duty station nurse."

He slumped into the dark blue fabric covered chair between his bed and the window, the drapes open to a still, cloudy, misty evening. He wanted so badly to curl up in some corner. For the first time in his life, Harrison felt utterly lost. "What was I afraid of? Oh! shit, those fuckin' class days . . . those fuckin' days. Fuck you, Bob. I am afraid . . . I *am* afraid. God, stinking, fucking afraid . . . my wife, my kid . . . almost killed . . . because they were with me . . . almost killed . . . fuckin' brave . . . how brave am I? Fuckin' afraid. Just a few hours ago, the world was a happy place for me and my family and now this fuckin' turn. My wife and son both injured. And Bob, probably dead. Fuckin' dream, yeah . . . the dream . . . oh! buddy . . . dead like all those we took out all those years. Why the hell am I crying? I'm so fuckin' scared . . . God . . . so fuckin' scared.

Something very wrong had happened with the mission. The fact that these events could happen to his family, to Bob, was a circumstance that he could never anticipate. "Maybe I should have, maybe I should have," he said to himself.

To that point in his career as a professional intelligence operative, his family had never been touched. Suddenly the battle was different, because the war was different. No longer was anyone less than a target in the new battleground; everyone around the real target, in fact, became a target. He knew he wouldn't remain idle. In time, he knew he would avenge those who had damaged his family and had taken out his friend.

First, he had to overcome this cold fear, a fear that only comes, he knew, when you watch your family almost taken away . . . his family the only thing he lived for. Harrison knew that as long as he was a target, he endangered his family. Having that knowledge, he was worried that he no longer had the edge, that extra dimension needed to continue in this alley war, as Bob so artfully described their work.

Yet, he also knew that if he was swayed by emotion, he was finished. Wasn't that what Bob instilled in him in his early training? "Emotional agents are dangerously wrong agents, and don't live long. Disciplined, focused agents are the successful ones and live longer." As hard as it would be, he had to put aside the emotional and deep trauma that he was experiencing. What alternative was there? What alternative was there? He couldn't abandon the mission, could he?

He reached over to the phone, dialing O for the hospital operator and asked her to call Commander Michael Robinson of Scotland Yard for Mr. David Harrison.

"Of course, sir. I'll be happy to do that for you," the cheery voice at the other end said. "I'll call you back directly."

As he replaced the phone on the receiver, he turned again, staring at his wife, realizing it was his career that had finally jeopardized his family. He had kept their lives separate, and nothing had ever interfered with this division. But this it was different, and he was also. As he continued to gaze at Betty, he murmured "Honey, I never thought it would get to this." He repeated "I'm sorry, I'm sorry" until the electronic tone of the phone sounded again, interrupting his slow and steady litany. He picked up the black push-button phone. "David Harrison."

"David, Michael Robinson here. I'm in my car coming directly to to see you and bring you up to date. Mary Auriello is to call you shortly. Anything you need?"

"Yeah, clothes. Can you send someone to the Carlton Tower to get them for me? I'm getting out of this hospital. Who's in charge?"

"I'll take care of the clothes request. We're lucky as to the investigating detective. It's Dean Goodwin, a young but aggressive bloke; he's bloody good, actually. Apparently, he's looking for the same man we are.

"The fellow took out two men at the Lowndes, one of whom, I believe, is your Colonel Boarders. Goodwin has a description of your assailant from the hotel security camera and it matches the one we have from a video that a tourist turned in to one of the investigating patrolmen. Also, I know that an intercept has been sent to Mary . . . but you know it goes directly to her . . . not shared at this end . . . so I don't know what it is . . . still doesn't trust the Brits . . . too many leaks this end, she keeps reminding me."

Rather than react to Robinson's comments, Harrison said, "You're certain it's Boarders?"

"Yes, he was one of the two found at the Lowndes. Mary asked that his body be removed to the Alconbury Air Force Base. I'm sorry, David; I know he was a friend and a man of great accomplishments. Mary's instructions to me are not to disclose any information on the colonel's death. We are, however, for the late news issuing a bulletin describing the assailant and have, of course, started our hunt for him. She believes, as I do, that he's still in London, although we've stepped up all surveillance at the airports, train as well as coach and channel ferry stations. It'll be difficult to spot him, so we must rely on his picture being televised and hope that someone will call in. I am bringing some preliminaries from Goodwin's initial investigation and he will be joining me to visit with you. Are you up to a short meeting?"

"Of course, I am. I want out of this hospital. How soon will you be here?

"Ten minutes."

"Good. See you then."

He looked over at Betty, saying quietly to himself, "I won't let anything like this happen to you again. Ever. I promise you that." As he began to get up from the chair to walk over to his wife, the electronic tone again sounded on the phone. This time, he knew who it would be.

"Mr. Harrison, a call for you from Ms. Auriello."

"David, how in the hell are you? The family?"

"You're a sound that I always want to hear, Mary. I'm fine, as are Betty and Tim. Oh! What the hell, Mary. I feel like shit . . . pure shit. Yeah. I know that Bob's dead. Robinson just told me. Some hit, Mary, some hit. Robinson and a Detective Goodwin are coming over with some preliminaries. I can't believe Bob is gone—hard to understand that, hard to understand . . . my wife and son hurt. Are you coming and when?" Harrison inquired, his voice breaking uncharacteristically.

"I'm about to take off for Alconbury, on my way to see you. You're okay, aren't you?"

"Yeah . . . maybe . . . maybe."

"David, I found myself sobbing in the park before coming back to the office for a meeting with the AG. What's there to say, David? Bob was the greatest. We both feel like shit now, David, but the time for grief will be later. You and I both know that. We have to conclude this mission, and soon, or some moronic *mafiya* salesman will get away with selling something he shouldn't have had in the first place. I briefed the AG and he thought that we should terminate the rest of the mission because of Boarders' death. I know that you know what my answer was to that. He was worried about the upcoming election. You know some crap about 'What if someone found out about Pentum?' and all that. No problem with our friend at the CIA, and I'll reach the president soon."

David smiled. He loved Mary's blunt, ruthless, truthfulness. Mary never changed, regardless. The mission was first and foremost, everything else secondary.

"Mary, it's hard to take. My family was almost taken out, Mary, I have to say, Mary, that maybe the edge to continue the mission—I don't know whether I have it anymore. I look at Betty and Tim, and but for me, they would be walking and laughing right now. It was me the fuckin' hit man was after, not them, but I was *with* them. He would have taken them out just to get me.

"I'm sorry, Mary . . . maybe we . . . you know . . . maybe we . . . should call it off. Without Bob—and in my condition—my family—I want to be with them now. You know I've never said that before. But now it's different. Very different."

"What am I hearing?" Mary's voice remained calm. She knew he was hurting, and there was no course other than to reason with him. "David Harrison bitter, despairing, when you should be indignant and scornful? Of course, you haven't lost the edge. Of course, you feel awful, weak, unsure. Let's face it, you don't watch your family wounded right in front of your own eyes every day. But, then, that's because we're lucky David, very, very lucky. All those places you've been—how many families in those places are protected from the crazies? None. Absolutely none. You know that as well as I do. I'm not going to get maudlin, but you figure that out.

"Okay? You want to leave? Fine. We'll call it quits. But that leaves unfinished business—a great deal of it. What about the contact? What about the bomb? How many people will get blown up if that thing is delivered? You know that for the three of us, life isn't a safe haven. You know that you believe in all we did. How many times have you turned near defeat to victory?"

"Mary, Mary, please, no pep talks. No lectures, please,—no admonition,—no call to the flag. I'm worn out and too old for this shit. Okay? I don't know if I want to continue to pay the price. You have to understand, Mary, just once, lay off the shit."

"No, not okay," she said, her voice rising. "Pity's out, David. It costs too much for us. I know that. But *we have already paid the price*. With both arms, David.

"I need your help. We don't have much time. This mission is going to be over by tomorrow night. I can't do it alone, and there's no one I can bring in. The cover for this mission is too deep. There's no one else. And we have two last things to do. David, are you going to help me?"

"Does the AG really have any influence over the president on this?

Would you listen, even if he told you to abort?"

"I thought I'd asked the question. Why do you always answer my question with one of your own? But who gives a shit? Oh, of course, I'd listen. I'm not a renegade. However, I won't abandon the contact and I won't let that nuke be delivered. The AG thinks he has some chits, but I don't care. The president won't change his mind. One thing he isn't: a coward. He's not that. We're going to finish this mission. We'll discuss that when I see you. Now, are you still on board or are we worried about whether you have the edge?"

"The contact never arrived at the theater," David responded, "but then if the contact did, I wouldn't have known anyway. Only Bob knew what the contact looked like."

"David, don't you ever answer a question? Why do you answer my question with something irrelevant," she laughed. "Yes, that's correct. You'll have to take over from Bob and sort that one out, David. We have to get her out. There's no question about that. None in my mind. In yours?"

"I wanted you to know how I feel. This is different, just different. You know that."

"Yes, I know that more than you, David, more than you. You on board? Are you? I want to know, David. Now." For a few moments, there was silence. She had never demanded anything of David, or for that matter, of Bob, before.

"Yes, Mary, I am, but I have to tell you, the man who turned defeat into victory is fuckin' scared, Mary, very frightened. I'm not kidding you, Mary, not at all, not at all."

"Good. We've got a lot to discuss, so get some rest and I'll see you in a few hours."

"What about this intercept that Robinson mentioned?"

"Thanks, David. I'll see you shortly. Did I ever tell you I hated to fly? I mean I get dizzy standing on a chair."

"Yeah, you did, when I was with you over Turkey in a thunderstorm. Even you turned pale, almost passed out, but then Bob and I had to jump out of the plane," Harrison said, laughing, as he remembered that night several years ago.

"Did you have to bring that up? You're scared? How do you think I feel now? Six hours in a flying aluminum tube, not my idea of a nice time. Oh, the intercept. You see why I don't trust the Brits, they can't stop talking. Yeah—I have it. I'll see you soon, David. Now sleep off that headache. I'll let you know what's in it when I see you."

"Good bye, Mary. Hurry across the water."

"I'll be at Alconbury around six this morning. Take care. See you then."

Mary couldn't lose another agent. Even if she'd told Harrison what the intercept showed, he was in no condition to go to 164 Cadogan Place, the locale of the intercepted call, and terminate the assassin. But then he would have to go alone, and in his condition—who knows? No, she couldn't take the chance now. Eliminating the *mafiya*'s hit man wouldn't solve the problem. No, she was after the big fish, and she needed to save the contact. For that, she needed Harrison.

The assassin would be given a reprieve for now. Maybe the Brits would catch him. She smiled as she adjusted her seat belt for the take-off. As soon as the plane was airborne, she would alert Robinson. She would give him a chance to redeem himself; perhaps he would catch the hit man.

The departure clock on the cabin wall indicated it was 6:30 p.m., Washington; the adjacent destination clock read 11:30 p.m., London. A third digital clock indicating the flight time automatically began as the plane lifted from the runway: 06:00 with the seconds and minutes rapidly descending. Mary settled in as she gazed at the dusk settling over Washington. She opened her brief case and took out a card she'd had plasticized and always carried in a pocket in the side of the case. She smiled as she read: "If we win, nobody will care. If we lose, there will be nobody to care." Winston Churchill. Below Churchill's name was written: "Actually I wrote this for him! Bob." Boarders had given her and David the card after the success of the Lebanon missions.

The powerful twin jet engines of the long range Citation Jet at full throttle, the all-dark gray plane lifted from a private airfield just outside Middleburg, Virginia, the only identifying mark on its tail N852A. As

Mary eyed the card, she knew how truthful those words rang with regard to the last Pentum mission she knew would ever be undertaken. Without Bob the indestructible bear, she was frightened. "You can always stop the beginnings, but once you start, there's no stopping," Boarders had said long ago in Paris, so very long ago. She heard the roll of thunder, and gripped the side arms of her seat as the plane gained speed and altitude.

She thought of the big smile of Boarders, one she would never see again. "Hey! little Mary, our real leader, did anyone ever tell you you're not bad looking?" Never the smile again, never. She closed her eyes, praying that the pilot would take them above the dark rain clouds quickly.

Moscow
Friday
Local Time: 8:00 p.m. (5:00 p.m., London)
Library of Dimitri Gravev's Dacha
Thirty kilometers southeast of Moscow, near the village of Barvikha

Dimitri moved politely but solemnly, with studied and considerate good manners, as he greeted the guests in his library. His impassive face hid his worry about whether the activity that Bradford had organized to be carried out in London would be accomplished. In these kinds of meetings, Dimitri was quiet and listened carefully. He made decisions calmly, never impulsively. The men—Prakash Farnak, the Iranian middle man headquartered in Moscow; Frederik von Hauser, a Swiss banker; Jomhori Shenasi, the Iranian ambassador in Moscow; and Maj. Gen. Yuri Nikolayev, together with Dimitri's aides, Sergei Mironov and Andrei Leskov—were seated around a large, lacquered mahogany table.

Dimitri's library was perhaps the most impressive room in his dacha. There was a sense of serene harmony in the room. This was where he preferred to hold his meetings and forge his business deals. From beams of mahogany of equal lengths, crossing the ceiling hung two ornate brass chandeliers, each with 32 electric candles, casting a glow across the fifteen-by-twenty-foot rectangular conference table. The floor was hand-laid cut slate from England, over which lay a large, silk, beige and green antique oriental carpet from Iran, or so the London dealer had told Dimitri and his wife, neither of whom really had the time or inclination to check out that bit of information.

The seats of the twelve chairs around the table were covered with a green damask, of a color virtually identical to the marble covering one-third of the walls of the thirty-five-by-forty-foot room. From the point where the marble ended, bookcases covered the walls to the ceiling height of twelve feet, but only on the left side of the room. The shelves held volumes of history and biographies of political leaders, many in English and in German, as well as in Russian.

Carefully arranged on the remaining three, dark mahogany paneled walls hung oil paintings of Russian pastoral scenes, all framed in similar, plain, golden frames. One was especially a favorite of Dimitri's, depicting the village in Khazakstan where he was born, and which he had commissioned a local artist to paint. The painting held the place of honor above the green marble mantle. There was little other furniture in the room, save for two hunter-green leather arm chairs flanking the fireplace, which was dark this evening. Behind the head of the table and directly opposite the fireplace stood an antique buffet table on which rested two electric brass candelabras. The hunter-green, fine wool drapes, which hung loosely from large corner brass rings on either side of the four eight-foot windows, were open. There never was a need to draw the drapes, because no one could get onto the property without first going through the security gate, about a mile from the main entrance. In any event, the library faced the heavily forested side of the property. By habit, Dimitri always liked to have drapes or curtains open. Although he rarely spoke about it, he was somewhat claustrophobic.

"Before we begin, I want to say how much I appreciate your waiting for me to come this evening. I like to spend time with my wife at the end of the day, as this is the only moment that I can get caught up on family matters. I trust that you found the food and drink to your satisfaction." Dimitri surveyed the seated gentlemen and addressed the housekeeper: "Please, Irina, bring us some fresh coffee and tea."

"Of course," replied Irina, as she cleared the remaining plates from the table. "I shall be but a moment."

"Thank you, Irina. You are most helpful."

"Ambassador Shenasi, Prakash Farnak, and of course, Frederik von Hauser, and General Nikolayev, you are welcome to my house. I understand from Sergei and Andrei that you have gone over the documents regarding the financial arrangement for this sale. Naturally, this is most important from our perspective. Do you still wish to purchase this device, Ambassador?" Dimitri asked, knowing what the response would be.

"Dimitri Gravev, we look around the room, and our friend and your colleague, Peter Bradford, is not here. Will he be joining us for the meeting?" Shenasi inquired.

"We had intended for him to be at this meeting, but an emergency has come up, and he will be late. If he is unable to come later, I shall discuss with him what transpired tonight."

"As you know, we have had several meetings with Peter, your assistant, Moussa Berdayev, and yourself. The selling price is firm at 350 million U.S. dollars; one half has already been delivered to Mr. von Hauser's bank to an account set up for one of your companies, and the other half will be transferred upon arrival of the device in Iran. In a phone conversation today, Peter indicated that this remains the arrangement between us. Further, the memorandum given to us by Peter at the last meeting regarding further purchases—have you decided on whether those are possible?"

Dimitri hid the anger that he felt because Bradford failed to tell him of the phone call, but replied, "Naturally, we should complete one business deal before we embark on others. So, the additional, extensive armaments listed on Peter's memorandum will require some discussion . . . at a later time. As I have just said, we must successfully complete this deal first before we embark on something else. Agreed?"

Without waiting for a response, Gravev continued, "What we have this evening is the only business arrangement. Nothing further at this point. But, what is important to us is that the origin of the purchase be hidden. General Yuri Nikolayev has assured me of this. Is that not so, General?"

"Yes, Dimitri, no one will know the source of the sale," General Nikolayev replied, staring past Dimitri and toward the montage of paintings on the wall behind Dimitri, a stare which did not go unnoticed by Dimitri.

"Good. That is essential if the sale is to go through. Ambassador Shenasi, have your technicians examined the device and found it to their satisfaction?"

"Yes," and he looked at Prakash Farnak, saying, "Actually, Prakash and General Nikolayev accompanied the technicians to the site in Turkmenistan and they conducted certain tests which indicated the device was operational. We are satisfied that the device will serve our purpose."

Ambassador Jomhori Shenasi, a lawyer educated both at the University of Teheran and also at Oxford, had joined the Khomeni movement when the revolutionary leader was in exile in Paris in the 1970s. He never appeared to be a mild person. A man of medium height and build, he had a rounded forehead, narrow but thick black eyebrows, and black eyes. His face had a dry, deep olive complexion and a fine mouth, with lips pursed so thin that they were revealed only when he spoke.

Before joining Khomeni in Paris, Shenasi lived in London and helped with a newspaper that circulated anti-shah propaganda to the Iranian community in London. At 50, his manners were impeccable toward Dimitri, but behind his courteous behavior lay a more sinister person. Upon his return to Iran, Khomeni appointed Jomhori to be Chief Magistrate of the Revolutionary Tribunal which tried many pro-shah supporters, supporters whose crime was that they were middle-class professionals and businessmen who declined to follow the rule of Khomeni. All were executed, exiled or jailed. When the courts were disbanded, Jamhori was first appointed ambassador to France, and then to Russia, when the Soviet Union collapsed in 1991.

Dimitri believed him to be brilliant and dedicated, but beyond that lacked any confidence in what the ambassador told him about his country's intended use of the device. Dimitri knew that the ambassador's wife and his two sons and one daughter were passengers in the ill-fated Iran Air Flight shot down in 1988 by a missile from the American cruiser,

Vincennes. The Ambassador recalled this incident as an example of what he termed the "evil ego of the U.S. devil." But Dimitri also believed that Jomhori loved power, for he appeared to relish the position he had during the tribunal days, when he could decide the fate of others. When Shenasi first met Dimitri, he quickly worked his early tribunal activities into the conversation, as if such a review of his terror would intimidate Dimitri. Dimitri never commented, changing the subject.

"And, General Nikolayev, the logistics for getting the device to Teheran? Are they in place?"

"Yes, Dimitri. They are. The plane has been provided by the Iranian Ambassador and will be waiting for us at an abandoned military field near Ashgabat, Turkmenistan. The device is still at your warehouse, awaiting your word to your manager that permission is granted by you to load it on the airplane."

"Thank you, my good friend and bank client, General Nikolayev," Dimitri replied now with a smile. "It is true, gentlemen. The general is an excellent client of the bank, and we like your business, General, always."

"Of course, Dimitri. Of course. We receive good service from you."

Maj. Gen. Yuri Nikolayev, about the same age as Dimitri, was rumored to have been involved in the abortive coup to replace Gorbachev in August 1991, which failed when the coup was crushed, the USSR collapsed, and Boris Yeltsin became President of Russia. After that fiasco, General Nikolayev retired and organized a trading company called Global Investments, Ltd. Although the title was grand, it was a one-man company. In fact, the general had no office and worked out of his central Moscow city apartment. He and Prakash Farnak, the Iranian middleman, spent many hours at Farnak's Metropol Hotel office.

Whenever arms from the old Soviet Union were marketed, it was he who had the contact with the successor Russian military and defense ministry. He was thought to have bought, at virtually give-away prices, many armaments, including battlefield missiles and light armored vehicles, from the Russian army that was leaving the eastern part of Germany. In addition, he maintained his contacts with all the successor republics, especially those in the Far East, where the old KGB had substantial influence in the governing bodies of those countries. General Nikolayev lived alone and was divorced. He had no children.

Dimitri had met him with Prakash Farnak when Bradford brought him along to Dimitri's office to discuss, for the first time, the nuclear sale to Iran. Dimitri recognized the magnitude of his activity, for much of the money for the general's business arrangements flowed through Dimitri's bank, Bank Alliance Russia.

"Prakash Farnak, you're spending good time at the Metropol? You don't want to lease space at one of my Republic Towers overlooking the Moscow River? I will charge you only $3,500 per square meter, a real bargain!"

"Do I get the best view of the river?" Prakash inquired sheepishly.

"Yes, and we have excellent security, just in case someone is after you, my friend. You know how dangerous they say Moscow is," Dmitri said, smiling as he continued the dialogue with Farnak.

"The security is provided by your company. Is it not, Dimitri?"

"Of course, we have the best in the country. We have never lost a tenant through death, other than by natural means," and with that everyone around the table laughed loudly, interrupted only by Irina placing a fresh pot of coffee and another of tea.

"Is that all, Dimitri Gravev?" she asked.

"Yes, thank you. And, please, we wish not to be disturbed for a while," Dimitri responded.

"Certainly," Irina left by the service door at the far right end of the room.

Prakash Farnak, had a high and receding forehead, an oval face with a rather long nose; he was olive in complexion and short in stature. He would make his guests happy with the least possible expenditure of sincerity. He was able to dazzle Russian businessmen with his opulent life style.

He had two suites at the five-star Moscow Metropol Hotel, one serving as his office and the other as his residence. Obviously funded by the Iranian government, he appeared stiff, yet captivated everyone by his charm in conversation. He always seemed to have a secret to hide and liked to flatter himself, giving himself the air of invincibility.

But no one, including Dimitri, could doubt his ability to get armaments for his clients. He was successful, and his network of arms supplies deep inside the Russian military was recognized, even by Dimitri. Dimitri had almost no contact with him until this venture, and he looked the other way when, over the years, Peter Bradford and his own cousin, Leonid Karanikov, did, from time to time, trade drugs for arms, especially through their contacts in Afghanistan, and he knew that both of them were close to Prakash. Dimitri knew the extent of the sales, but there was no reason for interfering unless that work impeded their own work for him.

The people who appreciated Prakash were those was needed him. Otherwise, he was despised. In reality, he didn't like Russians, and in private, disparaged them as fools, lacking in knowledge of the true worth of the products they were selling. He never knew how he would emerge from any negotiation, but one thing he did know was that he would make the most money. This was the third time Dimitri had met him.

"I see that our Swiss banker, as usual, has filled his plate with Russian sweets? My friend, Frederik, how do these compare to Swiss sweets? I'm sure, much sweeter?" and with that Dimitri raised his voice and pretended to be prepared for a surprise answer.

"These are much better, for these sweets are being served in your home. Anything served in your home is the best!" replied Frederik von Hauser. "What else could I say?" And the room broke out in laughter.

"Ah! Spoken like a diplomat, Frederik."

At 45, Frederik von Hauser was big but possessed no physique likely to inspire admiration. His body was shaped almost exactly like a barrel, in that it bulged at all the wrong places. He had no neck; his head sat immediately on his shoulders. His face was white and round; two big, pale blue eyes looked at the world with awe and timidity; his mouth was hidden beneath a carefully trimmed mustache and a bold segment of head rose above a ridge of sandy hair. Dimitri thought of him as a person devoid of anything heroic, but especially devoid of anything unkind. In character, he was the mildest and least offensive of men. He sold his banking skills to the highest bidder, and, as a Swiss banker, he fit perfectly well with the arrangements being discussed this evening.

He was Managing Director of Braun & Cie, a private Swiss bank with a limited and wealthy client base.

"But, Frederik, is our money in your bank still safe? I ask you, Frederik, as safe as it would be in my bank?" Dimitri said, speaking with a broad smile on his face.

"Not as safe as in your bank. We, in Switzerland, don't have your company providing our security," von Hauser replied. "When will you open a branch of your company in Zurich? We need you!" Again, everyone laughed.

"It is done. I shall have a branch of Bank Alliance Russia in Zurich and your bank will merge with mine. Enough said. It is done," Dimitri said, in a tone that was different from the humor just preceding. There was a moment of silence as everyone tried to understand the meaning of his remark. Then, after what seemed like a very long time, especially to von Hauser, Dimitri said, "Of course, Frederik, I was only joking, but it is a thought. We should discuss this at some point soon."

After some hesitation, von Hauser spoke somewhat carefully, "Yes, but there are so many legal barriers in Switzerland preventing this kind of merger. But we shall discuss, yes, we shall discuss it. It is an very interesting idea, Dimitri, a very interesting idea."

"More than an interesting idea, Frederik. We shall do it! I don't want to hear about barriers! All I hear from the West is barriers. Everyone wants to come to Russia and steal from us, and no one lets Russian companies go West. Why is that? We have Western banks right here in Moscow. Citibank. Now we have all heard of Citibank, haven't we? And they have a Zurich branch. Well, why not Bank Alliance Russia? Why not? The answer is that no one trusts us, but they only want to use us. Is Citibank really more secure than my bank? Only because the U.S. government will bail them out if something goes wrong. The Russian government would probably spit on us if we needed their help. Well, enough of this. Frederik, I am quite serious. I want a bank in Zurich. My own bank. I want to see Bank Alliance Russia's name on a building in Zurich. After all, we provide your private bank with over fifty percent of its deposits. Should that not mean something?" Dimitri inquired.

"Yes, you're our best customer, and we appreciate that. But Swiss law demands—"

Dimitri cut von Hauser off with an outburst that so contrasted with the earlier humor that it surprised even his aides. "Swiss law? What are you talking about? Swiss law? The Swiss law encourages deposits from foreign companies such as mine, and I might add, foreign individuals such as me, but they make it very difficult, if not impossible, for a bank such as mine to have a branch in Zurich. I shall have a branch there in due course. Mark my word, Frederik, mark my word," Dimitri said as he brought his hand down on the pad in front of him, causing the pencil at the top of the pad to fly and roll off the table.

As his aide Sergei reached for it, Dimitri said, "No, leave it, Sergei. I will pick it up myself. You are not my servant. I am my own servant."

And with that he reached down, picked up his pencil and rearranged it at the top of the pad. He looked at all the faces, wondering what was going through their heads, silently measuring them one by one: Farnak, "he would shit on his mother for money . . . and on me"; Shenasi, "a religious fanatic who will use the device. It won't be tested. It will be used"; Nikolayev, "a disgraced man with disgraced friends"; von Hauser, "can be bought for the highest amount." "But then," he thought to himself, "what other kinds of people would be in this business?" He was beginning to feel that he should stop the deal . . . no, although he did not like this, he was committed to go forward. Honor is important in business deals. Your word is honor and must be kept.

"Let us review the matter, Ambassador Shenasi," Dimitri quietly said. Everyone knew the meeting would now begin.

"Several months ago, on your behalf, Prakash Farnak approached Peter Bradford for assistance in locating a special weapon that he said your country needed. Peter's friendship and long standing relationship with General Nikolayev allowed for the location of the special armament. As you know, my bank is the repository of Prakash's funds and for that we are most thankful, Prakash. After those initial meetings, and again through Prakash, one of my companies was involved in the sale of certain armaments to a brother country of yours, Ambassador Shenasi.

"Although we were successful in delivering the required arms, the ship was destroyed just before arriving at its destination, a most unfortunate occurrence. I am concerned because the entire operation was a closely held-secret, and yet I believe agents from the United States knew everything and were able to destroy the ship, sinking its cargo and killing its crew, all innocent people. How certain are we that this will not occur again? Ambassador Shenasi, you indicated that you had an earlier conversation with Peter. Has anyone else had a conversation regarding this project with anyone else today?"

"I spoke with Ambassador Shenasi today," volunteered von Hauser. "But we were checking on the transfer of money necessary to complete the deal. I believe the funds are already at Credit Suisse, Zurich, under the name of an Iranian company, for which the ambassador has signatory power. The bank transfer request is already at the bank and is just awaiting the ambassador's approval."

"Yes, under our agreement, the device has to arrive in Iran, prior to the remaining funds being released to you, Mr. Gravev," the ambassador replied.

"Naturally, I spoke to Peter today," General Nikolayev said. "It was important to coordinate certain transportation details that I spoke about earlier this evening. The device is at your warehouse in Turkmenistan waiting to be moved to the airport, upon your approval."

"Peter and I had a conversation today about this meeting," said Prakash Farnak, "and we were just bringing each other up to date. As you know, we are most anxious to get the device to Iran per our agreement."

"Sergei Mironov, what does our agreement say about intended use?" asked Dimitri.

"Yes, Dimitri," responded Dimitri's young lawyer assistant. "We have a short one-and-one-half-page agreement. The last paragraph states that the device is for scientific and experimental purposes only. However, there is no penalty if the clause is violated."

"Very good, attorney Sergei, very good. There are no penalties. Ambassador Shenasi, does your country still intend to use the device for the purposes my friend Andrei just described?"

"Nothing has changed, Dimitri. Nothing has changed. My government will use the device as a test to demonstrate to the world that we have a nuclear weapon, just as the United States, France, the United Kingdom, of course Russia, Israel, Pakistan, India, and perhaps South Africa and maybe even Brazil do. What is it that makes others believe that Iran should not have the weapon, but all those I just listed can? The only country to ever use nuclear weapons was the United States. And the United States is the country that is trying desperately to prevent my country from having the weapon. Why? Because they want to protect Israel. The U.S. is not interested in any Muslim nation, except those that bow to it and receive tokens in return as payments for the oil we have.

"We intend to have the weapon. This purchase will only make it sooner, rather than later. And naturally, we thank you for working with us to achieve these goals."

Dimitri wished to appear calm, although he was annoyed. Nor did he wish to be insensitive to the business arrangement that had been worked out, but political lectures he certainly did not need nor appreciate.

"Ambassador Shenasi," Dimitri looked at him directly, "we are not here for a political discourse. We are here to execute a business deal and conclude arrangements for it. I understand what you are saying, but for me it is not relevant. Your politics are your own, but you would be making a dangerous mistake if you believe that I do not care whether a business deal is carried out precisely in accord with the agreement. I am interested in how the device is used, and I will know immediately if it is not used in accord with the arrangement that you and I have. I do not like surprises, Ambassador Shenasi.

"You would be making an even greater mistake of judgment if you seriously believe that if you violate the agreement there is nothing that I can do in return. Certainly there would be no further dealings with you or your country. I can assure you of that."

At that comment, the ambassador broke into the statement, saying caustically, "Dimitri Gravev, I know of your ability to seek vengeance and I do not intend to deviate from our agreement at all. Your threat, if it is one, is not necessary, and, frankly, is insulting."

As Dimitri's assistants, Sergei Mironov and Andrei Leskov, so well knew, when Dimitri got very angry, he became silent.

For several minutes he stared at the ambassador, saying nothing.

The silence in the room was broken only when Frederik von Hauser asked, "Dimitri, would you be kind enough to pass the coffee?"

After a moment of continued silence, Dimitri said, "Of course, Frederik. Anyone else? Frederik, after you, I shall have some, and I think the ambassador may need some too. Ambassador Shenasi, coffee?"

Without waiting for his reply, von Hauser turned to Shenasi, who was seated next to him, and poured some coffee for him, then for Dimitri, and lastly for himself.

The silence continued until Dimitri spoke, "Of course, Ambassador, we understand fully your view. We all wish you a long and prosperous life. I also understand that you may be promoted to Minister of Foreign Affairs. My good assistants have given me that information. That would be a grand appointment, and one that would be worthy for someone such as yourself, a very worthy appointment. I hope that you are successful in securing such a position. Now, I know your statement about threats was made in jest. Like you, I abhor threats. I think it more important to take action rather than give empty threats. Behavior is very difficult to change, as I am sure you agree. So a threat becomes meaningless when it is apparent that behavior will not change. The only solution is action."

Then, with his voice rising ever so slowly and looking directly at Shenasi, Dimitri continued, "You will live up to the agreement that you are signing this evening. I expect nothing less. If you have any problem living up to the agreement, then let us end the evening at this point and remain the friends that we are, rather than severe enemies if either one fails to live up to the agreement. Understood?" And, as he said that, he looked around the table and saw that the rest of the group were all staring at their pads of paper.

"Naturally, I understand. But, you must realize, Dimitri, that I cannot control my government once the device is in the country."

"You cannot control your government? You do not know how they ultimately will use the device? Come now, my friend. That is difficult to comprehend. You have stated that your government will use this for scientific and test purposes, nothing further."

"What I mean to say is that if our government is overthrown, although highly unlikely, the device may fall in the hands of the new government, and who knows what can happen. Right?"

"I am not worried about Iran being taken over by a new government. I am worried about the present government. I will need an addendum from your government agreeing with their ambassador about the use of the device. Can you obtain that for me? If your government were to use the device, it would create an impossible situation in the region ... impossible."

"Yes, I will obtain a clarification about the device's use. I have the authority to negotiate this purchase which is what I told Peter. He never asked for what you are now asking."

"Please get the document. I would like it by six a.m. tomorrow, which is when I arise. Send it by fax to my office in Moscow, and one of my aides will call me to tell me that it has arrived and read it to me. This is only fair."

"Agreed, it is only fair, but I wish Peter had told me about this before. Now, it may be difficult to explain to the foreign minister as well as to the president."

"I am sure you have brought them news before. This should come as no surprise. They are probably wondering why we did not ask for it in the first place."

"It shall be done."

"There is nothing further to discuss, gentlemen. We await the document. Once I have word of its receipt, I shall give the approval to airlift the device to Iran. If the ambassador gets me the required document, then I shall be satisfied, and there will be no delay for the flight to leave Turkmenistan. It is now ten p.m. and we all have had a heavy day, so we must get some rest. I understand that Ambassador Shenasi will take Frederik and Prakash home; General, you have your own car and driver... so we are set. By the way, Frederik, you are now staying at a different hotel, the Hotel Kempinski. You did not like the Penta?"

"Yes, I liked the Penta. But this is newer and my office suggested I stay there. It is closer—"

"Yes, I know, closer to the ambassador's office," interjected Dimitri. "You leave for Zurich this evening, Frederik?" Dimitri inquired.

"Yes, I have a charter flight waiting for me at Sheremetyevo."

"Ah! the joys of a private aircraft. In a few hours you will be in your own bed. Well, Frederik, a good flight to you," replied Dimitri.

Dimitri then rose, and, as he did, everyone else did. His aides headed toward the door and held it open as Dimitri shook each hand, standing by the door, saying good night to each.

He doubted that the Iranians would use the weapon as a test . . . but the document would protect him. If the Iranians wanted to lie, that was their problem. But he would never deal with them again, nor would he deal with Bradford again, but that removal was for another time.

On the Ring Road Returning to Moscow
Local Time: 10:00 p.m. (8:00 p.m., London)
Mercedes Limousine, Diplomatic Plates 786145M

"He must never know what we intend to do with the device. Understood? Frederik and Prakash?" Shenasi quietly said. "You are being paid handsomely for keeping this to yourselves. This arrogant Dimitri will get nothing. We shall have the weapon; Peter and the general have their money, and they both will be gone. There will be nothing Dimitri can do. Both of you will be gone as well. He will not be able to touch anyone, including me. Of course, Frederik and Prakash, you both have already received some of your funds, and more will be on the way. You have been very diligent in helping me and my government. That stupid document Dimitri wants will be drafted in my office tonight and sent to him. Dimitri is not as smart as he thinks, nor will he choose how we use the device. We have already decided that issue, and he can remain in the dark. We are pretending to pay him and that is all he has to know. Don't you agree, my friends?" Shenasi smiled.

Both von Hauser and Farnak nodded their heads as Shenasi continued, "The general is following us, I see, and he will join us at the office for some tea. We must make sure nothing will go wrong with the delivery tomorrow. The device is expected in Iran tomorrow evening. Nothing can stop these plans . . . nothing."

Unknown to the ambassador and the general, the black Volvo directly in front of the ambassador's limousine and the navy blue Audi much further back and behind the general's car were being driven by employees of Dimitri's security company. Dimitri would know where his recent guests would continue the meeting.

But he would not know the purpose of the meeting; he could only guess, and his guess would be right. Shenasi, von Hauser, Farnak, and Nikolayev were not having tea. They were trying to circumvent the additional requirement he had just placed on the sale. As he took the call from the driver of the lead car telling him of the arrival at the ambassador's residence of all four, he kept to himself his thoughts about the deal, about Bradford, and about the four who were continuing the meeting without him.

CHAPTER ELEVEN

Zurich
Friday
Local Time: 4:00 p.m. (3:00 p.m. London)
No. 64, Steinwiesstrasse, Apt. 10

Unable to suppress a shudder, her heart pounding, Svetlana left the taxi cab and walked into the wide marble vestibule of the five-storied apartment building in the middle of a quiet residential street. Weary from the tension that goes with any escape, exhausted by stress and the change in plans, she was even more distressed by the fact that she had been seen in Zurich, first by the business hustler Jess Stevens, and then by the grotesque friends, Anatoli and Sasha, of her lover Moussa. Why, she asked herself, was she really surprised? She had come to Zurich with Moussa, almost monthly for the last several years—as had his friends. Stevens was another matter. He followed whatever Russian money he could get his hands on . . . and many Russians made the pilgrimage to Zurich just to see their bankers.

But the fact is that she was seen. Nothing could change that reality, and now the consequences were unfolding. She knew at least one thing for certain, that her escape had been made known. To the hunters she had become the prey. Their energies would be further stimulated by the offer of rewards of whatever nature for her return, from Moussa, perhaps even from Peter Bradford, and the Moscow *vor* Dimitri Gravev. She would not be a forgotten fugitive.

Svetlana had entrusted her life and that of her mother to Colonel Boarders. She believed him, or she never would have started down the path that had led her to this curious and silent apartment building. Svetlana was under no illusions. She was a volunteer, and nothing is ever safe or certain for such a person.

To let herself into the front door, Svetlana used the larger of the two keys she had retrieved from the envelope taken from the bank deposit box. She avoided the elevator directly ahead because the elevator light indicated it was being used. Rather than wait, Svetlana walked the five floors of gray marble steps to apartment ten, which was directly to the left, at the top of the steps and at the end of a short corridor, painted light gray. A small skylight above the door to the apartment disguised an otherwise nondescript entryway with rich, bright, late afternoon sunlight. As she took the second key and inserted it into the lock, turning it sharply, she heard the lock bolt disengage, and she opened the plain gray door on which a small black and white plaque announced: Mr. and Mrs. Frederick Pentum, Apt. Ten.

She stood still, accustoming herself to the narrow, unlit apartment foyer, the only light coming through an arched opening leading from the foyer to the living room, where sunlight streamed through a oversized balcony glass double door... enough illumination for Svetlana to notice an ornately carved brass plate, resting in the middle of a long, narrow, rosewood table on which lay a small light blue envelope. Printed in neat lettering was her new name: "Helene LeFevre." Had Colonel Boarders been here? Had he? Such complete detail amazed and comforted her. It gave her a sense of protection.

She took the envelope and walked slowly through the archway into a grand living room, at one end of which a sliding-glass door opened onto a small balcony overlooking the front of the building, the street and a small garden below. She passed a sitting area where two off-white, flowered quilted fabric couches sat face-to-face, separated by a rectangular marble and oak coffee table, decorated with a generous arrangement of fresh flowers. The walls of the apartment were soft white, with the small wall space adjacent to the sliding door painted a muted green. Oak cube glass tables stood on either side of the couches holding simple wooden lamps with cream lampshades. Positioned about the room were lounge chairs of differing sizes. Although Svetlana found the room warm and comforting, she was in no disposition to enjoy its serene atmosphere. It is a sharp sting to understand reality. She couldn't unconscioulsy act, in tone and manner, as if she were really free, because that wasn't her condition.

At the other end of the room she noted a dining area with a large, round, glass table on a large oak cube, with six, modern, oak spindle chairs. Two brown-tinted, tall, fluted glass candlestick holders contained beige candles with a pale brown, unfilled, glass bowl centered between them. A smoke-brown glass buffet table stood against the far wall. Modern art lined the walls of both rooms. Normally, Svetlana would have been interested in such art, but now ignored it.

She slid the door silently along its tracks and stepped onto the flower filled balcony, sitting in one of the two wicker chairs separated by a small, wicker, glass-top table on which rested a small basket of potted lavender geraniums. On the left side of the balcony was a glass-top, wrought iron table where several green plants of various types sat on pewter plates; a large potted ficus grew in the opposite corner, close to Svetlana. She stared at the intricately designed oriental pot where the tree was placed, and then at the stark white apartment building across the street from which hung many flower boxes brimming with multicolored pansies. They gave the building a fairy tale appearance.

A large, stout, middle age, black haired woman was busily watering the flower boxes arranged on the top of her balcony rail at the same level as Sveltlana's apartment. She looked over to Svetlana, and waved vigorously.

Svetlana's heartbeats were now plainly audible to her—again she had been seen. "Who is that woman? Who? I don't recognize her. Should I? Have I ever seen her before? Have I? No? No? It is an innocent gesture . . . isn't it? Should I wave back? Should I go back into the apartment, pretending that I didn't see the greeting?. Is everyone now an adversary? What to do?" The outlines of what she had to do drew clearer, for the women kept waving vigorously, as if expecting a wave in return, before she would stop her gestures. Svetlana reluctantly raised her right hand to wave back meekly. After acknowledging the woman's greeting, Svetlana turned and went inside her own apartment.

Svetlana's senses now wandering, her hands trembling, she slowly lifted the flap of the envelope in her hand, noting that it had been only lightly sealed. She slipped out the light blue card where she read these typewritten words:

```
    Car keys are located in the desk drawer in the bedroom.
Car is located in the parking lot behind this building.
It is a black Volkswagen cabriolet, Zurich plates 145-698.
Drive to Einsiedeln, located approximately 50 kilometers
south of Zurich. You will go to the "Court" entrance of
the Monastery and ask for Abbot Hans Polzherr. Present
the small enclosed card to the Abbot. The Abbot will
arrange for your safekeeping. When you arrive at
Einsiedeln, call 589-5677 with this message:

This is your weather advisory. The sun will rise from the
northeast.

    We will come for you within twenty-four hours of the
phone call. You are to take the envelope and place this
message in it, seal the envelope, and place it back on
the hall table. Keep the small card.
                                      B.
```

Svetlana looked at the small blue card that had the word "Pentum" centered on it. Below the word was a small circle with an owl on one side and an eagle on the other, divided by a bold blue line. She gazed at the card for some time, trying to understand the significance of the circle, the owl, and the eagle when a loud and repetitive double ring of the phone broke her concentration.

Seconds turned into what seemed like minutes, until the rings stopped. Svetlana, standing in the open balcony doorway into the living room, stared at the phone on one of the small side tables next to the couch, knowing that she wouldn't pick it up. She had her instructions on the card; no one would be calling her. No one. After several double rings, she heard a woman's voice on the answering machine say: "We are not at home. Please leave a message." But the caller didn't leave a message. There was an abrupt click indicating that the calling party had hung up.

A vast stillness enveloped Svetlana. Then came the consciousness of the awful feeling of helplessness. Messages; no one at the other end of anonymous phone calls; more journeys; she couldn't put fright out of her heart. She wanted to scream, but no sounds came from her throat, only the whimper of someone overwhelmed with fear.

The words of Colonel Boarders rang in her ears. "If you come with me, Svetlana, I cannot promise you what you will be doing will be easy or lack danger. Nothing is safe, Svetlana, but I will do everything to minimize the threats to you and to your mother. I'll spare no effort in that regard . . . we need you . . . it will take courage, Svetlana . . . there is so little time. Are you willing to help us?"

"Are you willing to help us? Are you willing to help us?" Svetlana had answered "Yes, yes," but fright had taken what were noble words, subduing them into stupid, irrational ones. Courage of a final moment . . . she had to do what she must. It was too late to despair—to falter. She had promised, hadn't she? She would perform. Svetlana also knew she had to recover quickly, to call on reserves of resolution; she couldn't be timid. The woman's wave was friendly. . . a friendly wave; the phone call was probably innocent. In any event, nothing could be altered; she would continue; she had to continue.

Svetlana went inside, leaving the sliding door open, feeling the soft breezes beginning to come down from the mountains the late September afternoon. She wasn't one for moodiness, and the momentary depression made her angry that she had let herself into that state of mind. She would go to Einsiedeln, but first she would clean up, rest, and try to get something to drink and eat.

Then in a spontaneous moment, that comes only when fear is recognized and conquered, Svetlana began to laugh at herself and her situation. Her laughter became so hysterical she seemed to descend into insanity, but for her it was a release and the return to a balance that she needed in order to persevere. She wouldn't lose her patience and her logic. Moussa's and Dimitri's men were looking for her, but she was confident that Colonel Boarders would take care of them in his own way, and in his own time. She didn't know when, but she felt certain that he would. In the meantime, she needed a hot bath. She would take it quickly and she would be on her way.

Directly to the left was the cream colored bedroom, about three-quarters the size of the living area. As she entered, she unbuttoned her jacket, placing it on the small bed. The furnishings in the room were mostly varnished oak, giving the room a bright, light feeling. The wall-to-wall soft beige carpet was identical to the rest of the apartment. The unique bed headboard was curved, with built-in side tables. The lamps on either side of the bed were also oak with beige shades. There were no drapes on the window; stained window shutters opened to admit the afternoon sun, bathing the room in a brilliant light.

She quickly took off her slacks and underclothes, placing them and the bracelet her Aunt Yelena had given her so many years ago on the bed, then headed toward the bathroom, pleased to find that there was a bathtub rather than just a shower. The light-gray, marble-top bathroom counter displayed a variety of bathroom powders, soaps, bath gels, and perfumes. Svetlana opened a packet of bath gel and poured it into the tub as the hot water begin to flow. She looked into the mirrored chest above the sink and found mouth wash, toothbrushes, and razors, all in unopened wrappings.

As she looked at all the amenities, she wondered how many people had used the apartment. For a moment, her spirits sagged and she became frightened again, as she contemplated, "How many people have the key?" "Why would that matter anyway? Where would I go if someone opened the door?" She had made the irrevocable decision to continue, and worrying was not going to change that decision or diminish her fear. She accepted the unexpected obstacles and continued her trust in Colonel Boarders.

The steam from the hot water made Svetlana feel drowsy, and her nervousness began to dissipate. She slowly got into the bathtub, and felt the luxurious sensation of a soothing calmness that only a hot bath brings. Her head rested against the far end as she thought of nothing in particular and closed her eyes for a few moments of rest. No matter how hard she tried to forget, the misery of the images of Stevens, Anatoli and Sasha haunted her.

Then the phone began ringing again, the interminable double ring; the recording; again the click of the caller hanging up. "Perhaps a wrong number? No. . . ." Svetlana knew that in Zurich, if one knew the address, then telephone information would give out the phone number. "But how would anyone know that I am here . . . and in what apartment?"

Her brain throbbed. What was going to be a short respite was over. She had to continue her flight. She rose from the bath and began to hurriedly dry herself. There would be no interval from escape.

Zurich
Friday
Local Time: 4:30 p.m. (3:30 p.m., London)
Zurich City Taxi Company Dispatch Center

"This is Peiter Reichmann, manager, may I help you?" Reichmann was Swiss German. He was lazy, and perhaps a little dull, and by late afternoon, tired. And when he spoke, his voice was loud, because he couldn't properly modulate its volume. He kept his strength by eating small cookies and cakes that he bought every day on his way to work from the Sprugeli Confectionery store, where they knew him so well that when he walked in, they presented him with his selection for which he paid seven francs, five times a week without fail. He also never wanted to be disagreeable, which at times made him liked, and at other times, hated. But one thing he did correctly was to follow the rule book that he kept in front of him, carefully indexed, so that he could immediately give an answer to an irate customer, which was what he thought he had at the other end of the phone line. But this time, the caller was distraught and on the verge of panic, or so Reichmann thought.

"Hallo! Mr. Manager Reichmann. Yes, I am a tourist in town, Anatoli Shapov from Moscow!" Anatoli said loudly and in German. Then, lowering his voice, he continued, "Mr. Manager Reichmann, I must have some advice from you and that is why I have asked to speak to you, the esteemed manager, and one with authority! Thank you for taking the time to speak to me . . . a lowly tourist . . . and from Russia. Many people in Zurich do not like Russians and treat us unkindly . . . so, to hear your kind voice gives me confidence that you will be different."

"I am sorry that at times our Zurich citizenry do not treat you with respect, Mr. Shapov. It is not the Swiss way. But, of course, there are always exceptions. Now, how can I help you?" Reichmann's eagerness was evident.

"This is most embarrassing, for me to discuss with you over the phone, but I must. You see, I brought this young lady . . . you do understand what I mean, don't you . . . a young lady from Moscow; and . . . well, she decided that I wasn't . . . how shall I say this, in good order, well, I wasn't up to her standards, and so she left me stranded at the Schweizerhoff Hotel in a mood that . . . of course, you, as a man, would understand. This, after I had bought her the most beautiful ruby and diamond ring. Now, why would a young lady do this to me? I ask you, Mr. Manager Reichmann, why?" Anatoli said in a voice that sounded sad and naive.

"I do know what you mean. I have been divorced twice by bitches—" Unable to continue, Reichmann stopped talking for several moments. "Mr. Shapov, my God, what have I said? I am so sorry to have used that word over the phone, and I shouldn't have done so. Please forgive me, Mr. Shapov, please do. I'm not used to that kind of language. But, yes, I do understand that women can be unpleasant at times. I believe that it is easier for them to be wilfully miserable to a man than to acknowledge a genuine happiness, I suppose."

"It is reassuring to have someone comprehend what I'm saying. I'm most pleased. Well, now, Mr. Manager Reichmann, she was picked up by one of your company cabs, and as luck would have it, I wrote down the cab number. I would like to contact the driver to see if he would be kind enough to let me know where he took her. I pray, oh! Mr. Manager Reichmann, I pray that he didn't take her to the airport. I cannot lose her. I cannot! I don't want to be without her tonight! No, I can't be! That is why I brought her here to Zurich. But then, she was a country girl and they do act strange at times . . . you know, fearful about certain things," Anatoli nervously explained.

In a understanding manner, Reichmann replied, "My first wife was from a mountain village, and all she wanted to do was to have children, just like a cow, every nine months, she wanted her belly filled, and then we would start all over again. After six children in six years I called it quits. She actually screamed at me and called me unholy names, but I walked out and that was that," Reichmann replied courteously, but in a manner that indicated he wanted some understanding as well. "My second wife. . . ."

Anatoli interrupted, his voice rising "How tragic, Mr. Manager Reichmann. How could any woman do this to a man? So tragic. So very tragic. You don't deserve such behavior! No, you do not! But, now despite our mutual concerns, I must continue to solicit your help. Do you think that you can give me the name of the driver of cab number 4163A? This would be most kind to do this, most kind, and both of us who have suffered so much at the hands of country girls will get our revenge. Don't you agree?" Anatoli said.

"Of course. Yes, Cab number 4163A. One moment please." He flipped through the rule book and noted that cab numbers were to be given out only to the police or to someone who had lost an item in the cab, and could identify the item, and was calling to claim the item. Well, he said to himself, "He has lost his girl," and he smiled. Rule obeyed.

"Mr. Shapov, Cab number 4163A is being driven today by Rocco Scaleni. He's a guest worker from Italy and has been with us for over ten years. An excellent driver. Let me see if he is here because his shift ends in just a half hour." After a pause, Mr. Reichmann returned and announced with some authority, "He's here doing some paper work, and I have asked him to pick up the phone, Mr. Shapov. Yes, here he is."

With that, the phone went silent at Shapov's end of the line, but in a moment he heard a voice, speaking in German, "This is Rocco Scaleni, is there something I can do for you? Mr. Reichmann says you lost something in my cab? I have nothing to turn in but, please, let me know what you are looking for."

"A young woman, blond hair, about five-feet, four-inches tall, beautiful . . . and she left me in a huff. We had a lover's argument; I'm devastated. It is all my fault . . . yes, my fault! You picked her up at the front of the Schweitzerhof Hotel. Didn't you see me crying as she got into your cab? You must tell me that you didn't take her to the airport. I will jump into Lake Zurich if you did! Yes, I will do so, as I cannot live without her. My life is over without her! She must not leave me. You must help me. Please tell me that you didn't take her to the airport.

I beg you, Mr. Scaleni, I beg you . . . man to man, tell me."

"I remember her well. The most beautiful woman I drove today. No, I did not take her to the airport, but I took her to an apartment house, on Steinwiesstrasse, not too far from the Zurich Art museum. Number 64, I believe. She was so nice, and wanted to give me a good tip, but I don't take tips. You know in Zurich we provide good service and I don't expect a tip at all," he said eagerly.

"You're so good to me, Mr. Scaleni, I must send you something. Yes, it is done. I will send something for you and Mr. Reichmann. You're so good to me. You have saved me! Saved me from disaster! Love—of—love . . . you know what I mean," Anatoli pretended to cry, amidst nervous laughter.

"Yes, I do, and you are lucky to have such a fine woman. She is so fine and beautiful. Good luck, and no, don't send anything to us. This is our job," and with that cab driver Rocco Scaleni hung up.

As Anatoli placed the phone down, he turned to Sasha and said, "My, my Sasha, my old KGB skills have not failed me. They taught me how to be false, and it always works, Sasha, always works. My friend, I should have been an actor!" Anatoli said gleefully.

"Yes, you're right, but should we be doing this? Maybe this is what Moussa wants to happen. He may want to meet his girl alone. What if he gets angry at us? We'll be finished. Be careful Anatoli. You know his temper," Sasha worried.

"Yes, but, my instincts tell me she is running away, probably with someone else. We shall see. But, first, Anatoli, we must enjoy our two girls, and then we will be off. An hour or so will make no difference, I don't suppose. Besides, my dick is hard and I need to unload. What about you?" And, with that comment, they both broke into laughter and headed toward the bedroom roaring, "Girls, we are coming . . . we are coming . . . get it ready, get it ready for Anatoli and Sasha," Anatoli shouted.

Cyprus
Friday
Local Time: 6:00 p.m. (4:00 p.m., London)
Larnaca, Cyprus Sheraton Resort Hotel

Moussa Berdayev had come to Cyprus expecting that he would be alone with Svetlana for the weekend. He sometimes thought the only reason for his existence was to be with her. He loved her, not as he loved his wife who had given him a son, because "that was a village obligation," he thought to himself. No, he loved Svetlana as a man who had reached the pinnacle of ecstasy. There could be nothing like this feeling that he had when he was with her. Nothing. Not his village wife, nor the myriad girls he had shared in an orgy of sex with his cohorts, Anatoli Shapov and Sasha Rodinov.

Sometimes he felt afraid of Svetlana, afraid he couldn't control her. She was so silent at times, despite their love making which at times was ferocious, at least from his view. In that chaos of sheets and pillows, clasped together like a knot, their love was boundless, or so he thought. He would hold her in his arms and rock her with tender words and flattery as he entered her for the supreme ecstasy that he thought he brought to her and he knew he brought to himself. But she was always silent.

Those passionate moments were the happiest for him. He hoped for her too, but he never knew . . . the silence was all he ever received. She let him do anything to her smooth body, and in his eyes she reacted with happiness but without a sound, not like the other women, nothing, no sound whatsoever despite the intensity of their love making. He was proud to be with her. She had a bearing that no one possessed, not even Dimitri Gravev's wife.

And now she was gone. He knew she was gone. He couldn't bear this, not at all. He was profoundly in love with her and he would find her and bring her back. He had so tirelessly pursued her, and then this; his life would be a torment without her. She was never a reluctant love partner, only a silent one. Many time, tears would come to her eyes, and he surmised them to be the product of joy and rapture, not of sadness and gloom. Her fragility made him feel unbearable tenderness toward her. He always wanted to protect her, to clasp her in his arms, to sleep beside her, her legs twisted under his, so warm and vulnerable, with her hand resting on his chest. Now, she was gone.

"Oh, God, why is she gone? Maybe someone has done something terrible to her. Maybe someone is getting back at me for some reason, punishing me for what I do for Dimitri. But who?" he said to himself, as he began to sob.

"What is happening to me? Svetlana, you cannot do this to me. You can't!" He wouldn't delude himself into thinking that she had really gone from him. "No, you loved me too much . . . too much. I have done so much for you and your mother. Why would you leave me for another man? No, impossible!" he murmured to himself as he looked out to the Mediterranean Sea and the beach below. He had called Dimitri, who didn't appear to be concerned, telling him, in effect, to act like an iron man, that she would be back. But perhaps Dimitri was just trying to soothe him. Maybe Dimitri knew more but didn't want to tell him.

"No, impossible. What I am thinking? Dimitri would never do this to me. I must find her. She cannot leave me like this. No, she can't! Fuck you, Svetlana. Fuck you!"

Moussa looked at the bed on which he and Svetlana had shared their love making so many times, going over to it and taking one of the bed pillows and wrapping it around his arms remembering how he had held Svetlana, then throwing it on the floor, kicking it across the floor like a soccer ball. "I'll do this to you, you bitch . . . you fuckin' bitch." This was the suite that he had asked for because it offered a panoramic view of the sea, and he and Svetlana had enjoyed many sunsets from the balcony.

"Where are you, my Svetlana? Where are you? Why have you done this to me?" He walked over to the closets and started to feel her clothes one at a time, placing his nose to each and trying to reach her in this manner. Nothing had been touched. Even her mother's clothes were in the other bedroom on the other side of the suite. Had someone kidnaped them? But no message, nothing.

"Oh, Svetlana, you must come back. You can't do this . . . not you . . . no, please, no." As he began pacing the bedroom aimlessly, the ring of the phone broke the wave of sadness that had engulfed him.

"Hallo. This is Moussa."

"Moussa, this is Peter Bradford. I understand from Dimitri that Svetlana isn't on Cyprus. I'm very confused. She called me this morning and said she and her mother were having a nice time, and that they would be doing some shopping this afternoon. Then, just a few minutes ago, I received a call from an American businessman, Jess Stevens, who was in my office last week. He said that he thought that he'd seen Svetlana at the Zurich airport this morning, but that the woman denied that she was Svetlana. I don't know whether to believe him. Are Svetlana's clothes at the hotel?"

"Yes, nothing has been removed. I guess she took only her handbag," Moussa answered.

"Well then, Stevens is wrong. She must still be on Cyprus. Have you checked with the manager?" He knew otherwise. Stevens would gain nothing by lying about Svetlana's whereabouts.

"Yes," Moussa responded, "he said that Svetlana and her mother had gone to the clinic because her mother had a dizzy spell. I went to the clinic and found that Svetlana and her mother didn't register at all. I'm worried, Peter, very worried. You don't think that any of your deals—?"

"Absolutely not. Everyone has been paid for all the deliveries they made to me. No one is owed money. No one," Bradford was emphatic.

Moussa was relieved; it was known that Bradford was heavily into the drug trade, a business that Moussa could never understand why Dimitri allowed him to conduct . . . but that was between the two of them, he thought to himself.

"What time did Stevens call you, Peter?" Moussa inquired.

For a moment, Bradford was silent, but in that moment he decided to lie. In a hurried manner he said, "Moussa, I really don't have the exact time. It was just a few moments ago, but he said that he saw Svetlana at the Zurich airport this morning. I didn't ask him the time, but I shall call him back, and if I reach him, I shall call you immediately."

"Have you called Dimitri? You know he has his banker friends in Zurich. Maybe they can help us?" Moussa questioned.

"No, I haven't as yet, but I will do so right away after I ring off with you,"Bradford countered.

"Okay, please call me right back if you have anything. In the meantime, I shall book the first flight to Zurich. You can call my office if you don't reach me here. There is always someone there, and they will know how to reach me," replied Moussa.

"Yes, I shall do that. Don't worry, though. I'm sure she's fine and will be with you soon. It is unlike her to disappear like this," Bradford answered.

"One moment, Peter, the other line is ringing."

"This is the operator, Mr. Berdayev. There is an urgent call from Moscow for you. Shall I put it through?" the operator asked.

"Just a moment. I'll be right back. Hold the call just for a moment, please." Moussa clicked back to Peter.

"Peter, I have to leave now. I have another call. Do me a favor, call Dimitri with your information, and have him send someone to Svetlana's mother's apartment. Perhaps there may be some indications there. Thanks, and I'll see you soon." Moussa then pressed the button for the second line, saying, "Yes, send the call through now, please."

"Moussa, this is Igor, on duty at the bank tonight. We just received a call from Anatoli who is in Zurich, and he said that he saw Svetlana. I told him that can't be because you are to meet her in Cyprus. But, he said, no, he saw her at the Schweizerhoff Hotel. She said she was with you in Zurich. What is going on, Moussa?"

Without replying to Igor's question, Moussa directly asked: "Do you have Anatoli's number in Zurich?"

"Yes, he and Sasha Rodinov are at the Widder; the number is 446-2367 in Zurich. Do you want me to do anything at this end?"

"No, Igor, you have done well. Although I asked Bradford to call, I shall now call Dimitri and tell him myself. Then, I shall try to get on the next plane to Zurich," Moussa said, sounding dejected. He now knew she had left on her own. She had left him. She was escaping. His heart pounded with fury and hostility, despite his professed love for her.

Beads of perspiration were running down Moussa's forehead. He couldn't understand what was going on. A painful sensation of being surrounded by mystery came upon him. Nothing seemed correct. He had spoken to Svetlana, himself, just this morning and she appeared happy and excited that he was coming. "That was a ruse. She is a bitch, just like the others. A bitch. I'll cut her into pieces. Yes, that is what I will do. I will cut her into pieces and throw her into a garbage pit."

He picked up the phone and dialed Dimitri's dacha phone number. After several rings, the phone was answered. "Leo Sverdonov speaking. Yes, can I help you?"

"This is Moussa Berdayev in Cyprus. I must speak to Dimitri urgently."

"He cannot be disturbed because he is in a meeting and he said for no phone calls to get through. I can pass you on to Sergei Mironov if you wish."

Moussa did not want to talk to Dimitri's lawyer. He wanted to talk to Dimitri directly.

"No, can you take a message, however?"

"Certainly. What is it?"

"Tell Dimitri Gravev that I am going to Zurich and will be at the Baur au Lac hotel. I shall call him from there. Also, tell him that Svetlana is in Zurich and that Bradford told me this. It has been verified by Anatoli Shapov and Sasha Rodinov who also saw her in Zurich. Can you repeat the message, please?"

"Yes, of course." Almost verbatim, Sverdonov repeated the message. Dimitri's bodyguards were flawless, Moussa thought, and the message would be delivered without fail and without error.

"Thank you, and regards to Dimitri Gravev." Moussa hung up, more distraught than ever.

He walked over to the bureau and opened up the top drawer to see that Svetlana, as usual, had organized all her jewelry—jewelry that he had given to her, and he started to sob uncontrollably. "What have I done wrong that would make her leave me like this?"

He reached into the drawer and drew out a handful of necklaces, flinging them across the room. "This is what you'll get when I see you. I'll throw you across the room. You cannot leave me, my Svetlana. You are mine," he said as he then took the entire top drawer of the chest and smashed it against the wall. Walking over to the closet, he reached in and with both hands took her clothes, hangers and all, and threw them on the floor, walking in a disjointed fashion. In one vengeful fit of rage, he reached for some of the clothes, walked over to the balcony and threw them down eight stories, watching them flutter in the breeze as they finally settled on the ground below, several pieces flowing over to the swimming pool area.

Soon the phone rang as well as the door bell. He picked up the receiver and then hung up without bothering to hear who it was. He opened the door, and, as he strode out, he told the startled manager, "I'm leaving for the airport. Whatever the damage, put the costs on my credit card. You have the number." He left for the elevator, his heart racing with anger at himself and rage at Svetlana. "If you have left me, my Svetlana, I shall kill you," he said to himself. "Yes, I shall kill you." Moussa was thinking the unthinkable. Perhaps she was never in love with nor loyal to him. Humiliated and furious, he knew that something in his life had been destroyed forever . . . and that there was nothing he could change.

The idea of revenge came so naturally to him that for a moment he felt himself disassociated from himself, watching his own mood alter.

As he rode the elevator to the lobby, he did realized that his anger had colored his senses. He also recalled that he had forgotten to call Anatoli in Zurich. As he reached the lobby, he went directly to the concierge desk and asked to use the phone there. Rather than wait for a reply, he picked up the phone and dialed the operator, asking her to place the call and charge it to the suite he had just vacated. After a minute, the Hotel Widder operator came on the line.

"This is Moussa Berdayev for Mr. Anatoli Shapov, please."

"One moment and I shall see if he is in."

"Hallo," came a woman's voice.

"Is Anatoli there? This is Moussa."

"Moussa, my love, where are you? This is Tatyana. You must come immediately. Anatoli and Sasha are crazy. They have locked all our clothes in the closet and taken the key! We are bare—Nina and I, bare—not a stitch of clothes. We await you to come. Save us, Moussa! Save us from these horrible beasts. We need you!" Tatyana giggled.

"You're drunk and high, Tatyana. Where is Anatoli? Sasha?" Moussa asked curtly.

"They're screwing with your Svetlana, my Moussa. Your princess Svetlana," and with that she laughed uproariously.

"What? What are you saying? Do they know where Svetlana is? Tell me, Tatyana, or I'll have your breasts fed to the pigeons at Gorki Park. Tell me!"

"Then I shall get new ones. Anatoli and Sasha think these are too small. Oh, Moussa, but you never think they are small. You lick them all the time, my Moussa. And you lick me all over.

"Nina, Moussa said I can have new breasts. He's going to feed these little ones to the pigeons," and with that she continued laughing.

"You're high, you stupid bitch," he swore disgustingly. And yet, he knew he had done things to her that he had never done, nor ever would, to Svetlana. He could call Tatyana such names and all she did was laugh and beg for more. He never admitted it, but he loved the dirty language and the dirty sex he had with her.

"Oh, Moussa. You're calling me names. Why are you calling me names? Don't I make you happy anymore? Moussa, you are angry. Well, let me tell you something. Anatoli and Sasha are fuckin your Svetlana, right now. They saw her at the Schweitzerhof, came home, fucked us silly, and then left, locking our clothes in this closet. Shitheads! Just shitheads. That was about an hour ago, I think. We haven't heard from them since. And I don't know where they are now, you fucker. I'll tell them that you called, you fucker . . . yeah! You're just a fucker like them," and with that the phone went dead.

"Oh shit," he said loudly, and he walked out the front door. The the doorman hailed a cab for him.

It was almost seven. He knew there would be a few flights leaving directly for Zurich, and he would arrive by eleven. He was convinced now that Svetlana was in Zurich, but why? And with whom?

Moscow
Friday
Local Time: 7:00 p.m. (4:00 p.m., London)
Kropotkinskaya, 22, Apt. 70

Peter Bradford was but still somewhat nervous. He hadn't as yet heard from Boris Shenin, who should have arrived in London. Nevertheless, he was beginning to calm down slowly. The sex with his teenage girls had not been the best, but the powerful fear of death that had engulfed him with his severe dizzy spell had passed. There was no joy for him in this realization, only apprehension that it would occur again. Nevertheless, he felt good . . . at least as good as a man could be when he realizes that his sex urge is greater than his ability.

He knew also that he was very sick physically, but he wouldn't, he couldn't admit it. "Soon I will go to a doctor, yes, very soon," he said to himself, knowing, however, that his timidity wouldn't allow such a visit. He looked around the apartment one last time to make sure that he had forgotten nothing and headed toward the apartment door. Actually, he hadn't taken his briefcase from the car and his driver was still waiting downstairs, so this look was unnecessary.

Just as he reached the apartment door to leave, he realized that he had to call Dimitri as he had promised in his earlier conversation with Moussa. For a moment, he debated whether to do so. Although untruthful, he could say that he had received Jess Stevens' call after Dimitri had called and before Moussa had called. Not that it mattered. Bradford had no intention of staying in Moscow much longer. Yes, he had better call and tell Dimitri about the information that he had from Stevens. Bradford was distressed about making the call, but he knew he had to do it.

After several rings, the phone was answered at Dimitri's dacha. "Yes, can I help you?" came a voice at the other end that Bradford recognized as one of Dimitri's bodyguards, Leo Sverdonov.

"This is Peter Bradford. I would like to speak to Dimitri."

"I am sorry, Mr. Bradford, but Dimitri is in a meeting and asked that he not be disturbed. Do you wish to speak to Sergei Mironov? I can pass you on to him, if you wish, or take a message," came the response.

"No, that won't be necessary. Tell Dimitri that I have information that Svetlana Makorova is in Zurich, and I shall call him later this evening."

"I shall make sure that he gets the message. Anything else?"

"No, and thank you," Peter replied and hung up.

Bradford now understood that something was terribly wrong. At first, an interruption by Stevens' call was dismissed as unimportant. Now, after Moussa's phone call, it was clear that Svetlana was in Zurich rather than in Cyprus. She had never done anything like this before. No, this was not typical of her behavior. In a moment of dread and helplessness, he asked himself, "Has she left me, and what did she take? Oh! my God." He fled his apartment, running down the corridor and taking the sole elevator down to the lobby, rushing past the security counter without his usual greetings, and running to his car waiting for him on the street directly in front of the building. Struggling to regain his composure, he jumped into the back seat, shouting at his driver to take him to his office.

He was imagining the worst. He flung open his brief case and saw the tapes of Thursday's meetings, neatly in order and by time and day as noted in Svetlana's handwriting. A short burst of relief set in as he noted that she didn't take them with her. "But what about the computer files? Did she copy them? God, she must have copied the files. God, she must have copied the file," he said to himself. "Hurry, Yuri. Please hurry," he said, as panic began to set in. "Of course, no one knew of the Libyan sale but Dimitri, me, Moussa, Svetlana, and a few of Dimitri's assistants."

Bradford's mind was racing with thoughts. He blurted out, "She must have been the one who told the Americans . . . Harrison and Boarders. It had to be her. But how? How did she pass the information? How? The bitch is gone. My God! Dimitri won't have pity on me. Fuck him. I don't give a shit about him. After the Iranian sale, I'll be richer than . . . Oh! God. I hope it isn't so," he muttered as he continued to stare at the two tapes in his hands.

"She must have made copies. God, she must have made copies." Fright is an awful thing when it takes hold, as it was doing with Bradford. He couldn't control the despair that was overwhelming him. "But why would Svetlana do such a thing? I've treated her so well, all these years ... all the money ... the gifts ... the trips ... what more could she ask for? What more could she ask for? She has dishonored me, that bitch!"

It took 45 minutes to get to his office in central Moscow at Tverskaya. As his Mercedes stopped, his face worn and altered in every feature with the agony of a frightened child, he jumped out and ran up the steps to the building entrance, placing his security card in the slot, and waited for what seemed forever to hear the electronic code register and the door open. He kept trying to open it, prior to hearing the release, not realizing that this prolonged the problem. Finally, it opened and he ran past the guards, who looked in amazement at him as he approached the elevator bank, pressing the button, and again failing to realize he had to use his security card for entrance into the elevator bank.

"Mr. Peter Bradford," one of the guards shouted, "you have to use your card for entrance into the elevator. Don't press the button until you have used your card."

"Yes, oh yes, of course."

During the ride up, Peter's anxiety increased as he came to the realization that Svetlana had left for good, and she had probably been the one responsible for the Libyan disaster by giving information to the American security forces. He could think of no other explanation.

That understanding allowed him to calm down as he walked to his office door, took out his key and opened it. He flipped on the reception office lights and closed the door silently behind him. Standing for several moments, he knew what he was going to find when he checked the computer and the audio tapes. In fact, he said to himself, he didn't have to check anything.

He knew she had taken the information with her. Originally, her trip to Cyprus was to be the weekend before, but Svetlana postponed it on the ruse that her mother was ill. She left the night before, right after the meeting regarding the Iranian sale, and she must have taken the tapes with her. He knew that as he walked to the small closet behind his desk and next to the large picture of the Kremlin, carefully centered on that wall. He opened the closet door and saw the tape machine had the tapes that Svetlana had put in for Friday, labeled carefully. He took them out, and placed the ones from his brief case in the tape machine. He pressed "Play" and waited. Nothing came from the tape he'd taken from his brief case. He then replaced Friday's tape and started it. Voices from the most recent meetings emanated from the tapes, indicating that the system was working. He flung the empty tape on the floor. "That bitch! She took the originals and left me with nothing. I'll squeeze the last breath out of her, the bitch."

He went over to his computer and turned it on, signing on with his security code. It took but a moment for the system to tell him that all his files had been copied. Some had been copied some time earlier, but it was obvious that all the files regarding the business he did for Dimitri, as well as the drug and arms deals he did on the side, were copied. "She has everything. That bitch. Why would she do this to me? Why? I never abused her in any way. I never took advantage of her. In fact, I loved her. Why would she fuck me over in this fashion? Why?" He slumped into his chair, shaking his head in utter disbelief at what had occurred in so short a time. He had to decide what to tell Dimitri, if to tell him at all.

Angry and scornful, Bradford knew his luck had run out. The night would be a long one. He would repeat to himself, for many minutes, all the reasons he could summon for Svetlana's actions, and none would provide the necessary relief from what he knew to be a bitter fate. "Maybe I should leave, right now," he thought. "I have a bank account in Zug. Somehow, I could get word to my family . . . maybe just by post . . . but would Dimitri harm my wife and her sons? Probably not. Probably not. Who gives a damn? I don't care." Self preservation Bradford knew to be his mantra; he was a survivor because of that unshakeable attitude.

He knew he would leave.

Svetlana was gone and she had taken the *mafiya* secrets with her. He couldn't alter the fact. But as his mind churned, he thought of Moussa.

"She has left Moussa too! She was disloyal to Dimitri's favorite aide. He'll be in trouble too. Perhaps . . . yes, just perhaps . . . Dimitri will understand. But what if he doesn't?" Bradford knew that his mind was wandering and that the agony of a decision was upon him. He reached into his lower drawer and pulled out a bottle of Johnny Walker Black, stretching over on his desk for a glass on his water tray. He poured himself a full tumbler of scotch. The warmth of the flow down his throat eased his anxiety somewhat. His despair and desolation couldn't prevent what he had to do—call Dimitri and confirm the escape of Svetlana Makorova and to notify him of the computer disks. He couldn't tell Dimitri about the tapes, for Dimitri didn't know he had a taping system in the office.

"The nuke sale. Oh, shit . . . that money. The fuckers are giving me money to screw Dimitri on that deal. I can't leave now. No, that must go through. I have to act as if nothing is wrong. I have to be upset at Svetlana's leaving—furious, horrified, yes, that's how I must act . . . oh! damm you, Svetlana, you screwed my whole plan on this deal. Fuck, it's 7:30 and I haven't heard from Shenin from London; where the fuck is he? That hit man should have wiped out the two Americans by now. Where's the call? I'll remain silent about the tapes. Gravev won't know—I won't tell him. I won't tell him a thing. Not a fuckin thing! That way I protect myself, the nuke sale goes through, pocket the money, and leave. Fuck it, Svetlana. You fucked up everything—"

Bradford reached for the Johnny Walker Black bottle and poured himself another drink, and then another. "I fuckin' will say nothing . . . not a fuckin' thing . . . stick with Jess Stevens' call and that's all I know, all I know. She's gone, and I don't know why. Fuck it, Svetlana. I'm not stupid.

"God! You bitch! We had such a great thing going here . . . and now you've ruined everything, everything, you fuckin' bitch." If only he could last for a few more hours, get on that plane with the nuke and be off . . . if only he could last a few more hours—he had to project calmness. Nothing ever happened. Way back when he started his betrayal of the United States, in the early 1980s, his KGB handler had told him to act like a fighting cockroach which attacks even stronger opponents ruthlessly and defeats them by the vehemence and cleverness of its attack.

"Yeah—I'm that fighting cockroach now." He laughed, loudly and long.

CHAPTER TWELVE

The North Atlantic
Three Hours into the Flight Plan
Saturday
London Local Time: 3:00 a.m.
(Friday, 9:00 p.m., Washington)
AeroWorld Charter Flight 1001
On Route to Alconbury Royal Air Force Base, England

The repetition of the phone buzz didn't wake Mary from her deep sleep. After her calls to David Harrison and Michael Robinson, she had changed into a pale yellow jump suit, put on matching athletic socks, and reclined her seat to its maximum.

The exasperation and frustration that emanated from her meeting with the Attorney General were enough, she believed, to sink any rational person into a deep coma, if for no other reason than to escape from that man's incomprehensible attitude. As she settled into the reclined seat, she wondered what prompted a man like the AG to behave as he did. She had a concealed uneasiness about him from the first moment she had shaken his hand. The abuse of his first wife and probably that of his second was bad enough, but it was the insincere attitude not only toward others but also toward his own country that Mary found hard to comprehend. Mary believed he didn't give a shit about whether the country was protected *as long as he was protected.* He took self-preservation to its logical fuck-you conclusion. Patriotism? You've got to be joking.

"Whatever it takes, Mary. Whatever it takes" was his favorite expression. Mary thought this meant whatever it takes for success in the Pentum missions; the AG's interpretation was whatever it took for him to survive. At times, she thought the AG was in some unknown dimension, divorced from reality. His concerns about the Pentum missions bordered on lunacy, concerns that she had discussed with him these past four years, concerns that never seemed to fade away for Vennix.

He was the attorney general, after all, not some hack ward politico, although he acted that way from time to time. Didn't he understand that it was *his* president, the man that he helped put into office, who organized the Pentum missions? Where had he been? He knew well that all attempts to probe the Moscow *mafiya* center, until Boarders connected with the contact, seemed totally unproductive. Until the contact, the results of the U.S.'s penetration of the *mafiya* were meager at best—an honest appraisal would say nonexistent.

Mary wasn't going to abandon the contact under any circumstances, regardless of what the AG wanted. The AG was insignificant in her view; the contact was pivotal. Until the contact started to obtain information, nothing could be done to stop any sale of *mafiya* stolen ex-Soviet battlefield military missiles, some capable of sending nuclear warheads, let alone stop the sale of a nuke to a rogue country. With that last thought, Mary had drifted off into a heavy sleep that brought her welcome release from natural fatigue.

Her rest would be momentary.

On board the Cessna Citation 750 Executive Jet, the cabin attendant, Alice deWitt, gently touched Mary's right shoulder saying, "Ms. Auriello, there's a call for you . . . Ms. Auriello . . . the White House. The operator says it's urgent . . . Ms Auriello . . . wake up."

Mary slowly opened one eye, then the other, shaking off her sleep, all the while trying to understand what was being said. Without her contact lenses, she saw only a blur, finally discerning that she had a phone call. She slowly raised the back of her beige-colored, leather seat to a full upright position—gazing directly at Ms. deWitt, mumbling, "What is it?" She reached over to the adjacent seat for her glasses. As she put them on, everything came into focus, "Well, now I can see," she smiled at deWitt.

"There's a call for you from the White House, Ms. Auriello. The operator says it's urgent."

"Yes, of course, I'll take the call."

"The phone's directly on the table in front of you," deWitt said, touching the phone so Mary would find it. "Would you like some coffee? Juice?"

"Yes, thanks very much. Both. No cream or sugar in the coffee."

"I'll bring a warm danish, just in case."

"No, no, no danish. Please don't tempt me," she shouted to the departing deWitt.

Mary marveled at these charter flights. She knew that the crew was cleared for such trips and that they were specially trained by the Central Intelligence Agency, but the staff weren't employees of the CIA. They were employed by the charter company that had an exclusive contract with the CIA. The comfort was good and allowed her some time to rest and get organized for what was going to be a very long day. The pilots were all seasoned combat veterans with distinguished records. Many times, her flights took her over sensitive areas, and it was at those times that the experience of the flight crew was highlighted. But this wasn't one of those times. Other than the bumps during the turbulence, caused by a thunderstorm over Washington, it had been a smooth flight.

"Good morning. This is Mary Auriello."

"Good morning, Ms. Auriello. This is the White House operator. Hold one moment for the president."

"Well, the AG must have spoken to the chief. No other reason for the call," Mary said to herself.

"Hello, Mary. Enjoying your flight?" came a quiet, yet deep and sincere voice over the phone.

President Arthur William Steier, Mary believed, had an incredible mind; he always recognized situations and his memory was remarkable. His origins were simple. Abandoned by his father at the age of seven, he was raised by his mother's mother, because his own mother had a night supervisor's job at the local hospital in New Bern, North Carolina. But when she was with him, she doted on him and was instrumental in getting him into a school program for exceptionally bright children. It was his remarkable memory that was mostly responsible for his extraordinary school work. Although academics were his main strength, he did play sports and was an adequate baseball player—a game that he continued to followed assiduously. He received scholarships to both his undergraduate school, the University of North Carolina, and to his law school, Columbia. In both schools, he had excelled.

After a brief career as a corporate lawyer, he was elected at the age of thirty to the House of Representatives in North Carolina, where he remained for ten years. He won a bitter Democratic party primary for a vacancy in the U.S. Senate. His mentor at the time was his former law partner, and present attorney general, Bernard Vennix, who then became his chief of staff when he defeated the Republican incumbent, in what many believe to this day to have been one of the historic dirty campaigns in American political life: false accusations against his opponent, misleading advertisements about the opponent's positions, unlimited supplies of money, and a compliant press. The same approach, sanctioned by Vennix, was used to gain first his party's nomination for the U.S. presidency and then the presidency itself, both of which he won narrowly

Yet, despite the backing of his attorney general and campaign manager, President Steier appeared, to Mary at least, always an instrument of some reason. He was charismatic; he could move crowds with his passionate speeches. He was a gifted narrator who knew exactly how to reach his audience, explaining complex matters in simple language that his audience could understand. He had an infectious enthusiasm for life, especially in his early years for women, an enthusiasm which many of his critics called immoral.

He was slow and cautious when making a decision, but once he made up his mind, he never looked back; and Mary admired him for that. And yet, at times, he would grow anxious when matters were deviating from a plan. She chalked up this attitude to the fear of all politicians of defeat. But in him she discerned a note of panic, the few times she had to brief him about events that were unfolding other than as predicted.

He had a unique charm: he knew how to make people feel at ease. Never, to Mary at least, did he seem to get angry or feel insecure. He gave everybody the impression that he trusted each of them, and believed that what each of them was saying was true. What he never did was tell anyone what he really was thinking. His views remained unspoken until the last possible moment. Mary's briefings with him were always clinical; he asked few questions, but those he did were right on point. The one problem Mary had with him was his loyalty to his attorney general.

It was this president who, when he took office, was seriously concerned about the errant ex-Soviet Union military missiles and nuclear weapons. Treaties between nations aside, he knew, correctly, that those weapons would find their way into the hands of people he called the crazies. Diplomacy could do only so much, so he approved of the Pentum mission to stop the sale of those weapons. It would be an off-the-books mission without traceable government funding and without any traceable government official involved . . . except Mary and those whom she briefed: the President, the Attorney General, the Director of the FBI; and the Director of Central Intelligence.

All information would flow to Mary and she would be the focal point for the dissemination of it. In order to scramble effectively what little information she did dispense, her briefings were always one-on-one. She never, and would never, brief them as a group. Except for Mary, access to all intercepts and computer data was by means of the retina scan—the individual would have to go to a special room at the National Security Agency and be admitted via a scan of the person's eye. Only then would access be allowed. No one, to Mary's knowledge, ever tried to see the data at the NSA. In any event, any intercepts were deleted within twenty four hours of receipt, and Mary shredded any translation text given to her of the intercepts. No records. She abhorred them.

"Actually, I was enjoying my flight, Mr. President, and trying to get some sleep. What can I do for you, sir?" she asked in a solicitous tone.

"Bernie Vennix was here, and he told me about your conversation. By the way, how did you slip away without my knowing?" he asked as he began laughing.

"Connections," Mary responded, and with that the president's laughter became boisterous. But as quickly as his laughter came, it left and his tone turned soft, and serious.

"Mary, let me get to the pont of this call. Boarders' death is a profound loss. He was one of our best, if not the best covert operator. We know his skill, and you both know my belief in him, his actions and his wisdom in organizing Pentum. But with his death, and with Harrison injured, Bernie here believes that perhaps we should slow this down, if not cancel the remainder of the mission. Boarders was the key in all of this. I know, from what you've told me, that he structured the mission so as not to compromise the identity of the Moscow source, or for that matter any source, and certainly not compromise Pentum.

"I realize that you understand that we are now entering a political cycle, the presidential campaign, and so forth. I'm concerned that if anything goes wrong and we would be identified with Pentum, it would be devastating to me and to my campaign. Do you believe we should go forward?" It was a real question, asked as soothingly as the President could and, as usual, withholding any indication of his opinion.

"Without any doubt, Mr. President. It will succeed," replied Mary, matter of factly. "Harrison's injuries are minor and he will be meeting me in a few hours. In any event, the Pentum missions are always, Mr. President, as you know, designed to be star proof—if any one can be categorized as being a star. In other words, there is planned redundancy and contingency in the Pentum missions. Only by such planning can we be assured of success. Contingency planning includes the death of one of us, either of Boarders, Harrison, or me. This mission will be concluded successfully and shortly.

"You do know, Mr. President, that what Boarders accomplished was the penetration of the *mafiya* control point in Moscow. Bob's information, many times from tape recordings and computer disks that his contact gave him, was absolutely crucial in stopping the missile arrangement the *mafiya* Moscow leadership had made with Libya. The one that is being attempted now is a major sale—the sale of a nuclear weapon to Iran. In my view, Mr. President, we can't abandon the mission in any aspect. Our contact agent is a particularly capable and loyal one. In my view, we must use all our resources to rescue this person. You understand, I know, that when we recruit agents, that they believe we will not abandon them at the slightest whim. Frankly, the incompetence isn't on the contact's side; it will be incompetence on our side, if we abort the mission because Bob is no longer with us," Mary continued.

"I wish to be polite, sir, but I'm getting impatient with the rattle of one voice—that of your attorney general—who jumps ship at the moment something unexpected happens. Political campaigns aren't predictable, are they?

"Now, with regard to the political consequences," she continued, "if by some remote chance this government is identified as being the supporter of Pentum, such information can come only from the people that I brief . . . and from no one else. They are your appointments and they talk to the press. I never see the press and I talk to no one about Pentum. Access to Pentum is restricted to those individuals and all intercepted data is deleted within 24 hours after receipt. Records of Pentum are practically nonexistent. What records do exist are standard corporate documents at Pentum Trade and Investment offices in London, and that office is nothing more than a desk and an answering machine. All of this is to prevent leaks.

"Pentum isn't a mission of failed prospects, Mr. President. We have had great successes; it's taken time; but we haven't failed. But I'm beside the real issue, Mr. President. Bernie is afraid for reasons that I don't understand," Mary persisted.

The president admired Mary's direct, no-nonsense talk. She was a supreme realist but also an optimist, always confident. One thing was certain. She never joked with him. It was all business. He knew exactly how to take this attitude. He always listened, and in the four years that he was president, he had never said no to her, and she had never failed him.

"Bernie is strongly of the view that we should halt the mission," the president responded, ignoring her comments about his presidential campaign and about Vennix.

"Is he there with you?" Mary inquired.

"Yes, of course. I thought you knew that he was in the room with me."

"Perhaps you did tell me. Would you mind putting this conversation on the speaker? I want Bernie to hear what I have to say," Mary replied.

"No, Mary. I have no objection. Bernie. . . ."

"Good morning, Mary. You're saying some very nice things about me this early hour?" Vennix said indifferently.

"Good morning, Bernie. Very nice things, and truthful ones at that. I'm suggesting to the president, Bernie, that unless all reason fails us, there can be no turning back. We cannot let this brave contact, who has provided us with such valuable information, be set adrift. There should be no question about that.

"With regard to the nuclear item that we know is on its way to Iran, it would be a tragedy if that was delivered. Someone will have to convince me that such a delivery is in our national interest. The answer can never be that when things change, agents who help us must be left to fend for themselves. Nor can we throw up our hands and say, well, they will get the bomb anyway. With that mindset, which I believe Bernie has, why bother? Why bother with anything? There is an emptiness in such thinking, don't you agree, Mr. President?"

The President colored. "Mary, hold off on the personal attacks. They're unnecessary, and they aren't productive." He wished she would draw back a bit.

She did. "Of course, I certainly don't mean to attack Bernie's credibility, but you must know, Mr. President, Pentum has never been a favorite of Bernie's. First, he doesn't understand why we're engaging in this kind of activity; second, he doesn't understand why we are doing this outside the normal government channels; and third, he doesn't believe in this kind of preventive measure. His view is that whenever any rogue country gets the bomb, we have the capacity to take out the weapons and their manufacturing base. This is no doubt one possible way of meeting the problem, but it is the wrong way; it's not a thoughtful way. It's a hallucination. I don't see the international community backing us when we decide to bomb North Korea, Iraq, Iran, or Libya, whenever they get the bomb, with resultant loss of life and the radioactivity that will be released into the atmosphere. I still believe in prevention, don't you?

"I'm a Catholic," she continued, "and there was a chaplain at Smith

College who, speaking of something more personal, said it was important 'to stop the beginnings, because then you don't have to worry about the endings.' What we're doing here is 'stopping the beginnings.' The more we follow this path, the more we can rest easy. I would find it difficult to accept or recommend to you anything otherwise. The dark struggle Pentum was set up to defeat is not easy, Mr. President. It was never easy."

The thick silence lasted for at least a half minute, Mary noted, scanning the readouts on the three digital clocks in the front of the cabin. The destination clock read 5:45 a.m.; the pilot had clipped off fifteen minutes of flight time. The time remaining in flight clock read 2:45 hours. She had been respectful, but she wanted the president to know how she felt, regardless of whether Vennix was making grimaces, as she knew he probably was, while she was talking from the satellite phone. He had an annoying capacity to mimic the caller when the caller was on the speaker phone; Mary had seen that bizarre habit several times, reinforcing her belief that Vennix was anything but rational.

"Am I supposed to feel some hidden shame, Mary, because I disagree with you?" Vennix responded, his voice particularly harsh, grating like an instrument on a rough surface. The voice sounded awful to Mary, and she commented angrily.

"Hidden shame? No, you're not. It will be more than shameful if we abandon our contact and this mission. Bernie, I believe in Pentum. Do you understand that it will be over in less than twelve hours? Why are you so worried? Have you done something to prevent its success? *Don't think, sir, that I won't notice a betrayal . . . I will."*

"Wait a minute, Mary. You're going too, too far. Just who the hell do you think you're talking to? I'm as patriotic as you are. We just disagree. Can't you accept that? What's this talk about betrayal? I resent that inference," Vennix said curtly, his voice rising heatedly.

"Stop right there, Mary. . . Bernie . . . please, Mary . . . Bernie. I don't appreciate this kind of talk. It'll get us nowhere. Again, Bernie, give me your reasoning why we should opt out at this late moment. Mary, listen, and don't interrupt please."

"The fact is that Boarders is dead. He knows the identity of the contact

. . . only he. Harrison is injured and isn't usable. The nuke is going to get there, if not in this shipment, then tomorrow or the next day; the crazies will beg, borrow or steal one. The *mafiya* has the capacity to get other nukes and they will sell them. What if the press gets hold of the identity of Boarders, of Harrison—can you imagine what that will do to the campaign? Secret agents—secret contract agents—unknown to Congress and their oversight. Aren't we supposed to be telling Congress about our covert missions? Aren't we? If we distance ourselves now, we'll be on safer grounds. I'm afraid that we won't keep secret the identity of Boarders or Harrison, given the attacks in London, while the queen was there in the same theater as Harrison. It just won't sell. Someone will find out."

"Mary, I too am worried about the identification issue," President Steiner added. "It's very difficult, almost impossible, to keep anything secret for very long. I'm surprised we have been able to maintain the secrecy we have with Pentum. The way Boarders structured Pentum, it has certainly contained the information, no doubt about it, but there's always the chance that something from the attempt in London will surface."

"You're correct that the containment of the information has made for the success of the Pentum missions. And that control remains in place, Mr. President," Mary responded.

"Certainly, Bernie," she continued, "I understand your concerns, but I just don't think they're reasonable. First, you both know that Boarders and Harrison are not their real identities—which are shrouded in complete secrecy. Second, certain off-book funds have been used, but the funds are all accounted for and merged with other identifiable funds; original use of the funds is impossible to trace.

"Third, and more immediate to your concern, as I told you in your office, if anyone asks you to comment on the attempt on Harrison's life, say that he is a honorable businessman and that the United States abhors any attempt on any American wherever it takes place. There will be no information on Boarders, because he doesn't exist. His body has already been removed and is awaiting my arrival. I don't want to discuss at this time any more of the details regarding that matter . . .

but you should be aware that the identity of the murdered victim at the Lowndes Hotel won't be Boarders'. It'll be someone else's. I just don't see how there will be public knowledge of Boarders at all. The contact has certain instructions from Boarders, I am certain, and if the contact follows those instructions, the person will be identified and rescued. There should be no concern about that."

"I feel comfortable about what you're telling us, Mary," the president interrupted. "We know that the Pentum restrictions have prevented release of any information and they continue in place. That kind of containment is what has saved the program from the press and from the loose talk in this city.

"For that kind of success, Bernie, we should all be thankful. I know, Bernie, that you've been uncomfortable from the start, and I believe that you're more concerned about me and my political life and how anything may impact on that. I appreciate your attitude, but we are beyond that.

"Bernie, I have and continue to have an abiding belief in Pentum. Look at the results. Though, in all honesty, Mary, I'm still concerned that without Boarders, the originator of the Pentum missions, successful accomplishment will be difficult. It was he who knew all the details of the missions. Even you don't know the intricacies. I'm not criticizing the structure . . . but let me just say, I'm more cautious. I know that we can't broadcast successes in this kind of activity. Well, everyone really knows that we're behind the aborted missile delivery to Libya, especially since the Libyans blamed us. As I recall, our State Department said that the Libyans, again, are making us out to be the big devils. Privately, though, Mary and Bernie, I have had several calls from our European friends to congratulate me on that. I am silent of course, other than to say that we weren't involved. But, Mary, you must understand that these things don't go unnoticed. Let's move on, Mary. Give us the status of the proposed sale of the nuclear weapon to Iran."

"I can understand your concern," Mary replied, "As for the Pentum mission status, Mr. President, we know that a meeting took place in Moscow late yesterday evening regarding the delivery of the device. This comes on top of a meeting a week ago on the same subject. As you know, our contact is closely associated with an American businessman's office in Moscow and the front for much of the Moscow *vor* activities. This American, whose identity it is unnecessary to advance, has been disloyal to this country for a very long time, but the extent of that disloyalty never impinged on the real security concerns of the U.S. until now. In short hand, he's the sales manager for the delivery. We believe that delivery to Iran will occur this weekend. We will stop that delivery, Mr. President. Have no doubt about that whatsoever."

"You know the time and place of delivery?" the President asked.

"We'll have tapes of yesterday's Moscow meeting, and I am certain that we will obtain information about the delivery of the device—time and place," Mary replied. "I don't want to go into detail other than to advise you about these preliminaries. The original tapes are in Zurich, placed in a bank safety deposit box by our agent, and it is there that Harrison will be going to obtain the needed information. I received a coded message this afternoon indicating that the contact's mother would be arriving today. She has duplicates of the tapes and certain computer disks. This is the redundancy I spoke about earlier.

"Boarders was a master in that, in order to ensure success, he believed in contingency planning and fine tuned all such planning before any Pentum mission. Frankly, the planning is meticulous. The personnel accompanying the contact's mother are retired agents who have worked with Boarders on other missions. They will take care of her until I return. Because of the weather in Frankfurt, her plane was delayed, so her arrival occurred after I departed from Washington. In sum, Mr. President, the earlier tapes that Boarders was given a week ago clearly indicated that the delivery would take place this weekend. Yesterday's tapes will give us the precise location and time," Mary's responded.

"Bernie, I just don't think we can stop now. I just think it wouldn't be useful. Mary?" The president said her name in his soft voice, but he was unable to go on. She understood he was asking her for some help with Vennix.

Mary hesitated a moment. "Why not? Why not?" Mary said to herself. "Why not help the president? He's on my side."

"I won't take any chances, Mr. President," Mary's voice sounded uncharacteristically humble. "I'll continue to make sure nothing will surface that will in any way be untoward or embarrass anyone.

"Bernie, I know you feel otherwise, but I need your assistance now as well, Bernie. We're nearing the end of the president's most successful covert operation. I know you want the world to know, but not now, Bernie. The Pentum mission is just a fragment of history, and a good one, full of human greatness. I'm sorry if I offended you, Bernie. I really am," Mary practically drew blood from her tongue as she said it; but with the president on her side being magnanimous in victory wasn't an original thought but a good one, and she countered tersely with that.

"Bernie? . . ." the president asked.

"Good luck, Mary. Good luck. Hurry home," Vennix replied with little emotion in his voice and with a degree of curtness that indicated to Mary he was thinking just the opposite.

"Good luck. And I want to see you when you return. Don't take any chances, Mary. One loss is too many already. Confidence and faith in you and Pentum will be put to the test the next several hours, Mary. Beyond that, we don't need you and Harrison to do anything but to return safely," the president concluded. Mary knew he meant those comments in earnest.

"Mr. President, a personal matter. I want you to know that after the Pentum mission is concluded, I intend to submit my resignation to Bernie and to you. It's time for me to do something else. You're correct of course, when you said that it may be more difficult without Colonel Boarders. Not difficult in the execution stage of the mission, but in the personal stage. He was the greatest of the great and I will find it hard to work without him. I don't take this action lightly, Mr. President. But I hope that you'll understand."

"Mary, Mary—you're speaking from emotion . . . and probably exhaustion. Think about the decision more, and we can talk about it when you return. Okay?"

"Of course, Mr. President, but I don't think I'll change my mind. No, Mr. President, as soon as Pentum is completed, I hope you'll accept my decision," Mary replied.

"We'll talk further. Bernie, any final words for Mary?" the President inquired.

"No. Just good luck."

"See you in a day or so." The president hung up.

After the call, Mary had a sense of relief; a sense of gratitude that the president had decided to go forward with Pentum rather than pull the plug. And she felt a sense that, just maybe, Vennix would stop further clashes with her. She had made a gesture of peace; she had to wait for a return courtesy. It would be novel for Vennix to do so and, perhaps too difficult a challenge, but then again human nature does change, maybe, once in a while. She reclined her seat again, taking off her glasses, leaving the juice, coffee and danish untouched on a tray in front of her. The silence and stillness of the Citation jet quickly lulled her to sleep.

Washington, D.C.
Local Time: 10:45 p.m. (4:45 a.m. Saturday, London)
2570 Mills Run Road
Potomac, Maryland

"Don't think, sir, that I won't notice a betrayal; I will," with those words ringing in his ears, Bernard Vennix sat at his library desk, his shoulders bent, his face heavy lined and drawn, fiddling with his pen, pressing the top up and down watching the ball point come down, and then retract, a constant tremor in his mouth, as he repeated the words, "Don't think, sir, that I won't notice a betrayal; I will."

"Who the fuck do you think you are . . . you prima dona bitch? Women like you need a good fuck and hard fist against your jaw."

"'Don't think I won't notice a betrayal; I will,'" Vennix grimaced trying to mimic Mary, his voice trembling with agitation.

"Right in front of the president, the man *he,* yes *he* got elected president, she said those words—'Don't think, sir, I won't notice a betrayal; I will.' She knew what she was saying . . . she was threatening them *both* . . . she cornered them . . . that bitch . . . cornered them . . . yes, not only him, but also the president. Then that resignation crap . . . if anything did go wrong, she'd resign and blast everyone. 'I don't talk to the press. . . .' She would talk then. God, that woman thinks she's untouchable.

"I should have had her taken care of when I first came here . . . that first fuckin' briefing . . . no notes, and she said I couldn't take any notes. What the fuck is this? Who's running the department? I'm the Attorney General of the United States. 'You take notes, sir, and there is no mission. No notes, no records, no memory, no leaks.' What did I answer . . . I fuckin' agreed!"

If anything, Vennix knew he could not accept the humiliation that Mary hurled at him in front of the president. He felt his nerves set on edge; he had lost something . . . his honor, *in front of the president*.

"She knew exactly what she was doing. . . . 'Don't think I won't notice a betrayal; I will.' What the shit—right in front of the president!" He couldn't accept this and keep his dignity . . . nor could he accept the fact that she knew a secret about him that even the president didn't know. Mary didn't care about anyone's dignity, least of all his. "Just that Pentum crap . . . who gives a shit about that? She can't disgrace me this way. I mean, I'm the Attorney General of the United States . . . she can't do this to me . . . no, she can't." He picked up his phone.

"Dennis, I'm sorry to bother you this evening. I tried to call you earlier from my office, but there was no answer. Did you get my message?"

"I just got in myself from New York and haven't listened to my messages, Bernie. Is there something you need?"

"Yeah. I need you to do me a favor. . . ." With that call, Bernard Vennix ended whatever moral scruple remained in his person.

Dennis Eidenson had been hired by Vennix to plant false information and documents concerning Vennix's political opponents—in the present and in the earlier political campaigns. It was simple. By the time the person who was charged with the false information had time to respond, the information had already been disseminated. Charges, however false, are always remembered. It's the truth that is most often forgotten.

Eidenson had favorite news outlets that published what he called "his ball busters." He furnished tasteless and disgusting information—but many published it. In fact, even the larger newspapers would report the information by stating that "it was reported by" and name the newspaper, TV or radio outlet that was the source of the information. Eidenson paid handsomely for the placement of his crafted news. He now set out to smash Mary Auriello . . . and for his good friend and paymaster, Bernard Vennix, the Attorney General of the United States.

Washington, D.C.
Saturday
Local Time: Midnight (Saturday 5:00 a.m., London)
Talk Radio WWIT
Host: Peter Matheson
Syndicated throughout the eastern United States

"My friends, good evening! Midnight in the nation's capital, and do we have a story to start out the new day. It seems that a high-ranking Justice Department official—a woman—with a high security clearance—would you believe this?—has been seen in one of those alternate-life-style bars . . . you know, the ones that cater to women who like other women. Now, this administration is high on its cultural acceptance of diversity—but come on now, folks—a justice official with a high security clearance. I mean, let's face it, what secrets is she telling to her bed partner or maybe partners . . . what pillow talk is going on now? And the rumor is that she's involved in spy stuff that's illegal . . . Did you hear me folks? . . . Illegal. Who knows what's going on? We citizens don't know, and we should. Let me hear from you folks: 1-800-234-1111 . . . Dial that number right now. What's our country coming to?—security clearances to a woman who, I mean, maybe the woman she loves is from one of those countries that we don't like. Maybe she's in love with a spy and she doesn't know it. Love conquers all, they say. Folks: 1-800-234-1111 . . . Let's hear from you."

CNN monitors talk radio on a selected basis, choosing the program in accordance with the program ratings for the month monitored. The monitors are told to listen to the themes of the day to get a feel for what has the public's attention. Sarah Teller, a law student at American University, working part time for CNN, Washington, listened to the report and entered it into her computer terminal to be e-mailed to her editor. After the report she wrote—"Verify. Could be another one of Matheson's trash comments."

At one a.m., the editor reviewing matters for the morning news underlined her comment and transmitted it to a producer, who was asked to check with the Department of Justice Public Information office, first thing in the morning, noting, "You may have to call the PR rep at his home; office may be closed because of Saturday. Number in memory."

At six a.m., producer Michael McCorder eased into his chair and logged onto his computer. His first message was the request to call Department of Justice Public Affairs Information. Scanning his phone memory bank, he picked up the phone and called Michelle Stone, who, according to the memory, was the official to call on Saturday.

"Good morning, Michelle. I'm sorry to bother you so early, but this is Mike . . . Mike McCorder at CNN, and we're checking a report on Talk Radio WWIT on the Matheson show last night around midnight, and I quote: 'It seems that a high-ranking Justice Department official—a woman—with a high security clearance—would you believe this—has been seen in one of those alternate-life-style bars . . . you know, the ones that cater to women liking other women. Now, this administration is high on its cultural acceptance of diversity—but come on now, folks—a justice official with a high security clearance. I mean, let's face it, what secrets is she telling to her bed partner or maybe partners . . . what pillow talk is going on now?' There's more. Are you interested in hearing more?"

"Mike . . . is this some kind of a joke? Are you for real? You've got to be kidding. Is CNN really interested in this kind of crap?" Michelle Stone fumed.

"Are you denying the report?" McCorder asked.

"I'm saying it's crap. Pure crap. You have a slow news day or something?" Stone angrily replied.

"Michelle . . . come on now. I need a statement . . . are you going to give me a statement of denial or what? It may be crap. But is that what you want me to say?" McCorder persisted.

"I'll get back to you. Your direct dial number please," Michelle asked, lowering her voice, knowing that she had to work with this man.

"Direct Dial-1-800-345-9011," McCorder replied.

"I'll call within the hour. Don't send anything out on this crap. God, I can't believe you actually called me on this, Mike. Good bye."

Michelle Stone slammed the phone down on the receiver and turned to her husband, who was dressing to go jogging, saying, "Nick, some shithead called about another rumor—about a high ranking woman at Justice. It could only be about Mary Auriello. We don't have that many high-ranking women. It has to be her; something to the effect that she's been seen at some gay bar. This is the fourth call this morning. There seems to be some concerted effort here."

"You know what I think of the press, honey. They're shit," and he kissed her and left.

"But you're a sports reporter, for God's sake," she replied, as she heard him laughing while he went out the front door, closing it behind him.

She picked up her phone and dialed her boss, David Belden. Belden's voice mail came on and she left a message regarding the CNN call. But she had promised CNN she would call back in an hour. It was now 7:15; forty-five minutes to go. She decided to get up but purposely didn't turn on the TV. Finally, after what seemed like a longer period of time than it was, the phone rang and it was David Belden, the chief spokesman for the Department of Justice.

"David. You heard my message. Well? . . ." Michelle asked.

"It's shit. You know it and I know it, and that's what I want you to say. But let me check with Jonathan Coris, and get him in the loop. I'll be right back to you."

Michelle Stone knew what the answer would be. Coris, the AG's chief of staff, loved scandal as long as it didn't involve him but was targeted at someone the AG wanted to get rid of. If the call-back said to state,"We are looking into this"—that meant one thing. "Totally untrue and a fabrication" meant another. The first meant that the AG was out to axe someone. She hated her job when she knew this to be the case

THE PENTUM MISSION

... hated it.

Belden called her back within minutes. "Michelle, tell your friends in the media that "We are looking into the allegations, but will have nothing further to say until Monday. We don't believe the charges to be true, and thus we have to examine the facts, if there are any, behind the report."

"David," Michelle interjected, "that is such equivocation. It's the worst of both worlds. Are they trying to get rid of Mary Auriello? And why, for God's sake? She has every award that this government can give a civilian."

"Do your job, Michelle. That's the statement," Belden ordered.

Michelle called CNN back, knowing that once she read that statement to CNN, it would be broadcast. She felt sick. Mary had always cooperated with her; several times she had addressed the luncheon meetings of "Women Government Executives" for which Michelle had been Program Coordinator. She would wait until the last possible moment, yet she would have to do it. But first she had another call to make.

"Beverly, this is Michelle Stone, of the PR office. Sorry to bother you on a Saturday. Is Mary in town?" Michelle asked Beverly Peterson, Mary's secretary.

"No, she isn't in the city . . . and Michelle, but, I can get a message to her . . . if it's important."

"Well, it is. I've received a call from CNN and a few other news organizations regarding a report on Talk Radio WWIT that a senior Justice Department woman with a high security clearance has been seen in an alternative-life-style bar . . . and so on. A lot of nonsense . . . but—"

"What? Certainly, you'll immediately deny it and call their editors. You can't cooperate with this kind nonsense, Michelle. You can't. It's absurd. Why dignify such comments?" Peterson asked.

"The AG's authorized a statement to the effect that the department is looking into the charges," Michelle responded.

"What? You've got to be kidding, Michelle. Has the AG lost his head? He abhors Mary, but this has gone too far. You make that statement and I can assure you it will be the AG who will lose his job. He's gone too far."

"I'm sorry, Beverly. I truly am," Michelle replied.

"Do me a favor," Beverly asked. "Wait until the last moment."

"I will. I'm supposed to call it in around eight . . . but I'll call them and say we'll have the statement at 8:30. Does that help?"

"Thanks. Talk to you later," Beverly said, hanging up.

London
Saturday
Local Time: 3:00 a.m.
No. 164 Cadogan Place

Ruslan Ishaev lay on his stomach, his right arm tilted toward the shattered window, his head, resting on the floor—his feet in a pool of blood that had spread from under his head and neck and to the left of his body, covering the floor area directly and at the foot of the window. The room was in disarray as if it were the scene of some great struggle. The wall beneath the window was smeared with blood; splashes and streaks of blood smeared the shattered glass which lay on the floor. Ruslan's neck wounds were particularly deep—pieces of glass were still imbedded in his neck, hands, and face; great gashes cut across his face as if someone had taken a knife and repeatedly slashed his face haphazardly.

They all lingered by the body—Harrison, Robinson, Dean Goodwin and Goodwin's assistant, Dudley Arrison

It was Dean Goodwin who spoke first. His face, puffy with fatigue, his dark eyes generally good-natured and hopeful, were dreary and squinted slightly. It had never happened before: three murders in his station area, all connected by the man lying in the abandon of an unexplained death, surrounded by his own blood. Despite his calm demeanor, Goodwin began to feel a terror commingled with the most extraordinary feeling of relief. The murderer had been caught, but had the crime been solved? Why was Boarders murdered and why was an attempt made on Harrison's life?

"Mr. Harrison, is this the same man that made the attempt on your life last night? We're certain that he's the murderer of the two men at the Lowndes Hotel, and the various security videos at the hotel match the amateur video taken by a French tourist on the Strand, and given to the police. We need your identification, however, as well. Your ID will round out the identity check."

Harrison didn't immediately reply. He stood motionless, and at ease, his own face still displaying the marks of the violent blows he had received from the man whose body lay before him. He was weary, but not especially tired. "Battle, murder, death," he murmured to himself. He hadn't really slept after Robinson had taken him from the hospital directly to the hotel. So he welcomed the call from Robinson.

As soon as it became clear that the man at 169 Cadogan was the man that had killed Boarders and had attempted to murder Harrison and his family, Commander Robinson no longer felt it inappropriate to give the information to Harrison, despite Mary's admonition that David be told nothing if the *mafiya* hit man was found. She meant alive. She didn't want to endanger Harrison and she knew that David would go after the killer if he knew where to find him . . . and he would eliminate him. With Ruslan Ishaev dead, Mary's concern had ended.

The room was cold from the early morning wind gently moving the drawn drapes.

"Ghastly scene, isn't it, Dean? Ghastly scene, but who was he fighting? It appears he was either pushed into the window or somehow rushed into it pell-mell . . . all this glass . . . ghastly," Robinson commented, his own eyes burning from the lack of sleep, his face painfully long and haggard, his voice half exultant and half despairing. "Dean, who else could have been in this room with him? Who else?"

"Sir, I don't think anyone else was in the room,' replied Goodwin, "or if there were, the person floated on air. There are no bloody footprints; all the blood is underneath and near the body."

"Suicide?" Robinson seemed incredulous as he looked askance at Goodwin. "Doesn't make any sense, does it? The bloke runs right into the window. Maybe he was high on drugs or something? Maybe he thought the window was something or someone else ? Who knows? We'll get some answers soon," Goodwin said.

What David Harrison saw failed to upset, shock or alarm him. He thought to himself, he would have done worse if he had first found the man. Throughout the short conversation between Dean Goodwin and Commander Robinson, Harrison remained silent. His gaze, a sharp, peering intensity, clinical, like the deepness of his attention, seemed to increase, a cloud growing darker before a storm. Tangled, vital impressions came to Harrison as he looked at the body as if he were trying to recreate the deadly scene, to the end of which he was now a witness. It was clear that Ruslan had rushed headlong into the window, but why? What prompted him to do that? Someone trying to open the window? No, the room was up five stories and that would be impossible. Something frightened him? Another assassin? Frightened? Impossible. It didn't matter. The disfigured and marked man, his face filled with pieces of glass, was dead.

"Yes, Dean, he's the man," Harrison, breaking off the silence, answered. "Who killed him? I don't care. I only wish I had done it myself. That's all. This death was stolen from me. No, gentlemen, this isn't a triumph for me at all . . . no triumph," and Harrison began to walk toward the apartment exit door.

"Michael, do you still want Dean and me to go to Alconbury with you? We have a great deal of work to do here."

"No, I don't think it'll be necessary. You've found your man. No press announcement yet. We still have to sort this out. Pass any inquiries to the Yard, and they'll have instructions on how to handle it from there. Mum's the word now, gentlemen. Again, all inquiries to the Yard."

Goodwin looked relieved that he didn't have to go to Alconbury—more than a two-hour drive—and he had finished two shifts, now working on the third. He looked over to his assistant, Dudley Arrison, and said, "We're staying here." Arrison's eyes showed he also was happy at the thought of winding down their day in London.

"It's over for us, the case is over, isn't it Dean?" Arrison commented, his eyes frowning, as he saw Commander Robinson leave with Harrison. "By the way, who is this Harrison? Did you see the way he looked at the dead bloke and hear what he said: 'This death was stolen from me.' What the hell does that mean?"

"He's an American businessman . . . yeah . . . an American bloke who almost got his life snuffed out. . . . The case for us is over. . . . For him, Dudley . . . for him? . . . I'm not so sure. For him it may be just beginning."

CHAPTER THIRTEEN

Zurich
Friday
Local Time: 5:00 p.m. (4:00 p.m., London)
64, Steinwiesstrasse, Apt. 10

Svetlana froze as she heard the sharp sound of the apartment intercom buzzer. Drawing the large white bath towel closer around her damp body, folding it slightly over her breasts to hold the towel firmly, she stood still, feeling a chill pierce her bones. She began to shake . . . begging that the unwelcome, brash, intermittent buzz would turn out to be some horrible mistake. The buzzer went on periodically for several moments, then ceased. Svetlana stood still, waiting for the sharp, troubling note to echo again. Nothing. The only noise came from the gentle, late afternoon breeze flowing through the wide open balcony door, stirring the drawn drapes, and giving off a low whistle throughout the apartment.

Taking small steps, she slowly walked barefoot into the living room, the plush carpeting soaking up the moisture from her feet, stopping just in front of the balcony door. There, unable to see down to the street, she dropped to her hands and knees, cautiously crawling the few lengths onto the balcony floor, positioning herself at the corner where the left side of the balcony was attached to the longer front side by three metal bars fastened to the walls at ninety-degree angles. She peered through the bar openings down to the street, surprised to see the woman who had so eagerly waved at her earlier in the day, her broad frame cloaked in a brilliant pink dress, her black hair in a bun, and carrying a large paper sack, muttering, loudly and in German, rushing away from the entranceway to Svetlana's apartment building.

Svetlana's eyes followed the woman as she headed toward the

Mercedes parked directly in front of the building. One man was standing, his head bent down talking to the driver, when the woman interrupted their conversation. She had a document in her hand, perhaps a map, and was asking them for some information. The man turned to face the woman.

Horror and dread struck Svetlana's eyes. "My God, it is . . . oh! my God . . . Sasha? How did he find me here? My God! How did he find me here?" She mouthed the words, repeating them unconsciously to herself, but without sound . . . frantic. As she stared at him in astonished silence, she shuddered at the sight. "How could they know where I am staying? My God . . . oh! My God." It took Svetlana nearly a minute to control her fright. She crawled back into the living room, straightened herself, realizing that if the woman hadn't pressed the apartment house entry buzzer, Svetlana never would have known that Anatoli and Sasha were waiting for her. "But who was the woman?"—a question for which Svetlana would not get an immediate answer.

Svetlana went back to the bathroom, placed the soiled towels in the bathroom hamper, put on the same clothes she had worn since she had left Cyprus, brushed her hair hurriedly, ignored putting on any makeup, and then grabbed her purse, checking to see if she had her money, passport, credit cards and the note.

Following the instructions, she placed the note back into the envelope, sealed it, putting it on the foyer table as she quickly left the apartment. She kept the small blue calling card with the symbol which she couldn't yet decipher. Svetlana had to recover her calm state of mind, redoubling her caution as she realized the situation was far more serious than she had imagined when she first saw Anatoli and Sasha earlier in the day. She knew that she would be hunted, but she didn't imagine it would occur here, or now, or by these two vipers, of whose ruthlessness she was well aware.

Svetlana felt lonely and worried as she walked to the end of the corridor past the central stairway and the elevator to the far side of the fifth-floor corridor, where an exit sign was displayed on a door. She opened the door slowly and saw that it led to a narrow, light-gray, concrete stairway, dimly lit by a small oval light fixture centered in the ceiling of each landing, one flight heading obviously to the roof, and the other steps leading down. She started slowly down the steps, carefully silent. When she got to the first floor, she opened the door and was relieved to see that it led into a small foyer with a door marked laundry room, which was open, revealing a heavy woman with a head piled high with light hair, with a large bust, and with enormous hands holding a mass of laundry in an oversized basket.

She turned as she heard Svetlana close the door from the stairwell. "I'll be finished soon. Mrs. Hamerick has too many clothes. Too many clothes and they all have to be ironed! I'll be finished in ten minutes, if you would like to come down then."

"No, that is quite all right. I am on my way out," Svetlana replied.

The lady looked at Svetlana and snickered, "Anyway, you don't look as if you do much laundry," and she laughed uproariously.

"Can anyone come in through this door from the parking lot?" Svetlana asked.

"My, no. It is locked from the outside. Your front door key also opens this one. You know that security is tight here. Many important people live here . . . like you," and she laughed again.

Another door was labeled "mechanical" and a third marked "exit." Svetlana went to that door, opened it and immediately saw the black Volkswagen, parked directly opposite the exit door, where the note said it would be. There were three other cars in the modest, unpaved, gravel lot. The exit from the parking lot led via a small graveled alley on the left side of the apartment building directly to Steinwiesstrasse, the street where the apartment building's main lobby entrance was located.

Svetlana opened her purse, took out the keys, unlocked the car, and settled into the driver's seat. Her hands began to shake as she put the key into the ignition, realizing she didn't even know in which direction she was going. She opened the dashboard, and there found a large, plasticized map card carefully detailing, in bold red, the route from the apartment to Einsiedeln. She studied it for a moment and knew it would be easy because she had been on the various motor ways from Zurich when she and Moussa traveled outside the city, although she had never visited Einsiedeln. Her hopes and aspirations, which she had when she left Moscow, lay deep in the worry that was now overtaking her. She needed time, time to get to Einsiedeln, however long. She needed the time to continue her disrupted escape. Svetlana nerved herself to fear the worst, if only to soften the pain and anxiety which was increasingly sapping her strength.

The directions were clear. She placed the map card on the passenger side seat for easy reach. Then, putting the car into gear, she slowly began moving from the lot into the short alley leading to the street, where she stopped. She immediately noticed that the cars on both sides of the street were parked all in one direction, leaving only one narrow lane for traffic. The large black and white sign, at the end of the alley, and directly in front of her, had an arrow pointing one-way—the very direction she had to go. There was no traffic on the street and the directions on the map showed that she should turn left onto Steinweisstrasse, drive past her apartment entrance and toward the main thoroughfare three blocks away.

Svetlana put on her dark glasses. Then she took the green silk scarf she was wearing under the lapels of her jacket and placed it over her head, covering most of her long blond hair. There was little else she could do but drive out onto the street and exit onto the main thoroughfare.

As she started down the street, she noticed the woman was still engaged in conversation with Sasha, both looking at a large document she had placed on the hood of the Mercedes. Sasha was viewing at it intently, when he glanced up as he heard the approaching Volkswagen. Svetlana slowly accelerated her car, driving by them, staring straight ahead, trying to carefully navigate in the tightness of the one driving lane between the closely parked cars. At that moment, the woman moved to the other side of Sasha and closer to the street. The woman was reaching into her bag and bringing out another large document and as she began to open it and spread it on the hood, Sasha looked quizzically at the Volkswagen as it began to pass by. "The green scarf . . . it was the green scarf . . . was that Svetlana? Was it?"

Half-wild with anger as he judged it could only be her, Sasha shrieked as Svetlana's car went by, "Anatoli, Anatoli, that's Svetlana." He sputtered as he pushed the two documents off the hood of the car—"Clear the way, you hag. Clear the way." He shoved the woman away so forcibly that she slipped back and fell to the pavement. "Move, Anatoli! Move! Move!"

The woman rose quickly, grabbing the car's grill, steadying herself, running around to the driver's side, grabbing the handle, shouting, "Someone call the police! Police ! Help! Help!"

"Get the fuck off! Get the fuck off!" Anatoli screamed, punching her in the face through the open window as he pulled away from the curb, leaving the woman gasping on the pavement.

But Anatoli would be too late. Svetlana's Volkswagen had reached the end of the street and moved immediately onto the main four-lane thoroughfare at the end of Steinweisstrasse. She turned left onto the street, staying in the left lane. That lane would take her over the Quai Brücke, the bridge over the Limmath River, and continue for a short distance where she would get onto Nationalstrasse No. 3, the motor way out of Zurich. Normally this would have taken no more than three to five minutes, but the traffic was heavy because it was Friday evening and many people were heading to their mountain retreats. Svetlana had gone only four blocks when the light turned red, forcing her to stop; she was the first to go in her lane when the signal light would changed. Aside from the stop light, traffic was practically at a standstill.

It was the same for Anatoli, who was stuck three blocks behind Svetlana. "Get out of the car, Sasha. Get out . . . find her . . . get her . . . find the bitch," Anatoli said angrily.

Sasha left Anatoli's car and began jogging along the sidewalk on the left side of the road, reaching Svetlana's car just as the light turned green. He ran directly up the driver's side as Svetlana pulled away.

He shrieked, "You bitch, Stop! Get the fuck out! Get out." His burning eyes glared at her.

Svetlana fixed her gaze straight ahead and pulled away, leaving Sasha hanging on the door handle, dragging him for a few feet until he let go, still shouting at her. Several pedestrians, astonished at what they were seeing and at Sasha's screaming, tried to grab Sasha, but he shook them off, and ran back to Anatoli's car.

Because of the traffic jam, Anatoli had moved just one block. Sasha, perspiring and panting, jumped into the Mercedes, still muttering, "that bitch . . . that fuckin' bitch. She got away, Anatoli, got away again!" His body quivered with exasperation and anger.

"No matter, Sasha, I have Svetlana's license number, and we know the car is an old black Volkswagen. We shall find her, Sasha. Don't worry, my friend. You did well, and we will be the angels that destroy her. Not to worry, my friend, not to worry at all. In this traffic she won't get far. Not to worry, Sasha, not to worry," Anatoli repeated his litany with certainty.

The heavy traffic wound its way to the streetcar terminus just before the Quai Brücke, the bridge over the Limmath. Anatoli knew that would be the way Svetlana would take because it was the only crossing that made sense, if she was heading for the motor way out of the city, which he believed she was going to do. Cars had to go around the turnabout in order to head for several different streets emanating from the it.

Svetlana switched to the right lane to get into the correct road leading to the motor way. Now only a block behind her, Anatoli knew his instincts were correct. She was leaving the city. It was at this point that Anatoli clearly saw her, because he was on the slight incline looking down at the turnabout. "There she is, my friend. Yes, there is our little princess . . . dashing away like frightened deer. Yes, Sasha, we shall not lose her again."

He saw her drive over the bridge and tried to speed up in order to follow her. Again, the traffic was too heavy for him to catch up. It was clear to Anatoli that Svetlana was headed for the only motor way they could turn on to. He stayed on that route, driving several kilometers before he got on the motor way where he could see her car. She was headed south. In any case, he had caught up with her and was only four car-lengths behind.

"Relax, Sasha, my friend. We have her. We won't lose her. Relax. Call the girls and see what is going on," Anatoli asked. "Tell them we'll be late."

"I hope you're right, Anatoli. Svetlana is running away . . . yeah . . . the bitch is running away," Sasha commented as he picked up car phone, dialing the number of the Widder Hotel operator, who put him through to their room.

After several rings, a wispy, drunk voice came on. "Hallo. Hallo. I can't hear you. Do you want to fuck me?"

"This is Sasha, my love Tatyana."

"Sasha, where are you? We are waiting for you, my big dick man. I need you, now," Tatyana said.

"You'll get it soon enough, my love," Sasha replied. "But first, we have found Svetlana and are following her on the motor way south to San Bernadino. My love, did Moussa call?"

"Oh! my love. Did Moussa call? Oh! my love, he did! He threatened to cut my breasts off and feed them to the pigeons at Gorki Park. Oh! Sasha, come home. He's so cruel. I told him that you were fucking Svetlana, and she is sucking your dick. He is now very angry at you and Anatoli and said he'd kill you. He's on his way here from Cyprus, my love. Hurry home," and with that she hung up.

"Bitch! Fucking, drunken bitch!" he screamed as the phone went dead.

"What happened, my friend?" Anatoli asked.

"Moussa called our hotel and knows we found Svetlana. Tatyana said he is on his way here, but she was so drunk, she couldn't remember much more. I'm going to call Moussa's office and tell them where we are. I'll also call the Baur au Lac and leave a message for him there as well," Sasha, frustrated, said. "Somehow, we'll get to him . . . somehow."

"Well," Anatoli responded, "we now know that she really has left Moussa. I don't think this is something good that she's doing. Maybe she's hiding money for that bastard Bradford. Who knows? But I'm convinced she's running away, otherwise she wouldn't have lied to us and, look, she almost took your hand off just a few minutes ago. No, she's running away. Something is very wrong, my good friend, very wrong. Call Moussa's office."

Sasha quickly dialed Moussa's office in Moscow, left word what he and Anatoli were doing, and then called the receptionist at the Baur au Lac Hotel, leaving a message that they would contact Moussa later.

Anatoli soon caught up with Svetlana. The traffic on the motor way was heavy, but moving swiftly against the slower traffic in the right lane, and that was where he caught up with her. "There, Sasha, is the little princess, but we should stay a little behind. Let her think that she has cheated us of her good company. Sasha, I can guarantee you that when we catch her, Moussa will let us fuck her just like he does when the three of us are together . . . we fuck each girl the other has; yes, he will let us fuck her. Then he will kill her," Anatoli said with satisfaction.

"We'll stand triumphant! My friend, he'll reward us for all our help. We won't be treated like shit by him anymore, my friend. We'll be heroes in his eyes . . . real heroes," and Anatoli and Sasha laughed loudly, both repeating, over and over again, "Fuck Svetlana . . . Fuck Svetlana."

Svetlana, for her part, her weary day continuing, finally was on the motor way, relieved that she had eluded Sasha and Anatoli. Oblivious to the noise of the highway, she glanced repeatedly into the rearview mirror rather than concentrating on the passing cars. She accelerated to 100 kilometers per hour, passing green pastures along the lower hills, dotted with postcard-picture farm houses which she also failed to notice. She was having trouble quelling her anxiety. She had to get to Einsiedeln before they caught up with her. She knew then that Colonel Boarders would find her. She had to keep her trust in that fact.

As the kilometers melted away, she thought again of her mother and the long conversations she had about her father. She wanted to know more about her father, but her mother would only say,"You do not have to know. Sometimes, it is wise not to know . . . it is wise not to know everything, my daughter, really it is wise not to know everything, believe me. . . please believe me." Conversing with herself, aimlessly aloud as if her mother was sitting right next to her, Svetlana said, "Would I be here now, mother, if I had not taken the job with Peter Bradford, never met Moussa, never met Colonel Boarders? Oh! Mama, I want to be with you. I am so scared. Anatoli and Sasha . . . yes, even Moussa will kill me. I know that they will," she whispered, alone, in her car, tears of fear now streaming from her eyes. She kept up her speed, still not noticing Anatoli's Mercedes, her mind concentrating on the unknown that lay ahead. He was there, several car lengths behind.

It took thirty minutes to arrive at Einsiedeln, the exit ramp for the town from the motor way providing a sweeping view of the monastery below. Lines of cars and tour busses blocked the way in front of her, but she decided to follow them into the town. As the traffic slowed, she looked at the massive Benedictine monastery and church with awe, overwhelmed for a moment by its grandeur. The two towers were crowned with patriarchal crosses, with identical clocks in each citron-shaped tower. Between the towers, the facade of the church curved forward with the adjoining wings of the monastery on either side. The monastery was her destination, and she now knew this would be her last stop. As bells began to peel from the monastery church towers, Svetlana looked up to the twin towers and noted the time was six in the evening.

A short distance from the monastery, the traffic turned into a parking lot which was rapidly filling. She followed the line of buses and cars into this lot, but as she came to the entrance, a guard waved her off. The lot was already full. She was allowed to exit from the rear of the lot, however, and she found herself on the main street parallel to the monastery.

Throngs of pilgrims were streaming directly ahead toward the entrance to the monastery church, passing two arcades of religious stores that fronted a huge plaza leading to stairs to the church. She had difficulty maneuvering the car as the people spilled over from the sidewalks onto the street. She found a parking space on a side street four blocks from the monastery church. From there she walked toward the front of the church, joining the crowd of religious pilgrims making their way into the church.

Anatoli inched his car through the same street where Svetlana just driven several minutes before. Also looking for a parking space, Sasha searched the faces in the crowd for Svetlana's.

As Svetlana approached the open ten-foot double doors from which the odor of candles and incense filtered, she left the line of pilgrims entering the church. She walked along the outside of the monastery church along a small passageway and through a small archway into the main courtyard. Her solitary figure set against the building made her a target for Sasha who had been scanning the crowds from the car.

"There, there, Anatoli, the lady up there, on the side of the church—isn't that Svetlana? The green suit, scarf . . . isn't that her?" Sasha excitedly asked.

As he slowed the car to a stop, Anatoli looked out, but by then he saw just a glimpse of Svetlana as she entered the courtyard. "Sasha—it looked like her. I don't know . . . for sure. But not to worry, my friend. We have come this far for her. We won't leave without getting our hands on that cunt. No, we won't leave," he said, and again both laughed.

The courtyard, which Svetlana entered, was flanked on three sides by large, cream-colored gable houses, four and five stories in height, each side extending 100 meters. The joined gable houses formed a large square, open on only one side, and only through the archway she had just entered. She stood for a moment and admired how peaceful the courtyard enclosure was, masking the noise from the crowds of pilgrims entering the church proper.

There were only two doors to gain entrance into the monastery block of buildings. She walked to her left to the first of two entrances and noted that the first one was marked in German "Monastery Deliveries." Further down a second door was marked, also in German, "Court/Appointments." She slowly climbed the few steps to the door, reached for the large, black iron door handle and pushed the door which opened directly into a marble foyer. A larger than life statue of the founder of the Benedictine Order, St. Benedict, stood directly in the center of the foyer, bordered on either side by identical marble stairways to the second floor. Only one set of stairs, on the right, led to the lower level. No one was there, but directly to the right side of the foyer hung a wall phone with dialing instructions. Svetlana picked up the white phone and dialed zero.

Shortly, a male voice came over the speaker. "May I help you?"

"Yes, I am Helene LeFevre, and I am here to see the Abbot Hans Polzherr."

"One moment, please."

"Please wait, the abbot will be down momentarily to greet you. It will only be a minute or so."

For a moment, she looked at the statute of St. Benedict—not really knowing more about him than was written on the small plaque at the base of the statute, which, in German, read: "Let nothing be preferred to the work of God." The peaceful look on his face, the magnificence of the flowers that were placed on a small ledge surrounding the base, the silence of the room, all had a calming effect on Svetlana. She marveled at the silence. Not a sound from the outside came through the massive oak door which she had just entered, nor from the two-story-length windows on either side of the door. Time seemed to have stopped with the silence.

A rustle from above made her raise her eyes toward the right stairwell as she saw a brown robed figure quietly close the door behind him, descending, alone. The abbot's robe was tied by a double cream-colored rope belt, and he was wearing simple leather sandals. He appeared to Svetlana to be seventy, several inches taller than she, straight-backed, with gray-blue eyes, so clear, yet so smiling, and a coarse, ruddy complexion marred by age lines. He walked slowly and, as he reached the bottom of the stairs, he extended his hand, "Welcome, Helene LeFevre. How can we help you?"

"Thank you for seeing me, Abbot Polzherr." She drew out from her purse the small blue card with the symbol on it with the word "Pentum" printed below.

He looked at the card for a few moments, then at Svetlana. "I am happy you are here. We welcome any friend of Colonel Boarders. We never know when to expect his friends, but we are always happy to receive them. Please, come in." And for the first time since she left Moscow, she felt safe and secure. And so it would be for a while at least.

The abbot took her down a long cream-colored passageway lined by portraits of past clerics of the monastery. "These, Ms. LeFevre, are my predecessors. You can see I have had many. The church and abbey were founded some 1000 years ago. On the right side are the rooms, or cells as we call them, for my brother monks. We all keep a rigid schedule. We rise at three in the morning and are supposed to retire at eight in the evening, although, as you notice today, we have a special ceremony in the church, so it will be later."

"It is so peaceful . . . so wonderfully quiet." Svetlana said softly.

"That is part of the Benedictine life of piety, prayer, discipline, and generosity. We must be consistent in these ways."

"It is a harmonious life . . . a very beautiful life."

"Yes, it is, but we pray every day that we can continue to keep it as such," the abbot said. As they reached the end of the corridor, he motioned for her to turn right. "I am taking you to our guest quarters where you will be attended to by one of our lay workers. You know that we are an order of cloistered monks, although many of us teach and minister to the community as well. Ms. Marie Tohl is our administrator and heads the staff that keeps our monastery in good order. I wish we had the number of vocations to do all the work relating to the monastery ourselves, but those times are long gone. Modern temptations are too much sometimes, as you can imagine. So, we have to be diligent in our recruiting for brothers who will carry on our founder's work. And, you, Ms. LeFevre, do you profess a religion?"

"No, I can't say that I do. My parents, I believe, were Russian Orthodox, but I am not sure, and on my mother's side I think her family was Jewish; again I am not sure. Neither of my parents practiced religion. You know in our country it was forbidden—" and then she stopped in mid-sentence, forgetting for a moment that she was French. "I guess I really don't know what they were . . . but, no, I do not have any religion that I follow. Perhaps at some point I should. But not now," she said apologetically.

"I understand. Well, here we are." He opened a door to a foyer, and then on to another door that was marked, in German, "Administrator." He knocked and entered, revealing a spacious office which also overlooked the courtyard. Sitting at her computer, working, was a woman about fifty, tall and very thin, with jet black hair, a bold woman, it seemed, with deep, blue eyes. Behind her were three other women, perhaps in their forties, doing clerical work, Svetlana supposed. Again, she thought, how peaceful and quiet it was . . . even though everyone seemed busy.

"Excuse me, Ms. Tohl, we have a visitor for the evening. Ms.

LeFevre, I leave you in good hands. I wish you well . . . and I shall pray for you. Of course, you are welcome to come to the evening service, which will begin in a few minutes. But you may prefer to rest after so long a journey. You have sense, courage, and resolute will, Helene LeFevre, attributes that will always serve you well. We again welcome you."

"Good bye, Abbot Polzherr, and my thanks. I shall be very happy here, I am sure."

The abbot nodded to her and left.

"We have our guest suite just down the corridor from here," Marie Tohl said as she reached to shake Svetlana's hand. There was a serenity and dignity about her which, to Svetlana, awakened admiration and respect. Svetlana had the feeling that Marie Tohl was a brave woman. "I hope you will be comfortable. There is a phone, and we will bring your evening meal to you. The refectory is limited to the monks, as you can imagine. We are happy that you are here. Colonel Boarders has been most kind to us over the years, and we help him whenever we can. Please, come with me."

Within a few minutes, Svetlana stood in a small suite consisting of a spartan bedroom, sitting room, and bathroom. The rooms were all painted cream and the moldings were all stained dark oak. Oil portraits on the wall appeared to be scenes from the surrounding countryside. The floors in the suite were covered with soft, wool, muted-brown area carpets. The sitting room had a small, cream-colored fabric couch, two matching side chairs, and a mahogany desk with a straight-backed mahogany chair. A phone, a small electric clock, a pad of paper with the seal of the monastery at the top, and a cupful of sharpened pencils were neatly arranged on the desk. The bedroom had a single bed, one bed stand, and a small chest of drawers.

"If you need anything, please call me; my number is on the card by the phone, as is my home phone number. I am sorry there is no television or radio in the room, but I don't think you will be here long," said Marie Tohl. She smiled as spoke.

"I hope not. Perhaps less than twenty-four hours," Svetlana answered.

"We welcome you for whatever the length of time," Ms. Tohl said.

"I'll have a tray sent to your room within the half hour. You must be hungry."

"Yes, very." Svetlana smiled and shook Ms. Tohl's hand. "Oh! Marie, here are my car keys. I will not need the car any longer," and she reached into her purse, opened it, handing the keys to Tohl.

"Thank you. We'll pick up the car. It actually belongs to the monastery. We loan it to Colonel Boarders from time to time. Was it in good driving condition?" Tohl asked.

"Very good . . . fine condition. I had no problem. I parked it by a toy shop about four blocks along the main street fronting the church," Svetlana said.

"Good. Now if you need anything, please just call. Try to get some rest, if you can." As Ms. Tohl left, Svetlana headed for the desk and the phone to make her call. A small printed note on the base of the phone read, in German, that the phone was a direct outside line. She picked up the receiver and dialed 823-5671 and, after a moment, she heard a series of clicks indicating that the call was being transferred. Finally a voice came on stating, "The Pentum Trade and Investment Office is closed. Please leave a message at the sound of the tone." Svetlana waited for the signal and then said calmly, "This is your weather advisory. The sun will rise from the northeast." Then she hung up and went back to the bedroom and laid back down on the bed.

"Over. It is now over. They will come for me," she said to herself confidently.

Sasha had lost her in the crowd of pilgrims, but he was certain that he saw Svetlana enter the archway into the monastery office and residential complex. He knew she was there somewhere. "Okay, my friend. Let us call Moussa and see if he has arrived at the Baur au Lac. I think Svetlana has gone crazy, my friend. Maybe she will become a nun," and he started to laugh. "How stupid all these people are, going in to see an idol and light candles. How very stupid, my friend," Anatoli observed. Both of them just stared for several minutes as the throngs of pilgrims continued to grow and they could hear the sound of organ and choir music.

"We shall find her, my friend, Sasha. Yes, we shall find her." Anatoli and Sasha, despite the signs that said "No Parking," parked their car directly in front of the first hotel they saw—the Hotel Drei Könige—and went in. They would book rooms for the night, and wait. Their girlfriends would have to sleep alone tonight.

Moscow
Friday
Local Time: Midnight (9:00 p.m., London)
Dimitri Gravev's dacha
Thirty kilometers southeast of Moscow, near the village of Barvikha

Dimitri's usual state of mind was realistic and pragmatic. He now saw that the situation was deteriorating, and he knew, from experience, that once that pathway was taken, the end would be unpleasant. The calls from Bradford and Moussa telling him that Svetlana was not on Cyprus but was in fact in Zurich—when everyone believed she was in Cyprus—clearly indicated something serious had occurred. Further, there was no additional word from Bradford that the contract in London had been successful. Dimitri had no difficulty recognizing the obvious problem, and he had some suspicions as to what or who had caused the problem . . . but he needed more information . . . which he would try to get. But, if he found someone disloyal, it would be relentless warfare against that person.

"Dimitri, come and get some rest, please, Dimitri," his wife Olga said quietly. "Do you need anything, Dimitri? Tomorrow, you promised that we will go to visit Igor and see the twins. Remember we are going to spend the entire day with them. Did you get them some toys today, my Dimitri?" his wife asked.

He rose from his chair, going to where his wife was standing in the small sitting room adjacent to the bedroom. "Olga, yes, we will go. I bought one toy—a soccer ball—for both boys. They do not need two toys. We must teach them to be frugal, Olga. Frugal," he smiled as he said that.

"But the boys are only four!" Olga exclaimed.

"Yes, and they can kick the ball back and forth between them," Dimitri responded. "We shall have a good time with them. Have no fear, Olga. I hope you baked some sweets for them. Did you?" he winked at her as he said that, knowing she had over a dozen special sweets for the only set of twins in the family.

"No, I shall buy them." she said as he went over and kissed her.

"Olga, I shall go upstairs to my study and stay there for a short while. Then I shall be right down, directly."

"Dimitri, do not stay up late. You have not been sleeping lately, my husband. You must get your rest. Are we still going to America to visit Marya the week after next?"

"Yes, why not? We must see her and convince her to come back to Russia. We need her here in this country," Dimitri said with some force.

"Now, don't argue with her, Dimitri. Every time we see her, you argue with her. She has her own mind, and if she wants to stay in America, that should be fine, Dimitri, just fine," Olga replied.

"No arguments, I promise," he replied, knowing that as soon as he saw his daughter, he would start the process over again and ask when she planned to come back to Russia. But he didn't have the strength tonight to disagree with his wife. He needed to think of more pressing matters.

"I shall be down directly, Olga. I shall. Give me just a little time. I have to sort some things out and make some calls. Then I shall be down. Keep the bed warm," he said as he kissed her again. Age and the years had not dampened his love for her. She kept their children and grandchildren all together, remembering birthdays, school award days, sports, everything and always had a surprise for all the grandchildren. Olga provided a certain stability in the midst of his business life. He would sit with her every evening for a while and it would help him to relieve the tensions of the day. They always had much to say to one another, principally about the family.

Dimitri was thankful for all this good fortune, but his mind fixed on finding out why Svetlana was in Switzerland, taking with her some secrets of his organization. At least the secrets involved Bradford. It was likely that those disks contained all of Bradford's drug deals as well as the arms matters. He had earlier talked to his two sons, Nikolai and Gregor. All the businesses were running smoothly, and the only troubles with the bank were some minor tax disputes with the central bank that his lawyers would clear up. Only the arms transactions proved to be the irritant to what would otherwise be uneventful days. Everyone seemed to be working in a constructive fashion and making a great deal of money; no one tried to interfere from abroad. He needed some time to think about what was happening and who caused it to happen.

He walked down the dimly lit second-floor corridor to the open stairs to the third floor, passing the small kitchen adjacent to the housekeepers' sitting room. The housekeepers were having some tea and quiet conversation. As he passed by, Irina, one of the housekeepers, rose to greet him. "Dimitri Gravev, do you need anything? Tanya and I are just having some tea. I can bring you some tea if you wish."

"No, Irina, thank you very much, though."

"Does Mrs. Gravev wish anything?" Irina asked.

"No, she has gone to bed. Thank you for asking," he responded as he walked down the short corridor to his small study and library, both of which he enjoyed more than the formal library on the first floor.

The library and study were really one room separated by built-in bookcases. The bookcases framed a large open entranceway, on either side of which stood potted ferns in large green porcelain containers. Books were placed on either side, and the collection was mostly of Russian fiction. Scattered on all the bookshelves were various mementos that he had acquired over the years. The walls of the study were covered with antique maps of Russia. The largest map, directly behind Dimitri's mahogany table desk, was of modern Russia. The library walls were covered with a series of photos of his children and of his wife and him. Interspersed throughout were photos of him on some of his travels with General Secretary Brezhnev, including a framed photo directly centered on one wall, which Brezhnev autographed for him with the statement,"To my protector!" Dimitri was very proud of that photo.

Each room had a single highly polished brass chandelier with brass wall sconces—all with electric candle fixtures, which could be dimmed. The library had three burgundy leather wing chairs arranged around the double window facing the front of the house. A low, oval, gray marble table stood in front of the chairs on which lay several Russian newspapers. A phone also rested on the table. In addition to the large mahogany table desk and burgundy leather desk chair, a small burgundy couch sat in the office. On either side of the couch were two simple mahogany tables on which stood brass lamps with beige shades. The floors in both rooms were covered with burgundy-colored oriental carpets. On Dimitri's table desk he had placed a computer, which he rarely used, other than to update himself on certain financial data, and a telephone. A plain white paper pad and sharpened pencils were the only other items on the table desk. It was 11:00 p.m. in Tel Aviv and, despite the hour, he decided to call Arkady Mironov, his closest friend from his village days. Both were recruited into the USSR's army at the same time, and they had maintained a friendship ever since.

Arkady Mironov was Jewish. He had kept that fact hidden for many years while he was serving in the Soviet Army, where, like Dimitri, he was a bodyguard for Kremlin officials. He retired about the same time as Dimitri, but his rank at retirement was major, the same as Dimitri's. Notwithstanding this same rank, he always called Dimitri his "chief," and in fact he was. Dimitri was head of the Kremlin bodyguard force.

When he was able, in 1985, Arkady emigrated to Israel and, with assistance from Dimitri, started his own security service business. His company, Matra Enterprises, Ltd., was the largest security company in Israel and had a close relationship with Dimitri's German company which manufactured the security equipment Matra sold.

Matra had extensive dealings with many African countries, and through its own staff had trained many of the private security guards for several African political leaders, some of whom were military dictators. "But they paid their bills up front," Arkady used to say to Dimitri. It was this friendship that made Dimitri feel comfortable with hiring as an assistant Arkady's son, Sergei Mironov, a bright young lawyer educated in the United States and in France. Arkady wanted his son to get experience in the country of his birth, Russia, and after a year or two, to come back to Israel to work with him. Sergei told his father he wasn't ready to return to Israel, but wanted to remain in Russia. Arkady knew his son had fallen in love with a Russian girl and that was the real reason for his son's reluctance to come home.

After several rings, a groggy voice came on the line, "Yes, who is it? This is Arkady Mironov, and I hope this is important, or I'll have your balls for breakfast."

Dimitri laughed. His old friend never changed and always spoke the soldier's earthy language. "Arkady, it is me, your favorite Russian . . . after your son, of course—Dimitri Gravev."

"Shit! What time is it, my old leader? Where are you? What has happened to my son? I'll kill you with my bare hands if some shithead has harmed a hair on his head. You're supposed to take care of him, you bastard!" Arkady shouted and laughed at once.

"I answer your questions in the order received. It is 11:00 p.m.—early for you, in your city; I am at my dacha in Barvikha, you remember that village where the high party members had their dachas and we used to screw their secretaries, you, not me, used to screw their secretaries; your son is fine and in love with the most beautiful girl in Moscow, but you know there is a religious problem, and I am taking care of him, you bastard!" and Dimitri roared with laughter.

"Yeh! I remember Barvikha. You were so prim and prissy then. Are you still that way, my friend? Do you realize how much screwing you missed when you were young? Look at us now, old and decrepit . . . getting it hard takes twenty-four hours of sleep! That is why I am in bed so early, my friend Dimitri Gravev."

"For you, you old man. For me, only twenty-three hours! That is why I am still awake," Dimitri roared again. "But, my friend, what I have to talk to you about is very serious. I need some advice and some information. Are you now awake?"

"Let me go to another phone. Zelda will kill me if I stay here. She is wondering whom I am calling such names. It is Dimitri, my love, from Moscow. She says hallo to Olga and not to you. She is angry at you, you bastard, for waking her up. What can I do? I can't please my own wife. Life is over! Dimitri. Life is over! Hang on, my friend. I am going to the kitchen," and with that the phone went dead.

Dimitri knew he was taking chances that the phones would be tapped, but he had these phones checked periodically, and he assumed Arkady also had his phones similarly checked. In any event, short of flying to Israel, this was the only other option, and he had high confidence in Arkady.

A click sounded on his receiver, and he heard Arkady's booming voice, "My friend, I am in my kitchen, and I have poured myself some of that great vodka you keep sending me. So, tell me, my friend, what is the problem? How can I help?"

"Arkady, are you familiar with the shipment of arms that was blown up off the coast of Libya a few weeks ago?" asked Dimitri.

"Yes, of course, my friend. It was in all the newspapers. My friends in the Mossad tell me that the Americans were behind this, but there is absolutely no proof, none. The Mossad said it is a guess, but there is not one shed of evidence that the Americans were involved. For years, they told me the Americans have had a super secret group that assassinates people they don't like. Can you believe that, my friend? the Americans—like the Russians?" and he laughed for a moment. "But I will tell you though, my old comrade, they say your bank provided the funding for these arms, so the Americans, if they have this secret death squad, will target you. They won't let you live. Even the Russian government is now investigating your bank. Is it not?"

"Yes, my friend, but it is a tax issue and the lawyers are taking care of it. We will negotiate something, I am sure."

"Be careful. I am not as bright as you, my friend, but sometimes, other powers may force your government to revoke your license, and then where will you be?"

"They would not dare, I can assure you. I have a great deal of influence with this government. I won't lose any sleep over whether they will take away my banking license. It'll never happen."

"Be careful, my friend. I also hear that every idiot country around my little Israel is trying to get its hands on the bomb from Russia. The satellite surveillance is heavy on all the borders of Iran and Iraq. It's like they can't move anything without some satellite or local on the take finding out about the shipment."

"My friend, you know my American colleague, Peter Bradford?"

"Of course. Some day, you will have to tell me why you put up with that crawling scum. Remember that shit he use to give the KGB—I mean how much toilet paper the American Embassy used? Would you believe the KGB paid him? My friend, that is how corrupt we were at the time. Even the KGB had too much money . . . too much money. Shit, the old system was doomed from the start, was it not, my old comrade?

"But, Dimitri, I miss you so much! We do business together, but I don't see you—maybe once a year. Why? You must visit! That is an order, old comrade. Dimitri and I worry about what you are doing with this Bradford," Arkady said.

"Bradford has me in a deal now that I can't talk about but I really don't like. Today I learned that his secretary has gone alone to Zurich when she told everyone she was going to be in Cyprus with her boyfriend. Bradford just confirmed this by phone, but I have a feeling that he knew about it before he told me. She also took some computer disks from his office detailing certain financial transactions. What do you make of it, my friend?"

"Perhaps they are together in this defection. Do you know what is on the disks?"

"Vaguely. It would be funds he received for certain of the company projects . . . not the bank or my other companies . . . but special companies, if you understand."

"It connects you and the bank?" Arkady was anxious.

"I don't think so, but I am not sure. I have asked this to be checked out. You think he and his secretary are in this together?"

"Why not? Much money at stake?"

"A great deal."

"You must stop her and him, my friend. Without question. Can I help?"

"Perhaps later."

"My friend, my comrade, you should be careful. We are too old to make any bad deals and we have too much family. You understand?"

"Your family is fine, Arkady?"

"Yes. Yours?"

"Fine. Thank you, my old friend. I will see you soon. Don't worry about your son. He's better looking than you. And his bed is never cold!"

"I know that, Dimitri. Be careful. I am here if ever you need me. I am here always."

"I have no doubt about that . . . none. I love you for that, my friend. Good bye," Dimitri rang off.

Bradford would have to go as well as Svetlana. He would take care of Bradford; Moussa who should be in Zurich soon would find Svetlana. He was angry at himself that he allowed Bradford to convince him that these deals, although big profit makers, would be easy. They were not, and the Libyan missile business had attracted a great deal of attention . . . directly to his bank, according to Arkady. But he was committed to the Iranians. He would decide to handle that as well. He would not joint his wife in bed right away for fear all his tossing and turning would disturb her. He decided to lay down on the couch and doze. He knew that sleep would not be easy at this time.

The phone rang several times before Dimitri heard it—and this phone could only be answered by him. Again, it was a number that only a few people knew, and it rang only in his study. He walked over to the desk, trying to shake off the effects of the short nap, picked up the phone and it was his assistant, Andrei Leskov, the financial executive for Bank Alliance Russia and the supervisor of all the overseas representative offices.

"Yes," Dimitri quietly said.

"Dimitri Gravev, I hesitated to call you at this early hour, but I believe that you should know that our Washington representative was killed along with his two assistants tonight in a car bomb explosion in the garage of the office building; his home also was destroyed. Luckily his wife is in Moscow. Also, I just received word that Boris Shenin and his aide, Georgi Ivashkin, both were killed when the car they were riding in was in a crash on the way to London. This is similar to what happened to an earlier representative that we sent when we were checking on the Libyan matter. Again, Dimitri Gravev, I regret to disturb you, but I wanted you to know this information."

"Thank you, Andrei. Yes, thank you very much. We will find out who it is and respond accordingly. We will do some thinking overnight, then talk in the morning," Dimitri spoke quietly. "Please remind me tomorrow to call the fine wives of these three men. It is not a happy time for us, Andrei . . . not a happy one at all. Good night. I shall speak with you early tomorrow." He hung up, slowly walking out into the hallway, and down the stairs to his bedroom. Again, there would be little sleep tonight, just thinking . . . thinking . . . thinking. "There will be a solution," he said to himself. "There will be a solution."

AeroWorld Charter Flight 1001
Saturday
Local Time: 5:00 a.m.
On route to Alconbury Royal Air Force Base
Two hundred fifty kilometers north-northeast of London; five miles from Cambridge

This time, the smell of fresh coffee woke Mary from her short but deep sleep. She rose from her seat and walked to the galley where Alice deWitt, the cabin attendant, was preparing breakfast for her as well as for the crew.

"That's exactly what I need, Alice. May I take a cup . . . no cream or sugar . . . just plain, hot coffee?" Mary asked.

"Of course. It's decaf. I'll bring you breakfast in a moment . . . food service put on a western omelette or french toast or we have healthy cereal with a banana. What will it be for you?"

"Healthy—plus one small bit of french toast. I need a little real food. Who invented cereal anyway? Ugh!" Mary laughed as she took the cup and walked back to her seat.

She had to make another call before she changed for landing. It would be to Beke Santos. She looked at her watch and noted it was a little after 11:00 p.m. in Washington. Beke would still be up.

Mary sipped some coffee, her eyes looking out at the sparkling night sky with just the trace of dawn off on the horizon, a sliver of sunlight shimmering over the clouds. "All hope was not lost," she said to herself.

Misfortune hadn't begun with Bob's death. It had begun with the attorney general. She didn't regret her choice of words when she spoke to the president and the attorney general. Her bitterness was directed not at Steiner, a president whose instincts were correct, but at the AG, whose instincts were just the opposite. Regardless, Mary knew this would be a very dangerous trip and a dangerous day. Unlike every other mission she had been on, this ending was totally unplanned. In that fact, the AG was right. The mission finish would be different without Bob. Mary knew she had to be prepared to do more this time than would have been expected. It would be one long chase to stop the sale of the bomb. There would be no escaping heroes if she didn't succeed.

The phone was picked up on the third ring. "Good evening." The voice was low and soft. "Have you had a pleasant day?" Mary asked. In line with their custom, neither one would identify the other in the conversation.

"Yes, thank you for asking. The day has been very rewarding. I've accomplished everything."

"Good. May I call you later?"

"Yes. I'll be here all day . . . all day."

"Thank you." She was almost ready, now, to meet Dimitri Gravev, the Moscow *vor* leader. But before that, another signal had to be sent, and that she kept to herself.

Alice had waited until Mary was off the phone before bringing her the breakfast tray. "Mary, here you are . . . nice and hot and cold," she said laughing, noting the cold cereal and hot french toast.

"Alice, you're a dear. You did bring me a piece of french toast. Horrors . . . even some maple syrup. No, I won't use that at all!" Mary laughed.

"More coffee, Mary?"

"Just a little. And perhaps, a bit more juice. I'll need more Vitamin C for what is facing me the rest of this day. Thanks, Alice."

"We'll land at destination in about 45 minutes," Alice said.

"Right on schedule. Good."

"Actually, a little ahead of schedule."

"We must be on the right side of God today, wouldn't you say?" Mary sat back and for a few moments enjoyed both the cereal and the prohibited french toast.

CHAPTER FOURTEEN

Zurich
Friday
Local Time: Midnight
The Odeon

The night was clear and full of stars as Moussa Berdayev walked across the bridge that, unknown to him, Svetlana had crossed over just several hours earlier, as she fled Zurich, followed by his friends Anatoli and Sasha. He had arrived from Cyprus just an hour earlier, resigned to the idea that Svetlana was gone from him, probably for good. He had registered at the Baur au Lac Hotel, a small, but refined hotel at the end of the Bahnhofstrasse, where, for the past several years, he had maintained a suite that he and Svetlana had used often. From the suite they could look directly toward Lake Zurich. Svetlana always commented on the beauty of the view, visible from both the living area and the bedroom.

He needed to walk a few minutes, he thought to himself, just to sort out the puzzle of this whole matter of Svetlana and her recent behavior. These events were a craziness that he found hard to imagine. "We made love just a few days ago, Svetlana, and then you're gone. Why?" he asked himself. Tomorrow, he would drive to Einsiedeln to the hotel where his friends were staying. In Einsiedeln, he would plan to find Svetlana and end her life. There was little he could do today. He had been sick and nauseated most the night flight from Cyprus, and a strange emotion had overtaken his senses: he was afraid. His shirt, which he didn't change in the hotel, was soaked in sweat and clung to him. His heart pounded like a drum. For a moment, he leaned over the concrete bridge railing, thinking he would vomit.

He didn't want to do anything to Svetlana . . . nothing at all . . . but

Dimitri had told him in a call just as he arrived at the hotel that she had taken computer disks detailing information about the various business arrangements between Bank Alliance Russian and Bradford. Dimitri didn't know why and also suspected that Bradford would try to join her, but even that made little sense, for why would he need his own computer disks? He could have access to any of the funds in the accounts for which he had signatory authority—unless he had accounts of which no one knew and funds had been diverted into those accounts, as Dimitri thought.

But, then, Moussa wasn't really thinking of all this intrigue. He wanted to know why Svetlana had left him. "I'm not a terrible man, and I treated you with respect," he said to himself, as he joined the many pedestrians enjoying a beautiful fall evening, crossing the Quai Brücke over the Limmath River to the old part of Zurich with all its coffee houses, restaurants and shops.

Although it was midnight, there was much activity on a Friday evening. As Moussa went by the small dock just before crossing the bridge, he saw a tour boat embarking tourists for a midnight cruise on Lake Zurich. He glanced at a young couple holding hands with a joyous rapture on their faces, staring at them uncomfortably as they ascended the ramp to the boat deck. He raised his hands to his face, leaning over the bridge railing, trying to cover the tears that had come to his eyes. "Why? Svetlana, Why?"

He knew this would be a difficult time. At thirty, he felt that without Svetlana he would have little life ahead of him on which to build his future. For five years, she had been his light, his hope, his love, his entrance to a society that he only dreamed about. Her grace, polish, and manners made him feel he had succeeded in life. Moussa knew that he was losing precious moments of life, each minute without her, without knowing why she left. She provided the continuing mystery of woman that he so cherished in her. Although he had been with many women, when he made love to Svetlana, he always felt different. It was that difference that made him understand that the love he had for her was genuine. Suddenly, he had been humiliated by her abrupt departure, and he knew that he would be forever deprived of that love.

As he looked down into the Limmath River, stopping for the moment to admire the magnificence of the full moon shining on the water, he thought of the first time he saw Svetlana—her perfect nape, her round neck, soft shoulders caressed by long blond hair; beautiful smile and soft voice. "Svetlana, why are you doing this to me? You should not be doing this to me." He stared down, knowing that, for him, there would be no life after this great passion for Svetlana. The mark on his life left by his love for Svetlana would live beyond the time he spent with her. That painful truth was confronting him.

Two things were certain for him: she had shamed him by her departure and by taking information about the *mafiya* she shouldn't have. He would have to kill her for doing both.

Procrastination makes an unwelcome duty more so. Moussa lingered on the bridge longer than he should have and then decided to walk to a coffee house he had gone to many times with Svetlana, the Odeon, just a short distance from the Quai Brücke. He went into the coffee house, crowded with after-theater goers, his rage becoming depression and exhaustion which result from dwelling on something that couldn't be changed.

"Moussa Berdayev, what are you doing in Zurich without coming to my shop?" a voice shouted from the far corner of the one-room restaurant. Its cramped dark wood tables and bar full of patrons made movement virtually impossible. Moussa looked up and saw Saul Vellinoix, the Zurich jeweler he had visited several times to buy Svetlana specially made jewelry. In fact, he had ordered from Vellinoix a large five-carat diamond ring for the fifth anniversary of his meeting Svetlana. He was to pick it up in another month or so when he and Svetlana would be coming to Zurich for another holiday.

Moussa waved at Vellinoix and slowly made his way over to his table. As usual, the jeweler, dressed in a black silk shirt and black trousers, was surrounded by friends. He wore jewelry, mostly diamonds and emeralds, on his fingers, his wrists, and even a necklace around his neck—all, he said, for sale. "I am a walking shop," he would joke with anyone that commented on the jewelry he was wearing.

"My friend Moussa! Where is Svetlana, that beautiful creature? You are so lucky, so very lucky. Moussa, my dear friend, the diamond ring you commissioned me to make for Svetlana is beautiful. Svetlana will look even more magnificent wearing the ring. We shall finish it in a few days, and I shall call you in Moscow. But will you be here in Zurich? Moussa, you will be delighted at the result . . . impressed, I would say," Vellinoix said in a loud, booming voice. "By the way, Moussa, these are my friends from Lugano. Please meet Madame Elizabeth Grafte, Madame Eilda Farré, and Monsieur Phillipe Maret . . . all, like you, my clients. Come join us, my friend. Please," Vellinoix, asked, knowing that Moussa wouldn't and was less interested in remembering the names of his guests.

"Saul Vellinoix, I thank you for that, and it is good to meet your friends," he said as he nodded to the assemblage around Vellinoix. "I wish I could join you, but Svetlana is not with me. I think that she has left me," Moussa said, almost not thinking of what he was uttering, and not realizing he was also, except for Vellinoix, talking to complete strangers.

"What are you telling me? No, I do not believe this. No, under no circumstances will I believe what you are telling me! She is in love with you. I know that. I have seen it, Moussa. You are joking with poor Saul Vellinoix . . . Yes, joking! That beautiful creature . . . leaving you? Absolutely not! Perhaps she is sick and does not want you to know it. Not to worry, Moussa ; she will be back. I am sure. Do you know where she is, my friend?"

"Yes, at the monastery at Einsiedeln, I believe," Moussa replied quietly, lowering his head in supreme embarrassment.

"Einsiedeln! My God! Has she decided to go into the religious community? No, that would be impossible! It is a Benedictine Monastery, men only! Oh my God, Moussa. What is happening? She has lost her mind. She must have experienced something very tragic. What have you done? This can't be!" Vellinoix exclaimed as he looked incredulously at his guests, who remained silent. "I am absolutely shocked, my friend, shocked! She needs assistance, does she not? What can we do, my friend? What can we do? I ask you."

"I don't know. I just know she is there, and I am going to see her," Moussa said dejectedly.

"Moussa, my friend, for years that monastery provided safe haven for many escapees from Nazi Germany, and of course, lately, from the various Communist countries. It is a most holy place, Moussa, a most holy place. But why would she be going there? What have you done? What has she done? Can I help you both get together again?" Vellinoix kept asking Moussa, his questions fired in rapid succession in a tone bordering on worry and disbelief.

"No, nothing. I must go myself," he said, "and I must kill her." The last five words caused Vellinoix to take both of Moussa's hands into his. "What are you saying, my friend? You are joking, are you not?" For a few moments, Moussa just stared at Vellinoix, not realizing what he had just said. Vellinoix saw Moussa's mouth break into a strange, sharklike smile, his eyes taking on the appearance of violence and fury. For a moment, Vellinoix was frightened, his own hands shaking as he held onto Moussa.

"Yes, Saul Vellinoix, I shall kill the fuckin' bitch." Moussa pulled his hands away from those of Vellinoix and walked off, making his way through the crowd and into the crisp, cool September night.

Moussa Berdayev was never a loving, gentle child. Perhaps it was because his father, for reasons that no one knew, abandoned his mother and his two sisters. His father disappeared into the Ural Mountain foothills, near Perm, where Moussa was born, about 1,500 kilometers east of Moscow. His mother then moved in with her own mother and father. They lived in a two-room apartment. These were reserved for oil field workers who had retired, which his grandfather had done.

His fondest memories of his youth were the fishing trips on which his grandfather took him on the Kama River, which borders Perm. His grandmother was partially blind, and he had kind thoughts of her as well. He rarely saw his mother, who worked as a secretary in the city Communist Party offices, because her hours were especially long. Finally, when he was sixteen, his mother married a widowed, lower ranking Communist Party member who also worked for the city government. He had no children, so he welcomed Moussa and his sisters.

Moussa was surly in those years, but also recognized as an exceptionally intelligent young man. In school, he surpassed many of his schoolmates, and in fact was awarded several prizes for excellence in Soviet history and in mathematics. "Your son has a good mind," the principal of the school would remind his mother. Born in 1966, he received, upon graduation, an appointment to the Moscow State University—the only one in his school class of 300 to do so that year. That was in 1985, and he avoided military service because of this appointment. He studied mechanical engineering at the university but never went back to Perm for employment.

In 1990, he got a job as an interpreter/engineer for an American company renovating a Moscow hotel. It was during this time that he met Dimitri Gravev, whose security company was providing the necessary on-site construction security. Later he found out that one of Dimitri's companies was also a joint venture partner with the American contractor doing the renovation. When Dimitri came for an on-site visit, the American contractor was accompanied by Moussa who did all the translating, although later he also found out that Gravev understood and spoke English, but rarely chose to do so.

Dimitri was impressed with him, and when the construction project was over in late 1991, he asked Moussa to join his staff at BAR Ltd., the major subsidiary of Bank Alliance Russia. Soon Moussa was making visits to all the locations where BAR was, providing security, checking to see if the guards and supervisors were on duty, equipment was in order, the headquarters staff in place and functioning efficiently, and, importantly, that all clients paid for the service—and on time. It was a highly responsible job and gradually Dimitri brought him into discussions on other business arrangements that he was undertaking, primarily to see if Moussa could cope with more responsibility and decision making. He did; his suggestions were cogent, and many times Dimitri adopted what he proposed. Moussa agreed with Bradford, however, that the arms deals were good ones and provided extraordinary profits. Dimitri never liked the quickness of Moussa's agreeing with Bradford, but rationalized Moussa's behavior in that instance as his love for Svetlana.

Although Moussa never talked of fairness or compassion, he had a capacity for kindness, which he demonstrated not only to Svetlana and her mother but also to many others in the BAR headquarters office. He would recommend to Dimitri that special bonuses be given on a person's birthday or when a worker's child received an award. Some thought this an illusion to cover his darker side. Dimitri knew and accepted both sides of a complicated personality. Moussa was a prodigious worker and led a spartan life in Moscow.

But his personal habits were mixed. He knew that himself. Svetlana was something special to be treated specially. But his physical needs were at times so bizarre, and only he understood why. Yet even when he engaged in sexual acts as deviant as they were, his sexual release was never as complete as it was when he made love to Svetlana. He ignored his wife and son but provided for them in a material way. He was often passive but had a violent streak, which brought an admonishment from Dimitri, who, at times and only to himself, worried that Moussa was ill. But despite this thought, Dimitri used Moussa as an enforcer whenever the need arose. Moussa was an accomplished performer in the art of terror and murder. Moussa was, to Dimitri, hard, active, and fearless, inured to every peril—or so Dimitri thought.

Moussa walked back to the Baur au Lac in a torpid state. It is difficult to decide to murder someone. But, for Moussa, who had murdered before, once the decision was made, it was irreversible. His mind conjured up the unlikeliest plots and schemes in respect to Svetlana. He closed his eyes for a moment, inhaling with difficulty for a moment, trying to contain the wild feelings that were rapidly overcoming him.

"Svetlana, you slut, you whore. I'll get you Svetlana, my beauty," he shouted at no one in particular as he spit into the Limmath below. "I shall get you, cut you into pieces and feed you to the pigeons." Moussa had gone mad, but no one would know. As he crossed from the bridge onto the Bahnhofstrasse and into the main entrance of the hotel, his outward appearance was supremely calm.

He asked the concierge on duty quietly, "I will need a car to rent early tomorrow morning, around six a.m. Will that be possible? I realize the late hour, but can you arrange it for me?

"Of course, Mr. Berdayev. Of course. We shall have the car ready in the morning," the concierge said, noting to himself that Mr. Berdayev always tipped handsomely—and he would do so this time as well.

But first Moussa knew he would call Anatoli and Sasha's girls and have them come from their hotel to the Baur au Lac. He needed to have his frustrations released. As he entered his suite, with its opulent antique furniture culminating in the bedroom with a king-size canopied bed, his mind was disjointed. Moussa began to laugh, softly at first, then loudly, opening the window from the bedroom to the balcony and laughing boisterously. He knew he was descending into the hell only a rejected man feels, but did not care. He picked up the phone from the nightstand next to the bed and dialed the Widder Hotel. Within a few moments, a hazy voice came over the line. He recognized it as Tatyana, probably high on coke.

"Hallo. This is Tatyana. Anatoli is that you? We need your big dick. Nina and I need so badly to be fucked by a big dick; come home, my Anatoli."

"No, you bitch, this is Moussa. You'll have my dick instead. Come on over. I have the vodka cold, and my dick is hard for you both. I'll send a cab for you," Moussa said.

"Moussa, my true love. Yes, we will be right over. Oh! Moussa, send me to heaven tonight. I need to be in heaven with you. Be naked when Nina and I come. We will want you naked, so we can feel your dick right when we come in. Oh! Moussa, my love . . . you are in Zurich!" She hung up the phone.

Moussa next clicked the receiver for a dial tone and dialed the concierge to ask him to send a cab to the Widder and pick up the girls. Moussa would degenerate into an abyss of torment and he would call it pleasure.

But why not? Svetlana was gone and that was all that mattered. He never again would hear her laughter, smell the sweetness of the aroma of her skin and hair, feel her body, make love. He would no longer tremble with desire and surprise. It was over. He would seek his pleasure in slowly killing her, watching her beg for forgiveness. "You will learn, Svetlana, no one leaves me." The eternal flames of hell would envelope

Svetlana too. Her orifice which had brought him so much pleasure would be disfigured first. Then, he smiled to himself, he would slowly cut her fine skin, finally reaching her face. His hell was a place where bodies were ripped apart and that is what he would do to Svetlana. He knew that his perversions were taking over his logic and that there would be no turning back. His decline was pointed and complete.

**Moscow
Saturday
Local Time: 3:00 a.m. (Midnight, Friday, London)
Dimitri Gravev's dacha
Thirty kilometers southeast of Moscow, near the village of Barvikha**

There was no point trying to sleep, and Dimitri again quietly rose from his bed, attempting not to wake Olga. He rebuttoned the top two buttons of his gray silk pajama top, which by habit he always kept open when he went to sleep. He felt that it was important to have a more loose top when he was asleep. Dimitri took the covers and rearranged them so Olga would be covered. He slept so closely to her that when he would get up, the covers would be pushed away and her back would be exposed.

As he went over to the sitting room, he nursed no fantasies about the future. For a moment, he looked out the window toward the forest, lit by a full moon. The mist and rain had gone and the sky was now cloudless, the moonlight glancing off the evergreen forest. He stood there for several minutes, admiring the beauty of the night, thinking to himself that treachery had invaded his life—treachery from an unexpected source. Why would Svetlana take computer disks? She probably knew what was on those disks. She also knew of the accounts, the transfers, the entire operation from Bradford's perspective. What else did she take? There must have been something else. Svetlana never appeared frivolous. Why would she leave in this fashion?

He walked over to the small telephone table next to an easy chair, still standing as he peicked up the phone, and dialed Peter Bradford.

The phone rang several times and finally Bradford answered, his voice quivering and solemn. "Hallo . . . Hallo . . . who is this?"

"Peter, this is Dimitri. I am sorry to bother you so early in the morning, but I am having a great deal of trouble, as you can imagine, sleeping. Just a few minutes ago, I received a report from Andrei Leskov that the Bank's representative in Washington, D.C., was killed in a car bomb explosion as he was leaving his office car park. I was also told that Boris Shenin and Georgi Ivashkin, who, as you know, were on their way to London to find out whether the special operation was successful, were killed in an auto accident. The accident, to me, appears similar to the one that took our representatives in the Libyan matter. And now Svetlana is gone. These instances are too close to be isolated, would you not agree, Peter? And now we do not even know whether the special operation was a success. I fear it may not have been. My intuition tells me that Svetlana is somehow involved. What other explanation can there be? These appear strangely coincidental, do they not? It is difficult not to be suspicious, Peter, very difficult. What do you think, Peter?"

Bradford closed his eyes for a moment, trying to figure out what Dimitri meant. Dimitri never made an undeserving comment. He couldn't believe that the assassination attempt had failed. "The assassin was the best in the business," he said to himself, "the best in the business." Bradford was thinking about what Dimitri had just said, repeating it in his mind, and then responded. "Dimitri, I did not know whether the attempt had failed in London. I have had no reports. Now I understand why. I have absolutely no understanding about what went wrong in Washington. This is all astonishing, overwhelming for me. You may be correct, but I have no understanding whether there is a connection between all these events and whether Svetlana is involved, and if so, why. I do not believe that Svetlana is capable of turning against me, or for that matter, against you and Moussa. Svetlana is too loyal; she has been for five years. I believe this to be true, Dimitri, very true," Bradford said emphatically.

"Yes, these events are frightening. As for Svetlana, I have no doubt you trust her, Peter, but situations do change, and all I am trying to do is to find out what really happened. Now, do you have any idea why she would be leaving you? Any idea whatsoever? Or why she should be leaving Moussa? Please, give me your thoughts. I am unable to understand what is going on, Peter. There must be more to this story, don't you think?" Dimitri inquired.

"I don't know the answers to your questions. There is no reason for her to leave. We have been very generous to her, and you know, of course, that Moussa has as well. I just don't know, but I am worried about the disks," Bradford admitted.

"The disks. What is on them, Peter? What kind of information?"

Bradford decided at this point to continue the fabrication regarding the audio tapes. He fiddled with the phone cord and was silent for several moments, but his decision was unalterable: he would lie but at the same time he would shade the lie just a bit.

"Dimitri, let me go to another phone because I don't want to disturb Lydmila. A moment please," and Bradford placed the call on hold.

"Yes, that is what I will say. The disks contain synopses of meetings I had in my office. I dictated those to Svetlana who then wrote up short summaries of the decisions of the meetings. Yes, that makes sense," Bradford said to himself. As he walked to the living room, he repeated to himself what he would tell Dimitri. That way he could avoid having to tell Dimitri of the audio tapes, but he could tell him that Svetlana took summaries of the meetings. What could Dimitri do then? He could blame everything on Svetlana, but he couldn't answer the question why she left, taking with her the disks, and, as he knew, the audio tapes.

Bradford's wife always left the small desk lamp on in the living room, and, although he didn't have his glasses on, he had no trouble getting to the desk, a simple rosewood table he had purchased years earlier from an American state department employee. It was the only remembrance he had of the years that he spent helping to supervise the construction of the United States embassy in Moscow, other than the money he amassed as an informant for the KGB.

His home taping system worked only on this phone. When he would pick up the phone, the system would automatically start. Bradford had boxes of audio tapes stored in a locked closet in his bedroom. He rarely conducted business conversations from his home; he preferred his in-town apartment he had left just a few hours before.

"Hallo, Dimitri. Yes, I really don't understand why she left. Truly, I don't. The disks contain all the financial data, payments to everyone, from office supplies to payments for the contracts on certain goods, including the special projects in which I am involved. The disks also include summaries of all the meetings that we held in the office. Even for those meetings that Svetlana didn't attend, I would summarize the results for her and she would type the summaries into the computer," Bradford said, somewhat pleased with how the story sounded—so true, he thought to himself as he waited for Dimitri's reply.

"Summaries of meetings in your office? But, why, Peter?" Dimitri said, sounding incredulous.

"For reasons of accuracy. To make sure I carried out any decisions made, or to make sure others carried out decisions made. I think it is perfectly understandable. I see nothing wrong with doing this. You know I have many meetings, so I hope you understand," Bradford said softly.

"Yes, of course. I just wish I had known about your system, especially at meetings I attended in your office. As you well know, I always asked that no notes be taken of those meetings, unless I directed otherwise. So this method of yours comes as a surprise to me, although I can understand why summaries might be useful at times. The only problem is that the summaries would be put together by you and not reviewed by the others at the meetings, so it would be your recollection, which, bright as you are, might be inaccurate. Enough said. The damage is done. How far back do the disks go?" Dimitri asked.

"Several years," replied Bradford.

"Peter, how many years is 'several years?'" Dimitri inquired.

"I believe three years. Yes, I believe it is three years," Bradford's voice trailed off, knowing that now he was compounding the lies. The disks were for five years, contained all the data on money transfers to the various banks that Bradford used for his drug deals, as well as the arms deals he did, some without Dimitri's knowledge.

"Did the disks contain information on the Libyan matter?"

"Yes, they did."

"Did the disks contain information on the most recent project?"

"Yes."

"When did you have time to discuss with her the last meeting, just this past Thursday . . . in order to prepare a summary?"

Bradford now understood he had to continue the fabrication. "She did not leave until late afternoon. The summary I gave her was very sketchy because she was in a hurry to go home, to pick up her mother. I don't know if Moussa drove her to the airport or whether she had someone else do that. I just don't know."

"Peter, this is very, very unsettling. I hope that you will continue thinking of what she could possibly do with those disks and other information that she has."

"Certainly, I shall do that, but I am at a loss. Has Moussa arrived in Zurich to look for her?"

"Yes, he has arrived. I am sure that he will find her and that the situation will be clarified."

"I just have no idea why she left . . . absolutely none," Bradford said emphatically.

"Well, Peter, you can think about of all of this when you are on your flight with Ambassador Shenasi, General Nikolayev and Prakash Farnak. I understand the our banker friend, Frederik von Hauser, left for Zurich after our meeting. It is good that you are going with the team to Turkmenistan. That way, no one could accuse us of selling a faulty device. With you and the general on board, nothing could possibly go wrong. Of course, I still am waiting for the fax from the Iranians that what we are selling them will be used for scientific purposes only. I will receive that by six a.m. this morning, will I not, Peter?" Dimitri asked

"Yes, of course. You must," Peter agreed.

"Good. Your plane is a charter, and you can be a few minutes late if the fax does not arrive on time, but as of now you are scheduled to leave around eight a.m. The flight will take you directly to the airfield where the device will be loaded onto the plane. I believe that an Iranian air crew and plane are waiting at Ashgabat to take you on to Teheran, but of course, you know of all of this, so I don't know why I am repeating this information. Must be the early hour. Thank you, Peter. Don't forget to take your cell phone. I want frequent updates on your progress in the transfer of the device to the Iranians. You do understand the necessity for this, don't you?"

"Yes, of course."

"Thank you, Peter. I know you've worked hard on this project. It is sad that Svetlana has disturbed the matter, but this all will be solved in due course. Try to get a few hours sleep if you can. I will probably just stay in my easy chair and try to get a few moments of rest. I, too, shall try to figure out what is in Svetlana's mind, and why she left you. We don't want to let a world of business crumble over this Svetlana, do we, Peter?"

"Of course not, Dimitri. She'll be found. I'm confident of that," Bradford responded.

"I share your confidence, Peter. But, she must be found soon . . . very soon. "Dimitri placed the phone down on its holder.

He went to the kitchen and steeped some tea. The house was quiet, and he liked the silence. The moonlight through the foyer windows added to the peace of the early morning. He walked down the hallway and for a moment marveled at the modern and large kitchen. "How Mama would have enjoyed this," he said to himself, thinking back to the days of his youth, when his mother had a corner kitchen—literally, in one corner of the room was a small stove, sink, and, later on, a small refrigerator which worked on and off, plus a few shelves that his father had made. The wonderful odors from that corner remained always in his mind. He thought from time to time how lucky he was to have a father and mother so simple, yet so decent. He wondered if his children could define him and his wife in the same way. Maybe not, but he knew that Olga and he tried very hard to raise the family correctly. Whether they succeeded was for the future to advise.

He laughed to himself as he thought of the first time his mother saw his new dacha. "Dimitri, my son, why do you have all this space? It is too much. You should share it with other families. Look at this stove. Why six burners, my son, why?" And she was right in a way, very right. The saddest thing a son can do is to bury his mother. Mothers are to live forever, fathers not so long. Dimitri's mother died two years earlier, at the age of eighty-eight, exactly a year after her husband passed away. Dimitri was on a trip to Germany when he wife called with the news that his mother had died in her sleep. He went immediately to Kazakhstan, joining his wife and children, his brother and sister and other family members. His children saw him cry only twice: at his father's funeral and at his mother's. In both cases, he did so openly and without shame.

Irina kept an iron tea kettle full of water and on the stove all the time. On the counter adjacent to the stove was a large brass tea pot, with two tea bags ready to receive the hot water. Irina would always do this because many times the bodyguards would want something in the middle of the night, so it was always prepared for them. In addition, she left a plate full of sweets on the kitchen table in a covered dish. He turned on the burner, watched it flame immediately, went over to the cupboard and took out a cup and saucer, placing it on the kitchen table. He took the cover off the dish and looked at the sweet raisin bars that Irina had made, but he decided against them. After a few minutes, Dimitri went to the stove, poured the hot water into the tea pot, and let it steep for a while. He liked his tea strong. Then he poured it into this cup, watching the steam rise slowly.

Sitting down in one of the oak straight-backed kitchen chairs, he begin again to think why Svetlana left and why Peter never told him about the summaries. "This is very odd . . . doesn't make any sense. None whatsoever," he said to himself as he took his first sip of tea. The hot liquid going down his throat made him feel strangely relaxed, and for that he was thankful. He looked at the kitchen clock and saw that it was 3:30. He would take his tea upstairs and sit in his easy chair, trying to get some sleep. He knew that it would be fruitless to try to sleep back in his bed. This way, he would at least try to get a few moments of rest. The confusion in his mind was too great and he had to sort out much of the day's events. There had to be a reason for Svetlana's departure and for the three murders . . . yes, they were murders . . . there had to be a solid reason.

In his heart, he recognized it to be the hammer of treason.

London
Saturday
Local Time: 3:00 a.m.
Carlton Tower Hotel, The Landsdown Suite

He was weak and he knew it. The throbbing headache sapped all his energy and his going with Robinson to look at the dead body of Ruslan Ishaev added more turbulence to an already exhausting day. Relaxed and happy he was not. David Harrison's feelings immediately swerved after Mary's call. Until that point, he was ready to chuck it all—despite the training; his family was more important than anything in the world—anything.

"Where the fuck does Mary get that heart of steel? Does she ever care . . . ever care? What am I saying? She's the one that really cares. Me? Who the fuck knows now? She's the one who reminded me that we have never rejected or abandoned any contact, nor have we ever disengaged from any mission."

Harrison knew that there are moments when the bravest want a hand to help them, a voice to comfort them and urge them on. Mary was that voice. He was whining . . . that is what he was doing . . . whining. However preoccupied with the welfare of his wife and son, he could not let his life rust and rot because at this time, in this very hour of need, he decided, suddenly, consciously, to turn around and be a stranger to the part of his life for which he had trained. Regardless, he couldn't seek shelter from the storm.

"Fuck it, plain fuck . . . fuck . . . it must be this headache . . . and age. I'm fuckin' old." For a moment, he felt the heat of anger that he had wavered in his conversation with Mary . . . dithering like an old fool . . . emotional. *Pity is out*, Mary had said, and she was right.

"Where are those aspirin? I need them," Harrison mumbled to himself as he walked to the bathroom, looking for his toiletries kit. He fumbled for the bottle of aspirin and gobbled two with a full glass of water.

He thought about the difficult situation he and Mary were in. No, not Mary. He was the one in the difficult situation. Mary passionate, strong, a *believer;* he, a bloodied, frightened *shit.* "The noblest of aspirations is to lead someone to freedom." Wasn't that how, some twenty-five years ago, his first citation began when the Director of Central Intelligence, with the *fuckin' President* present, *with Boarders in attendance* . . . *"the noblest of aspirations"* . . . had spoken? And, he had almost fuckin' forgotten that.

These calculations flashed through his mind, not suddenly, but acutely and painfully. "What a fuckin' embarrassment to cry on Mary's shoulder. I mean, Harrison, what the fuck? How many have *you* killed? Where was all that *strength*? Where was all that *confidence?*" He knew the answer was Bob Boarders—that old bear—always there—always there—his rescue of Harrison from crazies in Iran, in the most silent and mysterious of missions. The helicopter swooped down and there was Bob, his hand outstretched. And that smile, "Sorry, David, air traffic control, you know we have to wait our turn. . . ." And the smile, and off they went, into the moonlit, cloudless night, skirting the inhospitable desert waste, hoping, praying that they would reach Turkey before being discovered, the sole, dark, unidentified fighter plane providing cover.

"Shit . . . what the fuck! Why did I unload my emotions on Mary? I can't be a coward. Let's face it, you talked tough at the sight of that shithead who snuffed Bob out, and almost took me, my fuckin' family out . . . but are you still tough? What does Mary really think of me now? What does she really think? She was the one doing the rescuing . . . and it was again, like Boarders, rescuing me . . . fuckin' me."

A few hours rest was what David Harrison needed, but he wouldn't get it. Robinson was downstairs waiting for him. He asked that he be dropped off at the hotel after the Cadogan Place visit, so he could make the one phone call the contingency plan required that he make, if something happened to Boarders. Once he made that call, he was still in the mission.

Pity is out, Mary had told him. Humbled and ashamed, he reached for the phone and dialed a number only he knew. After several rings, he heard the contact's voice saying, "This is your weather advisory.

The sun will rise in the northeast."

He hung up the phone and paused for a moment to ponder the voice he had just heard. It was not nervous, but serious, soft, and clear. The contact had arrived at the monastery and was at the safe house. He knew his assignment and he would carry it out. *Pity is out.* Fuck it, Mary knew how to use words . . . yeah . . . she knew how to use words. *Never mind yesterday* was her motto. It is today we have to worry about. He'd get some rest during the ride to Alconbury. There was no need to talk about anything with Robinson.

Harrison walked back to the bathroom, splashed some cold water on his face, grabbed a towel, holding it to his face for several moments, feeling the cold penetrate his eyes and skin. He would make it . . . yeah . . . he knew he would make it. *Pity is out . . . Pity is out.*

CHAPTER FIFTEEN

Saturday
Local Time: 6:00 a.m.
Approach and Clearance to Land at Alconbury Royal Air Force Base, England
100 kilometers north-northeast of London

The light of dawn was becoming clearer as Mary glanced out the windows, unable to admire the beautiful English countryside or the magical sunrise. The first streak of light stole into the east and threw a sliver of gold sunlight over the approach to Alconbury. Mary's thoughts were elsewhere. She had been led to Alconbury for a definite end to the Pentum mission, but she didn't know what that end would be.

Ceaselessly her mind was at work, picturing what the rest of the day would be like, her immediate conversations with Harrison and the trip that she had to take to Berlin. Strangely, she was in a calmer state of mind and spirit . . . primarily because the president had said to go forward . . . and that was precisely what she was doing. Nevertheless, she knew she might have been too harsh in her conversation with Harrison.

"He called on me to give him some understanding. But what could I do for him? Nothing. Nothing brings back the past. The past is destroyed. Is it any wonder? But he did suffer; suffering as few suffer, seeing his family nearly killed. I should have understood his torment. But what would that have changed? Nothing . . . absolutely nothing." Reality was what was important to her. She believed there was a profound truth in understanding that reality commands action; fantasy is for other worlds and other minds, not for her world or her mind. She wasn't some solitary traveler walking along unfamiliar streets. This mission would be concluded, and she was familiar with the streets that had to be walked.

Mary felt she had a purpose; her mind was resolved. And she knew Harrison was capable of further action; her momentary doubts quickly faded about that issue.

"Landing in ten minutes, Ms. Auriello," came the smooth voice of the captain. "We hope you had a nice flight." She smiled at his comment. It was a good flight with few bumps.

She had changed into a navy blue, tailored suit. The skirt was short, above her knees. For her stature she preferred short skirts. Her gold ear rings, in the shape of small sea shells, were a gift from her parents a year earlier when she turned forty. The ring she wore, a single solitary pearl surrounded by two bands of diamond chips, was given to her by her lover, Jim Foster, at the same time. The only make-up she used was soft red lipstick; her face was flawless, with high cheekbones, giving her a youthful look, which she attributed to genetics, namely being born to a mother of Irish and a father of Italian descent. Her wrist watch was too big for her small left wrist. It was one of the cheaper models. But it simultaneously showed two time zones. It was practical, but it certainly looked out of place with the rest of her ensemble.

As the plane's gear lowered for the landing at Alconbury, she thought of all those times that Colonel Boarders and David Harrison would be waiting at the end of the ramp: Boarders, with a big smile and great bear hug; Harrison, standing aside with his perpetual serious look, but twinkling gray-blue eyes, waiting to do likewise. But all those trips were to celebrate victories. Today it was different. It's never a happy occasion retrieving the remains of a friend. She would make sure that Boarders would receive a proper burial, a hero's burial, one that would erase the sordid death she wanted to forget.

Mary would remain at Alconbury, an active British military air field, for just a few hours. Her next stop would be Berlin. The plane touched down smoothly and slowed, turning off the main north-south runway onto the apron leading to the administrative building adjacent to the control tower. As the plane rolled to a gentle stop, Mary marveled at the orderly row of Harrier fighter jets. It was necessary to land at this base because noise restrictions closed London's Heathrow to air traffic until seven a.m. It was inconvenient, perhaps, but necessary, and time was crucial.

The front cabin door opened easily, as Alice deWitt, the cabin attendant, rotated the handle and pressed the release latch, lowering the steps electronically on the Citation jet.

"Get some rest. I believe arrangements have made at the officers' quarters for all of you," Mary said as she waited for the steps to fit in place before exiting the plane.

The pilots's compartment door opened and a lanky, gray-haired bulky man emerged. "Good flight, Mary. Right?" Captain Richards said.

"Yes, you managed to avoid all the turbulence and keep my anxiety for flying to a minimum. Thanks," Mary said. "How long will it take you to refuel, rest, and get me on to the next stop?"

"A couple of hours. Less if you're in a hurry. Is that what you want?" Richards asked.

"Yes, we'll leave at nine," Mary replied. She descended the steps, coatless in the September early morning dawn, her black briefcase hanging from her right shoulder, the expression on her face stern and sad. Whatever jet lag remained was wiped away by the crisp morning air.

His eyes shining between a disheveled head of hair and a rough beard, David Harrison moved directly to where the steps were being lowered. Commander Robinson was standing back by the administrative building entrance, alone. He waited, giving Mary and Harrison a chance to be together for a few moments. "Mary . . . Mary . . ." Harrison grabbed her, embracing her tightly, his face pale and severe.

"David, good to see you're still alive, and with a beard no less. Really, for one who's never lost a fight and now this—and in front of half of London!" she laughed as she hugged him in return, hiding her worry as he looked at him.

"I didn't lose. The other guy ran away," he said with a shrug.

"You look fine, David. How are Betty and Timothy?" Mary inquired.

"They're okay. Both should be out of the hospital by Monday, Tuesday, I'd think," David said, looking straight into Mary's face, his eyes tearless but sadder than if they had been full of tears. "I don't know for sure, really, but that's what the doctor told me."

Seeing his condition, Mary reached over and hugged him again, saying, "David ... David ... I know you've had to struggle more than you and I would like. But, David, we've been through so much. I need you. I can't do this without you. I tried very hard to go it alone, but I can't. I just can't." There was a pleading in Mary's voice, which made him feel as if she was speaking from her heart.

"We live in the shadows, David, in dark shadows, but we aren't cowards, never cowards. Whatever we may be, whatever we may have done, at least we don't surrender, David. We're not made for defeat, David. We can't do anything else. I can't and you can't," she whispered to him, as she hugged him.

Harrison held her tightly, quietly responding, "Mary, don't worry. I'll be fine." He loosened himself from her arms, turning, heading for Commander Robinson, who was standing about ten feet away, close to the door of the administrative building, finally saying, "Mary, you know Commander Robinson," as he pointed to Robinson.

"Indeed, I do. Commander, it's good to see you. Everything in order?" Mary asked.

"I hope so," Robinson replied with a smile, and with relief at being spared any of Mary's energetic vocabulary.

"And Colonel Boarders' body? "Mary asked.

"The van, with his casket, is parked directly behind this building. Do you wish to have it brought around and put onto your plane?" Robinson asked.

"No, not yet. You have the medical certificate regarding his death?"

"Yes, He died of a heart attack at the Pentum offices in London." Goodwin replied.

"Thanks, Commander. Thanks very much," Mary responded, relieved that he had carried out this assignment carefully and efficiently.

"Shall we go in?" Without saying more, Mary turned to Robinson who had already opened the building door and walked in.

The hall corridor was lined with old prints of the Royal Air Force squadron planes that had been stationed at Alconbury during World War II. Mary knew this airfield to have been the headquarters for flights that regularly supplied the resistance movement in Europe with agents and materiel during the Nazi occupation. The code name for that operation was "Carpetbagger," lifted from the annals of the U.S. after the Civil War. Mary thought the code name interesting and certainly descriptive.

As the group was walking down the corridor, a young airman hurried from the opposite end, carrying an envelope. He reached Commander Robinson. "Commander Robinson, I have a message for Ms. Auriello."

Without waiting for a response from Robinson, Mary interjected, "I'm Mary Auriello."

"A Beverly Peterson from your office called to say that it was urgent that you call her. She gave this number," and the airman handed Mary a folded slip of paper from the envelope.

"Thank you, Airman . . ." She paused, looking at his nameplate pinned to his left breast pocket and adding, ". . . Synder. I appreciate your bringing the message to me."

"Do you wish to make the call at this time, Mary?"

"In due course, Commander. Thanks, though."

The conference room they entered was sparsely furnished, with a large plain table of nondescript wood around which stood twelve worn, straight-backed gray metal chairs, with black leather backs and seats. On the side right wall were the framed insignias of the various squadrons stationed at Alconbury over the years. On the wall farthest from the head of the table hung a large map of England. A bank of six contiguous windows faced out toward the runways. Mary could see the Citation being towed to the refueling station.

"The anteroom is to the left," Robinson said, as he took Mary to a small room directly behind the head of the table.

"Thanks. I won't be but a moment. David, would you like to join me?"

"Yes, Mary . . . but let me grab some coffee and a muffin. You want one?" David asked as he walked down the to the end of the table where a small buffet had been set up with juice, a hot plate with a pot of coffee in its center, two large platters of breakfast breads, and a large bowl of cut fruit.

"Find some coffee for me. I ate on the plane, but I'll have some of that fruit later. Commander, excuse us." She went in the small room, followed by Harrison.

The anteroom held a small table with a phone almost directly in its middle, the cord coming up from the floor through a circular opening in the table. Three sharpened pencils lay neatly at the top of a large plain paper pad. There was one desk chair, similar to the chairs in the conference room, as well as a small, black, worn leather couch, positioned at the wall facing the double window behind the table desk, which also looked out at the runways. A matching side chair stood next to the end table at the right side of the couch. Apart from light coming in through the windows, the only other illumination was provided by one fluorescent ceiling fixture centered in the ceiling. A montage of watercolors depicting World War II dog fights hung on the wall above the couch. Mary sat on the couch, placing her briefcase next to her; Harrison sat in the side chair, placing the two coffees and plate of muffins on the adjacent table.

"I'm sorry I bothered you with all that emotional crap, Mary. I should've known better," Harrison said softly.

"I would've thought you strange if you didn't react the way you did. No matter, David. When this is all over, you and I are going to get really drunk. Promise?" Mary replied.

"Promise. Dead drunk," Harrison said as he rose from his chair and again hugged Mary.

"Before I get on this call to Beverly—it probably has to do with some crazy thing the AG has done," Mary said, shaking her head. "Let's review where we are."

"The contact, a woman, is now at the safe house outside of Zurich. You know that the mission protocol Bob had structured had me memorize the special phone number, plus the message code, if he wasn't around. I guess when he gave me the instructions, I never believed I would actually carry them out. Well, here we are.

"Anyway, I called and the contact left the correct message, sometime this morning, 'The sun will rise from the northeast,' meaning she was in the safe house outside Zurich. She was to do this if she was discovered while in Zurich. Obviously, something happened and that is why she

THE PENTUM MISSION

terminated her trip at the monastery at Einsiedeln. That's all I know, Mary," Harrison said.

"That's good news, David. At least we know she's still alive and in a safe location. She was to have the originals of certain audio tapes and also some bank documents, and the contact was to have placed them in a safety deposit box in Zurich, prior to going on to London," Mary replied. "The tapes she's bringing with her are the last meeting before the contact left. Frankly, I don't suspect that these will be different from the ones concerning the meetings on the Libyan sale—only, we'll have the Iranians now. Her boss, Bradford, has been a traitor for so long. He has to be taken out, David, and soon. I see no reason to change the mission protocol, which is to have you proceed to Zurich, change the accounts to show that Bradford has placed all the money for this Iranian deal into his personal account, and to get our contact out.

"I'm willing to bet that Bradford, along with the so-called banker, Frederik von Hauser, have both skimmed from Gravev. Von Hauser has to. He's into gambling and owes several million dollars to the casino at Monte Carlo. Here's the print-out of what he owes." Mary reached into her brief case and pulled out a spreadsheet with rows of figures. David rose from the chair as Mary handed him the sheet. "Show him this, and maybe he'll cooperate," Mary said. "The casino managers are about to go after him in a big way. As you can see, he's in hock $3.4 million," Mary said.

"Should I ask how you got those figures?" David asked, a large smile finally spreading across his face.

"The fruits of hard labor . . . and the skillful use of funds for services rendered," Mary countered, slightly laughing. "Come on, now, David. You and Bob invented the easiest manner in the world to obtain information: pay for it."

"Why did I ask?"

"I don't know." They both laughed loudly, finally breaking the cycle of gloom and worry.

"Bank Alliance Russia is the cover for these arms deals and von Hauser has been a banker with them for at least three years. It'll be easy to get him to cooperate. Whoever pays the most is his friend. Skillful use of resources. Am I right, or am I right? We'll see what's in the accounts of BAR that he hasn't already skimmed as bank fees and work from there."

"What about Gravev?" Harrison asked.

"He doesn't need this arms business and yet he sticks with Bradford, for reasons I can't understand. Maybe he's been overtaken by some sort of perverted loyalty to Bradford who helped him during the Communist days. But Gravev can only be in for greed, which is what everyone in this sordid business holds as their god. That's fine, except we don't want them to sell those weapons to anyone. To make sure that Gravev's cooperates when I see him in a few hours in Berlin—"

"Berlin? Mary, hey! when did you decide to go to Berlin?" Harrison interjected, uneasily, knowing that Mary made every decision with forethought.

"While on the plane. I decided that we have to get to Gravev and have him commit to no more arms sales and to surrender to us, in one form or another, Bradford. To make sure that he cooperates—and he's not stupid—I've had his daughter, a doctor on a student visa at Columbia University Hospital, detained for questioning. It appears that, based on a tip from someone in Washington," and with that Mary smiled broadly, "the Immigration people went by Dr. Marya Gravev's office and discovered a half ounce of cocaine in her purse. Need I say more?" Mary asked with satisfaction.

"You've done what? You've detained Russia's most powerful *mafiya* leader's daughter on trumped-up drug charges? And, on top of that you want him to surrender? Let's go back . . . the jet lag must have affected your thought process. Do you really think that he won't complain to the U.S. embassy, to his own government, to whomever, to get his daughter released?" Harrison asked, shaking his head, and taking another sip from his coffee cup.

"Ingenious, I thought. Don't you?"

"Very dangerous, Mary. Ingenious and dangerous. How long can you keep her under wraps?"

"About twenty-four hours maximum. That's why I'm going to Berlin to meet Dimitri Gravev."

"Have you already set up a meeting with Gravev?" Harrison asked, again shaking his head at how Mary organized this latest event.

"No, I'm about to, though. Why do you shake your head?"

"Mary, how in the hell are you going to get a meeting with one of the most guarded and secretive men in Russia?" Harrison asked uneasily. "I mean, you're resourceful, but do you really think he'll consider altering his behavior about this sale because of the threat to his daughter? Mary, come on now. He'll know it's a ruse."

"I know it's straining credulity, David, and that we're violating all our planning advice, but once that device is sold, it will be used, David. I can guarantee that, and all hell will break loose in the Middle East." Mary lowered her voice as she looked directly at David.

"Mary, you and I know that Bob's mission protocol didn't call for you to meet Gravev, but for him to do so with the tapes and the Bradford diversion of funds evidence. There was nothing in the mission about his daughter. You know that. No, you can't go. Gravev won't come and he won't come alone. You know that as well as I do," Harrison implored. "He'll kill you outright, and then worry about the repercussions. He'll claim you came to bribe him. Anything—and then the shit will hit when they find out the drugs were planted. Don't me tell who did it. I know our buddy in New York. There goes Pentum and there goes the mission. Right?"

"Wrong? We don't have time, David. You can't be in two places at the same time. Nice thought, but impossible. You have to go to Zurich, get the banker to change the accounts so Bradford is shown to have all the money, and get our contact out, safely. We have no idea who followed her, but it doesn't matter. Her life isn't her own, even if she's in the safe house. They'll do anything to get her."

"Mary, you've never done this. You're not trained for it. You know that. I'm the experienced hand at this. He may just call the bluff and wipe you out or, more likely, use you as a hostage to have his daughter released. It works both ways."

"Gravev won't harm me. I'm confident of that. He may ignore what I have to say and use his influence to get his daughter released. But, I have covered that. If my contact with the Immigration Service doesn't hear from me in New York by the end of today, he's to release Dr. Marya Gravev ... period ... no questions asked and with an apology. It's our only option to prevent the device from being delivered. What are the alternatives? Terminate the mission? Not go to Berlin? Not go to Zurich? I'm betting that Gravev, whatever his faults, will listen to his heart regarding his daughter. He won't like finding out that he has been betrayed by Bradford, and not just on this deal. The documents you'll send me will show that. Maybe even others that the banker has ... who knows?"

"Mary, I'm not so sure that Gravev will help us regarding the contact if he knows that she's the one ... as I suspect he does now. Bradford has probably told Gravev that the contact took the tapes and disks. Gravev will want them back. He'll have his own henchmen out, but whether he'll call them off, well, is anyone's guess."

"David, we're assuming that he knows what's on the computer disks as well as on the audio tapes. We shouldn't assume that. I'll mention both and see his reactions. I'm just willing to bet that Bradford, being the traitor he is, won't stop with stabbing his own country in the back; he'll forsake others as well. Regardless, you know we won't abort. Gravev is no angel. He probably approved the order to kill Bob and you. I don't know that for certain, but I'm sure he was aware of the decision.

"But what other alternative is available to us? The fact is that we need Gravev on our side, and Bob knew how to arrange for that eventuality. Bob's gone. It's only you and me. I'll go, David. I see no other choice. Unless there are some overriding reasons that you and I haven't come up with, David. We have to take this risk. At least, it's worth a try." Mary took out of her briefcase a legal size pad of paper which displayed one phone number. David knew she'd made up her mind. There would be no other opportunity. It was this avenue to pursue or nothing.

"It's 9:30 a.m. in Moscow time. He'll be up," Mary said.

"How are you going to reach him? Even our contact couldn't get his phone number ... other than the Bank Alliance central Moscow number," Harrison replied.

"Sometimes, David," Mary said, "as you so carefully teach at the National War College, sometimes the best approach in intelligence matters is the direct approach. So, following David Harrison's advice, here we go," Mary spoke with a smile, but her eyes were serious, intense.

She picked up the phone and dialed the operator. "This is Mary Auriello. I need to call overseas. Do I dial 9 and is there a special code?"

"Yes," the operator said. "After you dial 9, then dial your number, and before it rings, dial 889, our code for visitors, and you'll get through. If you have trouble, please let me know."

"Thank you," Mary replied, placing her hand on the dial tone button, depressing it once, and then releasing it for another tone. "Here we go, David. Let's see, dial 9, then 01 for overseas connection, 7 for Mother Russia, 095 for Moscow, 145-3000 for Bank Alliance Russia, then 889. It's working." She looked out the window, continuing, "Picture perfect day, David, wouldn't you say?"

David looked at her, mouthing silently, "You're crazy."

Mary laughed, "I know."

After several rings, a recording came on in Russian: "Bank Alliance Russia is closed. For emergencies, call 145-3011." "David, here, you're our Russian language expert. I think it's telling me that the bank's closed," she said as she handed the phone to Harrison.

"Yes, it's giving another number to call, however. Want me to dial and get to the right person?"

"Sure, you be my personal assistant," and both Harrison and Mary laughed, breaking the tension which was beginning to build as they both looked at the clock above the anteroom door. It now read 6:45—9:45 a.m. in Moscow. Harrison proceeded to dial the new number.

"Bank Alliance Russia Security Station. Name please," came the reply.

"This is David Harrison, Department of Justice, Washington, D.C., on behalf of Ms. Mary Auriello, also of the Department of Justice," Harrison said, speaking in Russian.

"Who? Would you mind repeating that?" the security officer asked.

"David Harrison, Department of Justice, Washington, D.C., on behalf of Ms. Mary Auriello. Urgent that Ms. Auriello speak to Mr. Dimitri

Gravev."

"One moment, please," and the line went silent.

After a few moments, a male voice came on the phone, identifying himself as Sergei Mironov, the legal assistant to Mr. Gravev. "Mr. Gravev is unable to come to the phone. Can I help you? Our bank is closed today, but is there anything I can do for you?" the voice spoke in perfect English. Rather than respond, Harrison turned the phone over to Mary. "He speaks English . . . legal assistant to Gravev . . . a Sergei Mironov."

"Sergei Mironov. This is Mary Auriello of the U.S. Department of Justice. I will say this only once. It is imperative that I speak immediately to Dimitri Gravev about his daughter, Dr. Marya Gravev, Columbia University Hospital, New York. We have detained her for drug possession. If he does not wish to talk to me, fine. Please advise him of what I just told you. I will be happy to wait for your response. I have a very short time, so I would suggest that you let me know whether I will be able to speak to Mr. Gravev. Mr. Mir—on—ov, it is the correct pronunciation of your name, isn't it?" Mary said brusquely.

"Yes, one moment . . . yes . . . the pronunciation of my name is correct. Please give me a minute. Please stay on the line."

Mary scribbled on the phone pad in front of her, "David, wipe off that smirk. I didn't take acting lessons at Smith for nothing."

Harrison leaned over and wrote, "Acting? You mean it."

Mary wrote back, "Right."

"Ms. Auriello, please wait another a moment. I will connect you. If we are disconnected, please call directly 235-8901, Moscow exchange." The phone did not go dead, but she heard a series of interconnection tones until the phone started to ring again, and a quiet, but deep voice came on the line.

"Ms. Auriello. This is Dimitri Gravev. I am sorry that my English is not good. Do you have a Russian translator with you? I would prefer to speak in Russian."

"He is here. I will have him pick up the other phone." David picked up the extension on the side table, adjacent to the couch, where he was now sitting.

"My translator is on the line. I will speak in English and then he will translate, if you desire," Mary said. "Mr. Gravev, I must inform you that the department has authorized the detention of your daughter, Dr. Marya Gravev, for possession of an illegal substance. In this case, it was a half ounce of cocaine. As you may know, she is on a teaching visa at the Columbia University Hospital in New York. This is a most serious matter, Mr. Gravev. But, because of your standing in the international financial community, and as a matter of courtesy due someone in your position, I was asked to deliver the message personally to you.

"Right this moment I am in London on my way to Berlin to meet with certain German officials regarding our two countries' efforts to combat terrorism. Is it possible for you to meet me in Berlin today? She paused briefly, so Gravev could digest the message. "Let's us say at two p.m.? My conferences with my German counterparts begin the following day, and I have a dinner with them this evening.

"I realize this is short notice, but I believe we should meet, alone of course, and in confidence, to discuss this matter, as well as another matter that I can review only on seeing you. We must keep this confidential, because I am sure you do not want anyone in Moscow to know about your daughter. But if you must check on me, please call the Russian National Security Council Director, Lt. General Yuri Balenko. He was in Washington just a few weeks ago, and we discussed our countries' mutual concerns regarding terrorism."

"Ms. Mary Auriello, you are reporting to me that your government has detained my daughter on a drug charge. This is insulting, and I resent this call. Why have I not heard from your embassy here in Moscow or from my own government? I shall call my daughter immediately. You cannot do this to my daughter, to me, to my family."

Mary interrupted, cutting him off, "Mr. Gravev, I have little time. If you have any questions about me, call your own government's security director, General Balenko. He knows me, and he knows I don't waste my time making calls when I don't feel the need to. Mr. Gravev, just so you understand, I will be in Berlin at the Four Seasons Hotel, and if you wish to discuss this issue as well as an even more important one, I would recommend that you be there. Sir, I strongly recommend you take that course of action. I hope that you understand my position." Her quickness and the passion of her response didn't surprise Harrison. He knew, however, that after each of Mary's strong and frank comments, intense silence followed. Gravev's reply would either be tumult or agreement. With Mary there never was any middle.

Gravev, alone, mulled over her remarks, furious that he was being addressed in such a fashion and by a woman. There was something intriguing about her voice. She spoke from conviction, from knowledge, from confidence. He knew Balenko, and there was no way he would ever call him and ask for any advice. If he made that call, all of Moscow's elite would know that the Moscow *vor* had a problem, a family one, and in the United States. No, he wouldn't check on Mary Auriello this way. And he would go to Berlin. He didn't like it. He wished to reject her invitation. For the moment, his vision was clouded by his anger. Yet he realized he had no choice. But what was the other matter she wished to discuss? What could that be?

"Mary Auriello, you leave me no choice. Do you?" Gravev softly responded. "I shall be in Berlin. What is the other matter? "

"A matter that you and I can solve with a minimum of discussion if we have goodwill and understanding on both our parts. I am sure that we can work everything out and that your daughter will be released as soon as you and I come to an agreement. Other than your calling General Balenko, we must keep this to ourselves, Dimitri. This visit is authorized by the highest levels of my government. You do understand, don't you?"

"We meet where in Berlin?"

"The Four Seasons Hotel. I shall see you at about two p.m. We shall have a good discussion alone. You will be coming alone, won't you? I shall be coming by myself," Mary said.

"Yes, I will be at the meeting alone, I never travel alone. You know, being a Russian bank president has its dangers. I travel with guards, but they will sit at another table. Is that satisfactory?"

"No. It is impossible. They can stay outside the restaurant at the hotel. You and I must meet alone. Dimitri. I must insist on that. I will be alone myself. If you cannot do this, we can not meet," Mary countered.

"I understand, Mary Auriello. Yes. I suppose it has to be if I am to meet you, correct?" Dimitri responded.

"Yes, alone, Mr. Gravev. That is the way our meeting must be held—one on one—you and me."

"I shall see you in Berlin at the Four Seasons Hotel, two p.m. Good bye," Dimitri said.

"Thank you, Dimitri Gravev. You will not be disappointed. See you this afternoon."

Mary rose from the couch and wandered to the window, looking out at the bright morning, watching an early morning flight of Harrier jets take off in tandem. "You know, David, I'm amazed how airplanes fly. Are we really supposed to be flying? Isn't it against all elements of physics? of gravity and the like?"

"You're worried, Mary, aren't you?" Harrison said, not responding to Mary's comments about flying.

"Oh, I don't know, David. He agreed too quickly. No comment, no argument. Just agreement. I know I'm good, but am I that good?" Mary asked, as she walked slowly back to the couch.

"Yeah, you are, Mary. You know, though, that all of this depends also on the bank signatory cards being changed for an account or accounts that Bradford was on, and you getting the information in time to show Gravev. You're cutting this too close, Mary. I have to get out of here. It'll take me an hour to London, Heathrow, then an hour and a half to Zurich. I should be there around ten," Harrison said.

"Too late. You have to get to Zurich now. You're not going to Heathrow. You're leaving from here," Mary emphasized.

"Well, that would make things much easier. Which plane out there do I fly?" Harrison asked.

"Pick one, "she smiled, "but before you go, I have to make one more call, to my office." Mary lifted the receiver off the phone and called her assistant Beverly at her home.

"Hallo," came an anxious voice.

"Mary. What's the problem, Beverly? Is it the AG?"

"Yes, it is," Peterson answered, "Mary, God, have I been waiting for your call." For several minutes Mary just listened, her face becoming uncharacteristically pale at what she heard.

"Thanks, Beverly. Don't worry. I'll let you know my schedule after I arrive in Berlin. And, thanks. Go back to bed now. By the way, what are you doing listening to that talk show host anyway?" Mary asked, laughing. "Talk to you later. Get some sleep."

"What was that all about, Mary?" Harrison asked.

"Nothing really—perhaps a little bothersome, though. Talk radio in D.C. is saying, and I quote, 'a high ranking Justice Department executive, with top security clearance, was seen in an alternative-life-style bar with another woman,' close quote. Well, David, talk radio broadcast the rumor, probably getting it from one of the AG's henchmen. Beverly is concerned that CNN will pick it up. Vennix knew I was going to resign after the mission was complete. He's making it appear as if my resignation will come as a result of the false rumor. That guy is a genuine asshole."

"Hey, hey, hey—wait a minute. You're resigning? What's this shit all about, Mary? Has Vennix lost all sense of reality? This mission is for real. Why this kind of distraction?" Harrison winced because he couldn't believe what he had just heard.

"There comes a time to move on, I suppose. It's hard for me to explain. I'm tired of fighting. It's been a constant struggle with Vennix about the Pentum missions. For openers, I'm not resigning until after Monday. And I'll sit down with the president, and the attorney general will apologize to me in front of him, and then issue a statement to that effect. Vennix won't get away with this. You know, David, you wonder what loyalty to one's nation means anymore when you have this kind of shit to contend with. You just wonder. Let's go. There's work to be done. He's shit, and let's treat him as such," Mary concluded, and she got up from the desk chair, opened the door, and headed directly toward the buffet.

Harrison followed, asking quietly, "Are you resigning after this ends?"

"Yes, I am."

"Commander Robinson, this is a most attractive breakfast," Mary said, as she reached over and filled a small porcelain plate with melon, strawberries, and a raisin scone. "Commander, we have a time crunch. David here has to be in Zurich in about two hours. Can you arrange for the base commander to release a transport jet to take him there?" Mary asked, her eyes widening as she spoke in an imploring fashion to Robinson.

"I can try," he replied. "Normally it would take some time. But I'll try."

"You command the queen's security detail. I'm sure you have some influence," and she went over, sitting next to him.

"Yes, I certainly will try," Robinson said as he left to go to the ante room that Mary had just vacated.

"David, you'll be going in a half hour. You'd better eat something. They won't have breakfast on your flight," Mary gently said.

"I'm worried about you, real worried," David said, leaning over to kiss her.

"So am I, David." For the first time, he saw water come to Mary's eyes.

Einsiedeln, Fifty kilometers south of Zurich
Saturday
Local Time: 9:30 a.m.
Restaurant of Drei Könige Hotel

Moussa placed two cubes of sugar into his coffee and stirred it aimlessly. He didn't drink from the cup. He just continued stirring the coffee, the spoon hitting the sides of the cup, making a short, high-pitched sound as if from a xylophone. He had called Anatoli and Sasha and told them he would be in Einsiedeln by nine. He was early, but he wouldn't disturb them. He had spent himself last night with the girls, and he was physically complete. He actually had a few hours of solid sleep, and, for reasons he couldn't explain, arose at six a.m. or so, dressed, and again took a walk over the Quai Brücke, along the Limmath for some distance, thinking of the times he and Svetlana had taken similar walks.

Early in the morning he had finally reached Dimitri, who reaffirmed that it was essential that he locate Svetlana and find out why she fled. Dimitri left it to him to decide what to do with Svetlana if she refused to tell him why she fled, taking the computer disks. "Ask her," Dimitri said to Moussa, "if she took any other information, any documents? My friend, Moussa," Dimitri counseled, "I do not know the full story yet. You must locate her and talk to her. If she refuses to talk, then you have to decide what to do. She may have a perfectly good reason she left. Who knows? Maybe she did not take anything. I am hearing this only from Bradford, so I really don't know. We must have the facts, Moussa, before we act hastily. Don't you agree, my friend?" Dimitri had thus cautioned him, correctly.

Moussa knew Svetlana was in Einsiedeln, and he knew his own temperament would harden. He would turn a deaf ear to any of her excuses. He would kill her. And he wouldn't change his mind. "Then, on the other hand," he said to himself, as he continued to stir the spoon in the coffee, "maybe there is a reason why she is in this stupid religious place. Maybe she has gone crazy, taking the computer information; maybe it is all a ruse." He would see. He also knew that she was too smart to do anything without planning.

"No, she is not sick. No, she is not sick," he silently repeated to himself. It must be something that Bradford asked her to do and she is not to tell anyone. "But, at this monastery, a religious place, no, this must be an escape," Moussa told himself. Knowing he was flustered, this matter perplexed him. This was uncharacteristic of her to leave. "Svetlana, you have always been faithful to me," he said to himself. "Why this? And your mother? Where is she?"

Moussa sat alone, waiting for his friends to come down. Most of the pilgrims had already left for the church and, in addition to Moussa, only two couples remained in the dining room, on whose walls hung large photographs of the monastery and church. Each table was covered with a white tablecloth; the paper place mats also had photographs of the monastery and church. Small vases of red and white carnations sat on all the fifteen tables in the small room.

Moussa stared at his coffee, which by this time had become cold. He pushed it aside and looked ahead.

"Sir, you did not like this coffee? It is too strong, perhaps?" asked the waitress, a rotund, pleasant looking lady, dressed in a bright yellow and white striped uniform.

"No, it is fine. I just let it get too cold. I'd like a hot cup again, however. I'm sorry that I let this cup get cold. I am," Moussa said, speaking softy.

"I'll bring you a fresh cup. You are here in Einsiedeln for the pilgrimage? The services this morning will be truly beautiful. Many have come from all over Europe to attend. You will be attending, no? I wish I could go, but here I work," the waitress said smiling.

"No, I don't think I will go to the services. Later on I may look into the church. Yes, that is what I will do. I will go look, but later on," Moussa replied.

"You should see the inside of the monastery church. It is memorable. Yes, you should see the church."

Just as the waitress departed, Anatoli and Sasha walked in. Both were shaved and dressed in suits. Moussa was taken aback by their appearance.

"Moussa, why didn't you come up last night? You are no friend! To screw yourself stupid with the girls while we are in church praying for your sins! We are no longer friends. Sasha and I leave right now!" Anatoli roared as he reached over to hug Moussa.

"Good," Moussa said, as he embraced him in return. "We are no longer friends, but you will still pray for me!" Sasha and Anatoli took the two other seats at the table, Sasha reaching immediately for a croissant, which he proceeded to eat, not bothering to put any butter or jam on it.

"And Svetlana?" Moussa asked.

"We know nothing more than what we told you. She is in the monastery. Actually, we took turns last night watching her car, which is parked just down the street. I don't think she has left the monastery. If she did, she didn't take her car."

"But then maybe she would not take her car," Moussa said. "Maybe she went out a back way."

"Perhaps, but Moussa, I don't think so. It will be difficult to locate her, though. The monastery is huge, and there are thousands of pilgrims there. You should know it will be difficult," Anatoli answered. "Nevertheless, yesterday I called the monastery and asked if I could use the library today. I asked to do research on the history of the monastery as a place of refuge. The monk who answered the phone said library access was by appointment only, and that most of the texts were in Latin or German, and to come at ten o'clock this morning.

"That is why, Moussa, the suits. We are dressed like professors! We are not even carrying our weapons! We will be pure with the monks. I am told that it is a sin to bring in a gun into a holy place. We do not want to sin; we are going to do some research in the monastery! Yes, Moussa, research. I also asked if there were any refugees now at the monastery. The man who answered the phone, a Father Gerhardt, said, he was not sure, but perhaps one. 'I believe a lady arrived, but I am not sure. From time to time, refugees come . . . not as much as before . . . but they do come,' the good father volunteered. I told him how generous it was to provide a place for them. He said that is what the religious order does, provides safe haven for refugees. So we must find where she is in that big building, Moussa. And we shall find out for you, our friend. But, you must let us screw her and have her suck our dicks!" Anatoli roared in laughter, joined by Sasha, who was already eating his second croissant.

Moussa didn't respond. His face flushed and his mouth contorted with anger. He was silent for several minutes. Never had Anatoli or Sasha failed to show respect to Svetlana. Because they both knew she had left him, they knew his reaction to that fact. She was his girl, and demanded respect, but the respect was gone . . . totally gone. She was like their own girls, to be screwed any way, anytime. Moussa wanted to care, he wanted so much to care, but he couldn't any more, he couldn't care. So, he quietly said, "Yes, you can have her, and then I destroy her, crushing her into little pieces and throwing her into the garbage."

"Sasha, did you hear that? We can have Svetlana, the princess," Anatoli exclaimed.

"But finding her will not be easy even for you, Anatoli, the KGB chameleon. I read the guide book. There are hundreds of rooms in that

THE PENTUM MISSION

monastery. Where do we start?" Sasha asked.

"At the library," Anatoli replied. "Moussa will you come with us?"

"I will not go with you. Look at how you are dressed. You have suits and ties and you look like the professors you're not. I am in jeans, shirt and leather jacket. I don't fit. No, I'll wander around the town. You check the library," Moussa said.

"Moussa, we'll start there. I promise you I shall find out where she is!" Anatoli said. "And you will reward us!"

"Yes, I shall reward you," Moussa replied. Depression had set in and Moussa was feeling this search would be futile. Everything was becoming meaningless and unreal. His two friends going to a monastery library to find Svetlana. Moussa wanted less to get Svetlana than to find out why she had left. "Why, Svetlana, did you leave?" he said aloud to Anatoli and Sasha.

"What," Sasha asked, "are you saying? Are you okay, Moussa, my friend?" Sasha said as he reached over to touch Moussa's arm.

For a time, no one spoke. Sasha took his arm away from Moussa and looked for guidance from Anatoli.

"We must go, Sasha," Anatoli said. "Yes, we have an appointment. Moussa, we must go. Here is the key to our room. We actually have two rooms, and the adjoining door is open. We shall see you later, my friend, and with good news. Let us go, Sasha, let us go." Anatoli and Sasha rose from the table, but Moussa still had neither lifted his eyes nor responded. Moussa was despairing, and Anatoli knew that it would be best to leave him alone.

Just as they reached the exit of the hotel restaurant, Moussa shouted, "Where is her car?" Startled by his loud voice, Anatoli turned and walked back to the table. Moussa stared at him, and again asked, this time much more quietly, "Where is her car?"

"It is four blocks down the street . . . the main street in front of the hotel . . . a black Volkswagen, Zurich plates. You can't miss it. It is parked right across from a children's toy shop. Anything else, my friend Moussa?" Anatoli asked.

"No, thank you. Good reading."

As Anatoli reached the door where Sasha had been standing waiting for him, Sasha whispered to Anatoli, "I think he is the one who is sick. But, I feel for him; he really loved her, I guess...."

"Yes, he did, but it's over, Sasha, over, and he will kill her."

Moussa sat at the table for several minutes. His shouts had caught the attention of the few other customers remaining in the restaurant. The noise was also heard by his waitress who came over and asked, "Would you like some breakfast now? A boiled egg, perhaps some toast or muffins?"

"No, nothing. More coffee and some juice." The waitress looked at the second cup she had brought him which, like the first, he had left untouched. But she said nothing. It was obvious that he was bothered, so she left, bringing him a fresh cup, and, although he didn't ask for it, a bowl of fresh strawberries.

"Thank you," Moussa said, as he looked at the bowl of strawberries and the fresh cup of coffee. He reached for his wallet, placed a twenty-franc Swiss note on the table and left, still touching nothing. He wanted to find the car, perhaps get in it and sit where Svetlana had been. Yes, he would find the car. He needed her so desperately now. "Don't you understand that I love you, Svetlana? Don't you understand that?" he thought to himself, as he left the restaurant, going into the lobby of the hotel. He could see the stream of pilgrims continuing into the monastery. But, no, it would not be for him. No church. No God. He turned right as he left the hotel, heading toward Svetlana's car.

Einsiedeln
Saturday
Local Time: 9:30 a.m.
Benedictine Monastery
Visitors' Suite

Marie Tohl handed Svetlana a sealed plain white envelope. "It is from Abbot Polzherr," she said. As Marie Tohl placed her breakfast tray on the table desk, Svetlana opened the envelope and read: "Dear Helene LeFevre. I have been informed that you will be leaving the monastery at six p.m. this evening. I shall bring Colonel Boarders' representative, a Mr. David Harrison, to you directly." The signature of the abbot appeared at the bottom. For some reason, Svetlana felt sad that she was leaving the monastery so soon. Last night's sleep was the soundest she had in a long time. The silence of her room, the peaceful countenance of the monastery, the star-filled night, all contributed to a serenity that she had never experienced. She was surrounded by silence, and for that she was thankful. "Silence is good therapy," she said to herself.

"Marie Tohl, is it possible that you could take me for a walk around the grounds and perhaps into the town? The courtyard is so beautiful. I looked at it from the windows for such a long time this morning. Would it also be possible to see the town? I would like to buy my mother a small souvenir of the monastery," Svetlana asked.

"I am sure that the abbot will give you some memento of your stay here. He does that for everyone who comes. But I will have to ask him whether it is permissible for you to leave the grounds," Tohl answered. "Let me go see him and I'll come back to you right away. I don't think there would be much of problem, but I am not sure of your status. Perhaps you would also like to see the church. It is a unique place, and I would be happy to accompany you."

"Yes, I would like that. I was reading about the monastery and church in the history book in the room," Svetlana said.

"Well, here is your breakfast. Let me see the abbot and I'll be back shortly. I hope you enjoy the breakfast as much as you apparently enjoyed the dinner—not a scrap left, according to Sister Mary Katherine. She was the one who delivered the tray last night," Marie Tohl replied.

"Oh! yes, she is such a pleasant person. I was starved," Svetlana replied.

"Well, let me be off, and I'll be right back."

As Svetlana walked over to the table where her breakfast tray had been placed, she stopped for a second, and decided to gaze out the window overlooking the courtyard and its careful landscaping. The courtyard was empty, save for two monks who had open prayer books in their hands and were walking in tandem. For the first time, she thought herself free. "This is a place I have longed for. How I wish the future to be the same," she thought to herself. She then walked back to the table, sat down, took off the tray cover and saw her breakfast of cereal, fresh orange juice and coffee.

She reached for a volume titled *Einsiedeln, The Monastery and Church of Our Lady of the Hermits*, opened it to page 89, and began to read "Inner Life." "This is a beautiful, quiet life. I can't believe that this place really exists," she said to herself. As she continued to read, she completely forgot about her breakfast until she heard a knock on the door. It was Marie Tohl.

"Ms. LeFevre. The abbot said that a short walk would be fine. I am to go with you, show you the church and then the small town, and perhaps have lunch at a cafe I know. But the Abbot asked that we not be gone too long. You should be resting in the monastery awaiting for your escort from Colonel Boarders who will come around six p.m. today," she said.

"That makes me happy, although it would be good for me to stay here for a few more days. It is so peaceful, and, after what I have been through, I need this kind of quiet time. But, I suspect that you have heard that before from many who come."

"But, it is always fine to hear it again. Well, now, you didn't like your breakfast?"

"Oh! I haven't touched a thing. I just got so involved in this book about the history of the monastery. It is such a unique place. How long have you worked here?"

"I've been at the monastery since 1968 when I fled what was then East Germany. I am one of the lucky ones, I suppose. The group I was with had bribed some boarder guards at a village crossing, about 200 kilometers south of Berlin, but just as I got through, the one guard we had bribed started shooting. Other guards came and shot all of the group of which I was a member. I was a lucky one and made my way here. I have no relatives because among the people the guards shot were my mother and father and my husband.

"But I shouldn't discuss myself. I live with the pain every day and I pray to God for an understanding of why I am here and they are all gone. And you? We are pleased to have anyone that Colonel Boarders is helping. He is a wonderful person. I have met him only a few times but he has such a quiet, confident nature. Have you met him?"

"Yes, I have worked with him for the past six months. It is he who arranged for my passage out of . . ." Svetlana stopped; she didn't know whether to continue.

"I understand. You don't have to tell me anything at all. I shouldn't have inquired. Anyway, it is now ten o'clock. Why don't I take you into the church even though a service is in progress, and then we'll walk to the town. It's a beautiful fall day. We're so lucky with the weather."

"Yes, we're very fortunate."

"Why don't you finish your breakfast first? I have more letters to sign and then we'll be off, say, in another thirty minutes?"

"That will be fine. I know that I'll enjoy the tour. Thank you; you're so generous," Svetlana responded.

Shortly after, Marie Tohl took Svetlana down the same corridor that Abbot Polzherr had led her just a day earlier. They walked down the same steps, past the statute of St. Benedict, and out into the courtyard. The day was fine, the sky a brilliant blue, the mountain air clear and bracing.

"You can see the forest extends nearly to the monastery's wall. It was in those woods that the founder of the monastery lived, as a hermit, over a thousand years ago. Slowly, and over a long period, the monastery and church were built, going through many different transformations to what we see today. Also attached to the monastery is a school, on the other side of the church. It used to be an all-boys school; now of course girls are admitted. So the monks are not only caretakers of the entire property, but teachers as well," Marie Tohl said as she and Svetlana walked slowly across the courtyard to the archway that would lead them out.

"I teach German literature to the senior students at the school. I enjoy the teaching very much, and the abbot has asked if I wish to teach full-time. I haven't made up my mind, but perhaps I shall take on that responsibility soon. Have you ever taught?"

"Oh, no, although I suppose that it would be interesting to do so. No, I actually have spent all my time since college as a secretary and translator. I have always been adept at languages, and that's why I went into translating. Perhaps, when this is over, I may go back to school. I just don't know yet. We'll have to see," Svetlana replied.

It took Svetlana and Marie just a few minutes to walk past the office wing of the monastery and then up a few steps into the front side door of the church. The 9:30 morning service was continuing in the main church, packed with pilgrims. A choir was singing a Latin chant as they entered the church vestibule.

"We'll stand in the back, and you can get a view of the magnificence of the church. This will give you an idea of the splendor of this building. It's a singular place," and with that Tohl opened the door from the vestibule into the main church. For a moment, Svetlana stood in awe at the splendor of the gold, pink and white of the ceiling frescoes. "All the frescoes depict aspects of the faith of our Church. At first, because they're so vast and complex in their depiction of events, the frescoes are overwhelming. Above us is the Redemption, beyond, the Resurrection, the Apocalypse, Noah's Ark and the Flood, the Flight from Sodom, and so on. Every time I come into the church, I see something that I failed to see before.

"Look, Svetlana, some of the walls are bright pink. The shining stucco, the marble, the bronze reliefs, the friezes, the gilded angels, all give us a joyful world that is, of course, our belief. So the depiction is accurate. And it is breathtaking, I have to admit," Tohl said.

"I've never seen anything like this in my life. Not anything. It's so inspiring. You're so fortunate to be at this place—yes, so very fortunate," Svetlana said.

"There's so much here in this church, but perhaps another time, when you're not in the situation you find yourself now. Yes, perhaps another time." As Tohl led her along the back of the church, she pointed out "The Lady Chapel of the Black Madonna" a large, free-standing, black marble interior chapel in the rear, centered in the main aisle

"You should know that many a wedding takes place in this chapel. It's supposed to be good luck, among other things." Tohl smiled as she and Svetlana stopped for a moment to view the gold panels on either side of the chapel. "As you'd suspect, there's much legend in faith and vice versa, and sometimes the two get confused. But I guess there can be nothing wrong with that."

"This is just overwhelming. Every corner of the ceiling and walls is filled with paintings . . . just overwhelming. It's hard for me to absorb the beauty of this place," Svetlana replied.

"It is for me as well." Marie led Svetlana back into the vestibule and out the left side door of church into the plaza directly in front. There, Marie first took Svetlana to the "Lady Fountain," a fountain in the middle of the plaza where many pilgrims drink a cup of water, believing the water to have holy attributes. "Again, this is either faith or legend or both, but you might as well have a drink from the fountain. One never knows, does one?" and Marie Tohl cupped her hands, placing them under one of the many fountain spigots from which water was flowing, and took a quick drink.

"My Aunt Elena believed in many things of the supernatural, and she many times foretold the future. I think she also would want me to drink from this fountain." Svetlana laughed as she took one cupped hand, filling it with a few drops of water, and swallowed. "I hope that it helps me," Svetlana said.

"I pray that it does, Svetlana. I shall pray that it brings you good health and happiness."

Crowds swirled around two elliptical arcades bordering the church plaza as the two women made their way toward the main street fronting the plaza. "Here, Svetlana, you may want to look at one of these stall stores for a gift for your mother," said Marie Tohl, directing Svetlana to one of the arcade shops.

"The book in my room, the history book about Einsiedeln; I believe my mother would like something like that. She loves to read, and a descriptive book would be the best, I suppose," Svetlana said. She then looked carefully at all the books written in German and picked a small one titled *Einsiedeln*. "I shall bring my mother here one day. She will like this place, I am sure."

"I hope that you do. I would like to meet her and certainly you can stay again at the monastery if you choose," Tohl replied. Svetlana paid for her purchase, and then she and Marie began to walk from the plaza to the main street fronting the monastery and church. "Einsiedeln is a very small town. We have many, many tourists come, and that is the reason for so many hotels, but the hotels are small and are really inexpensive. Pilgrims are not wealthy people but ordinary, and cannot afford anything expensive... such as you have in Zurich. But I always find walking a relaxing pleasure—always interesting, and always varied. There are so many things to see all the time, and it is always different. There are many shops and cafes along this street, nothing like Zurich, but still they are beautiful and have good quality items," Tohl said as she and Svetlana walked about a block until Marie stopped in front of a small dress shop.

"Would you like to go in? A friend of mine owns this shop. I am sure she would like the company. Few patrons shop when services are being held."

"Of course, I would like that very much. I may even buy something." Svetlana laughed. "I need undergarments!"

"Oh! that's right. You came without luggage. I should have known. I'm so sorry. I should have brought you some clothes myself," Marie Tohl opened the door for Svetlana to go in.

For a while, like a sleepwalker who had abruptly awakened, Moussa stared in disbelief. There was Svetlana with another woman, much older, walking down the street, a short single block from his hotel. It couldn't be. No, it couldn't be. If she had escaped, she wouldn't be walking so freely. What was happening? He closed his eyes, for a moment, then reopened them again seeing the blond hair, the striking face, the figure. "Svetlana, have I found you?" he muttered to himself. "But, what to do now? Wait for Anatoli and Sasha? Get her myself? What to do? And who is the other lady?"

Standing there, Moussa continued to stare in amazement. Perplexed by Svetlana's freedom, he couldn't understand what had happened. Had she really left him? Maybe she was just on a trip of her own. But then, how to explain the computer disks, the trip to Zurich, the apartment in Zurich? Logic flees when love or hatred takes over the mind. He started to advance slowly toward the shop Svetlana and her companion had just entered.

"There you are Svetlana," he said to himself. "You left without even talking to me. Maybe I would have been able to help . . . maybe. . . ." And he continued his slow walk toward her, almost too slow, as if he did not want to reach her, for he knew what the outcome would be once he reached her.

The shop was beautifully arranged. In its small light-blue and white interior stood several racks of dresses, blouses, skirts and two display cases, one filled with undergarments. Scarves hung on several circular racks on the display case. Shoppers could sit on a small chintz couch or in two matching chairs arranged on either side of the couch. There was a coffee table in front of the couch with several German fashion magazines for customers. A soft, subtle perfume permeated the shop.

"Marie, how good to see you, and the first one in the shop!" said Beatrice Selig.

"Yes, I'm here with a friend who would like to do some shopping. This is Helene LeFevre."

"This is such a pretty little shop and you have handsome clothes. If only I had time. . . ."

"Of course, we have some time. Do as you please, Helene. We have time," replied Tohl.

With that, Svetlana looked through the small rack of dresses, picking one simple navy blue one.

"May I try this on?" Svetlana asked.

"Of course. Here, let me take you to our dressing room," Selig said.

Moussa was watching this from across the street. He could see directly into the shop because the uncluttered shop window allowed a complete view of the inside. As he saw Svetlana move into the shop's interior with one of the women, he decided to enter.

He opened the door, and, as he did, Tohl said, "The shop owner will be right back. There are beautiful things here. You can pick something especially attractive for your wife or girlfriend. . . ."

"Yes, I intend to," Moussa said.

As Marie Tohl turned, Moussa moved behind her, covered her mouth with his left hand, and quickly snapped her neck, killing her instantly.

He carried her to the couch and laid her lengthways on it. Then he waited.

Shortly, Svetlana came out, followed by Beatrice Selig, the owner. "Well, what do you think?" she asked as she walked from around the rack of dresses.

"I like it very much," Moussa said.

There was a sudden silence before Svetlana shouted, "Moussa, my God, Moussa," and with that she ran toward the front door. Moussa grabbed her left arm, bringing her down, her head hitting the side of one of the display cases, stunning her for a moment. Beatrice Selig, trying to get to the couch to see the condition of her friend, was kicked from behind by Moussa, who held on to Svetlana. As he twisted her arm, Moussa went to Beatrice who was on the floor trying to get up. He kicked her in the head several times.

"Stop! Moussa, stop! I'll go with you. Stop! Stop!"

But he continued kicking until she stopped trying to get up. By then she was covered with blood, unmoving. Believing her dead, Moussa quietly said to Svetlana, "Come, my love. We will make love again."

Svetlana tried to turn her face away, but Moussa held it firmly in both hands, forcing her to look at him. It was a brutal kiss, his hands, one behind her back and the other reaching between her legs. Moussa's tongue tried to pry open her lips while his hand continued groping her legs. She kept her eyes open. Then both his hands moved, and he placed them around her neck. He began to squeeze her neck slowly as he kept kissing her violently. Finally, she stopped resisting, opened her mouth, and his hands fell away from her neck. Moussa was a machine gone awry. His eyes clouded, he ripped Svetlana's new dress off, pushing her to the floor. Silent, she crouched there limp.

"You cannot leave me. You cannot leave me. I love you. You know I do. I need you." He went over to the shop door, and locked it, turning off the lights. "You need me, Svetlana. I have not made love to you; that is the reason. I have not taken care of you like I should." Walking over to her, his body now shaking with anger, his penis rigid, he dragged Svetlana behind the couch. In one instant of madness he tore off her remaining clothes and he thrust himself into her, shouting all the while, "I love you, Svetlana. I love you." Svetlana did not move.

Moscow
Saturday
Local Time: 10:00 a.m.
Dacha of Dimitri Gravev
Thirty kilometers southeast of Moscow, near the village of Barvikha

Dimitri Gravev, to that moment, had felt confident that the day would be a family day, happy and animated. Earlier, precisely at six a.m., he had received the fax from the Iranian government regarding the use of the nuclear device which they certified would be used only for testing. Peter Bradford, Jomhori Shenasi, the Iranian Ambassador, and Prakash Farnak were on the charter transport plane bound for Turkmenistan—a full five-hour flight—so Dimitri believed he would have some free time. The call from Mary Auriello changed all of that. He certainly wouldn't call General Balenko of the National Security Council, whom Mary said she knew. That would be ridiculous. In any event, he wouldn't want Balenko to know he was meeting Mary Auriello. She knew that when she made her suggestion.

A call to his daughter's apartment in New York City went unanswered. Even the message machine had been turned off. But why would Marya be involved in drugs? Dimitri didn't know whether to tell his wife why he was going to Germany. If he told her about Marya, that would set off a chain of worry; she would call her sons and would pressure Dimitri into immediately going to New York when he couldn't.

He had to go to Berlin. He would make the trip under the guise of visiting with his German partner for an emergency. He would be back in Moscow that evening. It was a two-hour flight from Moscow to Berlin, and Bank Alliance Russia had its own plane, so he would go and come as he pleased. He would leave from Sheremetyevo at eleven a.m., which would give him plenty of time to arrive at the Berlin Four Seasons Hotel, and meet Mary Auriello. In the meantime he had one assignment for Sergei Mironov.

"Sergei, I do not wish to bother you, and I thank you for putting through the call from Mary Auriello. But, I shall have to leave for Berlin in a few hours. Can you get me some background on her? I don't know who your contacts are at the U.S. embassy or if the bank's computer system has such information, but please check."

"Yes, I will have to go to the office. I have a computer network that has information from a system called Lexis / Nexis. I'll type in her name to get background information for you. Do you need me to go to Berlin?"

"No, that will not be necessary. I will go with Viktor and Pyotr. I think they will be as unhappy as Olga will be. We thought we were going to have a family day today. I shall be back in the evening. I shall be meeting with this Mary Auriello at the Berlin Four Seasons Hotel. It is a matter involving the bank. I shall discuss it with you upon my return. Now, I must convince my wife that I have to go. Please call me, Sergei, before I leave with whatever information you have been able to obtain."

"Yes, I shall go to the office immediately and see what I can find out. Are you sure that you don't want me to come to Berlin with you?" Mironov asked.

"Positive," Dimitri replied.

CHAPTER SIXTEEN

Saturday
Local Time: 7:30 a. m.
Alconbury Royal Air Force Base, England
100 kilometers north-northeast of London

Mary watched Harrison's British Royal Air Force jet transport lift from the runway into the clear, blue morning sky, bound for Zurich, confident that he would follow through. The morning had become warmer, with little wind. Other than Harrison's flight, the airfield was strangely silent because the earlier flights of jet fighters were still on their training missions.

Fatigue was beginning to show. The snippets of sleep, although deep and sound, were too brief and too interrupted to help her much. What she wanted to do was to curl next to her lover, Jim Foster, and sleep, his comforting arms around her. That would happen later, she knew. The last leg of her journey was the most dangerous, and she required an absolute certainty of mind, and no actions or thoughts that would let her drift.

Beverly's call, concerning the talk radio host's comments about her, the work of Vennix, hurt her. Vennix was at his best when he tried to assassinate people's character by scattering half-formed half-truths, and, unless Mary was wrong, he had started the same process in an attempt to destroy her. She knew him to become fanatical when he started down that pathway. Until recently, she had been immune. No longer. She felt it painfully, but only for a moment. She gazed at the deserted runway, her eyes fixed on Harrison's plane as it faded away, a tiny speck on the blue horizon. A great loneliness entered her. And, as her own time to depart drew closer, she assumed that the harsher aspects of what Vennix was doing were attempts to disrupt her concentration. In that he was mistaken. There would be no distress, no apprehension, no silent fear. The sharpness of her response would soon emerge.

Wasn't there something pitiful in the sight of the Attorney General of the United States stumblingly trying to savage her? His poor, transparent attempt was disgusting. All she was trying to do was to carry out an intelligence mission, as she always had in the years before this AG. Vennix had no interest in the Pentum missions, even though the man he helped become president was the mission's main backer and, in fact, its initiator.

But then, Mary thought, the AG always looked at people with a mixture of superiority and condescension, certainly never with deference. His current occupation seemed an assault on her integrity, her reputation, her life. His hatred of Mary and his denial of the worth of the mission had become so overwhelming that, in her view, he'd lost all sense of balance. That's what hatred does. Long ago, after she had first met him, she'd become resolved to the situation of his dreary and imprudent behavior. Now he'd gone too far. Vennix would soon wish he'd known Mary better.

It was 2:30 a.m., Saturday, in Washington when Mary picked up the phone, dialing direct to Beke Santos' apartment. The conversation, as usual, would occur in code.

"Yes."

"Are you busy?"

"Yes. But I'll be free in five minutes. Can you call back at that time?"

"Yes, and thank you."

Beke Santos would go to the public phone booth in the lobby of his apartment building and wait for Mary to dial the number of the phone there. He put on his jeans, a sweat shirt and athletic shoes and rushed down to the reception area from his tenth-floor apartment. It was silent in the dimly lit art deco lobby of an elegantly restored building fronting Connecticut Ave. The night clerk watched his television, trying to stay awake. When he saw Santos, he nodded, as Beke went to the sole phone booth at the far right corner of the lobby seating area. Just as Santos got there and closed the door, the phone rang.

"Mary, are you okay?" he asked.

"Sorry to bother you again, Beke. Yeah, I'm okay. I understand that there was a segment on the midnight talk radio. You know the loud mouth, Peter Matheson. He calls himself the voice of America, a real joker, where he said that the most top level woman at the Justice Department was seen in an alternative-life-style bar. It'll be picked up, I suspect by CNN, and be broadcast probably on the noon news, your time. I'm not sure it's something they'd usually carry, but they will, I suspect. I guess it should come as no surprise to me that Vennix would try to do this, but I thought at least he'd wait until the mission is over. First it'll be this rumor, then something else. It'll go on for a little while, I suppose."

"What's the purpose of his doing this to you, Mary? My God, you've done so damn much . . . you, Bob and Harrison . . . so damn much and so successfully. I mean, where's this man's mind?"

"I don't know, Beke. He has his own reasons. But I can't let what he's doing go unchallenged. The man that he uses to spread this shit is Dennis Eidenson, who's on his personal payroll. And during the last presidential campaign, Vennix used this creep to feed stories to the press. If they reported them so they pleased Vennix, Eidenson would send gifts, substantial ones, in return for the favorable press. The mainstream press would avoid him; but some would pick up the stories and run with them, so he did ruin a great many. Now, I'm the target of the his damage attempt. I think you should visit him, don't you?"

"I think we should have a nice long talk," Santos replied, laughing at Mary's last comment.

"Beke, take your special briefcase with you. I'm sure you'll want to video record what he has to say. Take a large envelope with you as well. Fill it with some blank paper to make it seem as if there are photographs in it. Tell him that unless he puts a stop to the story about the 'high ranking department woman official that goes to alternative-life-style bars,' a photo will be distributed to his favorite newspapers.

"There's a catch, Beke. I don't have any photos. I know that they exist as part of the divorce decree granted to his first wife for abuse and violence against her. From what I gather, he used her as a punching bag. But no one really knows because the records have been sealed in the local court in Charlotte. He disliked me so much that this is his way of abusing me, especially because he can't hit me. I guess he realizes that would be a battery charge. I suppose he hopes to put my forthcoming resignation under a cloud.

"You may want to take a friend with you, just in case. He lives, as I recall, in a penthouse across the river in a building called Prospect House, just over Memorial Bridge."

"Mary, you quitting? Did I hear you correctly? You said you're resigning? Why? I can't believe that."

"I'm tired. With Bob dead and with all this backstabbing and second-guessing from Vennix, it makes little sense to continue, Beke. What's the purpose? I always thought we were doing something right and worthwhile. I don't want to be dragged into the hell that Vennix has made for himself by his own indecent actions. I'm just tired of hearing his footsteps behind me. You're probably saying, 'pretty timid excuse, pretty timid excuse.' But, when I decide to go is when I decide to go. No one sends me into a dark alley that I don't want to be walking through."

"Hell, Mary. You know we've been through so much. I understand. Times do change, I guess. What will the government do without you?"

"They'll manage. There'll be someone else."

"No, Mary, there'll never be someone else. You shouldn't let someone run you out."

"Vennix will go, and he'll go before me. Beke, how in the shit did we get off on this philosophical stuff? Do you know the building where Eidenson lives?"

"Yeah, I know the building. Double storied windows. He does have big bucks if he lives there. Single, married or what?"

"I remember a women he was escorting at one of Vennix's social functions, but I don't think he's married."

"Let me work on it, Mary. How much time do I have?"

"Noon your time, six p.m. my time. I'll soon leave for Berlin. I'll be at the Four Seasons Hotel in Berlin, phone number: 234-9845."

"I have it, Mary. Don't worry. He'll talk. I'll visit him around nine a.m. I guess you're six hours ahead, so it'll be your three p.m. "

"Thanks, Beke. This isn't a happy time for me. Not at all."

"We'll get what you need. It's nutty that you're trying to do your job, and this Vennix is trying to make sure you don't succeed. Only with this administration. Do they know which way is up?"

"He's the one that doesn't know the right way. Talk to you later, Beke."

"Take care, Mary. We can't lose you too."

One more call, some refreshments with Robinson, and Mary would be off. She hesitated as she reached for the phone on the table next to the couch. She twiddled the cord for some time before punching in the special home number in Potomac, Maryland, for the attorney general. The phone rang several times before a groggy voice answered. "Bernie Vennix here . . . hello. . . ."

"Bernie, good morning. This is Mary. Everything is progressing well here. . . ."

"There has to a better reason for your calling me at this hour, Mary. For God's sake, it's half past three in the morning!" he sighed as he mumbled.

"Well, I thought this would be one of those nights when you'd not be sleeping well but would be at your computer playing chess. You do remember you told me you suffered from insomnia," Mary said, with a whisper of regret for bothering him.

"What is it, Mary?" he answered.

"Bernie, I just wanted to know if you were aware of Matheson's talk radio show where he said that the top woman justice department official was found in an alternative-life-style bar, and doesn't this hurt national security, you know, pillow talk with whoever her female lover is. You know the shit that he airs on that program. Well, maybe you didn't listen to it. It's on at midnight.

"Anyway, I received a call here with the information. You don't think he was talking about me, do you? Are there other top justice department women officials besides me? I don't think so. So why do you think this rumor about me has started?"

"Come on, Mary! Are you bothering at this hour about a rumor on a talk radio show? You're showing how paranoid you are. I told the president that that's your problem. Really, Mary, why would I do something like that?"

Mary wondered what it was that he had said to the president. "I didn't say it was you. I only asked if you had any ideas about why or who could be spreading such a rumor. Your answer makes you sound paranoid. Anyway, sorry for the interruption. I just thought you were so upset that I convinced the president to go along with a mission that *he initiated and approved*, that you might have your henchmen, Dennis, spread such fantasy. It makes me feel much better that you're not involved. Thanks. Good bye, Bernie. See you in due course."

"I want you to know I don't even listen to the program, so I have no idea what you're talking about, and Dennis is no henchman. He's the best media consultant around. By the way, where are you now, Mary?"

"Above the clouds, Bernie, above the clouds. Good bye. See you soon."

These few words of Vennix could scarcely have been more ordinary, but the way he uttered them was so forced and unnatural, that Mary would have been surprised if what he was saying was true. She knew just the opposite. His was a lying voice.

Zurich
Saturday
Local Time: 11:00 a.m.
Kusnacht, suburb of Zurich
No. 55 Klossbach

From across the wide residential street, David Harrison viewed the mansion that overlooked Lake Zurich. An irregular structure of three stories, the house had a strong center structure flanked by two small wings, giving it a dramatic appearance. There was no doubt that Frederik von Hauser lived well. The house itself was a bit unique because most of the homes leading to von Hauser's were traditional. Von Hauser's three-storied, modern terraced house was stark white concrete with massive amounts of window space. A circular drive led to double, ten-foot, solid, dark gray doors. In the drive sat two cars—a Jaguar and a Mercedes—both hunter green.

His two-hour British Royal Air military flight from Alconbury had landed promptly at 10:30 a.m. at Dubendorf Swiss Airbase, twenty kilometers from Zurich, and through the arrangements of Commander Robinson, a car was available for his use. The drive into the city and on to the suburb of Kusnacht took only twenty minutes; Saturday morning traffic was light. Harrison had been to Zurich many times, but he didn't care to notice the sparkling sun shimmering on the lake as he sped toward Kusnacht. There would be time for enjoying scenery later, he thought.

Harrison had taken a calculated risk that von Hauser would be home that Saturday morning. Seeing two cars in the driveway, Harrison was confident that he was there. Just as Harrison parked his car, von Hauser, dressed in a bright red jogging outfit, opened the door and headed toward the right part of the lawn to begin his prerun warmups, oblivious to Harrison's navy blue Saab parked directly in front of the house on the opposite side of the street.

Harrison didn't wait for von Hauser to start his morning run. He walked up the driveway quickly, reaching von Hauser just as von Hauser saw him and turned back to the door, grasping immediately for the door knob to go back into his house. Harrison said quietly, "Mr. von Hauser, a moment, please."

"What is this?" von Hauser angrily demanded, keeping his hand on the door knob.

"I'm Peter Randolph and I need to talk to you concerning matters in Monte Carlo. May I come in?" Harrison countered, not raising his voice, as he stood directly in front of von Hauser.

Irritated, von Hauser responded, "I was expecting no one, and I don't know what you are talking about. Call my office on Monday and arrange for an appointment. As you can see, this is not a work day, and I would like to carry on with my morning routine."

"Mr. von Hauser," Harrison placed his right hand firmly on von Hauser's left arm, "this is a work day and we have to discuss many things. Shall we go in?"

"My wife is still sleeping," von Hauser interjected, his eyes darting to the left and right, his voice shaking.

"We won't disturb her at all, Frederik," Harrison said, using von Hauser's first name, hoping to calm his anxiety. "You and I have little time. Please, Frederik, we must talk and we must do so now," Harrison said softly. For a moment, von Hauser's eyes stopped their rapid movements as he stared directly at David, trying to decide what to do. Again speaking softly, Harrison said, "Frederik, it is important that we talk. It is very important for you and for your family."

Von Hauser looked into Harrison's eyes for a long moment and then slowly turned the front door knob, saying, "This is most irregular, most irregular. I did not receive any message from Monsieur Nouel, none whatsoever that you would be coming. Most irregular," he angrily shook his head as he opened the left side of the double doors, motioning for Harrison to walk in ahead of him.

"Thank you, Frederik. Thank you very much," Harrison smiled, as he walked ahead of von Hauser directly into a white-walled two-story foyer with a muted-gray marble floor. "Mr. Randolph, let's go into the kitchen where we can talk. It's my custom to make coffee for my wife because she normally gets up before I return from my run. It should be ready because I turned on the pot just before leaving. Would you like some?" von Hauser asked.

"Yes, thank you," said Harrison, not raising his voice as he followed von Hauser into the kitchen. The room was stark white, with open cabinetry. A center island held an electric coffee pot and the smell of fresh coffee permeated the room.

"Will you sit down?" von Hauser asked, as he pointed to the stainless steel cane back chairs carefully arranged around a highly lacquered white table. Anyone seated at the table could view Lake Zurich.

"You have a beautiful view," David said.

"Yes, I'm very lucky," von Hauser responded, his voice thin and strained.

"Do you take sugar or milk or both with your coffee?" von Hauser asked.

"No, just plain," Harrison responded.

"I also like my coffee black. Sugar or milk or both ruin the taste for me, and I guess for you as well," von Hauser replied, his tone remaining anxious as he walked to the kitchen table and placed a mug filled with coffee in front of Harrison. Then he sat directly opposite Harrison, placing his own mug to his mouth and sipping, rather than drinking the coffee. "It's too hot. You'll have to let it cool down, I suppose. Mr. Randolph, who are you, and what do you want?" von Hauser asked, lowering his head and staring at his coffee mug.

"I know I owe a great deal to the casino, but I have an arrangement to pay over time. Just this month, I gave them over hundred thousand francs. Monsieur Nouel appeared satisfied. So who really are you?" von Hauser inquired, gazing directly into Harrison's eyes.

Ignoring von Hauser's question, Harrison, again speaking softly, asked, "Would you like your three-million-plus dollar debt to the casino paid? Paid today?"

"What kind of nonsense is that?" von Hauser asked, his voice rising but without looking up from his mug of coffee.

"Frederik, your bank has several accounts for Dimitri Gravev, President of Bank Alliance Russia, and the chief *vor* leader of Moscow. Several of those corporate accounts also carry the signatory of Peter Bradford, his business partner. You were recently involved in a meeting in Moscow, where the sale to Iran of a special weapon was discussed. For the delivery of the weapon, 150 million dollars was transferred as down payment. We have an audio tape of that meeting. You are on that tape. The people I represent wish that the weapon not be delivered. Do you understand me?" Harrison inquired, again speaking very softly.

"Oh God!" von Hauser exclaimed as he slumped into his chair and covered his face with his hands. "What do you want me to do? Who are you? My God! Who are you?"

"That is unimportant. We have made arrangements to have your casino bill paid in full with an additional credit of one million U.S. dollars—both to take effect as soon as you make the necessary corrections to certain accounts involving Mr. Bradford at your bank. I want a print-out of those accounts. Frederik, I ask you to cooperate. You want to keep this beautiful house and not jeopardize your lifestyle. Your wife does not know of your habit, does she?" Von Hauser shook his head from side to side and turned toward the window looking aimlessly at the lake.

"Enough said, Frederik. We will go to the bank," Harrison demanded.

"You do not understand. I will be killed if I do this for you," von Hauser began insisting. "But then what do I tell Dimitri Gravev? He will want to know why I did not inform him earlier," von Hauser implored, lifting his head from his hands. Harrison saw tears in his eyes.

"Listen to me, Frederik," Harrison continued softly. "You tell Gravev the truth. You believed that you were carrying out his orders through Bradford. You never questioned those orders because of the close relationship between the two. I am sure he will understand. Nothing will happen to you or your family. You will be unharmed."

"Why will you not understand me, Mr. Randolph? Do you know if I cooperate with you, what this will mean? Do you know how this will ruin me? I don't think Dimitri will appreciate what I am doing. No, I don't think he will, but then I don't know . . . I just don't know," von Hauser said imploringly. "But maybe this all had to come to an end. What is the use of lying to myself? I am so tired, Mr. Randolph, or whatever your name is. I don't think you know what it is like to live this kind of deception. No, I don't think you understand. Yes, I will go with you," von Hauser said as he rose from his chair, perspiration appearing on his upper lip and forehead.

"Besides, what alternative do I have? If I don't cooperate with you, you will harm me. Am I right?" he asked and stared directly at Harrison.

Harrison didn't answer his question. He knew that eliminating von Hauser would accomplish nothing. He needed him.

"Frederik, I never would have bothered you but for the fact that you are now in business that will create a great deal of trouble for many, many people. Selling missiles and nuclear weapons differs from contraband drugs, paying inflated invoices, or creating false loans you know will never be repaid. No, what you are doing is much more dangerous. To stop this, we need your cooperation. You are essential, Frederik. You are the key. We need your help."

For several moments, von Hauser stared into his coffee cup, his hand now visibly shaking. "This is not proper. I don't even know who you are. This is very improper.

"Yet, I understand that I have no choice. You will kill me right here in my own home, if I do not go. Isn't that correct?"

"Yes," Harrison replied, this time coldly and without emotion.

"I understand," von Hauser said, as he rose from his chair and half held out his hand, which Harrison took firmly. As von Hauser closed the front door behind him and Harrison, both briskly walking to Harrison's car, von Hauser glanced back for a few seconds. Harrison looked at him and thought he saw von Hauser's lips move, forming a good bye.

As it was earlier when Harrison came to Kusnacht, the Zurich traffic was light, and the drive to von Hauser's downtown bank building took less than fifteen minutes. Neither Harrison nor von Hauser spoke. Banque Braun & Cie was housed in its own seven-storied building—a building of splendid proportions with two pillars framing the entrance, directly on the Bahnstrasse, the most prestigious street in Zurich. Von Hauser directed him to drive around the street, and as he motioned Harrison to go into the building garage, he handed Harrison a black key ring with a flat key that Harrison inserted into the security lock, raising the garage door.

Although the garage was empty, von Hauser said mechanically, "Park in number 21, please. That is my space."

Harrison slowly eased the car into the space, turned off the motor, and opened his door to get out. Von Hauser did not immediately do likewise. "I cannot do this. I cannot. This will be the end of me. This is forgery. This is not what I should do."

Harrison looked at him for a moment, silent, but, placing his hand tightly on von Hauser's arm, said, "Frederik, Let's go. I will do all I can to make sure nothing happens to you. I promise."

Von Hauser slumped into his seat, unmoving.

"We must go, and now, Frederik. Time is against us. The plane carrying the weapon is on its way. We must stop it. You cannot behave in this manner. That weapon can never be used, Frederik. You must help us stop this sale," Harrison said.

Von Hauser got out and stared at Harrison, his eyes filling with tears. "I am so afraid . . . so very afraid," von Hauser's voice broke with fear and helplessness.

"Frederik, we are helping you now with the funds, and we will help you when this is over," Harrison replied.

"Perhaps, but I don't think so."

The elevator bank was opposite the garage exit door. Von Hauser pressed the button and, in a moment, Harrison and von Hauser entered a glass elevator. Von Hauser pressed seven. The doors opened onto a carpeted corridor, and von Hauser briskly walked down to the end. He fumbled with his keys, opening the door where his name appeared in gold lettering, *Frederik von Hauser, Managing Director*. Without conversation, he headed directly to another door behind the reception desk and opened it without using a key, leaving the door open for Harrison to enter.

"Now what is it you want?"

"A printout of Peter Bradford's own personal accounts and the account that received the 150 million dollars; the transfer of that sum into Peter Bradford's account, back dated to when it originally came into the bank; and a printout of the same."

"Back dated?"

"Yes," Harrison replied.

"That will be somewhat difficult."

"I don't see why. The funds were transferred just two weeks ago . . . not two years ago," Harrison said.

"Of course. You are right," von Hauser said mechanically.

Harrison got up and positioned himself next to von Hauser so that he could see the monitor of von Hauser's computer.

"I will use the computer code for error in the account and have the funds immediately transferred to Bradford's. I will have to develop back-up data for the input. It will take a few minutes. The printout will not show the reason, but it will be dated on the date the funds were received in the bank. Since these statements are kept in the bank and not sent to the account holder, according to his instructions, it will be easy to make the switch." As he began the input into the computer, von

Hauser asked, "You're with the American security services, aren't you?"

"No, I am not."

"Only America is interested in stopping these sales. Most European countries are not interested at all. They are all doing business with Iran. I know. I have many accounts here with companies doing business in Iran. You must be working for the Americans. They are the only ones who care." He pressed the print button on his computer keyboard and out came a printout of Account No. A-3478-P. He took the five sheets from the printer, giving them to Harrison, who glanced at them.

"This Bradford liked money. This totals close to 300 million dollars. Has he been putting money into his own account that belongs to Bank Alliance?"

"Some of it, yes, but, apart from the 150 million dollars I just transferred into his account, the majority is from his trades in drugs and so forth," von Hauser replied.

"This is for you" Harrison pulled out a cashier's check made out to Frederik von Hauser for one million dollars, and a receipt for a wire transfer of three-and-one-half-million dollars to the Casino of Monte Carlo to be credited to von Hauser's account on the following day.

Von Hauser looked at the documents and folded them neatly, placing them into his right side pocket. "How did you know I would cooperate?" von Hauser asked, his face scowling.

Looking at him intently, Harrison said, "You earlier stated what you knew I would do. You had no option, Frederik, none." Again, Harrison's voice was level, without inflection.

"I guess I should say thank you for the money, but I know Bradford and Gravev will come after me. You didn't kill me, but they will. I know they will."

"No, they won't come after you. I can assure you of that. We won't forget your help. We'll do all we can to make sure no harm comes to you. But, now, I have to use your fax machine," Harrison said. "Later, we will discuss what protection you need."

"The fax is right in the reception area."

"I also need a plain piece of paper," Harrison said.

"Of course," and von Hauser reached into his drawer, handing

Harrison a blank sheet. He left the drawer open, staring for a moment at it.

As Harrison left and headed toward the reception area, he leaned over the desk, writing on the cover sheet: "To: The Berlin Four Seasons Hotel, Ms. Mary Auriello—Guest of the Hotel—scheduled to arrive today—hold for arrival. Five pages follow, all marked for Ms. Auriello. Deliver immediately. Total pages sent: six. Mary: per your request. See you soon. David."

Harrison didn't care who at the hotel saw these. Moreover, Mary wanted to show Gravev the actual documents from the bank, so encryption, even if available, was out of the question.

As he placed the six sheets into the fax machine and finished dialing the number, Harrison heard what could only be a shot. He rushed back into von Hauser's office. "Son of a bitch . . . son of a bitch . . . son of a bitch!" Von Hauser lay slumped in his chair, his head blown open by a shot through his mouth.

Harrison's memory of von Hauser mouthing "good bye" as they left his home earlier became all the more prophetic.

Einsiedeln
Saturday
Local Time: 11:00 a.m.
Library of the Monastery

It grew chill and dark in the library, or so it seemed to Anatoli and Sasha seated at the first of sixteen long tables directly in front of the solitary monk who worked at an even larger table before them. The walls of books seemed to have receded, leaving nothing but the shadows cast by the brilliant sunlight from the bank of windows that ran along one side, sending shafts of empty light into the great room. The monk who had escorted them into the library said little, bringing them the books with the comment, "I will be in the front, if you have any questions."

"Well, my friend, Anatoli," Sasha whispered, "we have been reading for an hour and a half and this place gives me the creeps. Should I tell you that I am afraid? Do you realize that no one else is in this room . . . and look at the size!"

"Do not worry, Sasha. You must be patient. We shall read on. Then we shall have some questions, but we must read. So, my friend, read, and don't turn the pages so quickly. I believe the monk is watching us. We must be serious. I do have several questions to ask the dear monk. Please continue reading, Sasha. I will go to him and ask."

"What will you ask him?" Sasha inquired.

"I will ask him if they have anything more recent . . . and maybe try to find out about Svetlana. Just read, Sasha. I will be right back."

Anatoli rose from his seat and walked up the center aisle that separated the rows of library tables. As Anatoli reached the table, the monk looked up and, before Anatoli could speak, he asked, "You have some questions? You need more reference material?"

"Yes. The historical material is very complete. But do you have any material, let us say, that would describe the last three years? I understand that you still provide refuge to those who are fleeing from political turmoil. Is that not so?" Anatoli inquired.

"Yes, of course. I shall bring you additional material. I have taken the liberty of informing the abbot that you are here on this research project. He will be down soon and will be happy to answer any of your questions, especially with regard to the subject as what the monastery is doing presently."

"Thank you. Interviewing the abbot will be a great honor," Anatoli responded, somewhat surprised that the abbot would come to talk to him and Sasha. But maybe, he thought, this library had so few visitors, the abbot would want to visit with researchers. Anatoli walked back to where Sasha sat, and, as he seated himself, leaned over to whisper to Sasha, "It looks good. The abbot will see us soon. I will find out where Svetlana is, and the abbot will tell us."

"The abbot is the number one man. Am I not correct? Why would he want to see us?"

"We are serious researchers, don't you remember? Now read, Sasha. Read. We will want to tell him what we think of this material."

From his vantage point behind bookcases on the alcove above the library, Abbot Polzherr looked at the two researchers with some amusement. He had been told of their inquiry as soon as it had been made, and he knew whom they were after. The abbot had heard the same story before. It was not the first time in the many years the monastery had been the locus of a hunt for someone it was sheltering. Usually, the hunters came after the hunted had left; this was unusual because these two had obviously traced his guest the day after her arrival. No matter—he would know how to take care of them.

He had received a call from Colonel Boarders' David Harrison whom he had met several times and knew his guest would be gone by six in the evening. He was concerned, however, that he had let her go into town with Marie Tohl just a short while earlier. "Well," he said to himself, "time to go in," and he walked down the hidden stairs that opened directly into the hall fronting the library. He opened the door slowly and approached Father Reichert, the librarian who was seated at the front table.

"Good morning, Father. I understand that our library guests have some questions."

"Yes, they do," Reichert responded with a slight smile, and rose from his seat, leading the abbot to where Anatoli and Sasha were seated.

Anatoli was the first to see the abbot approach the table where he and Sasha were reading. He had just turned the page and looked up for an instant to see a tall, older man come with the monk who brought them the research tools. "Sasha, number one is coming," he murmured. "Be serious."

"Mr. Anatoli Shapov and Mr. Sasha Rodinov, this is Abbot Polzherr," and the young monk left, returning to his table and his research.

"Gentlemen. I trust you are finding the material helpful. As you can see, we have many, many volumes on the history of this monastery. Certainly, much of our historical service has been to provide a safe sanctuary for those fleeing persecution. We have never ceased to do this, and we are honored that you are researching this vital topic. It is an unwritten part of our mission from our great founder, St. Benedict.

"Dear friends, do you know much about our founder? Please come with me to my office where we can discuss your project, and I would like to give you some material on our monastery and our church," Polzherr said, as he motioned for them to follow him.

"We thank you for your time, Abbot Polzherr."

"Well, it is seldom that we have researchers come from so far away. I understand that you are both from Russia, and, of course, we have had the benefit of many people from your country during the days when the Communists were in power. It was not a particularly bright period of civilization, would you not agree?"

"Yes, we would agree."

"You are former Communists?"

"Yes, but as you know, that was the only manner in which to advance in society."

"Of course, man does what it is expedient. The word of God is ignored—but then you are not here for a lecture about our faith. So we shall discuss your questions in my office." The abbot led Anatoli and Sasha from the library. They were silent as the abbot steered them through a maze of corridors, finally arriving at a small office which opened directly from the corridor. In the windowless office, a plain desk held several books neatly arranged. An oil painting of St. Benedict hung on the wall. Immediately in front of the desk stood two chairs. The floor was highly polished, without any carpeting.

"Where are you staying in our small town? There are so many hotels that cater to the pilgrims. I trust your accommodations are suitable."

"Yes, we are staying at the Hotel Drei Könige."

"Ah! yes, that is a lovely old hotel. You are most fortunate to have accommodations there. It is the most popular place. Well now, how is your research going? Oh, by the way, would you like some tea or coffee? I have not been a good host. I should have asked you that sooner, Mr. Shapov, Mr. Rodinov?"

"Nothing for me," Anatoli said. Taking Anatoli's lead, Sasha said the same.

"Well, now, I have to admit to you that I would like some hot tea. Would you mind if I just left you for a few moments and asked my fellow brother to obtain some for me?" Abbot Polzherr asked meekly.

"Of course, not, Father Abbot. Of course not," Anatoli responded.

Abbot Polzherr rose from his chair, going around the desk and to the office door directly behind where Anatoli and Sasha were seated. "By the way, gentlemen, you may wish to look at the pamphlets on the table. They contain information about the monastery and the church which may be of some help to you. You may have the booklets for your own personal collection if you wish. I shall be back in due course." Abbot Polzherr left, silently closing the door behind him.

Anatoli barely heard an audible click, but it was enough to make him realize that he and Sasha were locked in. "That's odd. I think he locked us in," Anatoli said as he headed toward the door and tried the door knob. "Sasha, we are locked in! By his fucking God, he locked us in!"

"I never thought he would believe your story that we were researchers. Just look at us. He knew what we were after. Now this, locked in. Yeah, you're a smart KGB master at lying. Well, friend, look were we are now. In a fucking church! And no way out! Look at this place, no windows, one door, no phone, just a few books on the desk. Nothing. Anatoli, you shit, what do we do now?" As he said that, the lights dimmed in the room and went out. They stood in total darkness.

"Oh, my God, that old man is going to torture us, kill us. Is he not supposed to be a priest?" Sasha shouted as he began to pound on the door, his hand increasing in its force, but to no avail. The six-inch, solid oak door wouldn't budge.

"We can't get out, Sasha. Save your breath. The old man will let us go when Svetlana is gone. He won't harm us. He can't harm us. He is a man of God," Anatoli said reassuringly.

"You have to be joking. This old man is a killer and he will kill us. Don't bet on getting out of here alive, my good KGB friend. Don't bet on it."

Einsiedeln
Local Time: 12:00 p.m.
The Shop of Beatrice Selig

Svetlana put on the green slacks and jacket she had worn since she left Cyprus. The torn skirt and blouse lay scattered about the floor as did her bra and panties. She bent over to pick them up, Moussa touching her back as she did. He put his arms around her body as he followed her into the dressing room where she placed the torn skirt and blouse on the chair. Moussa continued to talk to her as she put on her bra and panties, but she didn't respond. It was usual for Moussa to talk quietly after he had sex, and he was no different now, apologizing to Svetlana in a manner that indicated he had was insane. He was oblivious to the two bodies in the room, only encouraging Svetlana to get dressed because he wanted to take her to lunch at his hotel.

She left the dressing room and went into the small bathroom directly adjacent. Svetlana turned on the light over the mirror above the basin. She stared directly ahead, her face bruised on the left side from the force of Moussa's hand, her hair disheveled and her neck scratched. She turned on the cold water, cupping some in her hands and splashing it on her face.

As she looked up, she saw Moussa in the mirror, standing outside staring at her and saying, "I am sorry, Svetlana. I am very sorry."

She said nothing as she reached for the towel and dried her face. She ran her fingers through her hair, trying to put it in some order. She was barefoot, and walked back to where she had been raped, picking the shoes from behind the couch where Marie Tohl lay. Svetlana couldn't cry, and she didn't look. She walked over to the side chair and sat down.

As she reached down to put on her shoes, Moussa leaned over and took them from her. "Here, let me put them on," he said quietly. Rather than respond, Svetlana, staring ahead, felt the shoes being slipped on. She got up as he took her hand saying, "Svetlana, you are the most beautiful woman in the world. Let us go to the hotel and have champagne to celebrate our coming together."

He led her to the door, which he opened and guided her out into the bright sunshine where he took her tightly by the hand, and began walking toward the hotel, on a sidewalk crowded with pilgrims. "I am very happy now, Svetlana, very happy. And I want it to last forever," he said as he turned to look at her. She said nothing, staring silently straight ahead. She was thinking that only death would bring her the release for which she now prayed. Her life vanishing before her very eyes, she thought of nothing else.

Einsiedeln
Local Time: 12:30 p.m.
The Monastery
Abbot Polzherr's Office

"Both of them are in my prayer room ready for you, David. How is Colonel Boarders?" the abbot asked David. "We miss him. It has been six or seven months since we last saw him."

"Father Abbot, he is dead," David remarked quietly. "He died just yesterday evening in London."

"This is most shocking . . . most shocking. How did it occur?" Abbot Polzherr asked.

"He died at the hands of an assassin sent from Moscow. The contact that you are harboring is the one who provided information that we have needed to stop the crazies from selling missiles and nuclear weapons to other crazies."

"This news is not good, David. He was such a decent man. I just don't understand. He was so very careful at what he did. I shall have my brothers pray for him. This is most sad," Abbot Polzherr shook his head in disbelief. "David, the contact you came for is out getting some fresh air and should be back shortly. I sent her with Marie Tohl who was going to take her on a tour of the church and then, I believe, have lunch at one of the town cafes.

"But something further I must tell you. I have in my prayer room two gentlemen who claim to be researchers but obviously were looking for your Helene LeFevre. The two gentlemen are Russians going by

THE PENTUM MISSION   351

the names of Anatoli Shapov and Sasha Rodinov. They called the monastery and asked to do research in the library, which, of itself, is not unusual. But they also asked the brother answering the phone if the monastery had any refugees in residence. This was told to me immediately and, of course, we invited them in. You probably will want to talk to them. You have time because Marie said she and Ms. LeFevre would be back by two or three."

"Yes, I would like to talk to them. Very much so. If they are here, maybe others are also on their way to take Ms. LeFevre away. I would enjoy talking to them, one at a time."

"Right now, the lights are out in the prayer room. I suspect that they are in a state of panic."

"Father Abbot, have the lights turned on. I will go with you. I will need some help from your brothers."

"Of course, David. Shall we be on our way?"

Einsiedeln
Saturday
Local Time: 12:30 p.m.
The Abbot's Prayer Room

"Light! Anatoli, light!" Sasha exclaimed, as he rubbed his eyes with his hands.

"Fuck the lights. When Father Abbot walks in, I will tell him that this was most disappointing—to come into the monastery and then to have the lights turned off and the door locked."

"He will not let us go," Sasha said. "No, Anatoli, he will not let us go."

"What do you mean? Two against one. We can take him on. Come now, Sasha, stop trembling so much. You surprise me. Look how big you and I are. The old man is so frail. We can blow him over, Sasha. Have faith!" Anatoli laughed as he said "faith."

Sasha was standing by the door as he heard the knob open and in walked Father Abbot Polzherr alone. "I am sorry I was delayed, but an urgent matter came up that I had to attend to. Please, were you comfortable while I was gone?" Polzherr asked, looking at both as they approached him.

"Father Abbot, we wish to leave now. The lights were out and the door locked. This is most unusual, and we wish to leave," Anatoli said, shouting at the abbot.

"Of course. I had no idea that the lights were out. The door locked? This should have been fixed some time ago. I am so sorry, gentlemen. Our hospitality is not what it should be. Yes, you may leave. Let me escort you and, as we walk, you can ask me any questions."

Abbot Polzherr stayed by the door as he motioned Anatoli and Sasha to go forward. Another monk stood in the corridor, and bowed as Polzherr went by with his guests. As Polzherr entered the hallway, the monk in the corridor was joined by three other monks who were walking in prayer, coming from behind Abbot Polzherr, Anatoli and Sasha. The group of four monks walked silently. As the group approached the juncture of the hallway leading to the corridor housing the monks' individual sleeping cells, two monks went behind Anatoli and two behind Sasha.

"Father Abbot, what is going on?" Anatoli shouted as he struggled to get free. Sasha fell to his knees, shouting, "I told you, you fucking idiot, that he would not let us out. He is going to torture us ... oh! My God, he is going to torture us. You fool! We should have let Svetlana go and stayed with our own cunts."

Harrison was one of the monks that held on to Anatoli. He now knew they had been hunting Svetlana, and he would find out more. "Mr. Anatoli Shapov and Mr. Sasha Rodinov, you were not here to do research. You were dishonest. I have called the police who are on their way. In the meantime, you will be detained."

"We have done nothing wrong. What are you saying?" Anatoli shouted as he was dragged into the first room on the left side of the corridor. Sasha, sobbing and frantic, was taken to the room immediately next to Anatoli's.

Harrison looked directly at Anatoli seated on the bed. "Here is a pad of paper, Mr. Shapov. I want to know who is with you, what are you looking for, and where you are from. I would suggest you write everything down. I will be back shortly. I hope that you will cooperate."

"Fuck you, fuck you. And fuck your God." Anatoli spit at Harrison as he and the other monk left the room.

"I shall be back. You had better have everything written down," Harrison quietly said. Anatoli spit at him again, but Harrison closed the door behind him.

Harrison went directly to the next door and, as he opened it, found Sasha prone on the bed. David motioned for the two monks that were in the room guarding Sasha to leave. "Let us alone for a moment." With that, the two joined the other monk who was standing outside Anatoli's door, speaking with Abbot Polzherr.

"Mr. Sasha Rodinov, sit up, and sit up now," David ordered. Sasha raised his head and stared at Harrison. "You are not a priest, are you? You are here to kill me, are you not?" Sasha implored.

Ignoring the question, Harrison repeated, "Sit up, Mr. Sasha Rodinov ... now." Harrison started toward the bed from his position in front of the closed door. Seeing him approach, Sasha jumped up and headed toward him.

A monk's sleeping cell is very small, about ten feet by ten feet, and as he headed toward Harrison, Harrison stepped aside and Sasha ran into the door, sobbing, "You are going to kill me. That is what you are going to do. You are going to kill me. I know people like you. You are not a priest. No, you are not a priest," Sasha shouted hysterically.

Harrison again reached over to help him up, and Sasha recoiled. "No, leave me alone. What is it that you want?"

"Why were you here this morning? You were after Svetlana, were you not?" Harrison inquired.

"Who are you? Why do you want to know?" Sasha defiantly responded.

Again, Harrison ignored the question, repeating, "Were you after Svetlana?"

"Yes, we saw her in Zurich and she was supposed to be in Cyprus with her mother. It was by chance. We were on a holiday with our girls, and we saw Svetlana on the street."

"Why are you following her?"

"We called her friend who was supposed to meet her in Cyprus. He is now on his way here to get her. We saw her walk into this place, and that is why we are here. We wanted to get to her. I swear this is the truth. Please . . . please let me go."

"Who is her friend?"

"You would not know him. His name is Moussa Berdayev."

"Is he here now in Einsiedeln?"

"I don't know, but I think that he would be on his way. We told our girls in Zurich to tell him to meet us at the Hotel Drei Könige in town. He may be there now. I don't know."

"You have been very helpful," and, saying that, Harrison left.

It took but a few seconds to walk to the cell where Anatoli waited. As Harrison opened the door, Anatoli lunged out toward him. Anatoli, overweight and breathing heavily, fell on Harrison. The three monks standing with Abbot Polzherr rushed over to help Harrison. By this time he had taken hold of Anatoli's neck and was squeezing so severely that Anatoli rolled over off Harrison, who stayed with him, his hands still on Anatoli's neck. As Anatoli's eyes bulged and his breathing became erratic, Harrison let go, saying, "Where is the pad I gave you to write down your thoughts?" Gasping for breath, Anatoli again spit at Harrison. With one swift punch to Anatoli's face, Harrison broke the skin over Anatoli's eyes, causing blood to flow.

Stung, Anatoli shouted, "You're going to kill me. You fucker. You're going to kill me." Harrison got up, looking down at Anatoli who was now being helped to his feet by the three monks, and said quietly, "I told you to write everything on the pad of paper about why you are here. I will give you one more chance. There will be no more chances after that, Mr. Shapov. None. Do you understand what I am saying?"

Anatoli said nothing, but lowered his head and was led back into his room by the three monks guarding him. They placed him on the bed and locked the door behind as two took up positions in front of one room and two in front of Sasha's room. "Better get some chairs, gentlemen. It may be some time before I come back for your guests.

"I must get to the hotel, Father Abbot. I have a feeling that is where the boyfriend will be waiting for these two hoods who thought they were going to bring Svetlana back."

"Do you need help?" the abbot asked.

"No, I will do this myself." Harrison walked out, still wearing the habit of a Benedictine monk.

Einsiedeln
Local Time: Noon
The Boutique of Beatrice Selig

Evelyn Fontenot was looking forward to lunch with her sister. She had tried calling earlier but the line was busy, so she came a few minutes early just to be sure her sister could still have lunch with her. Slightly older than Beatrice Selig, she was proud that her sister had opened the shop some years earlier. It kept her sister busy, especially after her husband died. It was a dream come true for her sister to have this small boutique. She loved fashion but was worried that this very religious town would not support the kind of clothing she wanted to carry in the shop. After a while, however, she knew what clothing to buy for the many pilgrims and tourists that came into the town. She also selected clothes for many of her regular town customers.

Evelyn parked her car on the side of the shop right next to her sister's in the reserved space. She would enter through the front of the shop because her sister always kept the back delivery door locked. There had never been a robbery at the store and her sister liked everyone, including those delivering, to come through the front. In any event, she had few deliveries because her inventory was small. Evelyn walked the short distance around to the front and was startled to see the shade drawn down the front of the door with the lettering on the shade stating "Closed."

"Odd. My sister would have told me if she was closing." Evelyn looked through the display window directly into the shop and could see someone sprawled on the couch, but she couldn't make out who it was. Then her body started to tremble as she noticed what looked like another person on the floor and blood. "Oh! God of mercy! Oh! God of mercy," she started to shout. A few passersby stopped, looking quizzically.

Without saying anything further, Evelyn ran the few blocks to the policeman directing traffic in front of the church. "You must come! Please, you must come! I think my sister has had an accident, or something terrible has happened in the shop just up the street."

Officer Heinrich Axter took out his radio and called in to the station that there was need for another officer. Traffic was light and the automatic lights were working, so he went with Evelyn.

The scene at the shop was unlike anything he had ever seen. In fact, he had never seen a murder in Einsiedeln. Evelyn collapsed as she saw the bloodied corpse of her sister. The officer recognized Marie Tohl. Everyone in town knew the administrator of the abbey. He found it hard to understand what had happened. He again called into the station. "There are two severely injured women in Beatrice Selig's shop. Send ambulances immediately. I believe we have a robbery and possible murder... I don't know, but hurry, please hurry." The words sounded foreign in his mouth, as though someone else had been saying them.

CHAPTER SEVENTEEN

**Potomac, Maryland
Saturday
Local Time: 3:45 a.m.
2750 Mills Run Road**

"Above the clouds." Always the sarcastic comment, the demonstrated lack of respect. Why? Doesn't she know who I am? I'm the Attorney General of the United States." He repeated the litany over and over as if to convince himself that he was a quality person. "Fuckin' secrecy . . . always fuckin' secrecy . . . above the clouds . . . fuckin' bitch."

Vennix sat on the edge of his bed, holding the dead phone in his left hand, alone. No longer did he and his wife share the same bedroom. Several years earlier, because of his continued abuse of his second wife and her threat to take it public, he and she had come to an arrangement that was good for both. She received a generous financial settlement in return for continuing to live with him. This arrangement—separate personal lives and joint political lives— seemed to work well, although there were always rumors.

For a moment as he rose from his bed, he stood still, blinking. Something surged in him, making him almost afraid or, if not that, confused about what he had ordered done to Mary. No, not the diversion of the radio talk show; that he knew would be reported to her and would disturb her; she would connect to him. No, it was as if his nature were a horse taking the bit between its teeth in preparation for a furious gallop, trying to escape the constant whip applied by the jockey. He couldn't disconnect Mary's words from being whipped. "'Don't think I won't notice a betrayal; I will.' She said that right in front of the fuckin' president. And *he, of all people, listened to her.* 'Above the clouds.' Fuckin' secret, always secret, the fuckin' bitch. You're dead, Mary.

You arrive at the fuckin' hotel, and you are dead. They'll blame it on the fuckin' Russian *mafiya*, and no one will ever know . . . no one will ever know."

He turned and walked, his steps strangely shuffling, unsteady, unsure, to his bedroom window, looking out at the flood lit front yard, beyond it to a green darkness, no movement in sight. "You will live only today, Mary, only today. You won't notice that I did betray you." He opened the casement window, slowly winding the brass knob so that the right side panel opened fully. The wind had settled, leaving the night absolutely still.

Vennix began to rehearse what he would say in a statement about Mary's death: "A brave, brilliant young woman has met her death at the hands of a cowardly gang of Russian criminals. We shall devote all our energies to seeing that the perpetrators of this crime shall be found and brought to justice. The Russian Government has promised cooperation. This is a sad day for all of us at the department and for all Americans who value freedom." His mouth softly spoke the words, his mind curiously at ease, an unnatural calmness that comes with supreme happiness. He knew that *this* time it was not a deceptive dream or a mirage. No, Mary would not live out the day.

Vennix walked to the computer on his desk, reached over and turned it on. The glow from the screen cast a gray-blue light in an otherwise darkened room. Sitting down, his eyes wide open, Vennix placed his hands on the keyboard, clicking on the games program. He was ready to play chess in the cool, silent darkness.

Dennis Eidenson, his media consultant, left for Berlin the same time Mary left for London. He would make arrangements to take care of Mary. Hell was descending on Vennix, taking him to the darkness of a maddened mind as he kept mouthing the eulogy for Mary, "A brave young and brilliant woman has met her death. . . ." His sickness was complete and certain. "Checkmate, Mary. Checkmate, you fuckin' bitch."

THE PENTUM MISSION

Berlin
Saturday
Local Time: 1:00 p.m.
The Four Seasons Hotel
Charlottenstrasse, No. 49

Beverly Peterson, Mary's assistant, had again arranged the impossible. Mary could readily see that this five-star hotel was fully booked. Set in the most distinguished quarter of the city, the hotel had twice before had Mary as a guest: once when she addressed a conference on terrorism hosted by the German government, and the second time, when she met with German corporate officials on a matter involving the Middle East. The elegance and perfection of the marble, glass, and oriental-carpeted interior were unmatched. Mary wished that she could enjoy the amenities in this grand place.

The flight from Alconbury to Berlin was smooth and uneventful. The special flight crew needed rest so Beverly put them up at an airport hotel. Mary intended to depart late in the afternoon for London after meeting with Dimitri, flying on to the United States. She always anticipated a successful end to a mission. Negative vibes were alien to her body. Yet she was supremely realistic. There was no conflict of anxiety and exhilaration.

The only emotions she felt were fury at what Vennix was attempting to do and sadness at of the death of Boarders. No matter what happened, he was gone. Boarders' casket lay in the cargo hold of the chartered Citation jet. It would have been simpler to have left it at Alconbury, but no, she insisted that it go with her. Perhaps she felt a subconscious need to remain with him, ensuring a more graceful arrival in Washington. Whatever, he rested in the belly of the plane, silent and secure.

She would use her room for only a brief period. The room itself was decorated in muted colors of red and gray. The bed, covered with an overstuffed quilt, looked inviting, yet she knew that rest would come at another time and place.

What was already a complex day was becoming increasingly more confused and unpredictable. The receptionist had given her an envelope.

It contained the fax Harrison had sent from Zurich, detailing the information she needed to show Gravev, but perhaps even that was redundant. She had a persistent feeling that Dimitri would be rational and call off the insanity. To be sure, greed is insatiable, to be fed often. But for Gravev, greed made no sense. She believed that she could make him realize there was no upside to the arms sales to rogue countries and, regardless of the potential profit, he would pay an unacceptably high price for continuing.

What bothered Mary more was the other, unexpected bit of information she had received. The receptionist had informed her that, shortly after her arrival, a gentlemen had asked for her, but, following hotel policy, she had divulged no room number. The gentleman refused to leave any message and had left. The receptionist described the caller as tall, burly, with black hair and dark eyes, slightly bearded, dressed in a dark suit. What was memorable about the man was the left side of his mouth. It was turned up, as if corrected by surgery. He spoke without an accent, in German. Mary thought little of this, other than to say to herself, "He must be one of Gravev's henchmen. But do they speak without an accent?"

Normally she traveled in dimness and obscurity with virtually no one knowing her plans, except Beverly and those she would be meeting at her destination. Even then, however, the information shared with those expecting her would be released at the last possible moment.

She ran through the list of those who knew where she would be. Beverly, of course, would have told the director of Central Intelligence. He needed to know because the CIA charter flight crew had to file a flight plan for safety and tracking reasons, in case something happened to the flight. But that information would never be shared by the CIA without Mary's approval.

Also, Beverly knew about her hotel, as did Dimitri Gravev, whom she had told just this morning. Harrison? Santos? No one else knew she would be at this hotel. Even the flight crew didn't know until the plane landed in Berlin. "Oh! shit . . .Vennix knew she was leaving for London; she had told him that at yesterday's meeting in his office. But he didn't know her ultimate destination was Berlin . . . he must have obtained that information himself. But how? Beverly would've told her immediately if Vennix had asked her for the final destination. No, Mary surmised, the only way was to have his media consultant and all-round fixer, Dennis Eidenson, arrange for one of his private detective friends to place a tap on Beverly's home phone—that could be the only way he obtained her Berlin address.

No matter, she couldn't change what was happening. She was being watched, but she couldn't figure out why. Vennix was a fanatic, with an obsessive behavior pattern toward Mary thought obscene and judged to be the product of a confused mind. "I can't believe this irrational behavior. Aren't we on the same side? Doesn't he want me to succeed? He will betray me, that bastard."

She thought of all these things as she hurried to her room on the eighth floor She had bought a small overnight case with her which she opened on the bed, undressed, took a quick shower, changed into a dark red suit, and put on her pale red lipstick. Her jewelry remained the same but she changed into more different shoes, with a slightly lower heel. She pulled her hair back into a bun, fastening it with a matching red rosette. Then, glancing at her watch, noting that she had only a few minutes to reach the lobby to meet Gravev, she grabbed her black shoulder strapped briefcase, and rapidly walked out of the room, down the short, brightly lit, cream colored, oriental-carpeted corridor, taking the elevator to the lobby floor.

The lobby was not overly grand, but it was luxuriously decorated with teardrop chandeliers and stylish furniture. Luckily, it wasn't crowded. The patrons seemed to be seated in a lounge area directly to the left of the reception desk. With little difficulty Mary could see Gravev when he walked into the lobby. She would wait in the center reception area outside the restaurant. Few men would come into this hotel with bodyguards so she would recognize Dimitri—but then she would recognize him even if he came alone. She had a file on him with a picture from a public reception Dimitri had attended recently at the Kremlin.

The lounge featured several large overstuffed chairs. Mary's diminutive size made sitting in these pieces difficult. She wandered over to a grouping of tables on the left of the general seating area and alongside the large bank of windows that paralleled the entrance to the hotel, sitting at the table furthest from the entrance. The other seven tables were occupied.

When the waiter, a formal middle-age man in black tie, came over, she ordered a fresh orange juice and waited, reading slowly the bank data Harrison had sent her. "There truly is no honor among thieves," she thought to herself. Bradford had been systematically taking money from Dimitri without Dimitri's knowledge. Greed appeared to favor Bradford. What angered her was that Bradford sold himself, first to the KGB when he was working at the construction site for the United States embassy in Moscow, and then turned against Gravev, with whom he had been a partner all these years.

But, regardless of all their efforts, neither the FBI nor the CIA could tie him into anything untoward during the time he worked for the American contractor constructing the embassy. Whatever information he gave the KGB would be insignificant, in any event. Bradford might have thought he had useful information, but he didn't. He was never privy to real secrets. The most he could do was to pass on gossip. The KGB loved gossip, which was dutifully passed to the key Communist leadership. Bradford amassed some small change from those days, but it was obvious from the data Harrison had sent that the big bucks came from his association with Gravev.

Mary folded the data sheets and replaced them back in her case just as the waiter came over with her order. It was odd, she thought as she looked at him, quickly concluding that he was a different waiter from the one who took her order, but his mouth . . . his mouth on the left side, was just as described by the receptionist as the man who had asked for her earlier in the day. "No, it can't be . . . no . . . the tray he was carrying had both juice and a small plate covered with a silver top, as if concealing some food underneath. She had ordered no food.

Within moments, he reached Mary's table, and, holding his tray in his left hand, he placed a beverage napkin on the table.

"You certainly have changed, haven't you?" Mary asked.

"Madame, what do you mean?"

"You're not the waiter who took my order, are you?"

Just as he was about to take the glass of orange juice from the tray he was still holding, Mary rose, simultaneously putting both her hands under the edge of the small, round, marble top table, pushing it over, hitting the waiter's thighs, causing him to stumble backward, the orange juice and tray of tea sandwiches spilling over the floor and partially onto his trousers.

The waiter, surprised by Mary's action, leaned over to grab her, pushing her against the window, where she brought her knee up, kicking him the groin.

At this moment, several patrons rushed over, trying to restrain the waiter. From the crowd, two men emerged and quickly grabbed the waiter, yanking him back, at which point he let out a yell of pain because both his arms were twisted behind him. This effectively immobilized him, forcing him to his knees. Standing next to his bodyguards was Dimitri Gravev, who wryly asked, in heavily accented English, "Mary Auriello, do you always have people trying to kill you?" Then in Russian he told his bodyguards to keep the man a silent captive until the hotel security came.

"You did not touch the juice, did you?" Dimitri asked, a frown on his face.

"No, why?"

"Well, it probably was poison. I don't think he would have tried to shoot you here. Let me show you." He took the glass, still holding some juice drops, and handed it over to the waiter. "Drink this, you scum," Gravev ordered. The waiter turned his head away.

Mary was alternately embarrassed and furious. "Well, at least I know it was not you, Dimitri Gravev. But, I want to know who this person is. I very much want to know who sent him too."

The episode was brief, less than two minutes. Two hotel security guards arrived just as Dimitri's bodyguards took hold of the waiter. The crowd began to disperse as the hotel manager arrived. Gravev took charge, explaining in German what had happened and how his aides had foiled an attempt to harm Mary.

"Are you all right, Madame? Would you like to be seen by the hotel doctor? Perhaps you should," the manager explained, a worrisome look on this face.

Mary had recovered her composure. "There is nothing to be concerned about. When the police arrive, I'll make a statement. He's not one of your waiters, is he?" She inquired of the manager.

"No, he is not. I have no idea how he came to wait on you, Madame, but I shall find out immediately," the manger sheepishly responded. "This is most unsettling. I must apologize to you, Madame. Please let me know if I can be of any service. Most embarrassing, most embarrassing."

"Until the police come, my men will stay with this scum of a person," Gravev interjected, "to make sure he will not try to harm anyone again." What Gravev didn't say is that his aides would find out who the imposter was and why he tried to attack Mary. Mary didn't have to guess. Then, as she looked at the dispersing crowd, she thought she saw the unmistakable face of Vennix's media consultant, Dennis Eidenson, who disappeared just as quickly as Mary had seen him. No, it can't be. Vennix could not have arranged this. Vennix could not have betrayed me. He wouldn't dare. But, what if that was Eidenson. What if I have been betrayed.

"That bastard!"

"Me or him?" Gravev smilingly inquired.

"Someone who is not here, Dimitri Gravev. Someone who is not here, but if the bastard wants combat, he will have it." Mary put her arm through Dimitri's as she stood there, shaking with rage and embarrassment.

"Your briefcase, Madame," a porter said, handing it to her. It was still locked.

"Thank you, thank you very much," Mary responded, placing the long strap on her shoulder, the bag now resting on her right hip. "I guess I should clean up a bit if we are to go to the restaurant," she said, looking at her rumpled suit. "Oh, I forgot, I'm Mary Auriello of the United States Department of Justice, and you, you are Dimitri Gravev. Now, how is that for a formal introduction?" She laughed loudly.

"Well, Mary Auriello, I am Dimitri Gravev, President of Bank Alliance Russia. Now we meet formally. Okay? Not to worry though,

I'm not letting you go until my men come back. Who knows who is waiting out there to harm you? You would think this was Moscow," said Gravev, and with that he laughed loudly. "By the way, are you a Russian bank president?"

"No, but I am happy I am with one now. But, really, Dimitri, I have to freshen up a bit," Mary said. She took him again by the arm and walked past the reception desk and down a paneled corridor, the various wall tables holding large vases of fresh flowers, giving the corridor a spring like presence.

"You should be more careful, Mary Aureillo. That was a serious attempt on your life, not some ignorant attempt, but a planned one," Dimitri cautioned quietly. "Maybe you should travel with guards and not I."

"I know, Dimitri. I know who planned it," Mary replied as she swung open the door to a silent rest room with rose-petal wallpaper.

"I'll be outside," Gravev assured her. Glancing at him for a moment, Mary couldn't imagine how this solicitous man could be involved in the sale of missiles and nuclear weapons. Mary wasn't there to reformat her opinion about the deal this man was in charge of. "A moment's help doesn't make a lifelong friend," she had been told by her mother when still a child, and that advice remained good. Mary had to accomplish a mission, and she would.

She went to the wash basin, running cold water over her hands, and, taking a small hand towel, wetted it with cold water. She held it to her face for a few moments hoping to prevent a headache coming on.

She reached into her briefcase and pulled out a small comb, trying to straighten out her hair and repositioning the red rosette holding the hair in place. She walked over to the restroom lounge and sat down, her body shaking. Despite all her travels and numerous missions, she had never faced death before. Boarders and Harrison had, many times. But not her. She always came at the end of the mission, to meet them, to celebrate. Now she was alone, and, in one rare moment of uncertainty that she had never before experienced, she wondered aloud, "Maybe I can't do it anymore. Mmaybe I've really lost the edge— not David, but me."

Mary knew who the enemy was, and it was Vennix. The penalty she was paying was for underestimating the man's capacity for evil and hate. Hell itself wouldn't receive him; he was beyond reserving a place even there. She fought back tears, not of fright but of anger and disgust. She closed her eyes for several moments, struggling to compose herself.

Calm and assured, she strode out, a smile on her face. "Well, Dimitri Gravev, my new bodyguard! Thank you," and she leaned over and to her own surprise kissed him again on the cheek.

"This has been some opening to our meeting, Mary Auriello. Unexpected and, I must say, interesting. No one would believe me back in Moscow, even if I were to tell them. And two kisses from you. May I ask what more is in store for me?" Gravev said, a large smile again on his face.

"Conversation, drinks and lunch." Mary laughed.

"Well, so be it. Mary Auriello, my information is that you are the best spy in the United States. But I am not trying to kill you— and I should be for what you have done to my only daughter. So who is trying to kill you?"

Mary's laugh seemed easier than she felt. "It should be you, but it isn't. Let's eat. Better still, let's have a drink. I need it. And tell me, how did you know it was me?"

"Pictures. My staff had several pictures of you from some Interpol meetings, but there really is little information about you anywhere."

"Pictures? I take horrible photos. You must show them to me," Mary answered as she again placed her arm through Dimitri's. "Your English is very good. What's all this business about not having good English? That is just a ruse," Mary said, smiling and laughing.

"What means the word 'ruse'?"

"Oh, come on now, Dimitri, that means 'ploy.'"

"What means the word 'ploy'?" he asked as they reached the restaurant entryway.

"Dimitri, I know you know. It means 'deceit.'"

"Ah! Now I know."

"Shall we go in, Dimitri? We have business to attend to."

"Of course, Mary. Please, after you."

The tables in the restored, turn-of-the-century restaurant were discreetly set apart. The maitre d' escorted Mary and Dimitri to a table that flanked the large curved window overlooking the garden.

"Well, Mary Auriello, you lead a very interesting life . . . and you have escaped the clutches of a man for this long. If I were still single, I would not rest until I had you, Mary—not rest at all!"

"And, I would not rest until I had you," Mary responded.

"Spoken like a true woman!"

"Thank you again for helping me, for saving my life, which, I must admit, makes our business session more difficult. But now to that business, Dimtri, now to that business—perhaps more important even than my life." Mary's demeanor changed, and he noticed the sternness in her voice.

"Amazing," Gravev thought to himself. "She is almost killed, and yet she brushes it off as if it were just another incident. Amazing." Gravev knew Mary Auriello was not just the Deputy Assistant Attorney General of the United States, as her public biography read. That biography listed just that title and her educational credentials. Nothing else. No, Dimitri knew that she was more. This meeting proved to him that she was more than just some government functionary. But what was she really? What?

"I am glad I arrived when I did and was able to help. Now, Mary, you have information about my daughter and that to me is most important, most important. What is this about Dr. Marya Gravev? I do not believe that she would ever be involved in drugs. This is most unsettling. She is too good and too smart a woman. I am upset that she is being treated like a criminal. She is a heart surgeon, Mary Aureillo. Now, what, Mary, is really behind this?" Gravev looked directly at Mary, his voice soft but worried.

"She has been caught with a small amount of cocaine and, as you know, this is a violation of her visa to remain in the United States. But, Dimitri, I am trying to work out her release. Yet, you should know that the violation is serious . . . very serious," Mary replied looking at Dimitri, her eyes expressing sorrow and understanding.

"I don't believe the charge. Marya is a surgeon of high renown.

I have never know her to be involved in such matters. It is incomprehensible. Totally unbelievable. Mary, you did not come all this way to see me about my daughter on some made-up charges. I hope you believe that I am more intelligent than that. I am, of course, happy to work out something about Marya, but the information I have is that a visit from you means there are more important matters to discuss. Am I correct?" Gravev questioned.

"Yes, you are correct. Much more serious," Mary replied.

At that moment, the waiter, tall and dour, came over with the menus. "Madame, the menu," and he placed a large gold-rimmed, black folder in front of Mary. Mary looked up and, smiling, asked, "Are you really a waiter?" The waiter looked taken aback, and then, realizing whom he was talking to, answered with a simple, "Yes, I am a real waiter."

"Sir, for you," and he gave a menu to Dimitri. "Would you care for an aperitif before lunch? Perhaps a glass of wine?"

"Yes, we would like something to drink before lunch. Mary, what is your choice?"

"A dry martini, no olive and no twist." Mary responded.

"Vodka—no ice," Dimitri said to the waiter who dutifully wrote the order.

"Dimitri, to the point. You and your bank have been involved in trade matters which my government finds unacceptable." Dimitri turned his head, silent, looking out toward the front garden.

Mary continued, "We were able to stop the sale to Libya and we will stop the sale to Iran—with or without you, Dimitri. And while we are discussing this, please do explain to me why, Dimitri, you are in this business. You do not need the money. And, why on earth are you still in bed with Bradford? He both betrays his own country and steals from you as well."

Dimitri stared at Mary for several moments. "Certainly, I don't deny that Bradford and I are in business. What is this about his stealing from me?"

Before Mary could respond, the waiter came over, serving Mary and Dimitri their drinks. Mary reached over and raised her glass first. Dimitri reached over and raised his glass, "To you, Dimitri, my thanks for making sure I am still alive, and to a successful meeting between us in Berlin."

They clinked their glasses and each took a sip. Mary placed her glass down, Dimitri his, although he kept his hands around the glass, as if to warm its contents.

"Dimitri, this kind of business—with Libya and Iran—is also our business. My government does not like you selling destructive weapons to crazy people who, you must know, will use them. The people who buy these weapons don't buy them for any other purpose, Dimitri Gravev. They buy them to use them against those they do not like. I want you to help us, Dimitri, but, I will tell you directly, we will stop you regardless of whether you help. On this point, Dimitri, I want to convince you to help us prevent even further sales, not only by you, but by others as well."

Dimitri picked up his glass, slowly drinking from it. "Dear Mary, you know a great deal. Information you know could come only from someone close to me or to Bradford or perhaps to the purchasers. You know a great deal," Dimitri said, shaking his head.

"Yes, we do, Dimitri. We all live on this planet, Dimitri. We cannot escape that reality. We don't want to live in a place where nuclear weapons are flung at one another. You and I both know that the people you are dealing with lack the discipline, if I can call it that, that our two nations displayed through the cold war until now, Dimitri. You can't control the behavior of the purchaser, no matter what you believe. You must understand that once the weapon is on its way, you will be powerless to stop it from being used. You must understand this, Dimitri. The people you are selling the weapon to will use it and won't worry about it afterwards—or, worry about what happens to them afterwards."

Dimitri looked at his watch, realizing that Bradford's flight would be arriving shortly at Ashgabat, Turkmenistan, where it was four p.m. There an Iranian cargo jet plane would be waiting to take Bradford and the others, together with the cargo, on to Iran. The weapon would soon be loaded and on its way. Time was brief, very brief. Pleading with him, Mary was certainly sincere about both her information and her threats; and she was also probably right. He hated lectures, and she was lecturing. He could tell by the determination in her speech that if he did not comply, Mary Auriello, the woman he had just saved from harm, would make it difficult for his daughter and perhaps in other ways as well. Of that he was certain. Once the weapon was loaded on the plane and the flight took off for Iran, he would be powerless to stop it.

"Mary—" Dimitri stopped as the waiter came and asked, "Your order, Madame?"

"I shall have the potato and leek soup and the house salad with oil and vinegar dressing."

"And you, sir?"

"The same. Thank you. You are eating light, Mary. That is how you keep your figure," Dimitri said.

Mary shrugged off the compliment.

"No, no," Dimitri replied. He smiled. "First of all, Mary, You should understand that I am a strong believer in loyalty. Bradford helped me get started years ago. He knew all the mechanisms for getting money abroad; he introduced me to the few Western businessmen in Moscow during the old USSR days; he also had contacts with many in the government. So, realistically, without his help at the beginning, I probably would not have the success I have today," Dimitri explained.

"I understand loyalty, Dimitri. I only wish that I had it all the time. You just saw what happened to me. Someone has been disloyal to me. But that will not stop me from doing what I know to be right, stopping this sale. And I will stop the sale, Dimitri. You can stop this kind of activity in spite of your loyalty to Bradford. Look at what he has done. Look at this, Dimitri. Look at what your friend has done to you." And with that Mary turned over the five sheets of faxed bank computer statements Harrison had sent her from Zurich.

Dimitri took them and looked at them slowly, one at a time. The silence at the table was broken only by the waiter serving, first Mary her bowl of soup, then Dimitri.

"A traitor like Bradford, Dimitri, is never loyal . . . never. I am sure you understand that. It is hard for me to understand that you were unaware of what was going on. Bradford thinks only of himself. He was never loyal to you, Dimitri. Loyalty comes only from honorable people. And

Bradford is dishonorable," Mary said.

Dimitri took his soup spoon and slowly dipped into the silver rim china bowl, bringing the spoon to his lips, blowing on it for a moment, and then placing it in his mouth. He looked again out the window, gazing for some time. Mary said nothing.

Finally, Dimitri turned to Mary. "These are genuine documents, Mary. I can tell from the fax notations on the top of the pages they were faxed directly from the bank. I know that to be von Hauser's personal office fax number. How did you obtain them?"

"Come now, Dimitri. From the bank. Is it that important how I obtained them? It is the information that is crucial. Suffice it to say that you have them, and it is clear that Peter Bradford has been lying to you as well as stealing from you. Do you think that I fabricated these documents?"

Dimitri ignored Mary's outburst. "I went along with these arms deals because they appeared easy. The profit was not unsatisfactory. Bradford is the one who organized the deals, the people, everything. But it was I who gave the okay. It was I."

"Where is Bradford now?"

"On his way, with others, to effect the delivery to the customer."

"Will you stop the sale, Dimitri? Will you stop the sale?" Mary quietly asked.

Silence. Dimitri stared at Mary. Then, looking down at his glass and, picking it up, swallowed hard. "Yes, I will Mary. Yes, I will. How else do I get my daughter released?"

"How will you do this, Dimitri?" Mary asked, ignoring his question.

"Leave that to me, Mary. I do not believe that I have to tell you everything anymore than you have to tell me the true story about the bank documents," Gravev smiled. "Do I?"

"I guess not. But, if you call Bradford and tell him the deal has been canceled, he will realize that you know about him. In that case, he will probably flee to Iran after, of course, he delivers the merchandise. And, by the way, Dimitri, we have received audio tapes of all your meetings regarding the Libyan and Iranian meetings held in his office. Your loyal friend taped all his meetings, Dimitri, all."

Dimitri stunned, looked down at his drink, took his finger and begin to turn the sole ice cube in it, slowly bringing his finger out and wiping it with his napkin. Slowly, he raised his eyes to look at Mary, slowly saying, "So you are telling me he taped all the meetings? Well, now, Mary Auriello, your spy must be clever to get them from his office to you."

After several moments of silence, he looked an Mary and quietly said, "It was Svetlana Makorova. You knew everything that happened in that office. It was Svetlana Makorova. Wasn't it her? And Bradford, told me that he never had anything taped. What else did she take?" Dimitri's voice became almost inaudible.

"The computer discs as well. Yes, Dimitri, we know everything ," not answering his question about Svetlana.

"Audio tapes and computer discs. Enough evidence to embarrass me, right?"

"Yes. But the object is not to embarrass you. It is to stop this stupid sale to a country that will use the weapon."

"The Iranian government's correspondence that they would be using it only for scientific purposes is a piece of shit. Bradford is shit, and so is Svetlana. Stabbed in the back by all three. Right?" Dimitri insisted.

"The Iranian paper is a piece of shit. No doubt about that, Dimitri. And your correct about Bradford," Mary replied without commenting about Svetlana. "Scientific purposes? Dimitri, where have you been? They will use it. You could never have seriously believed that statement from the Iranians. I can't believe that you did. I don't mean to be too harsh, but that would have been fantasy. Dimitri Gravev, you must stop this shipment. My God, Dimitri, Bradford and the Iranians have treated you like a fool."

Dimitri again lowered his head, placing his spoon on the saucer. He stared at Mary for several moments, realizing that she was right. He had doubts about Bradford for some time, but this confirmed his doubts. "But, why Mary? Bradford made a great deal of money. Why would he do this to me?"

"Why not? Please, Dimitri. You must have known for some time about Bradford. Perhaps he wanted to be sure he would be taken care of in his old age. Who knows? Maybe he was just greedy. You must know that, Dimitri. You must. You are too bright a person not to understand . . . too bright."

"What will you do with the tapes and the discs?"

"Destroy them once the sale is aborted. Your daughter will be released as soon as I have your concurrence about the stopping the sale."

"Too bright? That is what you have said about me. Not bright enough to recognize the stab in the back by Bradford, and yes, Svetlana. It was her wasn't it?" Gravev again asked Mary.

Mary interrupted him, again not responding to the comment about Svetlana. "No, Dimitri, you are not stupid. You believe in loyalty. So do I . . . so do I. But, there are few people in your life that you can rely on to have that quality. You should not deceive yourself about that, Dimitri. Never deceive yourself about that. I have just lost one of those few people to one of your contract killers, Dimitri. Yet I sit across from you. Why? Because it is necessary for me, just as it was necessary for you to try to stop what we were doing. Look at me, Dimitri. I came alone. You can have one of your guards wipe me out right now. But what would that accomplish? Nothing. There will be others after me . . . and others after them. Why? Because what you are doing is too dangerous for mankind." Mary reached for his hand and, holding it tightly, said, "Dimitri, look at me. I keep up hope that there is some good we do in life. You must stop the sale, Dimitri. I must have your word, Dimitri. I must."

For all his logic and reason, wisdom and comprehension, he knew that he had to accede to Mary. It would be a painful plunge for him. Mary was right. The Iranians would use it, and it would be the beginning of a terrible conflict that would spill over to other countries. He did not know. He felt angry at himself for being—yes, he had to admit—stupid. So powerful and yet so stupid. Saying nothing to Mary, he reached into his inside suit jacket pocket, taking out his cellular phone.

She started to eat her soup, which by now, had become cold. She had not even touched her salad; food didn't interest her. She toyed with her soup for a while, before bringing the spoon to her mouth, half-filled.

After several moments, Dimitri began to push the buttons on his phone, soon speaking in Russian. The conversation took several minutes.

During this time Mary felt an uncharacteristic lack of security. She believed that Harrison was right. He knew Russian and would have understood the conversation. "But no matter," she thought to herself, "either Dimitri helps or not. If he doesn't, then there's nothing that can be done to me or to him."

Dimitri placed the phone back into his inside pocket and said, staring at Mary, "It is done. Finished. Period. About the tapes, discs and my daughter . . ."

"How is it being done? I must know."

Dimitri took out a pen from his shirt pocket. "You have a piece of paper?"

Mary reached for her purse and took out her note pad, ripping out one sheet, and handed it to Dimitri, who wrote: "The airfield is located south of Ashgabat. Your satellites can find it, Mary. Bradford, the Iranian Ambassador Jomhori Shenasi, General Nikolayev, and Prakash Farnak are all on the plane. They were to accompany the weapon to Iran. I may be stupid about Bradford, but I am not a fool either. In these kinds of matters, one has to be cautious. Unfortunately, there is criminal activity in that part of the country, and, unfortunately, the plane, bound for Teheran, has to obtain fuel there. In addition, the weapon has to be loaded on the plane. I understand from my office that the fuel taken on at the airport many times is contaminated, which can cause a plane to crash," Gravev spoke clinically.

"To be on the safe side," he continued, "I have also had my people contract out to a few of our friends who still have the Stinger missiles you gave to the Afghan rebels. They will use one of them to destroy the plane. You do realize that your Afghan friends sold many of them to others in the region. So either way, it will work, I assure you."

"Then, you must have suspected something. Otherwise, you would not have been so prepared. Right?"

"Bradford's Libyan mess made me cautious, as did some of his activity during the last several days with these four gentlemen. Something was lacking in the whole enterprise, and it became clear at our last meeting at my dacha that there was an undercurrent that I could not grasp. The Ambassador resisted, assuring me the weapon would not be used; there was silence from the others as well. Unusual, actually. Until our meeting today, I did not know for sure that Bradford was what you have disclosed to me. That is why I had taken some precautions. Let's say, I wasn't comfortable with him or the results of my last meeting with the group. Now, it is over. The sale has been stopped. Shall we now eat a real lunch, Mary? And what about this nonsense concerning my daughter? I am to be in New York in a few weeks, and I want to be able to see her."

"She will be free as soon as I verify what you have told me."

"You have satellites, don't you? And they are always over Iran. So have one of them swing by Turkmenistan and check it out. But, Mary, why bother? You have to trust me. Why would I not carry out what I said I was going to do? What advantage would it be to me? You have my daughter . . . and, Mary, I gave you my word."

"Yes, Dimitri, you have given me your word. When do you think the 'accident' will occur? I also assume that the triggering device is separate from the bomb. Correct?"

"Of course the triggering mechanism has been removed. The 'accident' will happen shortly after take off. What do you say in your business, Mary? Redundancy? If the missile doesn't do it, the contaminated fuel will," Dimitri said.

Even if she wanted to, she knew that she would be unable to call the National Security satellite control people to have them program one of the satellites to check out what he said would happen. She would have to trust him. He was right. There was no advantage to his continuing the sale to Iran . . . not any more.

"Oh, hell, let's have another drink, Dimitri. Only one though."

"One last thing, Mary. How did you get the tapes and disks? Was it Svetlana Makorova? She is the only one."

"I can't tell you, Dimitri. And why do you want to know? Bradford and his friends will soon go up in flames. His office will be destroyed. Right?"

"Yes, his office will be no more. But, if it is Svetlana, her lover, Moussa Berdayev, is now trying to find her. I am afraid that if he finds her, he will kill her."

"Where is he now?"

"He is in a town in Switzerland called Einsiedeln. Have you ever heard of it?"

"Yes, I know where it is."

Einsiedeln
Saturday
Local Time: 1:00 p.m.
Hotel Drei Könige
Room 710

Svetlana made a faint sound in her throat, without speaking or crying. Moussa had grown impatient with her silence and he struck her across the right check with the back of his hand.

"You must speak to me, my Svetlana. Why such silence?" he asked as he pushed her onto the bed. "Perhaps we should make love again. You are not speaking because you are not satisfied, my Svetlana. That is the reason. Of course, we must make love again," Moussa said smiling broadly at Svetlana.

Her blue eyes were wide open and fixed as she broke into a strange smile.

"Don't laugh at me, Svetlana," Moussa said angrily as he placed his hands on either side of her face and began to rock her head firmly from side to side. "Stop that smile." He again slapped her, this time much more forcefully, causing her to fall back onto the bed. "Do you think this is easy for me?" he said as he began to disrobe. "Do you think that anything but my love for you would have made me do what I just did? You know, until now, I have never been cruel and unfeeling to you. I am beginning to think that all these years you really hated me; you really had no feelings for me. Everything that I ever did was either for your or your mother's good. And, now, I know that you have never tried to understand the slightest thing about me or my deep love for you."

Svetlana's eyes remained fixed on the ceiling, her lips closed. She was beyond crying, beyond fear, beyond pain. She thought that dying would bring the release she wanted; she knew Moussa would continue to rape her and then kill her. For an instant she thought she saw her Aunt Yelana's face on the ceiling looking down on her and repeating, "Svetlana, bright as a golden star . . . Svetlana, my lovely Svetlana . . . do not concern yourself, Svetlana. I am here with you . . . I am always here with you." Svetlana felt the bracelet with the inscription, "Svetlana, bright as a golden star," that her aunt had given her so many years earlier and which she wore all the time.

Moussa, naked, flung out his arms toward her desperately, asking, "Why do you stare at the ceiling, Svetlana? Why do you not look at me? What have I done that you should run away?" He sat next to her on the bed, stroking her right bare arm and reaching for the bracelet which Svetlana's left hand was fingering. "Come, let me undress you again, my love. Here feel this. It is very hard and will make you happy."

He grabbed her left hand and placed it on his stiff penis. She let her hand drop back onto the bracelet. "Now, my Svetlana, I have told you to do something for me. You cannot just let your hand slip down. You used to hold it all the time. Don't you remember? Why are you toying with this piece of junk rather than with my cock? You must do as I say."

Moussa again took her left hand and placed it on his penis. Svetlana let it drop again, still staring at the ceiling.

"Listen to me Svetlana," he shouted to her, "Hold my cock in your hand or I will make you very sorry, my love." Again, he placed her hands on his penis, only to find her letting her hand listlessly drop again. In a fit of fury, he again slapped her across the face, repeating, as he did, "You bitch, touch my cock . . . touch my cock . . . do you hear me? Look at me!" Moussa stopped hitting her and took her face with both his hands, forcing it directly toward him.

Svetlana's face was stone white, and it showed no movement. She continued to fix her eyes as best she could on the ceiling. In silence, she thought, "I am ready to go see my Aunt Yelena . . . now. Oh! please, take me now. I ask you to get me now!" Svetlana pleaded.

Just as quickly as he succumbed into his madness, he retreated. Moussa seemed absorbed in some dream of his own. There was a strange air of concentration about him . . . the concentration that comes with hatred, and the weapon of hatred is death. Moussa's mind had gone into a darkness from which he knew he would never recover. It was over and he didn't care. He no longer needed Svetlana. She had betrayed him, which in his eyes was more important than her betrayal of the *mafiya*. There was no confusion in his mind now. It was deliberate madness, deliberately induced.

He walked over to the navy blue overstuffed chair where he had thrown his clothes and began muttering aloud. "My Svetlana," he said, "you know I will kill you. Perhaps slowly, so I can find out what you did with all the computer disks which Dimitri said you took from Peter. . . . Svetlana, did you ever fuck Peter? You know that he likes much younger women, though. Your cunt would be old for him, anyway. That is what I should do. I should cut out your cunt and send it to him. Yes, that is what I will do. . . ." Madness had now taken Moussa. "Oh, look, Svetlana, my cock has to go to bed now. But maybe I won't kill you, if you suck me. Yes, that is what you can do to save your life." Again, he walked over to Svetlana, straddled her breasts and held his penis directly over her mouth.

Svetlana's eyes remained fixed on the spot on the ceiling. "Come, my love, suck this. You would never do this, remember? Now it will be different. If you want to live, you must take it in your pretty mouth." Moussa stared at her, then blurted out, "You're fuckin' crazy. That is what you are. Crazy. But before I kill you, I am going to wait for Sasha and Anatoli. We will all have fun with you first. We will all fuck you at the same time. You will never be happier, bitch."

He rose from the bed and headed for the chair where his clothes were piled. Slowly he dressed, without looking at Svetlana. "Where there hell are Sasha and Anatoli? They said they would be here about noon . . . and look, it is after one o'clock," Moussa said to himself. Buttoning his shirt, he walked to the french doors that opened onto a small decorative balcony, just two-feet wide. There was no furniture on the balcony so Moussa walked out. He stared down, muttering loudly

THE PENTUM MISSION 379

to himself, "Stupid religious fools. Hey, people, this is what is important," as he unzipped his pants and pulled out his penis, stroking it slowly. His descent into hell was complete.

Moussa did not hear the hall entrance door open silently to the room which adjoined the one he was in. Sasha and Anatoli had reserved two adjoining rooms with the door between the room open for access into either room. David Harrison had just entered. He had heard no woman's voice, but he had heard Moussa's. He had taken the room keys from Sasha and Anatoli, and because both were marked with the separate room numbers, it was easy to enter the one that was unoccupied.

An assassin waits for an opportunity, and in David's experience, there always was an opportunity. The victim creates the opportunity many times unknowingly, but the opportunity is always there. Moussa created the opportunity by lingering on the balcony, mumbling incoherently to himself and staring down at the afternoon crowds immediately in front of the hotel. Svetlana did not notice Harrison silently go across the carpeted floor to where Moussa was standing.

It was a brief struggle. The moment Moussa sensed that someone was behind him, he felt the sharp pain of a knife plunged into his right kidney as he was pushed against the railing. It was only a matter of seconds before he lost his balance and fell the seven floors to the sidewalk below. The fall crushed most of his bones; his face hit the lamp post, severing part of his neck, so that when he hit the ground, his face was hanging to his body by loose skin. The screams of the passersby were muffled as Harrison closed the doors to the balcony.

Harrison approached Svetlana, whose eyes still stared at the ceiling. "Svetlana Makarova. I am David Harrison, and I work with Colonel Boarders. I am here to take you home." For a moment, Svetlana remained still. She continued to stare as David began to repeat himself. Svetlana turned her head slowly. A long mournful cry came out of her mouth, followed by gasps and a profusion of tears. She rose from the bed, burying her head in her hands, as she let out cries of one who had seen the deep well of terror. The ring of the phone punctured the silence of the room. Rather than answer, Harrison covered Svetlana with a blanket he had retrieved from the closet. The ringing stopped. The only sound was Svetlana's continued crying.

Berlin
Local Time: 3:00 p.m.
The Four Seasons Hotel
Restaurant, Main Level

"Miss Auriello, there is a phone call for you," the waiter said as he interrupted the conversation between Dimitri and Mary. "Would you like to take it at the maitre d' counter?"

"Yes, that will be fine. Dimitri, if you order desert, I'll have the same and some more coffee."

"Should I not follow you just in case someone else tries to take you to the heavens?"

"No, Dimitri, your boys have the only one. He is the only one." Mary knew this would be the call from Beke Santos. But she also knew that Santos would have been unable to find Dennis Eidenson. He was already in Berlin.

"This is Mary Auriello."

"Mary, Beke here. Nothing. He left for where you are on the direct flight to Berlin from New York. We got some interesting items from his apartment . . . nothing that you didn't suspect: whose payroll he was on, why he would be following you, whether he started the rumors here in D.C."

"He hired someone to take me out," Mary said matter of factly.

"What? What are you saying? Has he lost his mind? How screwy is this man back here?"

"I just don't know, Beke. People do crazy things, and maybe Vennix has flipped out. I just don't know. I'm leaving in three hours and will be back in the States early tomorrow. I'll see you then. Thanks for helping."

"Mary, don't take any more chances. Come right home. We can't lose you. I'll pick you up outside Middleburg, right? Call me from the plane."

"Okay and don't worry. I have the Russian *mafiya* guarding me," she laughed.

"Oh! shit. Wonders never cease, do they?"

"No, they don't. See you soon. And thanks," Mary replied.

"Bye, Mary . . . take care."

As Mary placed the phone down, she saw Dimitri's two aides walk toward the maitre d' desk looking satisfied. She waited for them. "Everything okay?" she asked.

The one who spoke English responded, "Everything is okay. But first, we must see Dimitri Gravev."

"Of course, come this way," said Mary, leading them to her table. Dimitri rose as he saw Mary followed by his two aides. "Here, Mary, sit. Viktor Kulikov and Pyotr Schtiloff, both of you sit down, too. Now tell us what has happened. Mary, you must forgive us if we speak Russian. I shall then tell you what they have said."

Mary did not have to understand Russian to know what they were telling Gravev . . . and she was humiliated that they were telling her betrayer was Dennis Eidenson, whom she knew was sent by Vennix. Confronted by Dimitri's aides and their obvious power, the would-be assassin confessed and repeated his confession in front of the Berlin police and the hotel security guards. He also identified Eidenson as the person who had hired him, and he had a card with Eidenson's name, as well as his room number at the hotel. After starting to outline the details for Mary, Dimitri excused his aides who went to an adjoining table to order their meal.

Dimitri slowly and quietly explained to Mary what she had suspected. The waiter, hired to take her out, was a former East German *spatzi* agent who had a private investigative firm in Berlin. He claimed that he was only to scare her on behalf of Eidenson, who claimed to have had a grudge against her. "In any event, Mary, that is the name of the man who tried to take you out. My men have it on tape, as do also the Berlin police. What will you do now?"

"Bring him to justice. That is the American way. Bring him to justice," Mary said, lowering her head, angry.

She had been betrayed.

CHAPTER EIGHTEEN

Saturday
Local Time: 6:00 p.m.
Former Soviet Military Airfield No. 4 (Abandoned)
Three hundred kilometers east of Ashgabat, capital of Turkmenistan

The fatigue after the five-hour flight from Moscow and the anxiety about his escape prevented Peter Bradford from conversing with his fellow passengers. Throughout most of the tedious flight each dozed, occupying his own row of two seats, in order to stretch out. The passengers were Jomhori Shenasi, the Iranian ambassador to the Russian Federation, Maj. Gen. Yuri Nikolayev, the retired ex-Soviet KGB operative, and Prakash Farnak, the Iranian middleman.

Bradford was the only one dressed in a gray suit, dress shirt and tie. Shenasi had on his djellabah, a solid black long robe, with a small round turban, also black, a double row of white piping running along the center of the turban. General Nikolayev wore black slacks, a blue open collar shirt and a black bomber style leather jacket. Farnak was dressed similarly to Nikolayev, the difference being he had a black turtleneck. Everyone had on black loafers of differing styles, with the exception of Shenasi who wore simple, plain black tie shoes.

The knowledge that Svetlana had betrayed him, had passed on all the intimate details of his office and his business arrangements for the past six months, continued to perplex him. He kept reminding himself how good he was to her; he couldn't understand why she consciously turned her back on him. Why? It couldn't have been money—he was generous to her, as was Moussa, her lover. All the tapes, computer disks, his entire business life was now in the hands of others. Regardless, there was no returning, and he hoped he would quickly forget his past.

The past would disappear as if it had never been. In such

THE PENTUM MISSION

circumstances, Bradford believed it would be contemptible if he didn't forget. After all, to whomever Svetlana gave the information, that person or persons knew everything . . . so, why not forget the past? "It's not relevant any more," he mused to himself. "Yes, the past isn't relevant. I don't give a shit why she took those fuckin' tapes and disks. They're no longer useful to me, and I'm on my way out with a load of cash." Satisfied with his rationale for his actions and but not knowing those those of Svetlana, he folded his arms across his chest, gazing out the window into a cloudless sky.

The plane, a Boeing 737 jetliner, had been reconfigured for Bank Alliance Russia. The interior was spacious and the seating comfortable. The front of the plane had seating, in a first-class configuration, for 12 people, behind which was a large space that could be used as a combination dining/board room. It was here that Bradford and the others took their luncheon upon departure from Moscow, one hour into the flight, on a table covered with white linen and set with china and silverware. Though the conversation among the four was muted and sparse, the only continuing noise, apart from the hum of the jet engines, was the faint clink of knives and forks as each cut into the baked peppered chicken, boiled potatoes, and green beans, everyone seemingly preoccupied with his own thoughts and worries.

The two female flight attendants were friendly and helpful throughout the flight and the meal carefully and beautifully served. But out of deference to Ambassador Shenasi's religious beliefs, no wine was served. At the instructions of Dimitri Gravev, the private BAR air fleet carried no hard liquor, only wine.

Behind the conference room was a spacious galley and behind that yet another seating area for a similar number of passengers, with a smaller galley at the rear of the plane. Restrooms were located at the front and rear of the aircraft. The crew were all Bank Alliance employees. Bradford had been on this plane, from time to time, when traveling inside Russia and the former countries of the Soviet Union. Yet he was unfamiliar with the crew of the plane.

What bothered Bradford was that this flight crew, which from his experience was usually composed of five—the pilot, the co-pilot and the flight engineer/security officer, and two flight attendants—was augmented by two other men, obvious security personnel, one of whom sat in the first row of seats behind the pilots' compartment, the other in the back cabin near the flight attendants' area. No one asked who they were, nor did they volunteer introductions. Both were dressed in formal, navy blue uniform and light blue turtleneck, with the BAR insignia on the their breast pocket, the wings above the insignia designating their assignment to the BAR air fleet.

Bank Alliance Russia had a fleet of five planes, one the personal plane of Dimitri Gravev. Company officials used the planes to supervise and inspect the many offices the bank maintained throughout Russia, as well as in surrounding countries, including Turkmenistan. The planes were the corporate color scheme of navy blue, white, and burnt gold, and displayed the insignia of Bank Alliance Russian, a stylized eagle, embossed on the jet's tail as well as on both forward panels facing the front passenger compartment. All the flight crews were former military pilots who had been retrained at the Boeing company's Seattle, Washington headquarters in order to pilot the aircraft by using Western avionics, the equipment that guided the planes accurately on their flights. Bradford felt safer on these planes than on the regular domestic air carriers. But that kind of safety was far from his mind.

As the Boeing jet began its long descent, Bradford looked out the window and was surprised that he didn't see the international airport at Ashgabat, the sprawling capital of that desert land, where he had several times finalized private drug deals. As the plane banked for its approach, what he saw from the air was a ridge of mountains, beyond which lay a great desert expanse. On the left intruded a series of low wooden buildings, of earthen color, the last of which was a stout, concrete, four-story structure that appeared to be a control tower. Wherever the plane was landing, it was not where he had been led to believe he would be going for the delivery of the device.

Tilted back in his seat, his eyes scanning the mountains in the distance, he felt utterly naked in his ability to control events. By degrees his anxiety and apprehension increasing, he worried that perhaps Gravev knew what he had planned. "It can't be. Svetlana would be betraying

THE PENTUM MISSION

him as well, wouldn't she? Wouldn't she?"

Self conscious, showing his nervousness by constantly rearranging the position of his wallet, first in one side of his jacket, which he had taken off during the flight and had just put back on, then in the other, his heart beating faster, he approached Prakash Farnak, whose eyes were shut as if in prayer. Bradford jostled him on the shoulder, sliding into the adjoining seat, asking, "Prakash . . . Prakash . . . do you recognize where we are landing? Do you know?" Bradford's voice was tense but timid.

"What Peter . . . what? I'm sorry I was concentrating on something. What is it? What did you ask me?" Farnak replied, now looking directly at Bradford.

"Do you recognize where we are landing? I don't. I thought we were going to Ashgabat to pick up the Iranian Airlines cargo jet. Isn't that what Shenasi said?" Bradford asked, his voice trembling.

Farnak looked out the window, then turned to Peter. "Of course, Peter, these mountains I know to be on the boarder with Iran—they're the Kopetdag, so we are really close to Ashgabat. Maybe it's a new approach to the field since they built the new airport. Who knows? Anyway, we are landing, which is good. The flight has been too long for me. I am not so much concerned as to where we land as I am to see the Iranian airliner with the cargo on. That should be your concern as well," Farnak said, softly admonishing Bradford.

In anticipation of landing, both Shenasi and General Nikolayev had moved from their seats two rows behind Bradford and Farnak, taking the seats directly behind.

Bradford, undeterred by Farnak's comment, turned around and asked, "General, do you know this area?" his voice continuing in the timid tremble that fearful people manifest.

"Well, we are certainly close to Iran. Am I not correct, Prakash?" General Nikolayev asked.

"Yes, we are on the border, no doubt about that, but I don't know the specifics. Ambassador Shenasi, we are near the Kopetdag range, am I not correct?" Prakash asked, turning around to address Shenasi.

"Yes . . . yes . . . yes, those are the Kopetdag mountains. Peter, come now, you do know the logistics for this transfer of the cargo?" Shenasi asked, irritated at Bradford's nervous demeanor. "Why, Peter, are you so troubled? General Nikolayev, our good friend, at last night's meeting with Dimitri, explained the logistics of the transfer of the device. Surely you know, even though you were not present at the meeting," Ambassador Shenasi continued.

"Well, yes, but I thought we were going on to Ashgabat but this landing pattern is not bringing us there. It looks to me as if we are going to land in the desert," Bradford quietly said, as he got up to walk to the front of the cabin to where the extra BAR air crew member was sitting, reading, and seemingly unconcerned.

"Captain, where are we? Are we not supposed to be at Ashgabat International Airport? Is something wrong? Weather?"

"No, nothing is wrong. But our flight plan is to land here and have your group disembark. Were you not told of this?" the crew member looked up from his book, his eyes focussing on Bradford's worried look.

"No, I don't believe so," said Bradford softly, his voice again cracking. This unknown destination was not what he had been told at all.

"Where are we?"

"This is a military airfield no longer in use. Your onward aircraft will be waiting for you upon our arrival, I believe. Is there a problem, sir?" The crew member closed his boo, and looked directly at Bradford with an expression that clearly said that there was no problem.

"No, none whatsoever, of course not. We were interested in where we were landing. We were of the impression we would be arriving at Ashgabat International," Bradford said, lying. "I will pass the information on to the others."

"In any event, sir, you should go back to your seat; the seat belt sign is on, and we will be landing shortly." Just as he said that, the soft voice of one of the female flight attendants came on and reminded the special passengers to place on their safety belts for landing at "your destination."

"Yes, certainly," Bradford said as he turned and walked rapidly toward his seat.

"Ambassador Shenasi, did you know where we were supposed to meet the flight that is to take us to Iran?"

"Yes, Peter. Why are you concerned? Please, sit down," Shenasi said, moving his hand in a fashion indicating that he wanted Peter to sit. "Friend Peter, Dimitri's assistant . . . his young assistant, the lawyer Sergei Mironov, he just told me to be at Moscow's Sheremetyevo, just like he told you and the others. Don't you remember we all met by the Aeroflot counter, and one of the BAR flight attendants took us out to the plane?

"Of course, earlier, this Mr. Mironov sent, by fax to my office, the coordinates for the airfield where the Iranian flight was to meet us and the approximate time our flight would arrive. He said that our flight and the Iran Air flight would fly to the airfield nearest where the device was located. So we are here. Mironov said you knew this, Peter, and that the transfer was to occur in the utmost secrecy. I assume that this airfield provides that kind of security. Peter, are you telling me you did not know this? What did Dimitri tell you? It is most unsettling to see you in such a worried state. Did you really think the transfer would occur at the International Airport in this country's capital? Come now, Peter, you are getting too unskilled in your thought process.

"Over those mountains, my dear friend, is my country, Iran. We are almost home, Peter, almost home."

"You must calm down, Peter," said Farnak. "It is most unlike you to be so disturbed. We will be on the ground momentarily, transfer to the other plane, and be off," Farnak said reassuredly.

Bradford knew none of this. Either Gravev had misled him, or Mironov was told to ignore him. Either way, it was a continued signal of displeasure. Rather than admit to his ignorance, he tried to offer an explanation. "I guess in the haste of getting all my office work done, before departure, I completely forgot that we were not going directly to Ashgabat. That, of course, makes no sense," Peter replied, trying to sound confident and secure.

General Nikolayev said nothing. He stared out the window, realizing there was no cotton warehouse here, or cotton fields. He knew you did not grow cotton in the desert, without canals and irrigation . . . and he saw nothing green from the airliner's window, just barren desert and inhospitable mountains. He had selected a totally different airfield, much closer to Ashgabat and to the warehouse where the nuclear device had been stored. It was difficult for him to believe that Gravev had the device shipped here, some 300 or more kilometers, in order to preserve secrecy and security, when the other field, similar to this, abandoned and unused, also would have served the purpose. He knew that this was not the way the transfer was to occur.

At the meeting at Gravev's dacha, when asked by Gravev if all the logistics were in place, General Nikolayev had responded in the affirmative, but he had not selected this field. He was familiar with most of the abandoned airfields in these eastern areas, because they were shipment points for many of his arms deals, and he knew some of them to be shipment points for Bradford's drug activities. The remote location wasn't the one he had selected.

Gravev had probably discovered the betrayal. Why be defiant now? Unarmed himself, with two armed security officers on the plane, what would defiance accomplish? He couldn't throw off these thoughts and feelings. There was nothing to resent. His KGB training was clear: if you're caught, you accept the consequences. Having himself practiced treachery, he knew its complexion, and he wasn't mistaken. His isolation was complete and final. He told no one, but resigned himself to a fate he knew was soon coming.

The Boeing jet made a smooth landing as it rolled past the abandoned series of weathered and decrepit buildings, taxiing to the control tower. A smaller jet, a kind that Bradford did not recognize, silver, without markings, was parked a short distance away from the tower where the BAR plane had stopped. Several trucks were stationed near the unmarked plane, and several armed men surrounded it.

From his airplane window vantage point Bradford recognized the arms as AK-47 automatic weapons; he had sold containers of them to whomever came to his office with cash. The supplies were that plentiful. None of the men were in uniform but were wearing the circular turban-like head gear of the mountain Turkmen.

THE PENTUM MISSION

As the jetliner rolled to a stop in front of the control tower, the pilot turned off the engine closest to the front exit stairs, but he kept his left wing engine idling. The officer who had sat in the first row of the front compartment lowered the automatic passenger steps and stood by the exit door. The flight attendants, who normally would have come forward, remained in their area. "Well, no matter," Bradford said to himself, trying to convince himself that everything would be fine.

Everyone was silent while departing, although the lone crew member at the exit door did manage a good bye. The desert air was cool, wisps of desert sand swirling like small whirlpools across the tarmac. The murmur of the wind down the mountains was constant but soft, not howling or distracting. In the clear blue sky, the mountains appeared closer than they really were. Desolation came to Bradford's nervous mind, a bleak, windswept location for the transfer.

As Farnak, the last one off the plane, stepped onto the tarmac, the jetliner's passenger steps retracted, the idling right wing engine revved up, and the plane turned and slowly went around the smaller jet, going down the apron for some distance before restarting its left wing engine, reaching full power in both engines in minutes. Bradford looked at the departing jet as it turned onto the only runway, the seal of BAR emblazoned on its tail. It soon took off, the sounds of its twin jet engines breaking the strange silence of the moment, banking right and heading southeast toward Ashgabat. The BAR plane had been on the ground fewer than five minutes.

"Welcome, gentlemen, I am Boris Rakhmanov." Rakhmanov was a tall man, strongly built, yet his features were small and refined. He had black, full hair, and clear black eyes. He welcomed them as he extended his hand to each. His long, dark brown leather overcoat was open to reveal that he was dressed in a dark brown suit, a brown and cream tie against a cream colored shirt, highlighting an otherwise somber appearance. "I am the manager for Dimitri Gravev's corporate holdings in this country," he said rather stiffly. "Would you like some refreshments before you board the aircraft for your next stop? I have some cold juice in one of the trucks, if you would like some."

"That is the plane from Iran?" Ambassador Shenasi asked, not responding to Rakhmanov's question.

"Yes, it arrived several hours ago. My men loaded the cargo, and it is ready to go. Although this airport is abandoned, I urge you to board quickly—there is much criminal activity here. As you can see, I have traveled here with an armed escort," he gestured, pointing to the five trucks, filled with armed men. Sadly, our country is now independent like Russia, but still, in these mountains, we have bandits who take advantage of the government's lack of control of these remote areas.

"Where is your warehouse?" General Nikolayev asked.

"Many kilometers from here. We flew the cargo into the airport early this afternoon, reloaded it onto the Iranian air jet, and, as you can see, it has been guarded by our friends in the region. This shipment has the utmost secrecy."

"Did you load it by hand? Or did you have mechanical equipment to hoist it onto this plane?" Nikolyaev pointed to the Iranian plane.

"It was not that difficult. We have two fork lifts in these trucks, and we used them to take the cargo from one plane and place it on another. In any event, it is on the flight you should now board." Rakhmanov paused and then continued, his eyes fixed on Nikolayev's. "Would you like to see the forklifts? Is that something that you feel necessary to view— instead of the cargo?"

"Of course not, I was just interested in how you moved such a heavy load from one plane to another. That's all." Nikolayev replied, walking toward the Iranian jet.

"Yes, but when we were here just several weeks ago, in Ashgabat, we were driven to a warehouse where the cargo was inspected," interjected Bradford, taking Rakhmanov's arm for attention.

"Absolutely. Again, for security purposes, and for utmost secrecy, we believe this is the best manner to handle the transfer, at this remote location. You know with the new international airport now open at Ashgabat and the great deal of air activity in that area, it would be difficult to have any secrecy there, would you not agree, Mr. Bradford? But the cargo is on the plane. Would you feel more comfortable if you checked whether what I am saying is true?"

"I would," answered Ambassador Shenasi.

THE PENTUM MISSION

"Fine, please, this way. Would you like to speak also to the Iranian crew? Perhaps you would like to talk to them about how we loaded the cargo and so forth. They observed the loading. But, please, this way," and he led the group a short distance, walking over cracked concrete and to the Iranian jet, the passenger steps locked in place.

A dark green uniformed man stood at the foot of the steps to the unmarked cargo jet. The Ambassador greeted him in Farsi and saluted; they hugged one another, exchanging kisses on each other's cheeks. Boris Rakhmanov stood at the bottom of the stairs, as Bradford's party, walking slowly up the steps, apart from each other, entered the jet, followed by the young military man who immediately retracted the passenger steps, sealing the entrance to the jet. As the steps begin to fold into the unmarked jet, Rakhmanov signaled the guards to walk back to the trucks and board them.

The interior of the Iranian cargojet was dimly lit. There were just four windows on the jet, two on either side of the cabin adjacent to the entrance. Bench-like seats ran along the side. The cargo could be seen ahead, strapped down, a large solid wooden crate, twenty feet by ten feet, with markings in Farsi and Russian indicating that the cargo was medical equipment. Three civilians, apparently technicians, as well as an equal number of uniformed security guards, were already on the plane and the ambassador spoke to them for several minutes.

Then he turned to Bradford, Farnak, and General Nikolayev, seated along the bench to the right of the entry door, addressing them. "Yes, the technicians and the guards saw the cargo loaded. Of course, we will check it when it is off-loaded and uncrated when we arrive in Teheran. I am confident that nothing is wrong here. We have paid for this purchase and I don't believe that Dimitri would be sending us medical equipment." Shenasi smiled as he pointed to the crate's markings. The slight joke broke the tension and everyone laughed nervously.

"Thanks to you, Peter, and to you, General Nikolayev and, of course, to our good friend Prakash. You have done so much for our country. I only wish that von Hauser were here to witness this historic event. No longer will we be unequal to our enemies, no longer." With that he spoke, again in Farsi, to the young military man, who went forward to the pilots' compartment.

In a few moments, the twin engine jets came to life. Peter couldn't see the trucks or the men that had surrounded the plane. He felt this was not how it was supposed to be. Bradford leaned to General Nikolayev, musing: "Well, we are on are way, General. Not as I had thought, but we are on our way."

"Not as I had imagined either, Peter. Why are we here anyway? Why do we have to accompany this . . . this . . . purchase?" he looked at Peter, hesitating before finishing the question.

"That is what Dimitri wanted to ensure that the delivery would be smooth," Peter replied.

"Perhaps . . . perhaps," the general replied, staring straight ahead.

Bradford had not recognized the man who identified himself as Gravev's manager, and he thought he knew all the top managers. But then he surmised the organization had grown so large, that maybe, just maybe, the man who introduced himself as Boris Rakhmanov was Gravev's corporate manager.

As the plane taxied for take off and his emotions grew more stable, he thought only of the 300 million dollars Gravev would never get. It would fill his pockets as well as those of the others on the plane except the ambassador, whose country was paying for something it wouldn't have for years without Bradford: a nuclear bomb. Besides, Bradford had to admit, the ambassador was not corrupt, only ruthless.

"Not to worry," Bradford told himself. "Of course, this is the way it should be." His seat on the bench allowed him to look at the control tower as the jet began its roll down the runway. He sat next to General Nikolayev. Next to him sat Farnak and, lastly, Ambassador Shenasi. The Iranian security crew and the technicians had seats directly opposite. As the plane gathered speed, Bradford wondered how busy this airfield was during the cold war, how many Russian pilots were stationed at this desolate base, so close to Iran, where the Americans had underwritten the massive military machine of the former shah.

As the plane took off, turning immediately right, its jet engines facing the tower, for an instant Bradford thought he saw a light flash, like a flash bulb, in the control tower, then another. "Taking pictures? Bradford, calm down. My God, calm down!" he thought, quietly turning to look at General Nikolayev, who stared straight ahead. Both Shenasi and Farnak had their eyes closed.

"Think it will be a smooth flight over the desert, General?" Bradford asked, trying to start a conversation. As the general turned to speak, the first of two Stinger heat-seeking ground-to-air missiles hit the plane. The first, targeted at the left engine, immediately tore off the section of the wing holding the engine, causing the plane to list at a forty-five-degree angle. The second hit the right engine, causing an explosion that tore off that wing, sending the plane into an uncontrolled spin. The truncated jet body fell like a bullet from a height of 1,500 meters, crashing south of the airfield's sole runway from which it had just taken off, creating a tremendous fireball on impact.

No one survived.

It was a seven p.m. local time.

Positioning their Stinger missiles earlier in the afternoon, even before the Iranian jet arrived, Rakhamanov's men had already calibrated their weapons accordingly. As the Iranian plane took off, they fired the first Stinger, quickly followed by the second. There was no way the flight could escape these high-velocity weapons heading toward their targets at supersonic speed. In order to record the attack for Gravev, a video camera had been placed in the tower, hidden until the plane taxied onto the runway. The video tape was sent by courier to Ashgabat, then on to Moscow, where it would arrive Sunday afternoon. As he saw the fireball blacken an otherwise cloudless dusk, Rakhmanov placed a call on the cellular phone to an assistant in Ashgabat. "Call Moscow and tell them that the deed is done." Sergei Mironov, who had been waiting by the phone most of the day, received the call at six p.m. He immediately called Berlin and reached Dimitri as he and Mary were finishing their meeting. Dimitri passed along the information to her, and the matter was closed.

An official report for Gravev was compiled by Boris Rakhmanov who stated in it that he and his crew had loaded the cargo onto the plane and greeted the passengers, making sure they boarded the onward bound aircraft. Because of banditry in the area, he and his escort left immediately after Bradford's group boarded the plane. That was the last he saw of them. As the five-truck convoy headed out from the abandoned airfield toward a small village just north of the field, he heard the explosion. He stopped the convoy and saw in the distance the large fireball.

They rushed back, driving as far as they could along the runway, continuing into the desert until they got to the crash site. There was nothing they could do except to watch the flames consume what remained of the plane. Rakhmanov took the convoy immediately to the village, some 40 kilometers away, where he notified the local militia leader, who said he would report it to headquarters at Ashgabat.

Dimitri Gravev accepted Rakhmanov's report and passed it on to the Iranian *chargé d'affaires* in Moscow. That was the last he heard of the incident. No further funds were transferred by the Iranian government, and the Iranians also did not ask for the return of the original deposit. Papers filed with von Hauser's bank by the Swiss and Russian attorneys for Bank Alliance Russia specified that Bradford left instructions that all of his accounts were trust accounts on behalf of BAR, and that his signatory was as trustee for the bank.

Later Dimitri would visit Zurich to meet the bank officials where he would pay his condolences for the untimely death of von Hauser, "a loyal friend of Bank Alliance Russian."

Washington, D.C.
Sunday
Local Time: 6:00 p.m.
The White House

Mary Auriello could have yielded to her impulse, which was to walk into the Oval Office and slap Bernarn Vennix, the Attorney General of the United States, in the face. Of course, she didn't. She wouldn't be given that opportunity.

She had left Berlin at six Saturday evening, the plane had refueled in London, and Mary was off to Washington, arriving early Sunday morning around eight. Two things were alive in her after the exhausting trip: her fury at the attempt on her life, and her exhilaration at being successful. Dimitri had pulled off what he had said he would; Svetlana Makorova was resting at the clinic in Eisiedeln; and Harrison would accompany her to the United States in a few days, after checking the condition of his own family.

She had no doubt about the veracity of what Gravev had told her in Berlin. Satellite imagery of the site would confirm that fact. Besides, she had no reason to doubt him. Gravev was clever, she thought, and had prepared two identical crates. The only marking difference was the letter "X" which would specify the correct crate to ship.

"Redundancy, Mary. Right?" he had told her when he related the full story.

Both crates were stored at his warehouse and both were taken by Rakhmanov to the alternative site he had selected. When Mironov gave him the number of the crate and left out the letter X, he knew which one to load onto the Iranian jet. The nuclear weapon was on its way back to Gravev's warehouse where it would remain, awaiting a charter Mary was sending from Turkey. It would be taken to the United States for dismantling. Mary was also convinced Gravev had some humanity after all. She believed he would leave the arms trade and, in fact, would work to prevent such sales. He appeared anxious to cooperate; Mary would see him in New York when he arrived in two weeks to see his daughter. Perhaps the glow of normalcy would return for a while, she hoped.

But a long sleep, and deep, intense love from her lover, Jim Foster, had failed to calm her anger at Vennix. One thing Mary could always do was forget for a moment and remember a lifetime. Vennix would be remembered for a lifetime.

Foster had driven her to the White House's east gate, where she was met by a Secret Service agent. Foster said he would wait for her at the Old Ebbitt Grill, a few blocks away. "Mary, are you sure you should be in jeans when you go to the White House," he laughed.

"Why not? Steiner's office said to come casual. Do you think this president will have a tie on at six on Sunday evening? I mean, Jim, his wife is out touring Asia. Besides, I have on my white virgin blouse and a Navy blazer, symbols of purity."

"Mary, you're awful!" and he leaned over to kiss her.

"I know," she said as she opened the car door, letting herself out. "See you at the Old Ebbitt Grill in an hour or so," she said.

A Secret Service agent escorted her, not to the oval office, but to a small elevator in the west wing that would take her to the president's private quarters and into a small library directly opposite the elevator. William Steiner was waiting for her alone, casually dressed in a light green polo shirt, khaki pants and brown loafers. No Bernard Vennix.

Before Mary could speak, President Steiner smiled, although Mary could see he looked worried, perhaps grim, the lines on his face making him look drawn and weary. When he reached her, he shook her hand, "Mary, my congratulations. Your actions are superb and heroic." He then leaned over and hugged her. "You can't believe how happy I was to get your call last night at the state dinner. I guess it was about ten or eleven and we winding things down a bit . . . actually, it was pretty boring. I suppose everyone thinks the president enjoys everything he does. Well, here's one secret: I hate state dinners. Now, I don't want to see that tidbit in any of tomorrow's papers! By the way, how is Harrison, his family?"

"Harrison is fine and his family is on the mend," Mary responded curtly. "About talking to reporters, you're addressing the wrong person. That's Bernie's role, and he relishes it. By the way, where is he? I'd like to see him. I've placed calls to his home and office and left word on voice mail, but he hasn't responded. You should know what he tried to do to me not only on the rumor mill of talk radio, but toying with my life in Berlin—both startling events, especially when you're supposed to be carrying out a mission supported by the president of the United States. Wouldn't you say that such behavior is odd? I really consider what he did a betrayal, wouldn't you?" Mary sat on the deep leather chair facing the couch where the president had been sitting. He had spread some papers and open books next to him on the couch.

For several moments, the president said nothing. "Would you like some coffee? A soft drink? Something more potent?"

"No. Mr. President. I don't. I want to know what, if anything, you intend to do about your attorney general. Or is my timing bad on this question? Maybe peculiar? Maybe I should be happy that I'm still alive and have carried out *a mission you approved.*"

"Mary . . . Mary . . . I don't know the full story, but Bernie was here earlier in the day. He submitted his resignation and left immediately for the Mayo Clinic."

"What're you saying? The Mayo Clinic? What kind of joke is that?"Mary interrupted the President without caring. "The Mayo Clinic, come now, Mr. President. What are we really talking about here? I'm eager to hear the rest of this silly tale."

"It's not silly, Mary. It's quite serious. This afternoon he told me the most bizarre story I have ever heard, about demons and devils. Frankly, Mary, I was embarrassed to listen to him. I believe that he has taken seriously ill . . . mentally ill." The president took Mary by the hand, and spoke gently, but with a firmness that hinted he was in command.

She didn't care. She was furious. Escaping to the Mayo Clinic? How transparent.

"In fact," he continued, "when he came, his doctor and wife were with him. It was obvious to me and to them that he had lost all sense of reality."

"What? When did this onset of illness begin? When he knew I was coming back alive? I don't mind his insults, Mr. President. I do mind his desire to see me dead.

"Mr. President, this man, your appointee, he not only had rumors spread about my personal life, but he also tried to have me taken out while I was in Berlin. Do you want to listen to a taped confession of the man who was caught . . . and caught by the person I thought was out to kill me, Dimitri Gravev, the Moscow *vor* leader. Bernie deserves to be in jail, period."

"Mary—Mary—Mary—no, no, no. I think he has been ill for some time—the pressure of the job and the reelection campaign. He has been spending too, too much time trying to keep up with all of his duties, and I don't make it easier for him at all with my constant demands. I have his resignation, effective tonight, and I have accepted it. The White

House Press Office will issue a release in time for the late evening news. He will undergo tests for a nervous breakdown, and I am sure they will recommend a long period at a private psychiatric hospital . . . a long period. . . ."

"Until the election is over, and you're in the White House for four more years. How convenient, wouldn't you say? Am I supposed to now believe that he's crazy! Where do you think I was born— someplace, someplace other than Earth? Mr. President, I saw him on Friday, talked to him on the phone Friday night in your office, again early Saturday morning. I think he knew exactly what he was doing all the time, sir, all the time. This convenient illness will melt away as soon as he believes I will melt away. This is outrageous, sir! He's in the gutter."

"He left this letter for you, Mary," the president said softly, avoiding a response to Mary's characterization. And with that the president reached for to a sealed envelope on the top of his papers piled on the couch. He rose and walked over to Mary, handing it to her. Mary stared at it for a while, then looked at the president, and then opened it. It was one-page, handwritten on the Vennixes' personal stationary. After she read it several times, she said, "Let me read it to you, Mr. President."

Sunday

Dear Mary,

I wanted you to know that I was responsible for the incident in Berlin last night, as well as the story making the rounds on talk radio.

For any harm that I have caused you, I am sorry. I know that you think this is all a ruse and that I really am not sick and am only doing this to avoid your understandable fury and disgust. But I am sick . . . very sick . . . probably have been for several years.

After I spoke to you early Saturday morning, I realized how my demons had taken over and I was no longer capable of living in a normal environment. Please accept this apology.

You have been the best the Department and this country have to offer. I regret if I have ever made your tasks harder and regret what I just did a few days ago. That will stay with me the rest of my life.

Regards,
Bernie

THE PENTUM MISSION

Mary looked up at the president who said, "Mary, he brought the letter with him and told me what he had done. I was shocked, stunned, still can't believe it."

"Here's what I think of this letter, which I know he didn't draft, Mr. President. This isn't his style, and if he's as sick as you claim, he wouldn't be able to write a coherent word," and with that she tore the letter into several pieces, crumpling the paper and carrying it over to a waste basket near the president's small library table.

Mary turned. "Mr. President, you should be outraged at what he tried to do to me and to the success of the mission. Bear in mind, sir, it is your mission as well as mine. I was only carrying out what you yourself correctly believed to be a priority in intelligence operations when you became president. Why would he try to circumvent *even you?*"

"Well, that reinforces my opinion, as shared by his personal physician and his wife, that he is a very sick man, Mary. You must believe me. I don't doubt that he is very sick, Mary. His actions towards you and others these last several months clearly indicate that his mind is not all together."

"Mr. President, let me repeat myself, just to make sure you and I understand what has happened to me. Bernie tried to have me murdered in Berlin... I can't imagine a more convenient way out than claiming that he's ill. He deserves to go to jail, Mr. President. I have an audio recording made by the Berlin police, among others, of a confession by a German private investigator who clearly states that Bernie's favorite media consultant, Dennis Eidenson, hired him to take me out... and with poison, no less. Now, if Bernie remotely believes that he's going to try to get out of this by feigning illness, then he truly is crazy.

"Mr. President, do you realize what he tried to do? I was saved by the *other side, the side that was supposed to get rid of me?*"

"In politics, Mary, loyalty transcends logic. I'm sure you understand that simple concept. He was loyal to me all these years. You have no idea what it is to run a presidential campaign and to win....Your Jim Foster, I've sent his name to the Senate to be a Court of Appeals judge, and I would have done that with or without knowing he's close to you. He's the best of the lot, brilliant, a man with a decent, human heart.

I'd put him on the high court, if there were a vacancy."

There was a pause.

"Now, what are you going to do about Bernie? About Dennis?" the president softly asked.

"Take care of them in due course."

"Where is Dennis? In a Berlin jail?"

"Last I heard he was. I should check on him to see how he is doing. I understand that he was seriously injured by Gravev's bodyguards before being turned over to the Berlin authorities. I don't even know if he is still alive. I will check on that."

"I suppose that he is receiving medical care."

"I would think so."

"He will live to stand trial, won't he?"

"I'm not sure of that. His injuries were severe."

"If he lives, do you know if his recovery will take long?"

"Several months; although I'm unsure whether he will live because of the extent of his injuries."

"And Vennix?" I don't suppose you'll bring any charges against him, now that he is in the hospital. Will you, Mary?"

"In due course, Mr. President. In due course."

"Trials are so messy and bring on so much publicity." He took the top off the decanter of gin, pouring slowly into a small crystal glass, then reaching over for some ice, placing two cubes in the glass, asking, "Just a splash of tonic?"

"Yes, Mr. President. "

"Just don't do anything until after the election, Mary." He laughed.

"I wouldn't think of it, sir. Never would've thought of that."